Phantasmagoria:
The Weird Fiction, Poetry, and Criticism of
Sir Walter Scott

The Hippocampus Press Classics of Gothic Horror Series

Edited by S. T. Joshi

Phantasmagoria
The Weird Fiction, Poetry, and Criticism of Sir Walter Scott

Edited by S. T. Joshi

Hippocampus Press

New York

Contents

Introduction

The work of Sir Walter Scott (1771–1832)—novels, short stories, poetry, even literary criticism—is so infused with weirdness that, in assembling a volume of his works pertaining to horror and the supernatural, it is difficult to decide what to exclude among his enormous output. He is best known for a series of historical works, the Waverley novels, that largely draw upon Scottish history and legend; as one critic noted, "Many ghosts flit through the pages of the Waverley novels."[1] Throughout his life he was drawn both to the weird folklore of his native Scotland and to literary Gothicism, whose birth and development in the late eighteenth and early nineteenth centuries he witnessed, and whose principles and effectiveness he analyzed in a series of trenchant review-articles.

Walter Scott was born on August 15, 1771, in Edinburgh, the ninth child of Walter Scott, a prominent solicitor, and Anna Rutherford Scott. As an infant he developed lameness in the right foot; and although his family spent a year in Bath in an attempted cure for him, he never gained the full use of the leg. After some private tutoring, he was sent to Edinburgh High School in 1779. The school emphasized classical learning (i.e., the study of Latin, Greek, and ancient history), but through tutors and on his own he also learned mathematics, French, and other subjects. A voracious reader, he discovered Thomas Percy's *Reliques of Early English Poetry* (1765) by around 1780. This landmark compilation of early ballads, many of them supernatural in theme, exercised a significant influence on the subsequent Gothic literary tradition. It is not surprising that around the same time Scott read Horace Walpole's *The Castle of Otranto* (1764), as this pioneering Gothic novel triggered the

---

1. Coleman O. Parsons, *Witchcraft and Demonology in Scott's Fiction* (Edinburgh: Oliver & Boyd, 1964), 112.

hundreds of novels that followed in its wake over the next sixty years. Scott went on to Edinburgh University, which he attended in two separate stints (1783–86, 1789–92). In the interim—indeed, all the way up to 1791—he worked as an apprentice to his father; but although Scott gained a law degree in 1792, he told his father he did not wish to follow in his footsteps and practice law.

Scott had begun writing poetry before his sixth birthday. As a young man, he developed a passion for two young women, first a girl named Jessie and then a fifteen-year-old girl, Williamina Belsches, a wealthy heiress. To impress her, Scott in 1796 translated the weird ballads of Gottfried August Bürger, "Lenore" (rendered by Scott under the title "William and Helen") and "Der wilde Jäger" (first published as "The Chase," then as "The Wild Huntsman"). These rousing ballads, fusing ghosts, apparitions, and romance, were published as a booklet; it constitutes Scott's first separate publication. Scott's courtship of Williamina was unsuccessful, and the next year he met and married Charlotte Carpenter (born Marguerite Charlotte Charpentier). Four of their children, two sons and two daughters, survived into adulthood.

Scott went on to translate other German ballads, notably Goethe's pungent brief lyric "Der Erlkönig" ("The Erl-King"). He also wrote ballads based on Scottish folklore, including "The Eve of St. John" and "Glenfinlas." The translations were reprinted in Matthew Gregory Lewis's poetry anthology *Tales of Terror* (1799), and then in a separate compilation, *Apology for Tales of Terror* (1799). Scott had met Lewis in Edinburgh in 1798. The Scottish ballads were included in Scott's own compilation, *Minstrelsy of the Scottish Border* (1802–03; 3 vols.), a pioneering anthology that brought Scott to the attention of the literary public throughout the United Kingdom and Europe.

His fame was only enhanced by the publication of *The Lay of the Last Minstrel* (1805) and numerous other book-length poems that followed. Many of these feature weird episodes and supernatural elements from folklore—brownies, wraiths, fairies, kelpies, and the like. Coleman O. Parsons writes of one such work:

> In *Marmion* (1808), Scott partially unfolds the mystery of his own reaction to the supernatural. He imagines that, after sitting on a necro-

mancer's grave, he muses over a "mystic lay" until he comes under its wild sway, hears unearthly voices "in the bittern's distant shriek," and recreates the unhallowed wizard-priest "Till from the task my brow I clear'd / And smiled to think that I had fear'd." The time, the place, the mood, and the poet's thoughts effect a very willing suspension of disbelief, which is pleasurably indulged before being revoked.[2]

The Lady of the Lake (1810)—inspired not by Arthurian lore, but by Scottish legendry—deals with a fairy princess and the human lovers who woo her.

In 1804 Scott and his family moved into a castle, Ashestiel, constructed in the Middle Ages and modified since then, lying about 25 miles southeast of Edinburgh, although he also maintained a three-story house in Edinburgh. He had become acquainted with many of the leading literary figures of the day, including William and Dorothy Wordsworth, S. T. Coleridge, Robert Southey, and, later, Lord Byron. For a time, indeed, there was a rivalry between Scott and Byron (who, like the Scotsman, was lame) for popularity among the British poets of the day. But literary disputes were the least of their concerns, for this entire period was darkened by the constant threat of an invasion of Great Britain by Napoleon. The invasion did not eventuate, but that did not prevent Scott from doing all he could to train himself and others for a battle between the two leading military powers in Europe.

When Scott's lease on Ashestiel expired, he moved his family to what he called a "cottage," Abbotsford, which he spent the next several years expanding, until it too became an imposing edifice. It was here that he completed his first novel, *Waverley* (1814), although he had begun it nearly a decade earlier. It was the first of his Waverley novels, a series of twenty-six novels spanning several centuries—from the eleventh to the eighteenth century—and set mainly in Scotland, although some traverse the known world, from Constantinople to Syria. They are not linked by plot or theme, but many of them, especially those set in the Middle Ages, draw upon the superstitions of the period and hence feature weird or supernatural episodes of various sorts.

---

2. Parsons, 59–60.

Scott, who himself attested to experiencing several ghost-sightings,[3] first ventured into weirdness in prose fiction with the brief sketch "Phantasmagoria" (1818). It is a slight piece that tells of a revenant that comes to a woman and speaks a prophecy regarding her son, who has gone into the army and for whose welfare she is deeply concerned. The piece has never been reprinted.[4] Another early piece, "Story of an Apparition" (*Blackwood's Edinburgh Magazine,* September 1818), was later rewritten and expanded into the effective tale "The Tapestried Chamber" (1828).

"Wandering Willie's Tale" is an insertion into the novel *Redgauntlet* (1824). This novel is set against the backdrop of the Jacobite rebellion—the quest of the followers of Prince Charles Edward Stuart, who claimed descent from James II (deposed in 1688 by William Orange, who then became King William III), to reclaim the English throne. Set in 1765, it tells of how Sir Hugh Redgauntlet attempted to revive the Jacobite cause, but failed. "Wandering Willie's Tale" (so labelled in the novel) is a tale told by the blind fiddler Willie Steenson, recounting the story of the mysterious death of Hugh's ancestor, Sir Robert Redgauntlet, and a tenant's apparent encounter with the Devil in disguise. The tale gains verisimilitude from its narration in Willie's dense Scots dialect—anticipating Robert Louis Stevenson's analogous device in the story "Thrawn Janet" (1881).

"My Aunt Margaret's Mirror" (1828) is Scott's most expansive tale of the supernatural. The focus here is on a magic mirror that provides a vision of a man's death. Scott himself heard an oral version of the tale from his own great-aunt, Margaret Swinton.[5] Other stories by Scott that are sometimes included in compilations of his weird work are consider-

---

3. Parsons, 105f.

4. A story published a few months earlier, "Narrative of a Fatal Event," has sometimes been reprinted under Scott's name; but it has been determined that "[William] Laidlaw was the primary author, with Scott perhaps having some editorial input." Tim Killick, "*Blackwood's* and the Boundaries of the Short Story," in *Romanticism and* Blackwood's Magazine: *"An Unprecedented Phenomenon,"* ed. Robert Morrison and Daniel S. Roberts (London: Palgrave Macmillan, 2013), 174n21.

5. See Parsons, 217.

ably less focused on the supernatural than the tales discussed above, hence have been omitted from this edition. "The Two Drovers" (1827) largely focuses on a dispute between two cattle drivers, leading one to kill the other; the only supernatural element being a prediction of the man's death by an old woman gifted with second sight. In "The Highland Widow" (1827), a widow wishes her son to follow in her dead husband's footsteps as a brigand; at one point the ghost of the father appears, but this is a small element in the overall narrative.

Scott's criticism of Gothic fiction deserves analysis in its own right. He had begun writing book reviews for the *Edinburgh Review* as early as 1804, but later gave up working for that paper because of political differences; he switched to writing for the *Quarterly Review,* newly established by the publisher John Murray. It was here, in 1810, that his review of Charles Robert Maturin's first novel, *Fatal Revenge* (1807), appeared. The long interval between the publication of the novel and the appearance of the review, and the lengthy, discursive nature of the review, are typical of the period. It is in this review that Scott articulates a point he makes repeatedly in his criticism of the Gothic novel. Specifically addressing the work of Ann Radcliffe (of whose work *Fatal Revenge* was a weak pastiche),[6] Scott points out the error of explaining away the seemingly supernatural events by natural means. The result can often seem contrived and unsatisfactory to the reader—a criticism that applies not only to the Radcliffian "explained supernatural" but to its unwitting successor, the "weird menace" story of the pulp magazines. Otherwise, Scott's evaluation of Maturin's novel is quite generous.

The same could be said for his analysis of Walpole's *The Castle of Otranto,* which originally appeared as an introduction to an 1811 reprint of the novel. This broad overview of Walpole's life and literary career focuses on that pioneering Gothic novel as both an effective tale of the supernatural and (implausibly) as an account "of domestic life and manners, during the feudal times, as might actually have existed, and to paint it checkered and agitated by the action of supernatural machinery,

---

6. H. P. Lovecraft referred to it as a "confused Radcliffian imitation." "Supernatural Horror in Literature" (1927), in *The Annotated Supernatural Horror in Literature* (New York: Hippocampus Press, 2nd ed. 2012), 39.

such as the superstition of the period received as matter of devout credulity." Suffice it to say that later commentators have not been quite as
charitable as Scott, although they have perforce recognized the seminal
role of the novel in fostering the entire Gothic movement.[7]

Scott's much more timely review of Mary Shelley's *Frankenstein*
(1818) is to some extent disappointing, as it largely consists of plot description; but at the outset he does broach, somewhat haltingly, the no-
tion that the novel constitutes an instance where scientific verisimilitude
takes the place of either pure supernaturalism or the Radcliffian "explained supernatural," and this is exactly what *Frankenstein* is about.

In 1821–24 Scott prepared a ten-volume edition of early British
novelists, with expansive bio-critical introductions. It was issued by his
longtime publisher, James Ballantyne, with whom he had become acquainted as early as his Edinburgh High School days.[8] This kind of editorial work was something Scott was comfortable with: earlier in his
career he had prepared an eighteen-volume edition of John Dryden's
complete works and a nineteen-volume edition of Jonathan Swift. The
Ballantyne Novelist's Library reprinted several of the prominent Gothic
novels of the period, including Walpole's *The Castle of Otranto,* five
novels by Ann Radcliffe, and Clara Reeve's *The Old English Baron.*
Accordingly, Scott wrote biographies of Walpole (a virtual reprint of his
introduction to *Otranto*), Reeve, and Radcliffe. Scott's introductions
were later gathered into a volume, *Lives of the Novelists* (1825).

These meticulously written pieces exhibit Scott's capacity for schol-
arly research and his acuity in critical judgment. He is perhaps more
charitable than he might otherwise have been, since he was clearly disin-
clined to speak harshly of authors or works that he was reprinting. But
his assessments are rarely off the mark, as when he mildly chastises
Reeve for unduly limiting the actions of her ghost in *The Old English*

---

7. Lovecraft, noting that *The Castle of Otranto* is "tedious, artificial, and melodra-
matic," concludes: "Such is the tale; flat, stilted, and altogether devoid of the true
cosmic horror which makes weird literature." *The Annotated Supernatural Horror
in Literature,* 34.

8. See Carola Oman, *The Wizard of the North: The Life of Sir Walter Scott*
(London: Hodder & Stoughton, 1973), 30.

Baron. He once again criticizes Radcliffe for her "explained supernaturalism," although in lesser compass than in his chapter on Walpole; and he finds an abundance of other virtues in Radcliffe's writing.

Scott's final essay on weird fiction—"On the Supernatural in Fictitious Composition" (*Foreign Quarterly Review,* July 1827)—is another pioneering article. This one addresses E. T. A. Hoffmann, and in the course of his discursive review-article he keenly focuses on Hoffmann as more an author of the grotesque than of the supernatural. Indeed, his provocative remark that "the grotesque in his compositions partly resembles the arabesque in painting" immediately brings to mind Edgar Allan Poe's landmark volume *Tales of the Grotesque and Arabesque* (1840). It is unlikely that Poe derived his title from Scott's review, although in his own preface to that volume Poe goes out of his way to repudiate any German influence on his work—by which he clearly refers to Hoffmann among others. Only toward the end of his essay does Scott devote any attention to "The Sandman," now Hoffmann's most celebrated story (thanks in no small part because it served as the basis for Sigmund Freud's essay on weird fiction, "The Uncanny" [1919]); but Scott's dismissal of this "wild and absurd story" is representative of his impatience with the extravagance and verbosity of Hoffmann's work.

Scott's *Letters on Demonology and Witchcraft* (1830) presents an interesting sidelight on his weird work. Taking a rigorously skeptical approach to the subject, he dismisses witchcraft fears as the product of superstition, ignorance of science, and (although the point is not stressed) deep-seated misogyny. Scott was, indeed, criticized by reviewers for being almost heretical in his skepticism, but he knew well that Scotland in particular was for centuries a notorious haven for witchcraft trials and accusations.

In the mid-1820s Scott suffered some financial troubles that resulted in his giving up the house in Edinburgh, but through hard work he eventually emerged out of debt. Toward the end of his life he oversaw the publication of a collected edition of his novels (1822–25). Suffering from poor health for the last several years of his life, he died at Abbotsford on September 21, 1832. But by then he had become established as one of Great Britain's most popular novelists, and such works as *Waverley, Ivanhoe,* and *The Fortunes of Nigel* were read by generations of young people well into the twentieth century. His son-in-law, John Gibson Lockhart, who had married Scott's daughter Sophia in 1820, wrote an exhaustive biography, *Memoirs of the Life of Sir Walter Scott, Bart.* (1837–38; 7 vols.), and critical attention has never been lacking.

Specifically within the realm of weird fiction, Scott can be seen as an author who built upon the Gothic work of Walpole, Radcliffe, and others and partially anticipated the work of Edgar Allan Poe by focusing on the short story as opposed to the novel as his chosen venue for supernatural conceptions. His ballad poetry was widely influential and might be said to have inspired writers as diverse as H. P. Lovecraft (whose "Psychopompos" [1918] bears some echoes of the tone and manner of Scott's longer poems) and Adam Bolivar, a contemporary balladeer whose scintillating work has brought renewed attention to this age-old form. His critical essays on weird writers are unfailingly acute and perspicacious, even if at times overly generous, and they helped to initiate the analysis of the nature and characteristics of weird writing that later critics such as Edith Birkhead, H. P. Lovecraft, Peter Penzoldt, and many others have followed. And, if nothing else, Scott's work, whether in prose or poetry, remains eminently readable, as its narrative drive and compelling characters leave a vivid impression long after the work is put aside.

—S. T. JOSHI

A Note on This Edition

The works included in this edition have been taken from various sources. The stories derive from their original appearances in magazines. The poems are taken from J. Logie Robertson's edition of *The Poetical Works of Sir Walter Scott* (Oxford University Press, 1916). The essays are taken from their original appearances in the *Ballantyne Novelist's Library* or, in the case of the essay on Hoffmann, from the *Foreign Quarterly Review.* Scott's inconsistent spelling and irregular punctuation, typical of the prose of the time, has been scrupulously maintained.

SHORT STORIES

Phantasmagoria

To the Veiled Conductor of Blackwood's Edinburgh Magazine.

Sir,
There are few things so much affected by the change of manners and circumstances, as the quality and the effect of evidence. Facts which our fathers were prepared to receive upon very slender and hearsay testimony, we are sometimes disposed to deny positively, even when fortified by all that the laws of evidence can do for them, by the confession of the perpetrator of wickedness, by the evidence of its victims, by the eye-sight and oath of impartial witnesses, and by all which could, in an ordinary case, "make faith," to use a phrase of the civilians, betwixt man and man. In the present day he would be hooted as an idiot, who would believe an old woman guilty of witchcraft, upon evidence, on the tenth part of which a Middlesex jury would find a man guilty of felony; and our ancestors would have pelted, as a Sadducee and an infidel, any one who, on the twentieth degree of testimony so rejected, would not have condemned the accused to faggots and tarr'd barrels.

To accommodate those who love the golden mean in judgment, or are inclined, with Giles Passamonte's ape, to pronounce the adventures in Montosinos's cave partly true and partly false, Dr. Ferriar of Manchester has invented a new mode of judging evidence with respect to those supernatural matters, in which, without impeaching the truth of the narrator, or even the veracity of the eyes to whose evidence he appeals, you may ascribe his supposed facts to the effects of preconceived ideas acting upon faulty or diseased organs.

I have, Sir, unfortunately no means of making myself the head of any new class of believers or infidels upon these mysterious points; for it is evident, that narrations of this marvellous complexion must be either true or false, or partly true, partly fictitious; and each of these classes have already their leaders and patrons. As, however, you, Sir, are yourself a mystical being, and, in the opinion of some, a nonentity, you cannot fail to be interested in examples referring to the mystical, and to that which, being hard of belief, is sometimes rejected as incredible. You are not, perhaps, being yourself a reserved personage, entitled to expect ample communication on the part of your correspondents; yet thus much I am willing to announce to you, as the preface to the present and future correspondence.

My father, Sir Michaelmas Shadow, lived in a glen, into which the sun does not shine above ten times a year, though we have no reason to complain of want of moisture. He was wont to say, that he was descended from the celebrated Simon Shadow, whom the renowned Sir John Falstaff desired to have in his regiment, in respect he was like to be a cool soldier, and refreshing to sit under after a hot day's march. My father abridged his days, by venturing out into the meridian sun (an hour remarkable for cutting short our family) with the purpose of paying his respects to an eclipse, which a rascally almanack-maker falsely announced as being on the point of rendering our globe a visit. I succeeded to him, Sir, in his retired habits, and his taste for the uncertain, undefined, and mysterious. Warned by my poor father's untimely fate, I never venture into broad day-light; but should you, sir, leave your bower at sun-rise or sun-set, like your prototype the veiled prophet of Moore, it is possible that you may meet and distinguish your correspondent by his tall slim figure, thin stilts of legs, and disproportioned feet. For I must inform you, in case of a disagreeable surprise, that my appearance reverses that of Michael Scott and the wizzards of old, from whom the devil is said to have stolen the shadow; whereas, in my case, it would seem he had stolen the substance, and left the shade to walk the earth without it.

My education and reading have been as fantastic as my person; and from a kindred propensity to those stories which, like the farther end of the bridge in Mirza's vision, are concealed by shadows, clouds, and darkness, they have been turned towards the occult sciences and mystical points of study. My library is furnished with authors who treat of the divining rod of the magical mirror, the weapon-salve, charms, lamens, sigils, christals, pentacles, talismans, and spells. My hereditary mansion, Castle Shadoway, has a tower, from which I can observe the stars (being something of an astrologer, like the valiant Guy Mannering) and a dungeon haunted by the restless ghost of a cooper, whilome confined there till his death by one of my ancestors, for having put two slight hoops on a barrel of March beer, by which the generous liquor was lost. This goblin shall hammer, dub-a-dub, scratch, rustle, and groan with any from the Hermitage Castle to Castle Girnigo, for an hundred pounds down play or pay. Besides this, I pretend to be acquainted with all spirits that walk the earth, swim the wave, or wing the sky; goblins, night-mares, hags, vampires, break-necks, black men and green women, familiars, puck-harries, Oberon, and all his moon-light dancers. The wandering Jew, the high-priest of the Rosy-cross, the genius of Socrates, the dæmon of Mascon, the drummer of Tedworth, are all known to me, with their real character, and essence, and true history. Besides these points of occult knowledge, my conversation has lain much among old spinsters and widows, who pardoned the disproportion between my club-feet and spindle-shanks, and my general resemblance to a skeleton hung in chains, in consideration of my conversational talents as an excellent listener. In this way, my mind, from youth upwards, has become stored with matter deep and perilous to read or narrate, which, with due effect, the hand of the clock should point to twelve, and the candles be in the snuff.

The time now approaches, Sir, that I must expect, in the course of nature, to fade away into that unknown and obscure state in which, as there is no light, there can of course be no shadow. I am unwilling so much current and excellent information should go with me to the darksome bourne. To your veiled and mysterious character, Sir, you are indebted, as I have already hinted, for the preference which I give to your work as the means of recording these marvels. You must not be apprehensive that I will overwhelm you with too many marvels at once, for I am aware, by experience, of the indigestion which arises after having, like Macbeth, "supp'd full with horrors." Farther, you may place absolute reliance upon the statements which I may give concerning my authorities. Trusting this offer may be acceptable, and that at a time when you are moving heaven and earth for furnishing instruction and amusement to your readers, you will not think the assistance of the inferior regions to be despised, I send you the first article of my treatise, which, with your permission, I entitle

Phantasmagoria.

"Come like shadows—so depart."

No I.

The incident which I am about to narrate, came to your present correspondent through the most appropriate channel for such information, by the narration, namely, of an old woman. I must however add, that though this old lady literally wore the black silk gown, small haunch-hoop, and triple ruffles, which form the apparel most proper to her denomination, yet in sense, spirit, wit, and intelligence, she greatly exceeded various individuals of her own class, who have been known to me, although their backs were clothed with purple robes or military uniforms, and their heads attired with cocked hats or three-tailed periwigs. I have not, in my own mind, the slightest doubt that she told the tale to me in the precise terms in which she received it from the person principally concerned. Whether it was to be believed in its full extent, as a supernatural visitation, she did not pretend to determine, but she strongly averred her conviction, that the lady to whom the event happened was a woman not easily to be imposed upon by her own imagination, however excited; and that the whole tone of her character, as well as the course of her life, exempted her from the slightest suspicion of an attempt to impose on others. Without farther preface, and without any effort at ornament or decoration, I proceed to my narration, only premising, that though I suppress the name of the lady, out of respect to surviving relations, yet it is well known to me.

A lady, wife to a gentleman of respectable property on the borders of Argyleshire, was, about the middle of the last century, left a widow, with the management of an embarrassed estate and the care of an only son. The young gentleman approached that period of life when it was necessary that he should be sent into the world in some active professional line. The natural inclination of the youth, like most others of that age and country, was to enter into the army, a disposition which his mother saw with anxiety, as all the perils of the military profession were aggravated to her imagination by maternal tenderness, and a sense of her own desolate situation. A circumstance however occurred, which induced her to grant her consent to her son's embracing this course of life with less reluctance than it would otherwise have been given.

A Highland gentleman, named Campbell (we suppress his designation), and nearly related to Mrs. ——, was about this time named to the command of one of the independent companies, levied for protecting the peace of the Highlands, and preventing the marauding parties in which the youth of the wilder clans were still occasionally exercised. These companies were called *Sidier-dhu,* i. e. black soldiers, to distinguish them from the *Sidier-roy,* or red soldiers, of the regular army; and hence, when embodied into a marching regiment (the well-known forty-second), the corps long retained, and still retains, the title of the Black Watch. At the period of the story the independent companies retained their original occupation, and were generally considered as only liable to do duty in their native country. Each of these corps consisted of about three hundred men, using the Highland garb and arms, and commanded by such gentlemen as the Brunswick government imagined they might repose confidence in. They were understood to engage only to serve in the Highlands, and no where else, and were looked upon rather as a kind of volunteers than as regular soldiers.

A service of this limited nature, which seemed to involve but little risk of actual danger, and which was to be exercised in his native country alone, was calculated to remove many of the objections which a beloved mother might be supposed to have against her only son entering into the army. She had also the highest reliance on the kindness and affection of her kinsman, Captain Campbell, who, while he offered to receive the young gentleman as a cadet into his independent company, gave her his solemn assurance to watch over him in every respect as his own son, and to prevent his being exposed to any unnecessary hazard until he should have attained the age and experience necessary for his own guidance. Mrs. ——, greatly reconciled to parting with her son, in consequence of these friendly assurances on the part of his future commander; it was arranged that the youth should join the company at a particular time; and in the mean while, Mrs. ——, who was then residing at Edinburgh, made the necessary preparations for his proper equipment.

These had been nearly completed, when Mrs. —— received a piece of melancholy intelligence, which again unsettled her resolution; and while it filled her with grief on account of her relation, awakened in the most cruel manner all the doubts and apprehensions which his promises had lulled to sleep. A body of Katerns, or freebooters, belonging, if I mistake not, to the country of Lochiel, had made a descent upon a neighbouring district of Argyleshire, and driven away a considerable *creagh,* or spoil of cattle. Captain Campbell, with such of his independent company as he could assemble upon a sudden alarm, set off in pursuit of the depredators, and after a fatiguing march came up with them. A slight skirmish took place, in course of which the cattle were recovered, but not before Captain Campbell had received a severe wound. It was not immediately, perhaps not necessarily, mortal, but was rendered so by want of shelter and surgical assistance, and the same account, which brought to Edinburgh an account of the skirmish, communicated to Mrs. — the death of her affectionate kinsman. To grief for his loss, she had now to add the painful recollection, that her son, if he pursued the line which had been resolved on, would be deprived of the aid, countenance, and advice, of the person to whose care, as to that of a father, she had resolved to confide him. And the very event, which was otherwise so much attended with grief and perplexity, served to shew that the service of the independent companies, however limited in extent, did not exempt those engaged in it from mortal peril. At the same time, there were many arguments against retracting her consent, or altering a plan in which so much progress had been already made; and she felt as if, on the one hand, she sacrificed her son's life, if she permitted him to join the corps on the other, that his honour or spirit might be called in question, by her obliging him to renounce the situation. These contending emotions threw her—a widow, with no one to advise her, and the mother of an only son whose fate depended upon her resolving wisely—into an agony of mind, which many readers may suppose will account satisfactorily for the following extraordinary apparition.

I need not remind my Edinburgh friends, that in ancient times their forefathers lived, as they do still in Paris, in *flats,* which have access by a common stair. The apartments occupied by Mrs. — were immediately above those of a family with whom she was intimate, and she was in the habit of drinking tea with them every evening. It was duskish, and she began to think that her agitation of mind had detained her beyond the hour at which she should have joined her friends, when, opening the door of her little parlour to leave her own lodging, she saw standing directly opposite to her in the passage, the exact resemblance of Captain Campbell, in his complete Highland dress, with belted plaid, dirk, pistols, pouch, and broad sword. Appalled at this vision, she started back, closed the door of the room, staggered backwards to a chair, and endeavoured to convince herself that the apparition she had seen was only the effect of a heated imagination. In this, being a woman of a strong mind, she partly succeeded, yet could not prevail upon herself again to open the door which seemed to divide her from the shade of her deceased relation, until she heard a tap on the floor beneath, which was the usual signal from her friendly neighbours to summon her to tea. On this she took courage, walked firmly to the door of the apartment, flung it open, and—again beheld the military spectre of the deceased officer of the Black Watch. He seemed to stand within a yard of her, and held his hand stretched out, not in a menacing manner, but as if to prevent her passing him. This was too much for human fortitude to endure, and she sunk down in the floor, with a noise which alarmed her friends below for her safety.

On their hastening up stairs, and entering Mrs. ——'s lodging, they saw nothing extraordinary in the passage; but in the parlour found the lady in strong hysterics. She was recalled to herself with difficulty, but concealed the extraordinary cause of her indisposition. Her friends naturally imputed it to the late unpleasant intelligence from Argyleshire, and remained with her till a late hour, endeavouring to amuse and relieve her mind. The hour of rest however arrived, and there was a necessity, (which Mrs. —— felt an alarming one,) that she should go to her solitary apartment. She had scarce set down the light which she held in her hand, and was in the act of composing her mind, ere addressing the Deity for protection during the perils of the night, when, turning her head, the vision she had seen in the passage was standing in the apartment. On this emergency she summoned up her courage, and addressing him by his name and surname, conjured him in the name of Heaven to tell her wherefore he thus haunted her. The apparition instantly answered, with a voice and manner in no respect differing from those proper to him while alive,—"Cousin, why did you not speak sooner,—my visit is but for your good,—your grief disturbs me in my grave,—and it is by permission of the Father of the fatherless and Husband of the widow, that I come to tell you not to be disheartened by my fate, but to pursue the line which, by my advice, you adopted for your son. He will find a protector more efficient, and as kind as I would have been; will rise high in the military profession, and live to close your eyes." With these words the figure, representing Captain Campbell, completely vanished.

Upon the point of her being decidedly awake and sensible, through her eyes and ears, of the presence and words of this apparition, Mrs. —— declared herself perfectly convinced. She said, when minutely questioned by the lady who told me the story, that his general appearance differed in no respect from that which he presented when in full life and health, but that in the last occasion, while she fixed her eyes on the spectre in terror and anxiety, yet with a curiosity which argued her to be somewhat familiarized with his presence, she observed a speck or two of blood upon his breast, ruffle, and band, which he seemed to conceal with his hand when he observed her looking at him. He changed his attitude more than once, but slightly, and without altering his general position.

The fate of the young gentleman in future life seemed to correspond with the prophecy. He entered the army, rose to considerable rank, and died in peace and honour, long after he had closed the eyes of the good old lady who had determined, or at least professed to have determined, his destination in life upon this marvellous suggestion.

It would have been easy for a skilful narrator to give this tale more effect, by a slight transference or trifling exaggeration of the circumstances. But the author has determined in this and future communications to limit himself strictly to his authorities, and rests your humble servant,

SIMON SHADOW.

The Story of an Apparition

Mr. Editor,

Observing that you have frequently introduced into your Miscellany popular fables collected from various quarters, I send you the following, which I solemnly protest is no invention of mine, but a ghost-story of natural growth, which I heard in conversation. If you can find room for it, it will probably afford more amusement than the Welsh superstitions you published some time ago, which were rather heavy. I am yours, &c. A. B.

About the fall of the leaf, in the year 1737, Colonel D— went to visit his friend Mr. N— at his country seat in the north of England. As this country seat was the scene of a very singular adventure, it may be proper to mention its antiquity and solemnity, which were fitted to keep in countenance the most sombre events. The following circumstances were well known in the family, and are said to have been related by one of its members to a lady much celebrated in the literary world, but now deceased.

Upon arriving at the house of his friend, Colonel D— found there many guests, who had already got possession of almost all the apartments. The chillness of an October evening, and the somewhat mournful aspect of nature, at that season, collected them, at an early hour, round the blazing hearth, where they thought no better amusement could be found than the ancient and well approved one of story-telling, for which all mankind seem to have a relish. I do not mean the practice of circulating abominable slanders against one's friends, but the harmless, drowsy, and good-natured recreation of retailing wonderful narratives, in which, if any ill is spoken, it is generally against such as are well able to bear it, namely, the enemy of mankind, and persons who, having committed atrocious crimes, are supposed, after death, to haunt the same spots to which their deeds have attached dismal recollections.

While these tales went round, the evening darkened apace, and the windows ceased any longer to contrast the small glimmerings of external twilight with the bright blaze of the hearth. The rustling of withered leaves, casually stirred by the wind, is always a melancholy sound, and, on this occasion, lent its aid to the superstitious impressions which were gaining force by each successive recital of prodigies. One member of the family began to relate a certain tradition, but he was suddenly stopped by their host, who exhibited signs of displeasure, and whispered something to him, at the same time turning his eyes upon Colonel D——. The story was accordingly broken off, and the company went to supper with their hair standing on end; but so transitory are human impressions, that in a few minutes they had all recovered their gayety, except the Colonel, who was unable to comprehend why any tradition should be concealed from him in particular.

When they separated to go to sleep, he was led by Mr. N—— (as the reader will probably anticipate), to a chamber at a great distance from the other bed-rooms, and which bore evident marks of having been newly opened after remaining long unoccupied. In order to dissipate the confined air of the place, a large wooden fire had been lighted, and the gloomy bed-curtains were tucked stiffly up in festoons. I have not heard whether there was tapestry in the room or not; but one thing is certain, that the room looked as dreary as any tapestry could have made it, even if it had been worked on purpose by Mrs. Ann Radcliffe herself. Romance writers generally decorate their imaginary walls with all the wisdom of Solomon; but, as I am unable to vouch for the truth of every particular mentioned in this story, I mean to relate the circumstances faithfully as they were told me, without calling in so wise a man to lend his countenance to them.

Mr. N—— made apologies to Colonel D—— for putting him into an apartment which was somewhat uncomfortable, and which was now opened only because all the rest were already filled. With these excuses, and other suitable compliments, he bade his guest good night, and went away with a good deal of seriousness in his countenance, leaving the door a-jar behind him.

Colonel D——, observing that the apartment was large and cold, and that but a small part of the floor was covered with carpet, endeavoured to shut the door, but found he could only close it half way. Some obstacle in the hinges, or the weight of the door pressing upon the floor, opposed his efforts. Nevertheless, being seized with some absurd fancies, he took the candle, and looked out. When he saw nothing, except the long passage and the vacant apartments beyond, he went to bed, leaving the remains of the fire still flickering upon the broad hearth, and gleaming now and then upon the door as it stood half open.

After the Colonel had lain for a long while, ruminating half asleep, and when the ashes were now nearly extinguished, he saw the figure of a woman glide in. No noise accompanied her steps. She advanced to the fire-place, and stood between him and the light, with her back towards him, so that he could not see her features. Upon observing her dress, he found that it exactly corresponded in appearance with the ancient silk robes represented in the pictures of English ladies of rank, painted three centuries ago. This circumstance filled him with a degree of terror which he had never experienced before. The stately garniture of times long past had a frightful meaning, when appearing, as it now did, not upon a canvass, but upon a moving shape, at midnight. Still endeavouring to shake off those impressions which benumbed him, he raised himself upon his arm, and faintly asked "who was there?" The phantom turned round–approached the bed–and fixed her eyes upon him; so that he now beheld a countenance where some of the worst passions of the living were blended with the cadaverous appearance of the dead. In the midst of traits which indicated noble birth and station, was seen a look of cruelty and perfidy, accompanied with a certain smile which betrayed even baser feelings. The approach of such a face near his own, was more than Colonel D—— could support; and when he rose next morning from a feverish and troubled sleep, he could not recollect how or when the accursed spectre had departed. When summoned to breakfast, he was asked how he had spent the night, and he endeavoured to conceal his agitation by a general answer, but took the first opportunity to inform his friend Mr. N——, that, having recollected a certain piece of business which waited him at London, he found it impossible to protract his visit a single night. Mr. N—— seemed surprised, and anxiously sought to discover whether any thing occurred to render him displeased with his reception; but finding that his guest was impenetrable, and that his remonstrances against his departure were in vain, he insisted upon shewing Colonel D—— the beauties of his country residence, after which he would reluctantly bid him farewell. In walking round the mansion, Colonel D——

was shewn the outside of the tower where he had slept, and vowed, mentally, never to enter it again. He was next led to a gallery of pictures, where Mr. N—— took much delight in displaying a complete series of family portraits, reaching back to a very remote era. Among the oldest, there was one of a lady. Colonel D—— had no sooner got a glimpse of it, than he cried out, "May I never leave this spot, if that is not she." Mr. N—— asked whom he meant? "The detestable phantom that stared me out of my senses last night;" and he related every particular that had occurred.

Mr. N——, overwhelmed with astonishment, confessed that to the room where his guest had slept, there was attached a certain tradition, pointing it out as having been, at a remote period, the scene of murder and incest. It had long obtained the repute of being haunted by the spirit of the lady, whose picture was before him; but there were some circumstances in her history so atrocious, that her name was seldom mentioned in his family, and his ancestors had always endeavoured as much as possible to draw a veil over her memory.

Wandering Willie's Tale

Ye maun have heard of Sir Robert Redgauntlet of that Ilk, who lived in these parts before the dear years. The country will lang mind him; and our fathers used to draw breath thick if ever they heard him named. He was out wi' the Hielandmen in Montrose's time; and again he was in the hills wi' Glencairn in the saxteen hundred and fifty-twa; and sae when King Charles the Second came in, wha was in sic favour as the Laird of Redgauntlet? He was knighted at Lonon court, wi' the King's ain sword; and being a red-hot prelatist, he came down here, rampauging like a lion, with commissions of lieutenancy, and of lunacy for what I ken, to put down a' the Whigs and Covenanters in the country. Wild wark they made of it; for the Whigs were as dour as the Cavaliers were fierce, and it was which should first tire the other. Redgauntlet was aye for the stronghand; and his name is kenn'd as wide in the country as Claverhouse's or Tam Dalyell's. Glen, nor dargle, nor mountain, nor cave, could hide the puir hill-folk when Redgauntlet was out with bugle and bloodhound after them, as if they had been sae mony deer. And troth when they fand them, they didna mak muckle mair ceremony than a Hielandman wi' a roe-buck—It was just, "Will ye tak the test?"—if not, "Make ready—present—fire!"—and there lay the recusant.

Far and wide was Sir Robert hated and feared. Men thought he had a direct compact with Satan—that he was proof against steel—and that bullets happed aff his buff-coat like hail-stanes from a hearth—that he had a mear that would turn a hare on the side of Carrifra-gawns—and muckle to the same purpose, of whilk mair anon. The best blessing they wared on him was, "De'il scowp wi' Redgauntlet!" He wasna a bad master to his ain folk though, and was weel aneugh liked by his tenants; and as for the lackies and troopers that raid out wi' him to the persecutions, as the Whigs ca'ad these killing times, they wad hae drunken themsels blind to his health at ony time.

Now ye are to ken that my gudesire lived on Redgauntlet's grund—they ca' the place Primrose-Knowe. We had lived on the grund, and under the Redgauntlets, since the riding days, and lang before. It was a pleasant bit; and I think the air is callerer and fresher there than onywhere else in the country. It's a' deserted now; and I sat on the broken door-cheek three days since, and was glad I couldna see the plight the place was in; but that's a' wide o' the mark. There dwelt my gudesire, Steenie Steenson, a rambling, rattling chiel' he had been in his young days, and could play weel on the pipes; he was famous at "Hoopers and Girders"—a' Cumberland couldna touch him at "Jockie Lattin"—and he had the finest finger for the back-lill between Berwick and Carlisle. The like o' Steenie wasna the sort that they made Whigs o'. And so he became a Tory, as they ca' it, which we now ca' Jacobites, just out of a kind of needcessity, that he might belang to some side or other. He had nae ill-will to the Whig bodies, and likedna to see the blude rin, though, being obliged to follow Sir Robert in hunting and hosting, watching and warding, he saw muckle mischief, and maybe did some, that he couldna avoid.

Now Steenie was a kind of favourite with his master, and kenn'd a' the folks about the castle, and was often sent for to play the pipes when they were at their merriment. Auld Dougal MacCallum, the butler, that had followed Sir Robert through gude and ill, thick and thin, pool and stream, was specially fond of the pipes, and aye gae my gudesire his gude word wi' the Laird; for Dougal could turn his master round his finger.

Weel, round came the Revolution, and it had like to have broken the hearts baith of Dougal and his master. But the change was not a'thegether sae great as they feared, and other folk thought for. The Whigs made an unca crawing what they wad do with their auld enemies, and in special wi' Sir Robert Redgauntlet. But there were ower mony great folks dipped in the same doings, to make a spick and span new warld. So Parliament passed it a' ower easy; and Sir Robert, bating that he was held to hunting foxes instead of Covenanters, remained just the man he was. His revel was as loud, and his hall as weel lighted, as ever it had been, though maybe he lacked the fines of the non-conformists, that used to come to stock larder and cellar; for it is certain he began to be keener about the rents than his tenants used to find him before, and they behoved to be prompt to the rent-day, or else the Laird wasna pleased. And he was sic an awsome body, that naebody cared to anger him; for the oaths he swore, and the rage that he used to get into, and the looks that he put on, made men sometimes think him a deevil incarnate.

Weel, my gudesire was nae manager—no that he was a very great misguider—but he hadna the saving gift, and he got twa terms rent in arrear. He got the first brash at Whitsunday put ower wi' fair words and piping; but when Martinmas came, there was a summons from the grund-officer to come wi' the rent on a day preceese, or else Steenie behoved to flit. Sair wark he had to get the siller; but he was weel-freended, and at last he got the haill scraped thegither—a thousand merks—the maist of it was from a neighbour they ca'd Laurie Lapraik—a sly tod. Laurie had walth o' gear—could hunt wi' the hound and rin wi' the hare—and be Whig or Tory, saunt or sinner, as the wind stood. He was a professor in this Revolution warld, but he liked an orra sound and a tune on the pipes weel aneugh at a byetime; and abune a', he thought he had gude security for the siller he lent my gudesire over the stocking at Primrose- Knowe.

Away trots my gudesire to Redgauntlet Castle wi' a heavy purse and a light heart, glad to be out of the Laird's danger. Weel, the first thing he learned at the Castle was, that Sir Robert had fretted himsell into a fit of the gout, because he did not appear before twelve o'clock. It wasna a'thegether for sake of the money, Dougal thought; but because he didna like to part wi' my gudesire aff the grund. Dougal was glad to see Steenie, and brought him into the great oak parlour, and there sat the Laird his leesome lane, excepting that he had beside him a great, ill-favoured jack-an-ape, that was a special pet of his; a cankered beast it was, and mony an ill natured trick it played—ill to please it was, and easily angered—ran about the hail castle, chattering and yowling, and pinching, and biting folk, specially before ill-weather, or disturbances in the state. Sir Robert ca'ad it Major Weir, after the warlock that was burned; and few folk liked either the name or the conditions of the creature—they thought there was something in it by ordinar—and my gudesire was not just easy in mind when the door shut on him, and he saw himsell in the room wi' naebody but the Laird, Dougal Mac-Callum, and the Major, a thing that hadna chanced to him before.

Sir Robert sat, or, I should say, lay, in a great armed chair, wi' his grand velvet gown, and his feet on a cradle; for he had baith gout and gravel, and his face looked as gash and ghastly as Satan's. Major Weir sat opposite to him, in a red-laced coat, and the Laird's wig on his head; and aye as Sir

Robert girned wi' pain, the jack-an-ape girned too, like a sheep's-head be-tween a pair of tangs—an ill-faur'd, fearsome couple they were. The Laird's buff-coat was hung on a pin behind him, and his broadsword and his pistols within reach; for he keepit up the auld fashion of having the weapons ready, and a horse saddled day and night, just as he used to do when he was able to loup on horseback, and away after ony of the hill-folk he could get speerings of. Some said it was for fear of the Whigs taking vengeance, but I judge it was just his auld custom—he wasna gien to fear onything. The rental-book, wi' its black cover and brass clasps, was lying beside him; and a book of sculduddry sangs was put betwixt the leaves, to keep it open at the place where it bore evidence against the Goodman of Primrose-Knowe, as behind the hand with his mails and duties. Sir Robert gave my gudesire a look, as if he would have withered his heart in his bosom. Ye maun ken he had a way of bending his brows, that men saw the visible mark of a horse-shoe in his forehead, deep-dinted, as if it had been stamped there.

"Are ye come light-handed, ye son of a toom whistle?" said Sir Robert. "Zounds! if you are—"

My gudesire, with as gude a countenance as he could put on, made a leg, and placed the bag of money on the table wi' a dash, like a man that does something clever. The Laird drew it to him hastily—"Is it all here, Steenie, man?"

"Your honour will find it right," said my gudesire.

"Here, Dougal," said the Laird, "gie Steenie a tass of brandy down stairs, till I count the siller and write the receipt."

But they werena weel out of the room, when Sir Robert gied a yelloch that garr'd the castle rock. Back ran Dougal—in flew the livery-men—yell on yell gied the Laird, ilk ane mair awfu' than the ither. My gudesire knew not whether to stand or flee, but he ventured back into the parlour, where a' was gaun hirdy-girdie—naebody to say 'come in' or 'gae out.' Terribly the Laird roared for cauld water to his feet, and wine to coo his throat; and, Hell, hell, hell, and its flames, was aye the word in his mouth. They brought him water, and when they plunged his swoln feet into the tub, he cried out it was burning; and folk say that it *did* bubble and sparkle like a seething cauldron. He flung the cup at Dougal's head, and said he had giv-en him blood instead of burgundy; and, sure aneugh, the lass washed clottered blood aff the carpet the neist day. The jack-an-ape they ca'd Major Weir, it jibbered and cried as if it was mocking its master; my gudesire's head was like to turn—he forgot baith siller and receipt, and down stairs he banged; but as he ran, the shrieks came faint and fainter; there was a deep-drawn shivering groan, and word gaed through the Castle, that the Laird was dead.

Weel, away came my gudesire, wi' his finger in his mouth, and his best hope was, that Dougal had seen the money-bag, and heard the Laird speak of writing the receipt. The young Laird, now Sir John, came from Edinburgh, to see things put to rights. Sir John and his father never gree'd weel—he had been bred an advocate, and afterwards sat in the last Scots Parliament and voted for the Union, having gotten, it was thought, a rug of the compensations—if his father could have come out of his grave, he would have brained him for it on his awn hearth-stane. Some thought it was easier counting with the auld rough Knight than the fair-spoken young ane—but mair of that anon.

Dougal MacCallum, poor body, neither grat nor graned, but gaed about the house looking like a corpse, but directing, as was his duty, a' the order of the grand funeral. Now, Dougal looked aye waur and waur when night was coming, and was aye the last to gang to his bed, whilk was in a little round just opposite the chamber of dais, whilk his master occupied while he was living, and where he now lay in as they ca'ad it, well-a-day! The night before the funeral, Dougal could keep his awn counsel nae langer; he came doun with his proud spirit, and fairly asked auld Hutcheon to sit in his room with him for an hour. When they were in the round, Dougal took ae tass of brandy to himsell, and gave another to Hutcheon, and wished him all health and lang life, and said that, for himsell, he wasna lang for this world; for that, every night since Sir Robert's death, his silver call had sounded from the state chamber, just as it used to do at nights in his lifetime, to call Dougal to help to turn him in his bed. Dougal said, that being alone with the dead on that floor of the tower, (for naebody cared to wake Sir Robert Redgauntlet like another corpse,) he had never daured to answer the call, but that now his conscience checked him for neglecting his duty; for, "though death breaks service," said MacCallum, "it shall never break my service to Sir Robert; and I will answer his next whistle, so be you will stand by me, Hutcheon."

Hutcheon had nae will to the wark, but he had stood by Dougal in battle and broil, and he wad not fail him at this pinch; so down the carles sat over a stoup of brandy, and Hutcheon, who was something of a clerk, would have read a chapter of the Bible; but Dougal would hear naething but a blaud of Davie Lindsay, whilk was the waur preparation.

When midnight came, and the house was quiet as the grave, sure aneugh the silver whistle sounded as sharp and shrill as if Sir Robert was blowing it, and up got the twa auld serving-men, and tottered into the room where the dead man lay. Hutcheon saw aneugh at the first glance; for there were torches in the room which shewed him the foul fiend, in his ain shape, sitting on the Laird's coffin! Over he cowped as if he had been dead. He could not tell how lang he lay in a trance at the door, but when he gathered himself, he cried on his neighbour, and getting no answer, raised the house, when Dougal was found lying dead within twa steps of the bed where his master's coffin was placed. As for the whistle, it was gaen anes and aye; but mony a time was it heard on the top of the house in the bartizan, and amang the auld chimnies and turrets, where the howlets have their nests. Sir John hushed the matter up, and the funeral passed over without mair bogle-wark.

But when a' was over, and the Laird was beginning to settle his affairs, every tenant was called up for his arrears, and my gudesire for the full sum that stood against him in the rental-book. Weel, away he trots to the Castle, to tell his story, and there he is introduced to Sir John, sitting in his father's chair, in deep mourning, with weepers and hanging cravat, and a small walking rapier by his side, instead of the auld broad-sword that had a hundred-weight of steel about it, what with blade, chape, and basket-hilt. I have heard their communing so often tauld ower, that I almost think I was there mysell, though I couldna be born at the time. (In fact, Alan, my companion mimicked, with a good deal of humour, the flattering, conciliating tone of the tenant's address, and the hypocritical melancholy of the Laird's reply. His grandfather, he said, had, while he spoke, his eye fixed on the rental-book, as if it were a mastiff-dog that he was afraid would spring up and bite him.)

"I wuss ye joy, sir, of the head-seat, and the white loaf, and the braid lairdship. Your father was a kind man to friends and followers; muckle grace to you, Sir John, to fill his shoon—his boots, I suld say, for he seldom wore shoon, unless it were muils when he had the gout."

"Ay, Steenie," quoth the Laird, sighing deeply, and putting his napkin to his een, "his was a sudden call, and he will be missed in the country; no time to set his house in order—weel prepared God-ward, no doubt, which is the root of the matter—but left us behind a tangled hesp to wind, Steenie.— Hem! hem! We maun go to business, Steenie; much to do, and little time to do it in."

Here he opened the fatal volume; I have heard of a thing they call Doomsday-book—I am clear it has been a rental of back-ganging tenants.

"Stephen," said Sir John, still in the same soft, sleekit tone of voice— "Stephen Stevenson, or Steenson, ye are down here for a year's rent behind the hand—due at last term."

Stephen. "Please your honour, Sir John, I paid it to your father."

Sir John. "Ye took a receipt then, doubtless, Stephen; and can produce it?"

Stephen. "Indeed I hadna time, an it like your honour; for nae sooner had I set doun the siller, and just as his honour, Sir Robert, that's gaen, drew it till him to count it, and write out the receipt, he was ta'en wi' the pains that removed him."

"That was unlucky," said Sir John, after a pause. "But ye maybe paid it in the presence of somebody. I want but a *talis qualis* evidence, Stephen. I would go ower strictly to work with no poor man."

Stephen. "Troth, Sir John, there was naebody in the room but Dougal MacCallum the butler. But, as your honour kens, he has e'en followed his auld master."

"Very unlucky again, Stephen," said Sir John, without altering his voice a single note. "The man to whom ye paid the money is dead—and the man who witnessed the payment is dead too—and the siller, which should have been to the fore, is neither seen nor heard tell of in the repositories. How am I to believe a' this?"

Stephen. "I dinna ken, your honour; but there is a bit memorandum note of the very coins; for, God help me! I had to borrow out of twenty purses; and I am sure that ilk man there set down will take his grit oath for what purpose I borrowed the money."

Sir John. "I have little doubt ye *borrowed* the money, Steenie. It is the *payment* that I want to have some proof of."

Stephen. "The siller maun be about the house, Sir John. And since your honour never got it, and his honour that was canna have taen it wi' him, maybe some of the family may have seen it."

Sir John. "We will examine the servants, Stephen; that is but reasonable."

But lackey and lass, and page and groom, all denied stoutly that they had ever seen such a bag of money as my gudesire described. What was waur, he had unluckily not mentioned to any living soul of them his purpose of paying his rent. Ae quean had noticed something under his arm, but she took it for the pipes.

Sir John Redgauntlet ordered the servants out of the room, and then said to my gudesire, "Now, Steenie, ye see you have fair play; and, as I have little doubt ye ken better where to find the siller than ony other body, I beg, in fair terms, and for your own sake, that you will end this fasherie; for, Stephen, ye maun pay or flitt."

"The Lord forgie your opinion," said Stephen, driven almost to his wits' end—"I am an honest man."

"So am I, Stephen," said his honour; "and so are all the folks in the house, I hope. But if there be a knave amongst us, it must be he that tells the story he cannot prove." He paused, and then added, mair sternly, "If I understand your trick, sir, you want to take advantage of some malicious reports concerning things in this family, and particularly respecting my father's sudden death, thereby to cheat me out of the money, and perhaps take away my character, by insinuating that I have received the rent I am demanding.—Where do you suppose this money to be?—I insist upon knowing."

My gudesire saw everything look so muckle against him, that he grew nearly desperate—however, he shifted from one foot to another, looked to every corner of the room, and made no answer.

"Speak out, sirrah," said the Laird, assuming a look of his father's, a very particular ane, which he had when he was angry—it seemed as if the wrinkles of his frown made that self-same fearful shape of a horse's shoe in the middle of his brow;—"Speak out, sir! I *will* know your thoughts;—do you suppose that I have this money?"

"Far be it frae me to say so," said Stephen.

"Do you charge any of my people with having taken it?"

"I wad be laith to charge them that may be innocent," said my gudesire; "and if there by any one that is guilty, I have nae proof."

"Somewhere the money must be, if there is a word of truth in your story," said Sir John; "I ask where you think it is—and demand a correct answer?"

"In hell, if you will have my thoughts of it," said my gudesire, driven to extremity,—"in hell! with your father and his silver whistle."

Down the stairs he ran, (for the parlour was nae place for him after such a word,) and he heard the Laird swearing blood and wounds behind him, as fast as ever did Sir Robert, and roaring for the baillie and the baron-officer.

Away rode my gudesire to his chief creditor, (him they ca'd Laurie Lapraik,) to try if he could make onything out of him; but when he tauld his story, he got but the warst word in his wame—thief, beggar, and dyvour, were the saftest terms; and to the boot of these hard terms, Laurie brought up the auld story of his dipping his hand in the blood of God's saints, just as if a tenant could have helped riding with the Laird, and that a laird like Sir Robert Redgauntlet. My gudesire was, by this time, far beyond the bounds of patience, and, while he and Laurie were at de'il speed the liars, he was wanchancie aneugh to abuse his doctrine as weel as the man, and said things that gar'd folks flesh grew that heard them;—he wasna just him-sell, and he had lived wi' a wild set in his day.

At last they parted, and my gudesire was to ride hame through the wood of Pitmurkie, that is a' fou of black firs, as they say.—I ken the wood, but the firs may be black or white for what I can tell.—At the entry of the wood there is a wild common, and on the edge of the common, a little lonely change-house, that was keepit then by an ostler-wife, they suld hae ca'd her Tibbie Faw, and there puir Steenie cried for a mutchkin of brandy, for he had had no refreshment the hail day. Tibbie was earnest wi' him to take a bite of meat, but he couldna think o't, nor would he take his foot out of the stirrup, and took off the brandy wholely at twa draughts, and named a toast at each:—the first was, the memory of Sir Robert Redgauntlet, and might he never lie quiet in his grave till he had righted his poor bond-tenant; and the second was, a health to Man's Enemy, if he would but get him back the pock of siller, or tell him what came o't, for he saw the hail world was like to regard him as a thief and a cheat, and he took that waur than even the ruin of his house and hauld.

On he rode, little caring where. It was a dark night turned, and the trees made it yet darker, and he let the beast take its ain road through the wood; when, all of a sudden, from tired and wearied that it was before, the nag began to spring, and flee, and stend, that my gudesire could hardly keep the saddle—Upon the whilk, a horseman, suddenly riding up beside him, said, "That's a mettle beast of yours, freend; will you sell him?"—So saying, he touched the horse's neck with his riding-wand, and it fell into its auld heigh-ho of a stumbling trot; "But his spunk's soon out of him, I think," continued the stranger, "and that is like mony a man's courage, that thinks he wad do great things till he come to the proof."

My gudesire scarce listened to this but spurred his horse, with "Gude e'en to you, freend."

But it's like the stranger was ane that does na lightly yield his point; for, ride as Steenie liked, he was aye beside him at the self-same pace. At last my gudesire, Steenie Steenson, grew half angry; and, to say the truth, half feared.

"What is that ye want with me, freend?" he said. "If ye be a robber, I have nae money; if ye be a leal man, wanting company, I have nae heart to mirth or speaking; and if ye want to ken the road, I scarce ken it mysell."

"If you will tell me your grief," said the stranger, "I am one that, though I have been sair misca'd in the world, am the only hand for helping my friends."

So my gudesire, to ease his ain heart, mair than from any hope of help, told him the story from beginning to end.

"It's a hard pinch," said the stranger; "but I think I can help you."

"If you could lend the money, sir, and take a lang day—I ken nae other help on earth," said my gudesire.

"But there may be some under the earth," said the stranger. "Come, I'll be frank wi' you; I could lend you the money on bond, but you would maybe scruple my terms. Now, I can tell you, that your auld Laird is disturbed in his grave by your curses, and the wailing of your family, and—if ye daur venture to go to see him, he will give you the receipt."

My gudesire's hair stood on end at this proposal, but he thought his companion might be some humoursome chield that was trying to frighten him, and might end with lending him the money. Besides, he was bauld wi' brandy, and desperate wi' distress; and he said, he had courage to go to the gate of hell, and a step farther, for that receipt.—The stranger laughed.

Weel, they rode on through the thickest of the wood, when, all of a sudden, the horse stopped at the door of a great house; and, but that he knew the place was ten miles off, my father would have thought he was at

Redgauntlet Castle. They rode into the outer court-yard, through the muckle faulding yetts, and aneath the auld portcullis; and the whole front of the house was lighted, and there were pipes and fiddles, and as much dancing and deray within as used to be in Sir Robert's house at Pace and Yule, and such high seasons. They lap off, and my gudesire, as seemed to him, fastened his horse to the very ring he had tied him to that morning, when he gaed to wait on the young Sir John.

"God!" said my father, "if Sir Robert's death be but a dream!"

He knocked at the ha' door, just as he wont, and his auld acquaintance, Dougal MacCallum, just after his wont, too,—came to open the door, and said, "Piper Steenie, are ye there, lad? Sir Robert has been crying for you."

My gudesire was like a man in a dream—he looked for the stranger, but he was gaen for the time. At last, he just tried to say, "Ha! Dougal Driveower, are ye living? I thought ye had been dead."

"Never fash yoursell wi' me," said Dougal, "but look to yoursell; and see ye tak naething frae onybody here, neither meat, drink, or siller, except just the receipt that is your ain."

So saying, he led the way out through halls and trances that were weel kenn'd to my gudesire, and into the auld oak parlour; and there was as much singing of profane sangs, and birling of red wine, and speaking blasphemy and sculduddry, as had ever been in Redgauntlet Castle when it was at the blythest.

But, Lord take us in keeping! what a set of ghastly revellers they were that sat round that table!—My gudesire kenn'd mony that had long before gane to their place. There was the fierce Middleton, and the dissolute Rothes, and the crafty Lauderdale; and Dalyell, with his bald head and a beard to his girdle; and Earlshall, with Cameron's blude on his hand; and wild Bonshaw, that tied blessed Mr. Cargill's limbs till the blude sprung; and Dumbarton Douglas, the twice-turned traitor baith to country and king. There was the Bluidy Advocate MacKenyie, who, for his wordly wit and wisdom, had been to the rest as a god. And there was Claverhouse, as beautiful as when he lived, with his long, dark, curled locks, streaming down to his laced buff-coat, and his left hand always on his right spule-blade, to hide the wound that the silver bullet had made. He sat apart from them all, and looked at them with a melancholy, haughty countenance; while the rest hallooed, and sung, and laughed, that the room rang. But their smiles were fearfully contorted from time to time; and their laughter passed into such wild sounds, as made my gudesire's very nails grow blue, and chilled the marrow in his banes.

They that waited at the table were just the wicked serving-men and troopers, that had done their work and wicked bidding on earth. There was the Lang Lad of the Nethertown, that helped to take Argyle; and the Bishop's summoner, that they called the De'il's Rattle-bag; and the wicked guardsmen, in their laced coats; and the savage Highland Amorites, that shed blood like water; and many a proud serving-man, haughty of heart and bloody of hand, cringing to the rich, and making them wickeder than they would be; grinding the poor to powder, when the rich had broken them to fragments. And mony, mony mair were coming and ganging, a' as busy in their vocation as if they had been alive.

Sir Robert Redgauntlet, in the midst of a' this fearful riot, cried, wi' a voice like thunder, on Steenie Piper, to come to the board-head where he was sitting; his legs stretched out before him, and swathed up with flannel, with his holster pistols aside him, and the great broad-sword rested against his chair, just as my gudesire had seen him the last time upon earth—the very cushion for the jack-an-ape was close to him, but the creature itsell was not there—it wasna its hour, it's likely; for he heard them say as he came forward, "Is not the Major come yet?" And another answered, "The jack-an-ape will be here betimes the morn." And when my gudesire came forward, Sir Robert, or his ghaist, or the deevil in his likeness, said, "Weel, piper, hae ye settled wi' my son for the year's rent?"

With much ado my father gat breath to say, that Sir John would not settle without his honour's receipt.

"Ye shall hae that for a tune of the pipes, Steenie," said the appearance of Sir Robert—"Play us up 'Weel hoddled, Luckie.'"

Now this was a tune my gudesire learned frae a warlock, that heard it when they were worshipping Satan at their meetings; and my gudesire had sometimes played it at the ranting suppers in Redgauntlet Castle, but never very willingly; and now he grew cauld at the very name of it, and said, for excuse, he hadna his pipes wi' him.

"MacCallum, ye limb of Beelzebub," said the fearfu' Sir Robert, "bring Steenie the pipes that I am keeping for him!"

MacCallum brought a pair of pipes might have served the piper of

Donald of the Isles. But he gave my gudesire a nudge as he offered them; and looking secretly and closely, Steenie saw that the chanter was of steel, and heated to a white heat; so he had fair warning not to trust his fingers with it. So he excused himself again, and said, he was faint and frightened, and had not wind aneugh to fill the bag.

"Then ye maun eat and drink, Steenie," said the figure; "for we do little else here; and it's ill speaking between a fou man and a fasting."

Now these were the very words that the bloody Earl of Douglas said to keep the King's messenger in hand, while he cut the head off MacLellan of Bombie, at the Threave Castle; and that put Steenie mair and mair on his guard. So he spoke up like a man, and said he came neither to eat, or drink, or make minstrelsy; but simply for his ain—to ken what was come o' the money he had paid, and to get a discharge for it; and he was so stout-hearted by this time, that he charged Sir Robert for conscience-sake—(he had no power to say the holy name)—and as he hoped for peace and rest, to spread no snares for him, but just to give him his ain.

The appearance gnashed its teeth and laughed, but it took from a large pocket-book the receipt, and handed it to Steenie. "Here is your receipt, ye pitiful cur; and for the money, my dog-whelp of a son may go look for it in the Cat's Cradle."

My gudesire uttered mony thanks, and was about to retire, when Sir Robert roared aloud, "Stop though, thou sack-doudling son of a whore! I am not done with thee. HERE we do nothing for nothing; and you must return on this very day twelvemonth, to pay your master the homage that you owe me for my protection."

My father's tongue was loosed of a suddenty, and he said aloud, "I refer mysell to God's pleasure, and not to yours."

He had no sooner uttered the word than all was dark around him; and he sunk on the earth with such a sudden shock, that he lost both breath and sense.

How lang Steenie lay there, he could not tell; but when he came to himsell, he was lying in the auld kirkyard of Redgauntlet parishine, just at the door of the family aisle, and the scutcheon of the auld knight, Sir Robert, hanging over his head. There was a deep morning fog on grass and gravestone around him, and his horse was feeding quietly beside the minister's twa cows. Steenie would have thought the whole was a dream, but he had the receipt in his hand, fairly written and signed by the auld Laird; only the last letters of his name were a little disorderly, written like one seized with sudden pain.

Sorely troubled in his mind, he left that dreary place, rode through the mist to Redgauntlet Castle, and with much ado he got speech of the Laird. "Well, you dyvour bankrupt," was the first word, "have you brought me my rent?"

"No," answered my gudesire, "I have not; but I have brought your honour Sir Robert's receipt for it."

"How, sirrah?—Sir Robert's receipt!—You told me he had not given you one."

"Will your honour please to see if that bit line is right?"

Sir John looked at every line, and at every letter, with much attention; and at last, at the date, which my gudesire had not observed,—*"From my appointed place,"* he read, *"this twenty-fifth of November."*—"What!—That is yesterday! Villain, thou must have gone to hell for this!"

"I got it from your honour's father—whether he be in heaven or hell, I know not," said Steenie.

"I will delate you for a warlock to the Privy Council!" said Sir John. "I will send you to your master, the devil, with the help of a tar-barrel and a torch!"

"I intend to delate mysell to the Presbytery," said Steenie, "and tell them all I have seen last night, whilk are things fitter for them to judge of than a borrel man like me."

Sir John paused, composed himsell, and desired to hear the full history; and my gudesire told it him from point to point, as I have told it you—word for word, neither more nor less.

Sir John was silent again for a long time, and at last he said, very composedly, "Steenie, this story of yours concerns the honour of many a noble family besides mine; and if it be a leasing-making, to keep yourself out of my danger, the least you can expect is to have a red-hot iron driven through your tongue, and that will be as bad as scauding your fingers wi' a red-hot chanter. But yet it may be true, Steenie; and if the money cast up, I will not know what to think of it.—But where shall we find the Cat's Cradle? There are cats enough about the old house, but I think they kitten without the ceremony of bed or cradle."

"We were best ask Hutcheon," said my gudesire; "he kens a' the odd corners about as weel as—another serving-man that is now gane, and that I wad not like to name."

Aweel, Hutcheon, when he was asked, told them, that a ruinous turret, lang disused, next to the clock-house, only accessible by a ladder, for the opening was on the outside, and far above the battlements, was called of old the Cat's Cradle.

"There will I go immediately," said Sir John; and he took (with what purpose, Heaven kens,) one of his father's pistols from the hall-table, where they had lain since the night he died, and hastened to the battlements.

It was a dangerous place to climb, for the ladder was auld and frail, and wanted ane or twa rounds. However, up got Sir John, and entered at the turret door; where his body stopped the only little light that was in the bit turret. Something flees at him wi' a vengeance, maist dang him back ower— bang gaed the knight's pistol, and Hutcheon, that held the ladder, and my gudesire that stood beside him, hears a loud skelloch. A minute after, Sir John flings the body of the jack-an-ape down to them, and cries that the siller is fund, and that they should come up and help him. And there was the bag of siller sure aneugh, and mony orra things besides, that had been missing for mony a day. And Sir John, when he had riped the turret weel, led my gudesire into the dining-parlour, and took him by the hand, and spoke kindly to him, and said he was sorry he should have doubted his word, and that he would hereafter be a good master to him, to make amends.

"And now, Steenie," said Sir John, "although this vision of yours tends, on the whole, to my father's credit, as an honest man, that he should, even after his death, desire to see justice done to a poor man like you, yet you are sensible that ill-dispositioned men might make bad constructions upon it, concerning his soul's health. So, I think, we had better lay the hail dir- dum on that ill-deedie creature, Major Weir, and say naething about your dream in the wood of Pitmurkie. You had taken ower mickle brandy to be very certain about onything; and, Steenie, this receipt, (his hand shook while he held it out)—it's but a queer kind of document, and we will do best, I think, to put it quietly in the fire."

"Od, but for as queer as it is, it's a' the voucher I have for my rent," said my gudesire, who was afraid, it may be, of losing the benefit of Sir Robert's discharge.

"I will bear the contents to your credit in the rental-book, and give you a discharge under my own hand," said Sir John, "and that on the spot. And, Steenie, if you can hold your tongue about this matter, you shall sit, from this term downward, at an easier rent."

"Mony thanks to your honour," said Steenie, who saw easily in what corner the wind sat; "doubtless I will be conformable to all your honour's commands; only I would willingly speak wi' some powerful minister on the subject, for I do not like the sort of soumons of appointment whilk you honour's father—"

"Do not call the phantom my father!" said Sir John, interrupting him.

"Weel, then, the thing that was so like him,"—said my gudesire; "he spoke of my coming back to him this time twelvemonth, and it's a weight on my conscience."

"Aweel, then," said Sir John, "if you be so much distressed in mind, you may speak to our minister of the parish; he is a douce man, regards the honour of our family, and the mair that he may look for some patronage from me."

Wi' that, my father readily agreed that the receipt should be burnt, and the Laird threw it into the chimney with his ain hand. Burn it would not for them, though; but away it flew up the lumm, wi' a lang train of sparks at its tail, and a hissing noise like a squib.

My gudesire gaed down to the Manse, and the minister, when he had heard the story, said, it was his real opinion, that though my gudesire had gaen very far in tampering with dangerous matters, yet, as he had refused the devil's arles, (for such was the offer of meat and drink), and had refused to do homage by piping at his bidding, he hoped, that if he held a circum-spect walk hereafter, Satan could take little advantage by what was come and gane. And, indeed, my gudesire, of his ain accord, lang forswore baith the pipes and brandy—it was not even till the year was out, and the fatal day passed, that he would so much as take the fiddle, or drink usquebaugh or tippenny.

Sir John made up his story about the jack-an-ape as he liked himsell; and some believe till this day there was no mair in the matter than the filch-ing nature of the brute. Indeed ye'll no hinder some to threap, that it was nane o' the Auld Enemy that Dougal and my gudesire saw in the Laird's room, but only that wanchancy creature, the Major, capering on the coffin;

and that, as to the blawing on the Laird's whistle that was heard after he was dead, the filthy brute could do that as weel as the Laird himsell, if no better. But Heaven kens the truth, whilk first came out by the minister's wife, after Sir John and her ain gudeman were baith in the moulds. And then my gudesire, wha was failed in his limbs, but not in his judgment or memory—at least nothing to speak of—was obliged to tell the real narrative to his friends, for the credit of his gude name. He might else have been charged for a warlock.

The Tapestried Chamber
or
The Lady in the Sacque

The following narrative is given from the pen, so far as memory permits, in the same character in which it was presented to the author's ear; nor has he claim to further praise, or to be more deeply censured, than in proportion to the good or bad judgment which he has employed in selecting his materials, as he has studiously avoided any attempt at ornament which might interfere with the simplicity of the tale.

At the same time it must be admitted, that the particular class of stories which turns on the marvellous, possesses a stronger influence when told, than when committed to print. The volume taken up at noonday, though rehearsing the same incidents, conveys a much more feeble impression, than is achieved by the voice of the speaker on a circle of fire-side auditors, who hang upon the narrative as the narrator details the minute incidents which serve to give it authenticity, and lowers his voice with an affectation of mystery while he approaches the fearful and wonderful part. It was with such advantages that the present writer heard the following events related, more than twenty years since, by the celebrated Miss Seward, of Lichfield, who, to her numerous accomplishments, added, in a remarkable degree, the power of narrative in private conversation. In its present form the tale must necessarily lose all the interest which was attached to it, by the flexible voice and intelligent features of the gifted narrator. Yet still, read aloud, to an undoubting audience by the doubtful light of the closing evening, or, in silence, by a decaying taper, and amidst the solitude of a half-lighted apartment, it may redeem its character as a good ghost-story. Miss Seward always affirmed that she had derived her information from an authentic source, although she suppressed the names of the two persons chiefly concerned. I will not avail myself of any particular I may have since received concerning the localities of the detail, but suffer them to rest under the same general description in which they were first related to me; and, for the same reason, I will not add to, or diminish the narrative, by any circumstance, whether moer or less material, but simply rehearse, as I heard it, a story of supernatural terror.

About the end of the American war, when the officers of Lord Cornwallis's army, which surrendered at Yorktown, and others, who had been made prisoners during the impolitic and ill-fated controversy, were returning to their own country, to relate their adventures, and repose themselves after their fatigues; there was amongst them a general officer, to whom Miss S. gave the name of Browne, but merely, as I understood, to save the inconvenience of introducing a nameless agent in the narrative. He was an officer of merit, as well as a gentleman of high consideration for family and attainments.

Some business had carried General Browne upon a tour through the western counties, when, in the conclusion of a morning stage, he found himself in the vicinity of a small country town, which presented a scene of uncommon beauty, and of a character peculiarly English.

The little town, with its stately old church, whose tower bore testimony to the devotion of ages long past, lay amidst pastures and corn-fields of small extent, but bounded and divided with hedge-row timber of great age and size. There were few marks of modern improvement. The environs of the place intimated neither the solitude of decay, nor the bustle of novelty; the houses were old, but in good repair; and the beautiful little river murmured freely on its way to the left of the town, neither restrained by a dam, nor bordered by a towing-path.

Upon a gentle eminence, nearly a mile to the southward of the town, were seen, amongst many venerable oaks and tangled thickets, the turrets of a castle, as old as the wars of York and Lancaster, but which seemed to have received important alterations during the age of Elizabeth and her successor. It had not been a place of great size; but whatever accommodation it formerly afforded, was, it must be supposed, still to be obtained within its walls; at least, such was the inference which General Browne drew from observing the smoke arise merrily from several of the ancient wreathed and carved chimney-stalks. The wall of the park ran alongside of the highway for two or three hundred yards; and through the different points by which the eye found glimpses into the woodland scenery, it seemed to be well stocked. Other points of view opened in succession; now a full one, of the front of the old castle, and now a side glimpse at its particular towers, the former rich in all the bizarrerie of the Elizabethan school, while the simple and solid strength of other parts of the building seemed to show that they had been raised more for defence than ostentation.

Delighted with the partial glimpses which he obtained of the castle through the woods and glades by which this ancient feudal fortress was surrounded, our military traveller was determined to inquire whether it might not deserve a nearer view, and whether it contained family pictures or other objects of curiosity worthy of a stranger's visit; when, leaving the vicinity of the park, he rolled through a clean and well-paved street, and stopped at the door of a well-frequented inn.

Before ordering horses to proceed on his journey, General Browne made inquiries concerning the proprietor of the chateau which had so attracted his admiration; and was equally surprised and pleased at hearing in reply a nobleman named, whom we shall call Lord Woodville. How fortunate! Much of Browne's early recollections, both at school, and at college, had been connected with young Woodville, whom, by a few questions, he now ascertained to be the same with the owner of this fair domain. He had been raised to the peerage by the decease of his father a few months before, and, as the general learned from the landlord, the term of mourning being ended, was now taking possession of his paternal estate, in the jovial season of merry autumn, accompanied by a select party of friends to enjoy the sports of a country famous for game.

This was delightful news to our traveller. Frank Woodville had been Browne's fag at Eton, and his chosen intimate at Christ Church; their pleasures and their tasks had been the same; and the honest soldier's heart warmed to find his early friend in possession of so delightful a residence, and of an estate, as the landlord assured him with a nod and a wink, fully adequate to maintain and add to his dignity. Nothing was more natural than that the traveller should suspend a journey, which there was nothing to render hurried, to pay a visit to an old friend under such agreeable circumstances.

The fresh horses, therefore, had only the brief task of conveying the general's travelling carriage to Woodville Castle. A porter admitted them at a modern gothic lodge, built in that style to correspond with the castle itself, and at the same time rang a bell to give warning of the approach of visitors. Apparently the sound of the bell had suspended the separation of the company, bent on the various amusements of the morning; for, on entering the court of the chateau, several young men were lounging about in their sporting dresses, looking at, and criticising, the dogs which the keepers held in readiness to attend their pastime. As General Browne alighted, the young lord came to the gate of the hall, and for an instant gazed, as at a stranger, upon the countenance of his friend, on which war, with its fatigues and its wounds, had made a great alteration. But the uncertainty lasted no longer than till the visitor had spoken, and the hearty greeting which followed was such as can only be exchanged betwixt those, who have passed together the merry days of careless boyhood or early youth.

"If I could have formed a wish, my dear Browne," said Lord Woodville, "it would have been to have you here, of all men, upon this occasion, which my friends are good enough to hold as a sort of holiday. Do not think you have been unwatched during the years you have been absent from us. I have traced you through your dangers, your triumphs, your misfortunes, and was delighted to see that, whether in victory or defeat, the name of my old friend was always distinguished with applause."

The general made a suitable reply, and congratulated his friend on his new dignities, and the possession of a place and domain so beautiful.

"Nay, you have seen nothing of it as yet," said Lord Woodville, "and I trust you do not mean to leave us till you are better acquainted with it. It is true, I confess, that my present party is pretty large, and the old house, like other places of the kind, does not possess so much accommodation as the extent of the outward walls appears to promise. But we can give you a comfortable old-fashioned room, and I venture to suppose that your campaigns have taught you to be glad of worse quarters."

The general shrugged his shoulders and laughed. "I presume," he said, "the worst apartment in your chateau is considerably superior to the old tobacco-cask, in which I was fain to take up my night's lodging when I was in the Bush, as the Virginians call it, with the light corps. There I lay, like Diogenes himself, so delighted with my covering from the element, that I made a vain attempt to have it rolled in to my next quarters; but my commander for the time would give way to no such luxurious provision, and I took farewell of my beloved cask with tears in my eyes."

"Well, then, since you do not fear your quarters," said Lord Woodville, "you will stay with me a week at least. Of guns, dogs, fishing-rods, flies, and means of sport by sea and land, we have enough and to spare: you cannot pitch on an amusement but we will find the means of pursuing it. But if you prefer the gun and pointers, I will go with you myself, and see whether you have mended your shooting since you have been amongst the Indians of the back settlements."

The general gladly accepted his friendly host's proposal in all its points. After a morning of manly exercise, the company met at dinner, where it was the delight of Lord Woodville to conduce to the display of the high properties of his recovered friend, so as to recommend him to his guests, most of whom were persons of distinction. He led General Browne to speak of the scenes he had witnessed; and as every word marked alike the brave officer and the sensible man, who retained possession of his cool judgment under the most imminent dangers, the company, looked upon the soldier with general respect, as on one who had proved himself possessed of an uncommon portion of personal courage; that attribute, of all others, of which every body desires to be thought possessed.

The day at Woodville Castle ended as usual in such mansions. The hospitality stopped within the limits of good order: music, in which the young lord was a proficient, succeeded to the circulation of the bottle: cards and billiards, for those who preferred such amusements, were in readiness: but the exercise of the morning required early hours, and not long after eleven o'clock the guests began to retire to their several apartments.

The young lord himself conducted his friend, General Browne, to the chamber destined for him, which answered the description he had given of it, being comfortable, but old-fashioned. The bed was of the massive form used in the end of the seventeenth century, and the curtains of faded silk, heavily trimmed with tarnished gold. But then the sheets, pillows, and blankets looked delightful to the campaigner, when he thought of his "mansion, the cask." There was an air of gloom in the tapestry hangings, which, with their worn-out graces, curtained the walls of the little chamber, and gently undulated as the autumnal breeze found its way through the ancient lattice-window, which pattered and whistled as the air gained entrance. The toilette, too, with its mirror, turbaned, after the manner of the beginning of the century, with a coiffure of murrey-coloured silk, and its hundred strange-shaped boxes, providing for arrangements which had been obsolete for more than fifty years, had an antique, and in so far a melancholy, aspect. But nothing could blaze more brightly and cheerfully than the two large wax candles; or if aught could rival them, it was the flaming, bickering fagots in the chimney, that sent at once their gleam and their warmth, through the snug apartment; which, notwithstanding the general antiquity of its appearance, was not wanting in the least convenience that modern habits rendered either necessary or desirable.

"This is an old-fashioned sleeping apartment, general," said the young lord, "but I hope you find nothing that makes you envy your old tobacco-cask."

"I am not particular respecting my lodgings," replied the general; "yet were I to make any choice, I would prefer this chamber by many degrees, to the gayer and more modern rooms of your family mansion. Believe me, that when I unite its modern air of comfort with its venerable antiquity, and recollect that it is your lordship's property, I shall feel in better quarters here, than if I were in the best hotel London could afford."

"I trust—I have no doubt—that you will find yourself as comfortable as I wish you, my dear general," said the young nobleman; and once more bidding his guest good night, he shook him by the hand, and withdrew.

The general once more looked round him, and internally congratulating himself on his return to peaceful life, the comforts of which were endeared by the recollection of the hardships and dangers he had lately sustained, undressed himself, and prepared for a luxurious night's rest.

Here, contrary to the custom of this species of tale, we leave the general in possession of his apartment until the next morning.

The company assembled for breakfast at an early hour, but without the appearance of General Browne, who seemed the guest that Lord Woodville was desirous of honouring above all whom his hospitality had assembled around him. He more than once expressed surprise at the general's absence, and at length sent a servant to make inquiry after him. The man brought back information that General Browne had been walking abroad since an early hour of the morning, in defiance of the weather, which was misty and ungenial.

"The custom of a solder,"—said the young nobleman to his friends; "many of them acquire habitual vigilance, and cannot sleep after the early hour at which their duty usually commands them to be alert."

Yet the explanation which Lord Woodville then offered to the company seemed hardly satisfactory to his own mind, and it was in a fit of silence and abstraction that he awaited the return of the general. It took place near an hour after the breakfast bell had rung. He looked fatigued and feverish. His hair, the powdering and arrangement of which was at this time one of the most important occupations of a man's whole day, and marked his fashion as much as, in the present time, the tying of a cravat, or the want of one, was dishevelled, uncurled, void of powder, and dank with dew. His clothes were huddled on with a careless negligence, remarkable in a military man, whose real or supposed duties are usually held to include some attention to the toilette; and his looks were haggard and ghastly in a peculiar degree.

"So you have stolen a march upon us this morning, my dear general," said Lord Woodville; "or you have not found your bed so much to your mind as I had hoped and you seemed to expect. How did you rest last night?"

"Oh, excellently well! remarkably well! never better in my life"—said General Browne rapidly, and yet with an air of embarrassment which was obvious to his friend. He then hastily swallowed a cup of tea, and, neglecting or refusing whatever else he was offered, seemed to fall into a fit of abstraction.

"You will take the gun to-day, general?" said his friend and host, but had to repeat the question twice ere he received the abrupt answer, "No, my lord; I am sorry I cannot have the honour of spending another day with your lordship: my post horses are ordered, and will be here directly."

All who were present showed surprise, and Lord Woodville immediately replied, "Post horses, my good friend! what can you possibly want with them, when you promised to stay with me quietly for at least a week?"

"I believe," said the general, obviously much embarrassed, "that I might, in the pleasure of my first meeting with your lordship, have said something about stopping here a few days; but I have since found it altogether impossible."

"That is very extraordinary," answered the young nobleman. "You seemed quite disengaged yesterday, and you cannot have had a summons to-day; for our post has not come up from town, and therefore you cannot have received any letters."

General Browne, without giving any further explanation, muttered something of indispensable business, and insisted on the absolute necessity of his departure in a manner which silenced all opposition on the part of his host, who saw that his resolution was taken, and forbore all further importunity.

"At least, however," he said, "permit me, my dear Browne, since go you will or must, to show you the view from the terrace, which the mist, that is now rising, will soon display."

He threw open a sash-window, and stepped down upon the terrace as he spoke. The general followed him mechanically, but seemed little to attend to what his host was saying, as, looking across an extended and rich prospect, he pointed out the different objects worthy of observation. Thus they moved on till Lord Woodville had attained his purpose of drawing his guest entirely apart from the rest of the company, when, turning round upon him with an air of great solemnity, he addressed him thus:

"Richard Browne, my old and very dear friend, we are now alone. Let me conjure you to answer me upon the word of a friend, and the honour of a soldier. How did you in reality rest during the night?"

"Most wretchedly indeed, my lord," answered the general, in the same tone of solemnity;—"so miserably, that I would not run the risk of such a second night, not only for all the lands belonging to this castle, but for all the country which I see from this elevated point of view."

"This is most extraordinary," said the young lord, as if speaking to himself; "then there must be something in the reports concerning that apartment." Again turning to the general, he said, "For God's sake, my dear friend, be candid with me, and let me know the disagreeable particulars which have befallen you under a roof where, with consent of the owner, you should have met nothing save comfort."

The General seemed distressed by this appeal, and paused a moment before he replied. "My dear lord," he at length said, "what happened to me last night is of a nature so peculiar and so unpleasant, that I could hardly bring myself to detail it even to your lordship, were it not that, independent of my wish to gratify any request of yours, I think that sincerity on my part may lead to some explanation about a circumstance equally painful and mysterious. To others, the communication I am about to make might place me in the light of a weak-minded, superstitious fool, who suffered his own imagination to delude and bewilder him; but you have known me in childhood and youth, and will not suspect me of having adopted in manhood, the feelings and frailties from which my early years were free." Here he paused, and his friend replied:

"Do not doubt my perfect confidence in the truth of your communication, however strange it may be," replied Lord Woodville; "I know your firmness of disposition too well, to suspect you could be made the object of imposition, and am aware that your honour and your friendship will equally deter you from exaggerating whatever you may have witnessed."

"Well, then," said the general, "I will proceed with my story as well as I can, relying upon your candour, and yet distinctly feeling that I would rather face a battery than recall to my mind the odious recollections of last night."

He paused a second time, and then perceiving that Lord Woodville remained silent and in an attitude of attention, he commenced, though not without obvious reluctance, the history of his night adventures in the Tapestried Chamber.

"I undressed and went to bed, so soon as your lordship left me yesterday evening; but the wood in the chimney, which nearly fronted my bed, blazed brightly and cheerfully, and, aided by a hundred recollections of my childhood and youth, which had been recalled by the unexpected pleasure of meeting your lordship, prevented me from falling immediately asleep. I ought, however, to say, that these reflections were all of a pleasant and agreeable kind, grounded on a sense of having for a time exchanged the labour, fatigues, and dangers of my profession, for the enjoyments of a peaceful life, and the reunion of those friendly and affectionate ties, which I had torn asunder at the rude summons of war.

"While such pleasing reflections were stealing over my mind, and gradually lulling me to slumber, I was suddenly aroused by a sound like that of the rustling of a silken gown, and the tapping of a pair of high-heeled shoes, as if a woman were walking in the apartment. Ere I could draw the curtain to see what the matter was, the figure of a little woman passed between the bed and the fire. The back of this form was turned to me, and I could observe, from the shoulders and neck, it was that of an old woman, whose dress was an old-fashioned gown, which, I think, ladies call a sacque—that is, a sort of robe completely loose in the body, but gathered into broad plaits upon the neck and shoulders, which fall down to the ground, and terminate in a species of train.

"I thought the intrusion singular enough, but never harboured for a moment the idea that what I saw was anything more than the mortal form of some old woman about the establishment, who had a fancy to dress like her grandmother, and who, having perhaps (as your lordship mentioned that you were rather straitened for room) been dislodged from her chamber for my accommodation, had forgotten the circumstances and returned by twelve, to her old haunt. Under this persuasion I moved myself in bed and coughed a little, to make the intruder sensible of my being in possession of the premises.—She turned slowly round, but, gracious heaven! my lord, what a countenance did she display to me! There was no longer any question what she was, or any thought of her being a living being. Upon a face which wore the fixed features of a corpse were imprinted the traces of the vilest and most hideous passions which had animated her while she lived. The body of some atrocious criminal seemed to have been given up from the grave, and the soul restored from the penal fire, in order to form, for a space, an union with the ancient accomplice of its guilt. I started up in bed, and sat upright, supporting myself on my palms, as I gazed on this horrible spectre. The hag made, as it seemed, a single and swift stride to the bed where I lay, and squatted herself down upon it, in precisely the same attitude which I had assumed in the extremity of horror, advancing her diabolical countenance within half a yard of mine, with a grin which seemed to intimate the malice and the derision of an incarnate fiend."

Here General Browne stopped, and wiped from his brow the cold perspiration with which the recollection of his horrible vision had covered it.

"My lord," he said, "I am no coward. I have been in all the mortal dangers incidental to my profession, and I may truly boast, that no man ever knew Richard Browne dishonour the sword he wears; but in these horrible circumstances, under the eyes, and, as it seemed, almost in the grasp of an incarnation of an evil spirit, all firmness forsook me, all manhood melted from me like wax in the furnace, and I felt my hair individually bristle. The current of my life-blood ceased to flow, and I sank back in a swoon, as very a victim to panic terror as ever was a village girl or a child of ten years old. How long I lay in this condition I cannot pretend to guess.

"But I was roused by the castle clock striking one, so loud that it seemed as if it were in the very room. It was some time before I dared open my eyes, lest they should again encounter the horrible spectacle. When, however, I summoned courage to look up, she was no longer visible. My first idea was to pull my bell, wake the servants, and remove to a garret or a hay-loft, to be ensured against a second visitation. Nay, I will confess the truth, that my resolution was altered, not by the shame of exposing myself, but by the fear that, as the bell-cord hung by the chimney, I might, in making my way to it, be again crossed by the fiendish hag, who, I figured to myself, might be still lurking about some corner of the apartment.

"I will not pretend to describe what hot and cold fever-fits tormented me for the rest of the night, through broken sleep, weary vigils, and that dubious state which forms the neutral ground between them. An hundred terrible objects appeared to haunt me; but there was the great difference betwixt the vision which I have described, and those which followed, that I knew the last to be deceptions of my own fancy and over-excited nerves.

"Day at last appeared, and I rose from my bed ill in health, and humiliated in mind. I was ashamed of myself as a man and a soldier, and still more so, at feeling my own extreme desire to escape from the haunted apartment, which, however, conquered all other considerations; so that, huddling on my clothes with the most careless haste, I made my escape from your lordship's mansion, to seek in the open air some relief to my nervous system, shaken as it was by this horrible rencounter with a visitant, for such I must believe her, from the other world. Your lordship has now heard the cause of my discomposure, and of my sudden desire to leave your hospitable castle. In other places I trust we may often meet; but God protect me from ever spending a second night under that roof!"

Strange as the general's tale was, he spoke with such a deep air of conviction, that it cut short all the usual commentaries which are made on such stories. Lord Woodville never once asked him if he was sure he did not dream of the apparition, or suggested any of the possibilities by which it is fashionable to explain apparitions,—wild vagaries of the fancy, or deceptions of the optic nerves. On the contrary, he seemed deeply impressed with the truth and reality of what he had heard; and, after a considerable pause, regretted, with much appearance of sincerity, that his early friend should in his house have suffered so severely.

"I am the more sorry for your pain, my dear Browne," he continued, "that it is the unhappy, though most unexpected, result of an experiment of my own. You must know that, for my father and grandfather's time, at least, the apartment which was assigned to you last night, had been shut on account of reports that it was disturbed by supernatural sights and noises. When I came, a few weeks since, into possession of the estate, I thought the accommodation, which the castle afforded for my friends, was not extensive enough to permit the inhabitants of the invisible world to retain possession of a comfortable sleeping-apartment. I therefore caused the Tapestried Chamber, as we call it, to be opened; and, without destroying its air of antiquity, I had such new articles of furniture placed in it as became the modern times. Yet, as the opinion that the room was haunted very strongly prevailed among the domestics, and was also known in the neighbourhood and to many of my friends, I feared some prejudice might be entertained by the first occupant of the Tapestried Chamber, which might tend to revive the evil report which it had laboured under, and so disappoint my purpose of rendering it a useful part of the house. I must confess, my dear Browne, that your arrival yesterday, agreeable to me for a thousand reasons besides, seemed the most favourable opportunity of removing the unpleasant rumours which attached to the room, since your courage was indubitable, and your mind free of any pre-occupation on the subject. I could not, therefore, have chosen a more fitting subject for my experiment."

"Upon my life," said General Browne, somewhat hastily, "I am infinitely obliged to your lordship—very particularly indebted indeed. I am likely to remember for some time the consequences of the experiment, as your lordship is pleased to call it."

"Nay, now you are unjust, my dear friend," said Lord Woodville. "You have only to reflect for a single moment, in order to be convinced that I could not augur the possibility of the pain to which you have been so unhappily exposed. I was yesterday morning a complete sceptic on the subject of supernatural appearances. Nay, I am sure that had I told you what was said about that room, those very reports would have induced you, by your own choice, to select it for your accommodation. It was my misfortune, perhaps my error, but really cannot be termed my fault, that you have been afflicted so strangely."

"Strangely indeed!" said the general, resuming his good temper; "and I acknowledge that I have no right to be offended with your lordship for treating me like what I used to think myself—a man of some firmness and courage.—But I see my post horses are arrived, and I must not detain your lordship from your amusement."

"Nay, my old friend," said Lord Woodville, "since you cannot stay with us another day, which, indeed, I can no longer urge, give me at least half an hour more. You used to love pictures, and I have a gallery of portraits, some of them by Vandyke, representing ancestry to whom this property and castle formerly belonged. I think that several of them will strike you as possessing merit."

General Browne accepted the invitation, though somewhat unwillingly. It was evident he was not to breathe freely or at ease, till he left Woodville Castle far behind him. He could not refuse his friend's invitation, however; and the less so, that he was a little ashamed of the peevishness which he had displayed towards his well-meaning entertainer.

The general, therefore, followed Lord Woodville through several rooms, into a long gallery hung with pictures, which the latter pointed out to his guest, telling the names, and giving some account of the personages whose portraits presented themselves in progression. General Browne was but little interested in the details which these accounts conveyed to him. They were, indeed, of the kind which are usually found in an old family gallery. Here, was a cavalier who had ruined the estate in the royal cause; there, was a fine lady who had reinstated it by contracting a match with a wealthy round-head. There, hung a gallant who had been in danger for corresponding with the exiled court at St. Germain's; here, one who had taken arms for William at the revolution; and there, a third that had thrown his weight alternately into the scale of whig and tory.

While Lord Woodville was cramming these words into his guest's hear, "against the stomach of his sense," they gained the middle of the gallery, when he beheld General Browne suddenly start, and assume an attitude of the utmost surprise, not unmixed with fear, as his eyes were caught and suddenly riveted by a portrait of an old lady in a sacque, the fashionable dress of the end of the seventeenth century.

"There she is!" he exclaimed—"there she is, in form and features, though inferior in demoniac expression to, the accursed hag who visited me last night."

"If that be the case," said the young nobleman, "there can remain no longer any doubt of the horrible reality of your apparition. That is the picture of a wretched ancestress of mine, of whose crimes a black and fearful catalogue is recorded in a family history in my charter-chest. The recital of them would be too horrible: it is enough to say, that in yon fatal apartment incest, and unnatural murder, were committed. I will restore it to the solitude to which the better judgment of those who preceded me had consigned it; and never shall any one, so long as I can prevent it, be exposed to a repetition of the supernatural horrors which could shake such courage as yours."

Thus the friends, who had met with such glee, parted in a very different mood; Lord Woodville to command the tapestried chamber to be unmantled, and the door built up; and General Browne to seek in some less beautiful country, and with some less dignified friend, forgetfulness of the painful night which he had passed in Woodville Castle.

My Aunt Margaret's Mirror

"There are times
When Fancy plays her gambols, in despite
Even of our watchful senses, when in sooth
Substance seems shadow, shadow substance seems,
When the broad, palpable, and mark'd partition
'Twixt that which is and is not, seems dissolved,
As if the mental eye gain'd power to gaze
Beyond the limits of the existing world.
Such hours of shadowy dreams I better love
Than all the gross realities of life."

ANONYMOUS

My Aunt Margaret was one of that respected sisterhood, upon whom devolve all the trouble and solicitude incidental to the possession of children, excepting only that which attends their entrance into the world. We were a large family, of very different dispositions and constitutions. Some were dull and peevish—they were sent to Aunt Margaret to be amused; some were rude, romping, and boisterous—they were sent to Aunt Margaret to be kept quiet, or rather, that their noise might be removed out of hearing: those who were indisposed were sent with the prospect of being nursed—those who were stubborn, with the hope of their being subdued by the kindness of Aunt Margaret's discipline: in short, she had all the various duties of a mother, without the credit and dignity of the maternal character. The busy scene of her various cares is now over—of the invalids and the robust, the kind and the rough, the peevish and pleased children, who thronged her little parlour from morning to night, not one now remains alive but myself; who, afflicted by early infirmity, was one of the most delicate of her nurselings, yet, nevertheless, have outlived them all.

It is still my custom, and shall be so while I have the use of my limbs, to visit my respected relation at least three times a week. Her abode is about half a mile from the suburbs of the town in which I reside; and is accessible, not only by the high road, from which it stands at some distance, but by means of a green-sward foot-path, leading through some pretty meadows. I have so little left to torment me in life, that it is one of my greatest vexations to know that several of these sequestered fields have been devoted as sites for building. In that which is nearest the town, wheel-barrows have been at work for several weeks in such numbers, that, I verily believe, its whole surface, to the depth of at least eighteen inches, was mounted in these monotrochs at the same moment, and in the act of being transported from one place to another. Huge triangular piles of planks are also reared in different parts of the devoted messuage; and a little group of trees, that still grace the eastern end, which rises in a gentle ascent, have just received warning to quit, expressed by a daub of white paint, and are to give place to a curious grove of chimneys.

It would, perhaps, hurt others in my situation to reflect that this little range of pasturage once belonged to my father (whose family was of some consideration in the world), and was sold by patches to remedy distresses in which he involved himself in an attempt by commercial adventure to redeem his diminished fortune. While the building scheme was in full operation, this circumstance was often pointed out to me by the class of friends who are anxious that no part of your misfortunes should escape your observation. "Such pasture ground!—lying at the very town's-end—in turnips and potatoes, the parks would bring £20 per acre, and if leased for building—O, it was a gold mine!—And all sold for an old song out of the ancient possessor's hands." My comforters cannot bring me to repine much on this subject. If I could be allowed to look back on the past without interruption, I could willingly give up the enjoyment of present income, and the hope of future profit, to those who have purchased what my father sold. I regret the alteration of the ground only because it destroys associations, and I would more willingly (I think) see the Earl's Closes in the hands of strangers, retaining their sylvan appearance, than know them for my own, if torn up by agriculture, or covered with buildings. Mine are the sensations of poor Logan:

"The horrid plough has rased the green
      Where yet a child I stray'd;
The axe has fell'd the hawthorn screen,
      The school-boy's summer shade."

I hope, however, the threatened devastation will not be consummated in my day. Although the adventurous spirit of times short while since passed gave rise to the undertaking, I have been encouraged to think that the subsequent changes have so far damped the spirit of speculation, that the rest of the woodland foot-path leading to Aunt Margaret's retreat will be left undisturbed for her time and mine. I am interested in this, for every step of the way, after I have passed through the green already mentioned, has for me something of early remembrance:—There is the stile at which I can recollect a cross child's maid upbraiding me with my infirmity, as she lifted me coarsely and carelessly over the flinty steps, which my brothers traversed with shout and bound. I remember the suppressed bitterness of the moment, and, conscious of my own inferiority, the feeling of envy with which I regarded the easy movements and elastic steps of my more happily formed brethren. Alas! these goodly barks have all perished on life's wide ocean, and only that which seemed so little sea-worthy, as the naval phrase goes, has reached the port when the tempest is over. Then there is the pool, where, manœuvring our little navy, constructed out of the broad water-flags, my elder brother fell in, was scarce saved from the watery element, to die under Nelson's banner. There is the hazel copse, also, in which my brother Henry used to gather nuts; thinking little that he was to die in an Indian jungle in quest of rupees.

There is so much more of remembrance about the little walk, that,—as I stop, rest on my crutch-headed cane, and look round with that species of comparison between the thing I was and that which I now am,—it almost induces me to doubt my own identity; until I find myself in face of the honey-suckle porch of Aunt Margaret's dwelling, with its irregularity of front, and its odd projecting latticed windows; where the workmen seem to have made a study that no one of them should resemble another, in form, size, or in the old-fashioned stone entablature, and labels, which adorn them. This tenement, once the manor-house of Earl's Closes, we still retain a slight hold upon; for, in some family arrangements, it had been settled upon Aunt Margaret during the term of her life. Upon this frail tenure depends, in a great measure, the last shadow of the family of Bothwell of Earl's Closes, and their last slight connexion with their paternal inheritance. The only representative will then be an infirm old man, moving not unwillingly to the grave, which has devoured all that were dear to his affections.

When I have indulged such thoughts for a minute or two, I enter the mansion, which is said to have been the gatehouse only of the original building, and find one being on whom time seems to have made little impression; for the Aunt Margaret of to-day bears the same proportional age to the Aunt Margaret of my early youth, that the boy of ten years old does to the man of (by'r Lady!) some fifty-six years. The old lady's invariable costume has doubtless some share in confirming one in the opinion, that time has stood still with Aunt Margaret.

The brown or chocolate-coloured silk gown, with ruffles of the same stuff at the elbow, within which are others of Mechlin lace—the black silk gloves, or mitts, the white hair combed back upon a roll, and the cap of spotless cambric, which closes around the venerable countenance, as they were not the costume of 1780, so neither were they that of 1826; they are altogether a style peculiar to the individual Aunt Margaret. There she still sits, as she sat thirty years since, with her wheel or the stocking, which she works by the fire in winter and by the window in summer; or, perhaps, venturing as far as the porch in an unusually fine summer evening. Her frame, like some well-constructed piece of mechanics, still performs the operations for which it had seemed destined; going its round with an activity which is gradually diminished, yet indicating no probability that it will soon come to a period.

The solicitude and affection which had made Aunt Margaret the willing slave to the inflictions of a whole nursery have now for their object the health and comfort of one old and infirm man; the last remaining relative of her family, and the only one who can still find interest in the traditional stores which she hoards; as some miser hides the gold which he desires that no one should enjoy after his death.

My conversation with Aunt Margaret generally relates little either to the present or to the future: for the passing day we possess as much as we require, and we neither of us wish for more; and for that which is to follow we have on this side of the grave neither hopes, nor fears, nor anxiety. We therefore naturally look back to the past; and forget the present fallen fortunes and declined importance of our family, in recalling the hours when it was wealthy and prosperous.

With this slight introduction, the reader will know as much of Aunt Margaret and her nephew as is necessary to comprehend the following conversation and narrative.

Last week, when, late in a summer evening, I went to call on the old lady to whom my reader is now introduced, I was received by her with all her usual affection and benignity; while, at the same time, she seemed abstracted and disposed to silence. I asked her the reason. "They have been clearing out the old chapel," she said; "John Clayhudgeons having, it seems, discovered that the stuff within,—being, I suppose, the remains of our ancestors,—was excellent for top-dressing the meadows."

Here I started up with more alacrity than I have displayed for some years; but sate down while my aunt added, laying her hand upon my sleeve, "The chapel has been long considered as common ground, my dear, and used for a penfold, and what objection can we have to the man for employing what is his own, to his own profit? Besides, I did speak to him, and he very readily and civilly promised, that, if he found bones or monuments, they should be carefully respected and reinstated; and what more could I ask? So, the first stone they found bore the name of Margaret Bothwell, 1585, and I have caused it to be laid carefully aside, as I think it betokens death; and having served my namesake two hundred years, it has just been cast up in time to do me the same good turn. My house has been long put in order, as far as the small earthly concerns require it, but who shall say that their account with Heaven is sufficiently revised?"

"After what you have said, aunt," I replied, "perhaps I ought to take my hat and go away, and so I should, but that there is on this occasion a little alloy mingled with our devotion. To think of death at all times is a duty—to suppose it nearer, from the finding of an old gravestone is superstition; and you, with your strong useful common sense, which was so long the prop of a fallen family, are the last person whom I should have suspected of such weakness."

"Neither would I have deserved your suspicions, kinsman," answered Aunt Margaret, "if we were speaking of any incident occurring in the actual business of human life. But for all this, I have a sense of superstition about me, which I do not wish to part with. It is a feeling which separates me from this age, and links me with that to which I am hastening; and even when it seems, as now, to lead me to the brink of the grave, and bids me gaze on it, I do not love that it should be dispelled. It soothes my imagination, without influencing my reason or conduct."

"I profess, my good lady," replied I, "that had any one but you made such a declaration, I should have thought it as capricious as that of the clergyman who, without vindicating his false reading, preferred, from habit's sake, his old Mumpsimus to the modern Sumpsimus."

"Well," answered my aunt, "I must explain my inconsistency in this particular, by comparing it to another. I am, as you know, a piece of that old-fashioned thing called a Jacobite; but I am so in sentiment and feeling only; for a more loyal subject never joined in prayers for the health and wealth of George the Fourth, whom God long preserve! But I dare say that kind-hearted Sovereign would not deem that an old woman did him much injury, if she leaned back in her arm-chair, just in such a twilight as this, and thought of the high-mettled men, whose sense of duty called to arms against his grandfather; and how, in a cause which they deemed that of their rightful prince and country—

'They fought till their hand to the broadsword was glued,
They fought against fortune with hearts unsubdued.'

Do not come at such a moment, when my head is full of plaids, pibrochs, and claymores, and ask my reason to admit what, I am afraid, it cannot deny,—I mean, that the public advantage peremptorily demanded that these things should cease to exist. I cannot, indeed, refuse to allow the justice of your reasoning; but yet, being convinced against my will, you will gain little by your motion. You might as well read to an infatuated lover the catalogue of his mistress's imperfections; for, when he has been compelled to listen to the summary, you will only get for answer, that 'he lo'es her a' the better."

I was not sorry to have changed the gloomy train of Aunt Margaret's thoughts, and replied in the same tone, "Well, I can't help being persuaded that our good King is the more sure of Mrs. Bothwell's loyal affection, that he has the Stuart right of birth, as well as the Act of Succession in his favour."

"Perhaps my attachment, were its source of consequence, might be found warmer for the union of the rights you mention," said Aunt Margaret; "but upon my word, it would be as sincere if the King's right were founded only on the will of the nation, as declared at the Revolution. I am none of your *jure divino* folks."

"And a Jacobite notwithstanding."

"And a Jacobite notwithstanding; or rather, I will give you leave to call me one of the party which, in Queen Anne's time, were called *Whimsicals;* because they were sometimes operated upon by feelings, sometimes by principle. After all, it is very hard that you will not allow an old woman to be as inconsistent in her political sentiments, as mankind in general show themselves in all the various courses of life; since you cannot point out one of them, in which the passions and prejudices of those who pursue it are not perpetually carrying us away from the path which our reason points out."

"True, aunt; but you are a wilful wanderer, who should be forced back into the right path."

"Spare me, I entreat you," replied Aunt Margaret. "You remember the Gaelic song, though I dare say I mispronounce the words—

> 'Hatil mohatil, na dowski mi.'
> 'I am asleep, do not waken me.'

I tell you, kinsman, that the sort of waking dreams which my imagination spins out, in what your favourite Wordsworth calls 'moods of my own mind,' are worth all the rest of my more active days. Then, instead of looking forwards, as I did in youth, and forming for myself fairy palaces, upon the verge of the grave, I turn my eyes backward upon the days, and manners, of my better time; and the sad, yet soothing recollections, come so close and interesting, that I almost think it sacrilege to be wiser or more rational, or less prejudiced, than those to whom I looked up in my younger years."

"I think I now understand what you mean," I answered, "and can comprehend why you should occasionally prefer the twilight of illusion to the steady light of reason."

"Where there is no task," she rejoined, "to be performed, we may sit in the dark if we like it—if we go to work, we must ring for candles."

"And amidst such shadowy and doubtful light," continued I, "imagination frames her enchanted and enchanting visions, and sometimes passes them upon the senses for reality."

"Yes," said Aunt Margaret, who is a well-read woman, "to those who resemble the translator of Tasso,

> 'Prevailing poet, whose undoubting mind
> Believed the magic wonders which he sung.'

It is not required for this purpose, that you should be sensible of the painful horrors, which an actual belief in such prodigies inflicts—such a belief, now-a-days, belongs only to fools and children. It is not necessary, that your ears should tingle, and your complexion change, like that of Theodore, at the approach of the spectral huntsman. All that is indispensable for the enjoyment of the milder feeling of supernatural awe is, that you should be susceptible of the slight shuddering which creeps over you, when you hear a tale of terror—that well-vouched tale which the narrator, having first expressed his general disbelief of all such legendary lore, selects and produces, as having something in it which he has been always obliged to give up as inexplicable. Another symptom is, a momentary hesitation to look round you, when the interest of the narrative is at the highest; and the third, a desire to avoid looking into a mirror, when you are alone in your chamber, for the evening. I mean such are signs which indicate the crisis, when a female imagination is in due temperature to enjoy a ghost story. I do not pretend to describe those which express the same disposition in a gentleman."

"This last symptom, dear aunt, of shunning the mirror, seems likely to be a rare occurrence amongst the fair sex."

"You are a novice in toilette fashions, my dear cousin. All women consult the looking-glass with anxiety, before they go into company; but when they return home, the mirror has not the same charm. The die has been cast—the party has been successful or unsuccessful, in the impression which she desired to make. But, without going deeper into the mysteries of the dressing-table, I will tell you that I, myself, like many other honest folks, do not like to see the blank black front of a large mirror in a room dimly lighted, and where the reflection of the candle seems rather to lose itself in the deep obscurity of the glass, than to be reflected back again into the apartment. That space of inky darkness seems to be a field for Fancy to play her revels in. She may call up other features to meet us, instead of the reflection of our own; or, as in the spells of Hallowe'en, which we learned in childhood, some unknown form may be seen peeping over our shoulder. In short, when I am in a ghost-seeing humour, I make my hand-maiden draw the green curtains over the mirror, before I go into the room, so that she may have the first shock of the apparition, if there be any to be seen. But to tell you the truth, this dislike to look into a mirror in particular times and places has, I believe, its original foundation in a story, which came to me by tradition from my grandmother, who was a party concerned in the scene of which I will now tell you."

THE MIRROR.

Chapter I.

You are fond (said my aunt) of sketches of the society which has passed away. I wish I could describe to you Sir Philip Forester, the 'Chartered Libertine' of Scottish good company, about the end of the last century. I never saw him, indeed, but my mother's traditions were full of his wit, gallantry, and dissipation. This gay knight flourished about the end of the seventeenth and beginning of the eighteenth century. He was the Sir Charles Easy and the Lovelace of his day and country: renowned for the number of duels he had fought, and the successful intrigues which he had carried on. The supremacy which he had attained in the fashionable world was absolute; and when we combine it with one or two anecdotes, for which, 'if laws were made for every degree,' he ought certainly to have been hanged, the popularity of such a person really serves to show, either, that the present times are much more decent, if not more virtuous, than they formerly were; or, that high breeding then was of more difficult attainment than that which is now so called; and, consequently, entitled the successful professor to a proportional degree of plenary indulgences and privileges. No beau of this day could have borne out so ugly a story as that of Pretty Peggy Grindstone, the miller's daughter at Sillermills—it had well nigh made work for the Lord Advocate. But it hurt Sir Philip Forester no more than the hail hurts the hearth-stone. He was as well received in society as ever, and dined with the Duke of A—— the day the poor girl was buried. She died of heart-break. But that has nothing to do with my story.

Now, you must listen to a single word upon kith, kin, and ally; I promise you I will not be prolix. But it is necessary to the authenticity of my legend, that you should know that Sir Philip Forester, with his handsome
person, elegant accomplishments, and fashionable manners, married the
younger Miss Falconer, of King's-Copland. The elder sister of this lady had
previously become the wife of my grandfather, Sir Geoffrey Bothwell, and
brought into our family a good fortune. Miss Jemima, or Miss Jemmie Falconer, as she was usually called, had also about ten thousand pounds ster-
ling; then thought a very handsome portion indeed.

The two sisters were extremely different, though each had their admirers while they remained single. Lady Bothwell had some touch of the old
King's-Copland blood about her. She was bold, though not to the degree of
audacity: ambitious, and desirous to raise her house and family; and was, as
has been said, a considerable spur to my grandfather, who was otherwise an
indolent man; but whom, unless he has been slandered, his lady's influence
involved in some political matters which had been more wisely let alone.
She was a woman of high principle, however, and masculine good sense, as
some of her letters testify, which are still in my wainscot cabinet.

Jemmie Falconer was the reverse of her sister in every respect. Her
understanding did not reach above the ordinary pitch, if, indeed, she could
be said to have attained it. Her beauty, while it lasted, consisted, in a great
measure, of delicacy of complexion and regularity of features, without any
peculiar force of expression. Even these charms faded under the sufferings
attendant on an ill-sorted match. She was passionately attached to her husband, by whom she was treated with a callous, yet polite, indifference;
which, to one whose heart was as tender as her judgment was weak, was
more painful perhaps than absolute ill-usage. Sir Philip was a voluptuary,
that is, a completely selfish egotist: whose disposition and character resembled the rapier he wore, polished, keen, and brilliant, but inflexible and
unpitying. As he observed carefully all the usual forms towards his lady, he
had the art to deprive her even of the compassion of the world; and useless
and unavailing as that may be while actually possessed by the sufferer, it is,
to a mind like Lady Forester's, most painful to know she has it not.

The tattle of society did its best to place the peccant husband above the
suffering wife. Some called her a poor spiritless thing, and declared, that,
with a little of her sister's spirit, she might have brought to reason any Sir

Philip whatsoever, were it the termagant Falconbridge himself. But the greater part of their acquaintance affected candour, and saw faults on both sides; though, in fact, there only existed the oppressor and the oppressed. The tone of such critics was—"To be sure, no one will justify Sir Philip Forester, but then we all know Sir Philip, and Jemmie Falconer might have known what she had to expect from the beginning.—What made her set her cap at Sir Philip?—He would never have looked at her if she had not thrown herself at his head, with her poor ten thousand pounds. I am sure, if it is money he wanted, she spoiled his market. I know where Sir Philip could have done much better.—And then, if she *would* have the man, could not she try to make him more comfortable at home, and have his friends oftener, and not plague him with the squalling children, and take care all was handsome and in good style about the house? I declare I think Sir Philip would have made a very domestic man, with a woman who knew how to manage him."

Now these fair critics, in raising their profound edifice of domestic felicity, did not recollect that the corner-stone was wanting; and that to receive good company with good cheer, the means of the banquet ought to have been furnished by Sir Philip; whose income (dilapidated as it was) was not equal to the display of hospitality required, and at the same time to the supply of the good knight's *menus plaisirs.* So, in spite of all that was so sagely suggested by female friends, Sir Philip carried his good humour every where abroad, and left at home a solitary mansion, and a pining spouse.

At length, inconvenienced in his money affairs, and tired even of the short time which he spent in his own dull house, Sir Philip Forester determined to take a trip to the continent, in the capacity of a volunteer. It was then common for men of fashion to do so; and our knight perhaps was of opinion that a touch of the military character, just enough to exalt, but not render pedantic, his qualities as a *beau garçon,* was necessary to maintain possession of the elevated situation which he held in the ranks of fashion.

Sir Philip's resolution threw his wife into agonies of terror, by which the worthy baronet was so much annoyed that, contrary to his wont, he took some trouble to soothe her apprehensions; and once more brought her to shed tears, in which sorrow was not altogether unmingled with pleasure. Lady Bothwell asked, as a favour, Sir Philip's permission to receive her sister and her family into her own house during his absence on the continent. Sir

Philip readily assented to a proposition which saved expense, silenced the foolish people who might have talked of a deserted wife and family, and gratified Lady Bothwell; for whom he felt some respect, as for one who often spoke to him, always with freedom, and sometimes with severity, without being deterred either by his raillery, or the *prestige* of his reputation.

A day or two before Sir Philip's departure, Lady Bothwell took the liberty of asking him, in her sister's presence, the direct question, which his timid wife had often desired, but never ventured, to put to him.

"Pray, Sir Philip, what route do you take when you reach the continent?"

"I go from Leith to Helvoet by a packet with advices."

"That I comprehend perfectly," said Lady Bothwell drily; "but you do not mean to remain long at Helvoet, I presume, and I should like to know what is your next object?"

"You ask me, my dear lady," answered Sir Philip, "a question which I have not dared to ask myself. The answer depends on the fate of war. I shall, of course, go to head-quarters, wherever they may happen to be for the time; deliver my letters of introduction; learn as much of the noble art of war as may suffice a poor interloping amateur; and then take a glance at the sort of thing of which we read so much in the Gazette."

"And I trust, Sir Philip," said Lady Bothwell, "that you will remember that you are a husband and a father; and that though you think fit to indulge this military fancy, you will not let it hurry you into dangers which it is certainly unnecessary for any save professional persons to encounter."

"Lady Bothwell does me too much honour," replied the adventurous knight, "in regarding such a circumstance with the slightest interest. But to soothe your flattering anxiety, I trust your ladyship will recollect, that I cannot expose to hazard the venerable and paternal character which you so obligingly recommend to my protection, without putting in some peril an honest fellow, called Philip Forester, with whom I have kept company for thirty years, and with whom, though some folk consider him a coxcomb, I have not the least desire to part."

"Well, Sir Philip, you are the best judge of your own affairs; I have little right to interfere—you are not my husband."

"God forbid!"—said Sir Philip hastily; instantly adding, however, "God forbid that I should deprive my friend Sir Geoffrey of so inestimable a treasure."

"But you are my sister's husband," replied the lady; "and I suppose you are aware of her present distress of mind—"

"If hearing of nothing else from morning to night can make me aware of it," said Sir Philip, "I should know something of the matter."

"I do not pretend to reply to your wit, Sir Philip," answered Lady Bothwell; "but you must be sensible that all this distress is on account of apprehensions for your personal safety."

"In that case, I am surprised that Lady Bothwell, at least, should give herself so much trouble upon so insignificant a subject."

"My sister's interest may account for my being anxious to learn something of Sir Philip Forester's motions; about which otherwise, I know, he would not wish me to concern myself: I have a brother's safety too to be anxious for."

"You mean Major Falconer, your brother by the mother's side:—What can he possibly have to do with our present agreeable conversation?"

"You have had words together, Sir Philip," said Lady Bothwell.

"Naturally; we are connexions," replied Sir Philip, "and as such have always had the usual intercourse."

"That is an evasion of the subject," answered the lady. "By words, I mean angry words, on the subject of your usage of your wife."

"If," replied Sir Philip Forester, "you suppose Major Falconer simple enough to intrude his advice upon me, Lady Bothwell, in my domestic matters, you are indeed warranted in believing that I might possibly be so far displeased with the interference, as to request him to reserve his advice till it was asked."

"And, being on these terms, you are going to join the very army in which my brother Falconer is now serving."

"No man knows the path of honour better than Major Falconer," said Sir Philip. "An aspirant after fame, like me, cannot choose a better guide than his footsteps."

Lady Bothwell rose and went to the window, the tears gushing from her eyes.

"And this heartless raillery," she said, "is all the consideration that is to be given to our apprehensions of a quarrel which may bring on the most terrible consequences? Good God! of what can men's hearts be made, who can thus dally with the agony of others?"

Sir Philip Forester was moved; he laid aside the mocking tone in which he had hitherto spoken.

"Dear Lady Bothwell," he said, taking her reluctant hand, "we are both wrong:—you are too deeply serious; I, perhaps, too little so. The dispute I had with Major Falconer was of no earthly consequence. Had anything occurred betwixt us that ought to have been settled *par voie du fait,* as we say in France, neither of us are persons that are likely to postpone such a meeting. Permit me to say, that, were it generally known that you or my Lady Forester are apprehensive of such a catastrophe, it might be the very means of bringing about what would not otherwise be likely to happen. I know your good sense, Lady Bothwell, and that you will understand me when I say, that really my affairs require my absence for some months;—this Jemima cannot understand; it is a perpetual recurrence of questions, why can you not do this, or that, or the third thing; and when you have proved to her that her expedients are totally ineffectual, you have just to begin the whole round again. Now, do you tell her, dear Lady Bothwell, that *you* are satisfied. She is, you must confess, one of those persons with whom authority goes farther than reasoning. Do but repose a little confidence in me, and you shall see how amply I will repay it."

Lady Bothwell shook her head, as one but half satisfied. "How difficult it is to extend confidence, when the basis on which it ought to rest has been so much shaken! But I will do my best to make Jemima easy; and farther, I can only say, that for keeping your present purpose I hold you responsible both to God and man."

"Do not fear that I will deceive you," said Sir Philip; "the safest conveyance to me will be through the general post-office, Helvoetsluys, where I will take care to leave orders for forwarding my letters. As for Falconer, our only encounter will be over a bottle of Burgundy; so make yourself perfectly easy on his score."

Lady Bothwell could *not* make herself easy; yet she was sensible that her sister hurt her own cause by *taking on,* as the maid-servants call it, too vehemently; and by showing before every stranger, by manner and sometimes by words also, a dissatisfaction with her husband's journey, that was sure to come to his ears, and equally certain to displease him. But there was no help for this domestic dissension, which ended only with the day of separation.

I am sorry I cannot tell, with precision, the year in which Sir Philip Forester went over to Flanders; but it was one of those in which the campaign opened with extraordinary fury; and many bloody, though indecisive, skirmishes were fought between the French on the one side, and the allies on the other. In all our modern improvements there are none, perhaps, greater than in the accuracy and speed with which intelligence is transmitted from any scene of action to those in this country whom it may concern. During Marlborough's campaigns, the sufferings of the many who had relations in, or along with, the army, were greatly augmented by the suspense in which they were detained for weeks, after they had heard of bloody battles, in which, in all probability, those for whom their bosoms throbbed with anxiety had been personally engaged. Amongst those who were most agonized by this state of uncertainty, was the, I had almost said deserted, wife of the gay Sir Philip Forester. A single letter had informed her of his arrival on the continent—no others were received. One notice occurred in the newspapers, in which Volunteer Sir Philip Forester was mentioned as having been entrusted with a dangerous reconnoissance, which he had executed with the greatest courage, dexterity, and intelligence, and received the thanks of the commanding officer. The sense of his having acquired distinction brought a momentary glow into the lady's pale cheek; but it was instantly lost in ashen whiteness at the recollection of his danger. After this they had no news whatever, neither from Sir Philip, nor even from their brother Falconer. The case of Lady Forester was not indeed different from that of hundreds in the same situation; but a feeble mind is necessarily an irritable one, and the suspense which some bear with constitutional indifference or philosophical resignation, and some with a disposition to believe and hope the best, was intolerable to Lady Forester, at once solitary and sensitive, low-spirited, and devoid of strength of mind, whether natural or acquired.

Chapter II.

As she received no further news of Sir Philip, whether directly or indirectly, his unfortunate lady began now to feel a sort of consolation, even in those careless habits which had so often given her pain. "He is so thoughtless," she repeated a hundred times a day to her sister, "he never writes when things are going on smoothly; it is his way: had anything happened he would have informed us."

Lady Bothwell listened to her sister without attempting to console her. Probably she might be of opinion, that even the worst intelligence which could be received from Flanders might not be without some touch of consolation; and that the Dowager Lady Forester, if so she was doomed to be called, might have a source of happiness unknown to the wife of the gayest and finest gentleman in Scotland. This conviction became stronger as they learned from inquiries made at head-quarters, that Sir Philip was no longer with the army; though whether he had been taken or slain in some of those skirmishes which were perpetually occurring, and in which he loved to distinguish himself, or whether he had, for some unknown reason or capricious change of mind, voluntarily left the service, none of his countrymen in the camp of the allies could form even a conjecture. Meantime his creditors at home became clamorous, entered into possession of his property, and threatened his person, should he be rash enough to return to Scotland. These additional disadvantages aggravated Lady Bothwell's displeasure against the fugitive husband; while her sister saw nothing in any of them, save what tended to increase her grief for the absence of him whom her imagination now represented,—as it had before marriage,—gallant, gay, and affectionate.

About this period there appeared in Edinburgh a man of singular appearance and pretensions. He was commonly called the Paduan Doctor, from having received his education at that famous university. He was supposed to possess some rare receipts in medicine, with which, it was affirmed, he had wrought remarkable cures. But though, on the one hand, the physicians of Edinburgh termed him an empiric, there were many persons, and among them some of the clergy, who, while they admitted the truth of the cures and the force of his remedies, alleged that Doctor Baptista Damiotti made use of charms and unlawful arts in order to obtain success in his practice. The resorting to him was even solemnly preached against, as a seeking of health from idols, and a trusting to the help which was to come from Egypt. But the protection which the Paduan doctor received from some friends of interest and consequence enabled him to set these imputations at defiance, and to assume, even in the city of Edinburgh, famed as it was for abhorrence of witches and necromancers, the dangerous character

of an expounder of futurity. It was at length rumoured, that, for a certain gratification, which of course was not an inconsiderable one, Doctor Baptista
Damiotti could tell the fate of the absent, and even show his visitors the
personal form of their absent friends, and the action in which they were engaged at the moment. This rumour came to the ears of Lady Forester, who
had reached that pitch of mental agony in which the sufferer will do any
thing, or endure any thing, that suspense may be converted into certainty.

Gentle and timid in most cases, her state of mind made her equally ob-
stinate and reckless, and it was with no small surprise and alarm that her
sister, Lady Bothwell, heard her express a resolution to visit this man of art,
and learn from him the fate of her husband. Lady Bothwell remonstrated
on the improbability that such pretensions as those of this foreigner could
be founded in anything but imposture.

"I care not," said the deserted wife, "what degree of ridicule I may incur: if there be any one chance out of a hundred that I may obtain some
certainty of my husband's fate, I would not miss that chance for whatever
else the world can offer me."

Lady Bothwell next urged the unlawfulness of resorting to such sources
of forbidden knowledge.

"Sister," replied the sufferer, "he who is dying of thirst cannot refrain
from drinking even poisoned water. She who suffers under suspense must
seek information, even were the powers which offer it unhallowed and infernal. I go to learn my fate alone; and this very evening will I know it: the
sun that rises to-morrow shall find me, if not more happy, at least more resigned."

"Sister," said Lady Bothwell, "if you are determined upon this wild step,
you shall not go alone. If this man be an impostor, you may be too much agitated by your feelings to detect his villainy. If, which I cannot believe, there
be any truth in what he pretends, you shall not be exposed alone to a communication of so extraordinary a nature. I will go with you, if indeed you determine to go. But yet re-consider your project and renounce inquiries
which cannot be prosecuted without guilt, and perhaps without danger."

Lady Forester threw herself into her sister's arms, and, clasping her to
her bosom, thanked her a hundred times for the offer of her company;
while she declined with a melancholy gesture the friendly advice with which
it was accompanied.

When the hour of twilight arrived,—which was the period when the Paduan doctor was understood to receive the visits of those who came to consult with him,—the two ladies left their apartments in the Canongate of Edinburgh, having their dress arranged like that of women of an inferior description, and their plaids disposed around their faces as they were worn by the same class; for, in those days of aristocracy, the quality of the wearer was generally indicated by the manner in which her plaid was disposed, as well as by the fineness of its texture. It was Lady Bothwell who had suggested this species of disguise, partly to avoid observation as they should go to the conjurer's house, and partly in order to make trial of his penetration by appearing before him in a feigned character. Lady Forester's servant, of tried fidelity, had been employed by her to propitiate the doctor by a suitable fee, and a story intimating that a soldier's wife desired to know the fate of her husband; a subject upon which, in all probability, the sage was very frequently consulted.

To the last moment, when the palace clock struck eight, Lady Bothwell earnestly watched her sister, in hopes that she might retreat from her rash undertaking; but as mildness, and even timidity, is capable at times of vehement and fixed purposes, she found Lady Forester resolutely unmoved and determined when the moment of departure arrived. Ill satisfied with the expedition, but determined not to leave her sister at such a crisis, Lady Bothwell accompanied Lady Forester through more than one obscure street and lane, the servant walking before, and acting as their guide. At length he suddenly turned into a narrow court, and knocked at an arched door, which seemed to belong to a building of some antiquity. It opened, though no one appeared to act as porter; and the servant stepping aside from the entrance, motioned the ladies to enter. They had no sooner done so, than it shut, and excluded their guide. The two ladies found themselves in a small vestibule, illuminated by a dim lamp, and having, when the door was closed, no communication with the external light or air. The door of an inner apartment, partly open, was at the further side of the vestibule.

"We must not hesitate now, Jemima," said Lady Bothwell, and walked forwards into the inner room, where, surrounded by books, maps, philosophical utensils, and other implements of peculiar shape and appearance, they found the man of art.

There was nothing very peculiar in the Italian's appearance. He had the dark complexion and marked feature of his country, seemed about fifty years old, and was handsomely, but plainly, dressed in a full suit of black clothes, which was then the universal costume of the medical profession. Large wax-lights, in silver sconces, illuminated the apartment, which was reasonably furnished. He rose as the ladies entered; and, notwithstanding the inferiority of their dress, received them with the marked respect due to their quality, and which foreigners are usually punctilious in rendering to those to whom such honours are due.

Lady Bothwell endeavoured to maintain her proposed incognito; and, as the doctor ushered them to the upper end of the room, made a motion declining his courtesy, as unfitted for their condition. "We are poor people, sir," she said; "only my sister's distress has brought us to consult your worship whether—"

He smiled as he interrupted her—"I am aware, madam, of your sister's distress, and its cause; I am aware, also, that I am honoured with a visit from two ladies of the highest consideration—Lady Bothwell and Lady Forester. If I could not distinguish them from the class of society which their present dress would indicate, there would be small possibility of my being able to gratify them by giving the information which they come to seek."

"I can easily understand," said Lady Bothwell—

"Pardon my boldness to interrupt you, mi-lady," cried the Italian; "your ladyship was about to say, that you could easily understand that I had got possession of your names by means of your domestic. But in thinking so, you do injustice to the fidelity of your servant, and I may add, to the skill of one who is also not less your humble servant—Baptista Damiotti."

"I have no intention to do either, sir," said Lady Bothwell, maintaining a tone of composure, though somewhat surprised, "but the situation is something new to me. If you know who we are, you also know, sir, what brought us here."

"Curiosity to know the fate of a Scottish gentleman of rank, now, or lately upon the continent," answered the seer; "his name is Il Cavaliero Philippo Forester; a gentleman who has the honour to be husband to this lady, and, with your ladyship's permission for using plain language, the misfortune not to value as it deserves that inestimable advantage."

Lady Forester sighed deeply, and Lady Bothwell replied—

"Since you know our object without our telling it, the only question that remains is, whether you have the power to relieve my sister's anxiety."

"I have, madam," answered the Paduan scholar; "but there is still a previous inquiry. Have you the courage to behold with your own eyes what the Cavaliero Philippo Forester is now doing? or will you take it on my report?"

"That question my sister must answer for herself," said Lady Bothwell.

"With my own eyes will I endure to see whatever you have power to show me," said Lady Forester, with the same determined spirit which had stimulated her since her resolution was taken upon this subject.

"There may be danger in it."

"If gold can compensate the risk," said Lady Forester, taking out her purse.

"I do not such things for the purpose of gain," answered the foreigner. "I dare not turn my art to such a purpose. If I take the gold of the wealthy, it is but to bestow it on the poor; nor do I ever accept more than the sum I have already received from your servant. Put up your purse, madam; an adept needs not your gold."

Lady Bothwell, considering this rejection of her sister's offer as a mere trick of an empiric, to induce her to press a larger sum upon him, and willing that the scene should be commenced and ended, offered some gold in turn, observing that it was only to enlarge the sphere of his charity.

"Let Lady Bothwell enlarge the sphere of her own charity," said the Paduan, "not merely in giving of alms, in which I know she is not deficient, but in judging the character of others; and let her oblige Baptista Damiotti by believing him honest till she shall discover him to be a knave. Do not be surprised, madam, if I speak in answer to your thoughts rather than your expressions, and tell me once more whether you have courage to look on what I am prepared to show?"

"I own, sir," said Lady Bothwell, "that your words strike me with some sense of fear; but whatever my sister desires to witness I will not shrink from witnessing along with her."

"Nay, the danger only consists in the risk of your resolution failing you. The sight can only last for the space of seven minutes; and should you interrupt the vision by speaking a single word, not only would the charm be broken, but some danger might result to the spectators. But if you can remain steadily silent for the seven minutes, your curiosity will be gratified without the slightest risk; and for this I will engage my honour."

Internally Lady Bothwell thought the security was but an indifferent one; but she suppressed the suspicion, as if she had believed that the adept, whose dark features wore a half-formed smile, could in reality read even her most secret reflections. A solemn pause then ensued, until Lady Forester gathered courage enough to reply to the physician, as he termed himself, that she would abide with firmness and silence the sight which he had promised to exhibit to them. Upon this, he made them a low obeisance, and saying he went to prepare matters to meet their wish, left the apartment. The two sisters, hand in hand, as if seeking by that close union to divert any danger which might threaten them, sat down on two seats in immediate contact with each other: Jemima seeking support in the manly and habitual courage of Lady Bothwell; and she, on the other hand, more agitated than she had expected, endeavouring to fortify herself by the desperate resolution which circumstances had forced her sister to assume. The one perhaps said to herself, that her sister never feared any thing; and the other might reflect, that what so feeble a minded woman as Jemima did not fear, could not properly be a subject of apprehension to a person of firmness and resolution like her own.

In a few moments the thoughts of both were diverted from their own situation, by a strain of music so singularly sweet and solemn, that, while it seemed calculated to avert or dispel any feeling unconnected with its harmony, increased, at the same time, the solemn excitation which the preceding interview was calculated to produce. The music was that of some instrument with which they were unacquainted; but circumstances afterwards led my ancestress to believe that it was that of the harmonica, which she heard at a much later period in life.

When these heaven-born sounds had ceased, a door opened in the upper end of the apartment, and they saw Damiotti, standing at the head of two or three steps, sign to them to advance. His dress was so different from that which he had worn a few minutes before, that they could hardly recognise him; and the deadly paleness of his countenance, and a certain stern rigidity of muscles, like that of one whose mind is made up to some strange and daring action, had totally changed the somewhat sarcastic expression with which he had previously regarded them both, and particularly Lady

Bothwell. He was barefooted, excepting a species of sandals in the antique fashion; his legs were naked beneath the knee; above them he wore hose, and a doublet of dark crimson silk close to his body; and over that a flowing loose robe, something resembling a surplice, of snow-white linen: his throat and neck were uncovered, and his long, straight, black hair was carefully combed down at full length.

As the ladies approached at his bidding, he showed no gesture of that ceremonious courtesy of which he had been formerly lavish. On the contrary, he made the signal of advance with an air of command; and when, arm in arm, and with insecure steps, the sisters approached the spot where he stood, it was with a warning frown that he pressed his fingers to his lips, as if reiterating his condition of absolute silence, while, stalking before them, he led the way into the next apartment.

This was a large room, hung with black, as if for a funeral. At the upper end was a table, or rather a species of altar, covered with the same lugubrious colour, on which lay divers objects resembling the usual implements of sorcery. These objects were not indeed visible as they advanced into the apartment; for the light which displayed them, being only that of two expiring lamps, was extremely faint.—The master—to use the Italian phrase for persons of this description—approached the upper end of the room with a genuflexion like that of a catholic to the crucifix, and at the same time crossed himself. The ladies followed in silence, and arm in arm. Two or three low broad steps led to a platform in front of the altar, or what resembled such. Here the sage took his stand, and placed the ladies beside him, once more earnestly repeating by signs his injunctions of silence. The Italian then, extending his bare arm from under his linen vestment, pointed with his forefinger to five large flambeaux, or torches, placed on each side of the altar. They took fire successively at the approach of his hand, or rather of his finger, and spread a strong light through the room. By this the visitors could discern that, on the seeming altar, were disposed two naked swords laid crosswise; a large open book, which they conceived to be a copy of the Holy Scriptures, but in a language to them unknown; and beside this mysterious volume was placed a human skull. But what struck the sisters most was a very tall and broad mirror, which occupied all the space behind the altar, and, illumined by the lighted torches, reflected the mysterious articles which were laid upon it.

The master then placed himself between the two ladies, and, pointing to the mirror, took each by the hand, but without speaking a syllable. They gazed intently on the polished and sable space to which he had directed their attention. Suddenly the surface assumed a new and singular appearance. It no longer simply reflected the objects before it, but, as if it had self-contained scenery of its own, objects began to appear within it, at first in a disorderly, indistinct, and miscellaneous manner, like form arranging itself out of chaos; at length, in distinct and defined shape and symmetry. It was thus that, after some shifting of light and darkness over the face of the wonderful glass, a long perspective of arches and columns began to arrange itself on its sides, and a vaulted roof on the upper part of it; till, after many oscillations, the whole vision gained a fixed and stationary appearance, representing the interior of a foreign church. The pillars were stately, and hung with scutcheons; the arches were lofty and magnificent; the floor was lettered with funeral inscriptions. But there were no separate shrines, no images, no display of chalice or crucifix on the altar. It was, therefore, a Protestant church upon the continent. A clergyman dressed in the Geneva gown and band stood by the communion-table, and, with the Bible opened before him, and his clerk awaiting in the background, seemed prepared to perform some service of the church to which he belonged.

At length, there entered the middle aisle of the building a numerous party, which appeared to be a bridal one, as a lady and gentleman walked first, hand in hand, followed by a large concourse of persons of both sexes, gaily, nay richly, attired. The bride, whose features they could distinctly see, seemed not more than sixteen years old, and extremely beautiful. The bridegroom, for some seconds, moved rather with his shoulder towards them, and his face averted; but his elegance of form and step struck the sisters at once with the same apprehension. As he turned his face suddenly, it was frightfully realised, and they saw, in the gay bridegroom before them, Sir Philip Forester. His wife uttered an imperfect exclamation, at the sound of which the whole scene stirred and seemed to separate.

"I could compare it to nothing," said Lady Bothwell while recounting the wonderful tale, "but to the dispersion of the reflection offered by a deep and calm pool, when a stone is suddenly cast into it, and the shadows become dissipated and broken." The master pressed both the ladies' hands severely, as if to remind them of their promise, and of the danger which they incurred.

The exclamation died away on Lady Forester's tongue, without attaining perfect utterance, and the scene in the glass, after the fluctuation of a minute, again resumed to the eye its former appearance of a real scene, existing within the mirror, as if represented in a picture, save that the figures were moveable instead of being stationary.

The representation of Sir Philip Forester, now distinctly visible in form and feature, was seen to lead on towards the clergyman that beautiful girl, who advanced at once with diffidence, and with a species of affectionate pride. In the meantime, and just as the clergyman had arranged the bridal company before him, and seemed about to commence the service, another group of persons, of whom two or three were officers, entered the church. They moved, at first, forward, as though they came to witness the bridal ceremony, but suddenly one of the officers, whose back was towards the spectators, detached himself from his companions, and rushed hastily towards the marriage party; when the whole of them turned towards him, as if attracted by some exclamation which had accompanied his advance. Suddenly the intruder drew his sword; the bridegroom unsheathed his own, and made towards him; swords were also drawn by other individuals, both of the marriage party, and of those who had last entered. They fell into a sort of confusion, the clergyman, and some elder and graver persons, labouring apparently to keep the peace, while the hotter spirits on both sides brandished their weapons. But now, the period of brief space during which the soothsayer, as he pretended, was permitted to exhibit his art, was arrived. The fumes again mixed together, and dissolved gradually from observation; the vaults and columns of the church rolled asunder and disappeared; and the front of the mirror reflected nothing save the blazing torches, and the melancholy apparatus placed on the altar or table before it.

The doctor led the ladies, who greatly required his support, into the apartment from whence they came; where wine, essences, and other means of restoring suspended animation, had been provided during his absence. He motioned them to chairs, which they occupied in silence; Lady Forester, in particular, wringing her hands, and casting her eyes up to heaven, but without speaking a word, as if the spell had been still before her eyes.

"And what we have seen is even now acting?" said Lady Bothwell, collecting herself with difficulty.

"That," answered Baptista Damiotti, "I cannot justly, or with certainty, say. But it is either now acting, or has been acted, during a short space before this. It is the last remarkable transaction in which the Cavalier Forester has been engaged."

Lady Bothwell then expressed anxiety concerning her sister, whose altered countenance, and apparent unconsciousness of what passed around her, excited her apprehensions how it might be possible to convey her home.

"I have prepared for that," answered the adept; "I have directed the servant to bring your equipage as near to this place as the narrowness of the street will permit. Fear not for your sister; but give her, when you return home, this composing draught, and she will be better to-morrow morning. Few," he added, in a melancholy tone, "leave this house as well in health as they entered it. Such being the consequence of seeking knowledge by mysterious means, I leave you to judge the condition of those who have the power of gratifying such irregular curiosity. Farewell, and forget not the potion."

"I will give her nothing that comes from you," said Lady Bothwell; "I have seen enough of your art already. Perhaps you would poison us both to conceal your own necromancy. But we are persons who want neither the means of making our wrongs known, nor the assistance of friends to right them."

"You have had no wrongs from me, madam," said the adept. "You sought one who is little grateful for such honour. He seeks no one, and only gives responses to those who invite and call upon him. After all, you have but learned a little sooner the evil which you must still be doomed to endure. I hear your servant's step at the door, and will detain your ladyship and Lady Forester no longer. The next packet from the continent will explain what you have already partly witnessed. Let it not, if I may advise, pass too suddenly into your sister's hands."

So saying, he bid Lady Bothwell good night. She went, lighted by the adept, to the vestibule, where he hastily threw a black cloak over his singular dress, and opening the door, entrusted his visitors to the care of the servant. It was with difficulty that Lady Bothwell sustained her sister to the carriage, though it was only twenty steps distant. When they arrived at home, Lady Forester required medical assistance. The physician of the family attended, and shook his head on feeling her pulse.

"Here has been," he said, "a violent and sudden shock on the nerves. I must know how it has happened."

Lady Bothwell admitted they had visited the conjurer, and that Lady

Forester had received some bad news respecting her husband, Sir Philip.

"That rascally quack would make my fortune were he to stay in Edinburgh," said the graduate; "this is the seventh nervous case I have heard of his making for me, and all by effect of terror." He next examined the composing draught which Lady Bothwell had unconsciously brought in her hand, tasted it, and pronounced it very germane to the matter, and what would save an application to the apothecary. He then paused, and looking at Lady Bothwell very significantly, at length added, "I suppose I must not ask your ladyship anything about this Italian warlock's proceedings?"

"Indeed, doctor," answered Lady Bothwell, "I consider what passed as confidential; and though the man may be a rogue, yet, as we were fools enough to consult him, we should, I think, be honest to keep his counsel."

"*May* be a knave—come," said the doctor, "I am glad to hear your ladyship allows such a possibility in anything that comes from Italy."

"What comes from Italy may be as good as what comes from Hanover, doctor. But you and I will remain good friends, and that it may be so, we will say nothing of whig or tory."

"Not I," said the doctor, receiving his fee and taking his hat, "a Carolus serves my purpose as well as a Willielmus. But I should like to know why old Lady Saint Ringan's, and all that set, go about wasting their decayed lungs in puffing this foreign fellow."

"Aye—you had best set him down a Jesuit, as Scrub says." On these terms they parted.

The poor patient—whose nerves, from an extraordinary state of tension, had at length become relaxed in as extraordinary a degree—continued to struggle with a sort of imbecility, the growth of superstitious terror, when the shocking tidings were brought from Holland, which fulfilled even her worst expectations.

They were sent by the celebrated Earl of Stair, and contained the melancholy event of a duel betwixt Sir Philip Forester, and his wife's half-brother, Captain Falconer, of the Scotch-Dutch, as they were then called, in which the latter had been killed. The cause of quarrel rendered the incident still more shocking. It seemed that Sir Philip had left the army suddenly, in consequence of being unable to pay a very considerable sum, which he had lost to another volunteer at play. He had changed his name, and taken up his residence at Rotterdam, where he had insinuated himself into the good graces of an ancient and rich burgomaster, and by his handsome person and graceful manners captivated the affections of his only child, a very young person of great beauty, and the heiress of much wealth. Delighted with the specious attractions of his proposed son-in-law, the wealthy merchant—whose idea of the British character was too high to admit of his taking any precaution to acquire evidence of his condition and circumstances—gave his consent to the marriage. It was about to be celebrated in the principal church of the city, when it was interrupted by a singular occurrence.

Captain Falconer having been detached to Rotterdam to bring up a part of the brigade of Scottish auxiliaries, who were in quarters there, a person of consideration in the town, to whom he had been formerly known, proposed to him for amusement to go to the high church, to see a countryman of his own married to the daughter of a wealthy burgomaster. Captain Falconer went accordingly, accompanied by his Dutch acquaintance, with a party of his friends, and two or three officers of the Scotch brigade. His astonishment may be conceived when he saw his own brother-in-law, a married man, on the point of leading to the altar the innocent and beautiful creature, upon whom he was about to practise a bat, and unmanly deceit. He proclaimed his villainy on the spot, and the marriage was interrupted of course. But against the opinion of more thinking men, who considered Sir Philip Forester as having thrown himself out of the rank of men of honour, Captain Falconer admitted him to the privilege of such, accepted a challenge from him, and in the rencounter received a mortal wound. Such are the ways of Heaven, mysterious in our eyes. Lady Forester never recovered the shock of this dismal intelligence.

"And did this tragedy," said I, "take place exactly at the time when the scene in the mirror was exhibited?"

"It is hard to be obliged to maim one's story," answered my aunt; "but, to speak the truth, it happened some days sooner than the apparition was exhibited."

"And so there remained a possibility," said I, "that by some secret and speedy communication the artist might have received early intelligence of that incident."

"The incredulous pretended so," replied my aunt.

"What became of the adept?" demanded I.

"Why, a warrant came down shortly afterwards to arrest him for high-treason, as an agent of the Chevalier St. George; and Lady Bothwell, recollecting the hints which had escaped the doctor, an ardent friend of the Protestant succession, did then call to remembrance, that this man was chiefly *proné* among the ancient matrons of her own political persuasion. It certainly seemed probable that intelligence from the continent, which could easily have been transmitted by an active and powerful agent, might have enabled him to prepare such a scene of phantasmagoria as she herself witnessed. Yet there were so many difficulties in assigning a natural explanation, that, to the day of her death, she remained in great doubt on the subject, and much disposed to cut the Gordian knot by admitting the existence of supernatural agency."

"But, my dear aunt," said I, "what became of the man of skill?"

"Oh, he was too good a fortune-teller not to be able to foresee that his own destiny would be tragical if he waited the arrival of the man with the silver greyhound upon his sleeve. He made, as we say, a moonlight flitting, and was nowhere to be seen or heard of. Some noise there was about papers or letters found in the house, but it died away, and Doctor Baptista Damiotti was soon as little talked of as Galen or Hippocrates."

"And Sir Philip Forester," said I, "did he too vanish for ever from the public scene?"

"No," replied my kind informer. "He was heard of once more, and it was upon a remarkable occasion. It is said that we Scots, when there was such a nation in existence, have, among our full peck of virtues, one or two little barleycorns of vice. In particular, it is alleged that we rarely forgive, and never forget, any injuries received; that we used to make an idol of our resentment, as poor Lady Constance did of her grief; and are addicted, as Burns says, to 'Nursing our wrath to keep it warm.' Lady Bothwell was not without feeling; and, I believe, nothing whatever, scarce the restoration of the Stuart line, could have happened so delicious to her feelings as an opportunity of being revenged on Sir Philip Forester, for the deep and double injury which had deprived her of a sister and of a brother. But nothing was heard or known till many a year had passed away."

At length—it was on a Fastern's E'en (Shrovetide) assembly, at which the whole fashion of Edinburgh attended, full and frequent, and when Lady

Bothwell had a seat amongst the lady patronesses, that one of the attendants on the company whispered into her ear, that a gentleman wished to speak with her in private.

"In private? and in an assembly-room?—he must be mad—tell him to call upon me to-morrow morning."

"I said so, my lady," answered the man; "but he desired me to give you this paper."

She undid the billet, which was curiously folded and sealed. It only bore the words, *"On business of life and death,"* written in a hand which she had never seen before. Suddenly it occurred to her that it might concern the safety of some of her political friends; she therefore followed the messenger to a small apartment where the refreshments were prepared, and from which the general company was excluded. She found an old man, who at her approach rose up and bowed profoundly. His appearance indicated a broken constitution, and his dress, though sedulously rendered conforming to the etiquette of a ball-room, was worn and tarnished, and hung in folds about his emaciated person. Lady Bothwell was about to feel for her purse, expecting to get rid of the supplicant at the expense of a little money, but some fear of a mistake arrested her purpose. She therefore gave the man leisure to explain himself.

"I have the honour to speak with the Lady Bothwell?"

"I am Lady Bothwell; allow me to say that this is no time or place for long explanations.—What are your commands with me?"

"Your ladyship," said the old man, "had once a sister."

"True; whom I loved as my own soul."

"And a brother."

"The bravest, the kindest, the most affectionate," said Lady Bothwell.

"Both these beloved relatives you lost by the fault of an unfortunate man," continued the stranger.

"By the crime of an unnatural, bloody-minded murderer," said the lady.

"I am answered," replied the old man, bowing, as if to withdraw.

"Stop, sir, I command you," said Lady Bothwell.—"Who are you, that, at such a place and time, come to recall these horrible recollections? I insist upon knowing."

"I am one who intends Lady Bothwell no injury; but, on the contrary, to offer her the means of doing a deed of Christian charity which the world would wonder at, and which Heaven would reward; but I find her in no temper for such a sacrifice as I was prepared to ask."

"Speak out, sir; what is your meaning?" said Lady Bothwell.

"The wretch that has wronged you so deeply," rejoined the stranger, "is now on his deathbed. His days have been days of misery, his nights have been sleepless hours of anguish—yet he cannot die without your forgiveness. His life has been an unremitting penance—yet he dares not part from his burthen while your curses load his soul."

"Tell him," said Lady Bothwell sternly, "to ask pardon of that Being whom he has so greatly offended; not of an erring mortal like myself. What could my forgiveness avail him?"

"Much," answered the old man. "It will be an earnest of that which he may then venture to ask from his Creator, lady, and from yours. Remember, Lady Bothwell, you too have a deathbed to look forward to; your soul may, all human souls must, feel the awe of facing the judgment-seat, with the wounds of an untented conscience, raw, and rankling—what thought would it be then that should whisper, 'I have given no mercy, how then shall I ask it?'"

"Man, whosoever thou mayst be," replied Lady Bothwell, "urge me not so cruelly. It would be but blasphemous hypocrisy to utter with my lips the words which every throb of my heart protests against. They would open the earth and give to light the wasted form of my sister—the bloody form of my murdered brother.—Forgive him?—Never, never!"

"Great God!" cried the old man, holding up his hands; "is it thus the worms which thou hast called out of dust obey the commands of their Maker? Farewell, proud and unforgiving woman. Exult that thou hast added to a death in want and pain the agonies of religious despair; but never again mock Heaven by petitioning for the pardon which thou hast refused to grant."

He was turning from her.

"Stop," she exclaimed; "I will try; yes, I will try to pardon him."

"Gracious lady," said the old man, "you will relieve the over-burdened soul which dare not sever itself from its sinful companion of earth without being at peace with you. What do I know—your forgiveness may perhaps preserve for penitence the dregs of a wretched life."

"Ha!" said the lady, as a sudden light broke on her, "it is the villain himself." And grasping Sir Philip Forester, for it was he, and no other, by the collar, she raised a cry of "Murder, murder! seize the murderer!"

At an exclamation so singular, in such a place, the company thronged into the apartment, but Sir Philip Forester was no longer there. He had forcibly extricated himself from Lady Bothwell's hold, and had run out of the apartment which opened on the landing-place of the stair. There seemed no escape in that direction, for there were several persons coming up the steps, and others descending. But the unfortunate man was desperate. He threw himself over the balustrade, and alighted safely in the lobby, through a leap of fifteen feet at least, then dashed into the street, and was lost in darkness. Some of the Bothwell family made pursuit, and had they come up with the fugitive they might have perhaps slain him; for in those days men's blood ran warm in their veins. But the police did not interfere; the matter most criminal having happened long since, and in a foreign land. Indeed it was always thought that this extraordinary scene originated in a hypocritical experiment, by which Sir Philip desired to ascertain whether he might return to his native country in safety from the resentment of a family which he had injured so deeply. As the result fell out so contrary to his wishes, he is believed to have returned to the continent, and there died in exile. So closed the tale of the MYSTERIOUS MIRROR.

POEMS

William and Helen

From heavy dreams fair Helen rose,
    And eyed the dawning red:
"Alas, my love, thou tarriest long!
    O art thou false or dead?"

With gallant Fred'rick's princely power
    He sought the bold Crusade;
But not a word from Judah's wars
    Told Helen how he sped.

With Paynim and with Saracen
    At length a truce was made,
And every knight return'd to dry
    The tears his love had shed.

Our gallant host was homeward bound
    With many a song of joy;
Green waved the laurel in each plume,
    The badge of victory.

And old and young, and sire and son,
    To meet them crowd the way,
With shouts, and mirth, and melody,
    The debt of love to pay.

Full many a maid her true-love met,
    And sobb'd in his embrace,
And flutt'ring joy in tears and smiles
    Array'd full many a face.

Nor joy nor smile for Helen sad;
    She sought the host in vain;
For none could tell her William's fate,
    If faithless, or if slain.

The martial band is past and gone;
    She rends her raven hair,
And in distraction's bitter mood
    She weeps with wild despair.

"O rise, my child," her mother said,
    "Nor sorrow thus in vain;
A perjured lover's fleeting heart
    No tears recall again."

"O mother, what is gone, is gone,
    What's lost for ever lorn:
Death, death alone can comfort me;
    O had I ne'er been born!

"O break, my heart—O break at once!
    Drink my life-blood, Despair!
No joy remains on earth for me,
    For me in heaven no share."

"O enter not in judgment, Lord!"
    The pious mother prays;
"Impute not guilt to thy frail child!
    She knows not what she says.

"O say thy pater noster, child!
    O turn to God and grace!
His will, that turn'd thy bliss to bale,
    Can change thy bale to bliss."

"O mother, mother, what is bliss?
    O mother, what is bale?

My William's love was heaven on earth,
    Without it earth is hell.

"Why should I pray to ruthless Heaven,
    Since my loved William's slain?
I only pray'd for William's sake,
    And all my prayers were vain."

"O take the sacrament, my child,
    And check these tears that flow;
By resignation's humble prayer,
    O hallow'd be thy woe!"

"No sacrament can quench this fire,
    Or slake this scorching pain;
No sacrament can bid the dead
    Arise and live again.

"O break, my heart—O break at once!
    Be thou my god, Despair!
Heaven's heaviest blow has fallen on me,
    And vain each fruitless prayer."

"O enter not in judgment, Lord,
    With thy frail child of clay!
She knows not what her tongue has spoke;
    Impute it not, I pray!

"Forbear, my child, this desperate woe,
    And turn to God and grace;
Well can devotion's heavenly glow
    Convert thy bale to bliss."

"O mother, mother, what is bliss?
    O mother, what is bale?
Without my William what were heaven,
    Or with him what were hell?"

Wild she arraigns the eternal doom,
    Upbraids each sacred power,
Till, spent, she sought her silent room,
    All in the lonely tower.

She beat her breast, she wrung her hands,
    Till sun and day were o'er,
And through the glimmering lattice shone
    The twinkling of the star.

Then, crash! the heavy drawbridge fell
    That o'er the moat was hung;
And, clatter! clatter! on its boards
    The hoof of courser rung.

The clank of echoing steel was heard
    As off the rider bounded;
And slowly on the winding stair
    A heavy footstep sounded.

And hark! and hark! a knock—tap! tap!
    A rustling stifled noise;
Door-latch and tinkling staples ring;
    At length a whispering voice:

"Awake, awake, arise, my love!
    How, Helen, dost thou fare?
Wak'st thou, or sleep'st? laugh'st thou, or weep'st?
    Hast thought on me, my fair?"

"My love! my love!—so late by night!
    I waked, I wept for thee:
Much have I borne since dawn of morn;
    Where, William, couldst thou be?"

"We saddle late—from Hungary
    I rode since darkness fell;

And to its bourne we both return
    Before the matin-bell."

"O rest this night within my arms,
    And warm thee in their fold!
Chill howls through hawthorn bush the wind:
    My love is deadly cold."

"Let the wind howl through hawthorn bush!
    This night we must away;
The steed is wight, the spur is bright;
    I cannot stay till day.

"Busk, busk, and boune! thou mount'st behind
    Upon my black barb steed:
O'er stock and stile, a hundred miles,
    We haste to bridal bed."

"To-night—to-night a hundred miles?
    O dearest William, stay!
The bell strikes twelve—dark, dismal hour!
    O wait, my love, till day!"

"Look here, look here—the moon shines clear—
    Full fast I ween we ride;
Mount and away! for ere the day
    We reach our bridal bed.

"The black barb snorts, the bridle rings;
    Haste, busk, and boune, and seat thee!
The feast is made, the chamber spread,
    The bridal guests await thee."

Strong love prevail'd. She busks, she bounes,
    She mounts the barb behind,
And round her darling William's waist
    Her lily arms she twined.

And, hurry! hurry! off they rode,
    As fast as fast might be;
Spurn'd from the courser's thundering heels
    The flashing pebbles flee.

And on the right, and on the left,
    Ere they could snatch a view,
Fast, fast each mountain, mead, and plain,
    And cot, and castle flew.

"Sit fast—dost fear? The moon shines clear;
    Fleet goes my barb—keep hold!
Fear'st thou?" "O no!" she faintly said;
    "But why so stern and cold?

"What yonder rings? what yonder sings?
    Why shrieks the owlet grey?"
"'Tis death-bells' clang, 'tis funeral song,
    The body to the clay.

"With song and clang, at morrow's dawn,
    Ye may inter the dead:
To-night I ride, with my young bride,
    To deck our bridal bed.

"Come with thy choir, thou coffin'd guest,
    To swell our nuptial song!
Come, priest, to bless our marriage feast!
    Come all, come all along!"

Ceased clang and song; down sunk the bier;
    The shrouded corpse arose;
And, hurry! hurry! all the train
    The thundering steed pursues.

And, forward! forward! on they go;
    High snorts the straining steed;

Thick pants the rider's labouring breath,
 As headlong on they speed.

"O William, why this savage haste?
 And where thy bridal bed?"
"'Tis distant far, low, damp, and chill,
 And narrow, trustless maid."

"No room for me?" "Enough for both;
 Speed, speed, my barb, thy course!"
O'er thundering bridge, through boiling surge
 He drove the furious horse.

Tramp! tramp! along the land they rode,
 Splash! splash! along the sea;
The scourge is wight, the spur is bright,
 The flashing pebbles flee.

Fled past on right and left how fast
 Each forest, grove, and bower!
On right and left fled past how fast
 Each city, town, and tower!

"Dost fear? dost fear? The moon shines clear,
 Dost fear to ride with me?
Hurrah! hurrah! the dead can ride!"
 "O William, let them be!

"See there, see there! What yonder swings,
 And creaks 'mid whistling rain?"
"Gibbet and steel, th' accursed wheel;
 A murderer in his chain.

"Hollo! thou felon, follow here:
 To bridal bed we ride;
And thou shalt prance a fetter dance
 Before me and my bride."

And, hurry! hurry! clash! clash! clash!
    The wasted form descends;
And fleet as wind through hazel bush
    The wild career attends.

Tramp! tramp! along the land they rode,
    Splash! splash! along the sea;
The scourge is red, the spur drops blood,
    The flashing pebbles flee.

How fled what moonshine faintly show'd!
    How fled what darkness hid!
How fled the earth beneath their feet,
    The heaven above their head!

"Dost fear? dost fear? The moon shines clear,
    And well the dead can ride;
Does faithful Helen fear for them?"
    "O leave in peace the dead!"

"Barb! barb! methinks I hear the cock;
    The sand will soon be run:
Barb! barb! I smell the morning air;
    The race is wellnigh done."

Tramp! tramp! along the land they rode,
    Splash! splash! along the sea;
The scourge is red, the spur drops blood,
    The flashing pebbles flee.

"Hurrah! hurrah! well ride the dead;
    The bride, the bride is come;
And soon we reach the bridal bed,
    For, Helen, here's my home."

Reluctant on its rusty hinge
    Revolved an iron door,

And by the pale moon's setting beam
    Were seen a church and tower.

With many a shriek and cry, whiz round
    The birds of midnight, scared;
And rustling like autumnal leaves
    Unhallow'd ghosts were heard.

O'er many a tomb and tombstone pale
    He spurr'd the fiery horse,
Till sudden at an open grave
    He check'd the wondrous course.

The falling gauntlet quits the rein,
    Down drops the casque of steel,
The cuirass leaves his shrinking side,
    The spur his gory heel.

The eyes desert the naked skull,
    The mould'ring flesh the bone,
Till Helen's lily arms entwine
    A ghastly skeleton.

The furious barb snorts fire and foam,
    And, with a fearful bound,
Dissolves at once in empty air,
    And leaves her on the ground.

Half seen by fits, by fits half heard,
    Pale spectres flit along,
Wheel round the maid in dismal dance,
    And howl the funeral song;

"E'en when the heart's with anguish cleft,
    Revere the doom of Heaven!
Her soul is from her body reft;
    Her spirit be forgiven!"

The Wild Huntsman

The Wildgrave winds his bugle-horn,
    To horse, to horse! halloo, halloo!
His fiery courser snuffs the morn,
    And thronging serfs their lord pursue.

The eager pack, from couples freed,
    Dash through the bush, the brier, the brake;
While, answering hound, and horn, and steed,
    The mountain echoes startling wake.

The beams of God's own hallow'd day
    Had painted yonder spire with gold,
And, calling sinful man to pray,
    Loud, long, and deep the bell had toll'd.

But still the Wildgrave onward rides;
    Halloo, halloo! and, hark again!
When, spurring from opposing sides,
    Two Stranger Horsemen join the train.

Who was each Stranger, left and right,
    Well may I guess, but dare not tell;
The right-hand steed was silver white,
    The left, the swarthy hue of hell.

The right-hand Horseman, young and fair,
    His smile was like the morn of May;
The left, from eye of tawny glare,
    Shot midnight lightning's lurid ray.

He waved his huntsman's cap on high,
　　Cried, "Welcome, welcome, noble lord!
What sport can earth, or sea, or sky,
　　To match the princely chase, afford?"

"Cease thy loud bugle's clanging knell,"
　　Cried the fair youth, with silver voice;
"And for devotion's choral swell,
　　Exchange the rude unhallow'd noise.

"To-day, the ill-omen'd chase forbear,
　　Yon bell yet summons to the fane;
To-day the Warning Spirit hear,
　　To-morrow thou mayst mourn in vain."

"Away, and sweep the glades along!"
　　The Sable Hunter hoarse replies;
"To muttering monks leave matin-song,
　　And bells, and books, and mysteries."

The Wildgrave spurr'd his ardent steed,
　　And, launching forward with a bound,
Who, for thy drowsy priestlike rede,
　　Would leave the jovial horn and hound?

"Hence, if our manly sport offend!
　　With pious fools go chant and pray:
Well hast thou spoke, my dark-brow'd friend:
　　Halloo, halloo! and hark away!"

The Wildgrave spurr'd his courser light,
　　O'er moss and moor, o'er holt and hill;
And on the left and on the right,
　　Each Stranger Horseman follow'd still.

Upsprings, from yonder tangled thorn,
　　A stag more white than mountain snow;

And louder rung the Wildgrave's horn,
 "Hark forward, forward! holla, ho!"

A heedless wretch has cross'd the way;
 He gasps the thundering hoofs below;—
But, live who can, or die who may,
 Still, "forward, forward!" on they go.

See, where you simple fences meet,
 A field with Autumn's blessings crown'd:
See, prostrate at the Wildgrave's feet,
 A husbandman with toil embrown'd:

"O mercy, mercy, noble lord!
 Spare the poor's pittance," was his cry,
"Earn'd by the sweat these brows have pour'd,
 In scorching hour of fierce July."

Earnest the right-hand Stranger pleads,
 The left still cheering to the prey;
The impetuous Earl no warning heeds,
 But furious holds the onward way.

"Away, thou hound! so basely born,
 Or dread the scourge's echoing blow!"
Then loudly rung his bugle-horn,
 "Hark forward, forward! holla, ho!"

So said, so done: A single bound
 Clears the poor labourer's humble pale;
Wild follows man, and horse, and hound,
 Like dark December's stormy gale.

And man and horse, and hound and horn,
 Destructive sweep the field along;
While, joying o'er the wasted corn,
 Fell Famine marks the maddening throng.

Again uprous'd, the timorous prey
    Scours moss and moor, and holt and hill;
Hard run, he feels his strength decay,
    And trusts for life his simple skill.

Too dangerous solitude appear'd;
    He seeks the shelter of the crowd;
Amid the flock''s domestic herd
    His harmless head he hopes to shroud.

O'er moss and moor, and holt and hill,
    His track the steady blood-hounds trace;
O'er moss and moor, unwearied still,
    The furious Earl pursues the chase.

Full lowly did the herdsman fall;
    "O spare, thou noble Baron, spare
These herds, a widow's little all;
    These flocks, an orphan's fleecy care!"

Earnest the right-hand Stranger pleads,
    The left still cheering to the prey;
The Earl nor prayer nor pity heeds,
    But furious keeps the onward way.

"Unmanner'd dog! To stop my sport
    Vain were thy cant and beggar whine,
Though human spirits, of thy sort,
    Were tenants of these carrion kine!"

Again he winds his bugle-horn,
    "Hark forward, forward! holla, ho!"
And through the herd, in ruthless scorn,
    He cheers his furious hounds to go.

In heaps the throttled victims fall;
    Down sinks their mangled herdsman near;

The murderous cries the stag appal,
    Again he starts, new-nerved by fear.

With blood besmear'd, and white with foam,
    While big the tears of anguish pour,
He seeks, amid the forest's gloom,
    The humble hermit's hallow'd bower.

But man and horse, and horn and hound,
    Fast rattling on his traces go;
The sacred chapel rung around
    With, "Hark away! and, holla, ho!"

All mild, amid the rout profane,
    The holy hermit pour'd his prayer;
"Forbear with blood God's house to stain;
    Revere his altar, and forbear!

"The meanest brute has rights to plead,
    Which, wrong'd by cruelty, or pride,
Draw vengeance on the ruthless head:
    Be warn'd at length, and turn aside."

Still the Fair Horseman anxious pleads;
    The Black, wild whooping, points the prey:
Alas! the Earl no warning heeds,
    But frantic keeps the forward way.

"Holy or not, or right or wrong,
    Thy altar, and its rites, I spurn;
Not sainted martyrs' sacred song,
    Not God himself, shall make me turn!"

He spurs his horse, he winds his horn,
    "Hark forward, forward! holla, ho!"
But off, on whirlwind's pinions borne,
    The stag, the hut, the hermit, go.

And horse and man, and horn and hound,
    And clamour of the chase, was gone;
For hoofs, and howls, and bugle-sound,
    A deadly silence reign'd alone.

Wild gazed the affrighted Earl around;
    He strove in vain to wake his horn,
In vain to call: for not a sound
    Could from his anxious lips be borne.

He listens for his trusty hounds;
    No distant baying reach'd his ears:
His courser, rooted to the ground,
    The quickening spur unmindful bears.

Still dark and darker frown the shades,
    Dark as the darkness of the grave;
And not a sound the still invades,
    Save what a distant torrent gave.

High o'er the sinner's humbled head
    At length the solemn silence broke;
And, from a cloud of swarthy red,
    The awful voice of thunder spoke.

"Oppressor of creation fair!
    Apostate Spirits' harden'd tool!
Scorner of God! Scourge of the poor!
    The measure of thy cup is full.

"Be chased for ever through the wood;
    For ever roam the affrighted wild;
And let thy fate instruct the proud,
    God's meanest creature is his child."

'Twas hush'd: One flash, of sombre glare,
    With yellow tinged the forests brown;

Uprose the Wildgrave's bristling hair,
    And horror chill'd each nerve and bone.

Cold pour'd the sweat in freezing rill;
    A rising wind began to sing;
And louder, louder, louder still,
    Brought storm and tempest on its wing.

Earth heard the call; her entrails rend;
    From yawning rifts, with many a yell,
Mix'd with sulphureous flames, ascend
    The misbegotten dogs of hell.

What ghastly Huntsman next arose,
    Well may I guess, but dare not tell;
His eye like midnight lightning glows,
    His steed the swarthy hue of hell.

The Wildgrave flies o'er bush and thorn,
    With many a shriek of helpless woe;
Behind him hound, and horse, and horn,
    And "Hark away!" and "Holla, ho!"

With wild despair's reverted eye,
    Close, close behind, he marks the throng.
With bloody fangs and eager cry;
    In frantic fear he scours along.

Still, still shall last the dreadful chase,
    Till time itself shall have an end;
By day, they scour earth's cavern'd space,
    At midnight's witching hour, ascend.

This is the horn, and hound, and horse,
    That oft the lated peasant hears;
Appall'd, he signs the frequent cross,
    When the wild din invades his ears.

The wakeful priest oft drops a tear
   For human pride, for human woe,
When, at his midnight mass, he hears
   The infernal cry of "Holla, ho!"

The Fire-King

"The blessing of the evil genii, which are curses, were upon him."
                                              —*Eastern Tale.*

B old knights and fair dames, to my harp give an ear,
Of love, and of war, and of wonder to hear;
And you haply may sigh, in the midst of your glee,
At the tale of Count Albert, and fair Rosalie.

O see you that castle, so strong and so high?
And see you that lady, the tear in her eye?
And see you that palmer, from Palestine's land,
The shell on his hat, and the staff in his hand?

"Now palmer, grey palmer, O tell unto me,
What news bring you home from the Holy Countrie?
And how goes the warfare by Galilee's strand?
And how fare our nobles, the flower of the land?"

"O well goes the warfare by Galilee's wave,
For Gilead, and Nablous, and Ramah we have;
And well fare our nobles by Mount Lebanon,
For the Heathen have lost, and the Christians have won."

A fair chain of gold 'mid her ringlets there hung;
O'er the palmer's grey locks the fair chain has she flung:
"O palmer, grey palmer, this chain be thy fee,
For the news thou hast brought from the Holy Countrie.

"And, palmer, good palmer, by Galilee's wave,
O saw ye Count Albert, the gentle and brave?

When the Crescent went back, and the Red-cross rush'd on,
O saw ye him foremost on Mount Lebanon?"

"O lady, fair lady, the tree green it grows;
O lady, fair lady, the stream pure it flows;
Your castle stands strong, and your hopes soar on high;
But, lady, fair lady, all blossoms to die.

"The green boughs they wither, the thunderbolt falls,
It leaves of your castle but levin-scorch'd walls;
The pure stream runs muddy; the gay hope is gone;
Count Albert is prisoner on Mount Lebanon."

O she's ta'en a horse, should be fleet at her speed;
And she's ta'en a sword, should be sharp at her need;
And she has ta'en shipping for Palestine's land,
To ransom Count Albert from Soldanrie's hand.

Small thought had Count Albert on fair Rosalie,
Small thought on his faith, or his knighthood, had he:
A heathenish damsel his light heart had won,
The Soldan's fair daughter of Mount Lebanon.

"O Christian, brave Christian, my love wouldst thou be,
Three things must thou do ere I hearken to thee:
Our laws and our worship on thee shalt thou take;
And this thou shalt first do for Zulema's sake.

"And, next, in the cavern, where burns evermore
The mystical flame which the Curdmans adore,
Alone, and in silence, three nights shalt thou wake;
And this thou shalt next do for Zulema's sake.

"And, last, thou shalt aid us with counsel and hand,
To drive the Frank robber from Palestine's land;
For my lord and my love then Count Albert I'll take,
When all this is accomplish'd for Zulema's sake."

He has thrown by his helmet, and cross-handled sword,
Renouncing his knighthood, denying his Lord;
He has ta'en the green caftan, and turban put on,
For the love of the maiden of fair Lebanon.

And in the dread cavern, deep deep under ground,
Which fifty steel gates and steel portals surround,
He has watch'd until daybreak, but sight saw he none,
Save the flame burning bright on its altar of stone.

Amazed was the Princess, the Soldan amazed,
Sore murmur'd the priests as on Albert they gazed;
They search'd all his garments, and, under his weeds,
They found, and took from him, his rosary beads.

Again in the cavern, deep deep under ground,
He watch'd the lone night, while the winds whistled round;
Far off was their murmur, it came not more nigh,
The flame burn'd unmoved, and nought else did he spy.

Loud murmur'd the priests, and amazed was the King,
While many dark spells of their witchcraft they sing;
They search'd Albert's body, and, lo! on his breast
Was the sign of the Cross, by his father impress'd.

The priests they erase it with care and with pain,
And the recreant return'd to the cavern again;
But, as he descended, a whisper there fell:
It was his good angel, who bade him farewell!

High bristled his hair, his heart flutter'd and beat,
And he turn'd him five steps, half resolved to retreat;
But his heart it was harden'd, his purpose was gone,
When he thought of the Maiden of fair Lebanon.

Scarce pass'd he the archway, the threshold scarce trode,
When the winds from the four points of heaven were abroad,

They made each steel portal to rattle and ring,
And, borne on the blast, came the dread Fire-King.

Full sore rock'd the cavern whene'er he drew nigh,
The fire on the altar blazed bickering and high;
In volcanic explosions the mountains proclaim
The dreadful approach of the Monarch of Flame.

Unmeasured in height, undistinguish'd in form,
His breath it was lightning, his voice it was storm;
I ween the stout heart of Count Albert was tame,
When he saw in his terrors the Monarch of Flame.

In his hand a broad falchion blue-glimmer'd through smoke,
And Mount Lebanon shook as the monarch he spoke:
"With this brand shalt thou conquer, thus long, and no more,
Till thou bend to the Cross, and the Virgin adore."

The cloud-shrouded Arm gives the weapon; and see!
The recreant receives the charm'd gift on his knee:
The thunders growl distant, and faint gleam the fires,
As, borne on the whirlwind, the phantom retires.

Count Albert has arm'd him the Paynim among,
Though his heart it was false, yet his arm it was strong;
And the Red-cross wax'd faint, and the Crescent came on,
From the day he commanded on Mount Lebanon.

From Lebanon's forests to Galilee's wave,
The sands of Samaar drank the blood of the brave;
Till the Knights of the Temple, and Knights of Saint John,
With Salem's King Baldwin, against him came on.

The war-cymbals clatter'd, the trumpets replied,
The lances were couch'd, and they closed on each side;
And horsemen and horses Count Albert o'erthrew,
Till he pierced the thick tumult King Baldwin unto.

Against the charm'd blade which Count Albert did wield,
The fence had been vain of the King's Red-cross shield;
But a Page thrust him forward the monarch before,
And cleft the proud turban the renegade wore.

So fell was the dint, that Count Albert stoop'd low
Before the cross'd shield, to his steel saddlebow;
And scarce had he bent to the Red-cross his head,
"Bonne Grace, Notre Dame!" he unwittingly said.

Sore sigh'd the charm'd sword, for its virtue was o'er,
It sprung from his grasp, and was never seen more;
But true men have said, that the lightning's red wing
Did waft back the brand to the dread Fire-King.

He clench'd his set teeth, and his gauntleted hand;
He stretch'd, with one buffet, that Page on the strand.
As back from the stripling the broken casque roll'd,
You might see the blue eyes, and the ringlets of gold.

Short time had Count Albert in horror to stare
On those death-swimming eyeballs, that blood-clotted hair;
For down came the Templars, like Cedron in flood,
And dyed their long lances in Saracen blood.

The Saracens, Curdmans, and Ishmaelites yield
To the scallop, the saltier, and crossleted shield;
And the eagles were gorged with the infidel dead,
From Bethsaida's fountains to Naphthali's head.

The battle is over on Bethsaida's plain.
Oh, who is yon Paynim lies stretch'd 'mid the slain?
And who is yon Page lying cold at his knee?
Oh, who but Count Albert and fair Rosalie!

The Lady was buried in Salem's bless'd bound,
The Count he was left to the vulture and hound:
Her soul to high mercy Our Lady did bring;
His went on the blast to the dread Fire-King.

Yet many a minstrel, in harping, can tell,
How the Red-cross it conquer'd, the Crescent it fell:
And lords and gay ladies have sigh'd, 'mid their glee,
At the tale of Count Albert and fair Rosalie.

The Erl-King

From the German of Goethe

O, who rides by night thro' the woodland so wild?
It is the fond father embracing his child;
And close the boy nestles within his loved arm,
To hold himself fast, and to keep himself warm.

"O father, see yonder! see yonder!" he says;
"My boy, upon what dost thou fearfully gaze?"
"O, 'tis the Erl-King with his crown and his shroud."
"No, my son, it is but a dark wreath of the cloud."

(*The Erl-King speaks.*)

"O come and go with me, thou loveliest child;
By many a gay sport shall thy time be beguiled;
My mother keeps for thee full many a fair toy,
And many a fine flower shall she pluck for my boy."

"O father, my father, and did you not hear
The Erl-King whisper so low in my ear?"
"Be still, my heart's darling—my child, be at ease;
It was but the wild blast as it sung thro' the trees."

Erl-King.

"O wilt thou go with me, thou loveliest boy?
My daughter shall tend thee with care and with joy;
She shall bear thee so lightly thro' wet and thro' wild,
And press thee, and kiss thee, and sing to my child."

"O father, my father, and saw you not plain
  The Erl-King's pale daughter glide past thro' the rain?"
"O yes, my loved treasure, I knew it full soon;
  It was the grey willow that danced to the moon."

Erl-King.

"O come and go with roe, no longer delay,
  Or else, silly child, I will drag thee away."
"O father! O father! now, now, keep your hold,
  The Erl-King has seized me—his grasp is so cold!"

Sore trembled the father; he spurr'd thro' the wild,
Clasping close to his bosom his shuddering child;
He reaches his dwelling in doubt and in dread,
But, clasp'd to his bosom, the infant was dead.

The Eve of St. John

The Baron of Smaylho'me rose with day,
    He spurred his courser on,
Without stop or stay, down the rocky way,
    That leads to Brotherstone.

He went not with the bold Buccleuch,
    His banner broad to rear;
He went not 'gainst the English yew
    To lift the Scottish spear.

Yet his plate-jack was braced, and his helmet was laced,
    And his vaunt-brace of proof he wore;
At his saddle-gerthe was a good steel sperthe,
    Full ten pound weight and more.

The Baron return'd in three days' space,
    And his looks were sad and sour;
And weary was his courser's pace,
    As he reach'd his rocky tower.

He came not from where Ancram Moor
    Ran red with English blood;
Where the Douglas true and the bold Buccleuch
    'Gainst keen Lord Evers stood.

Yet was his helmet hack'd and hew'd,
    His acton pierced and tore,
His axe and his dagger with blood imbrued,—
    But it was not English gore.

He lighted at the Chapellage,
    He held him close and still;
And he whistled thrice for his little foot-page,
    His name was English Will.

"Come thou hither, my little foot-page,
    Come hither to my knee;
Though thou art young, and tender of age,
    I think thou art true to me.

"Come, tell me all that thou hast seen,
    And look thou tell me true!
Since I from Smaylho'me tower have been,
    What did thy lady do?"

"My lady each night sought the lonely light
    That burns on the wild Watchfold;
For, from height to height, the beacons bright
    Of the English foemen told.

"The bittern clamour'd from the moss,
    The wind blew loud and shrill;
Yet the craggy pathway she did cross
    To the eiry Beacon Hill.

"I watch'd her steps, and silent came
    Where she sat her on a stone;
No watchman stood by the dreary flame,
    It burned all alone.

"The second night I kept her in sight
    Till to the fire she came,
And, by Mary's might! an armed Knight
    Stood by the lonely flame.

"And many a word that warlike lord
    Did speak to my lady there;

But the rain fell fast, and loud blew the blast,
    And I heard not what they were.

"The third night there the sky was fair,
    And the mountain-blast was still,
As again I watch'd the secret pair
    On the lonesome Beacon Hill.

"And I heard her name the midnight hour,
    And name this holy eve,
And say 'Come this night to thy lady's bower;
    Ask no bold Baron's leave.

"'He lifts his spear with the bold Buccleuch;
    His lady is all alone;
The door she'll undo to her knight so true
    On the eve of good Saint John.'

"'I cannot come, I must not come,
    I dare not come to thee;
On the eve of Saint John I must wander alone,
    In thy bower I may not be.'

"'Now out on thee, fainthearted knight!
    Thou shouldst not say me nay;
For the eve is sweet, and when lovers meet
    Is worth the whole summer's day.

"'And I'll chain the blood-hound, and the warder shall not sound,
    And rushes shall be strew'd on the stair;
So, by the black rood-stone, and by holy Saint John,
    I conjure thee, my love, to be there!'

"'Though the blood-hound be mute, and the rush beneath my foot,
    And the warder his bugle should not blow,
Yet there sleepeth a priest in the chamber to the east,
    And my footstep he would know.

"'O, fear not the priest, who sleepeth to the east,
        For to Dryburgh the way he has ta'en;
And there to say mass, till three days do pass,
        For the soul of a knight that is slayne.'

"He turn'd him around, and grimly he frown'd,
        Then he laugh'd right scornfully—
'He who says the mass-rite for the soul of that knight
        May as well say mass for me.

"'At the lone midnight hour, when bad spirits have power,
        In thy chamber will I be.'
With that he was gone, and my lady left alone,
        And no more did I see."

Then changed, I trow, was that bold Baron's brow,
        From the dark to the blood-red high—
"Now tell me the mien of the knight thou hast seen,
        For, by Mary, he shall die!"

"His arms shone full bright in the beacon's red light;
        His plume it was scarlet and blue;
On his shield was a hound in a silver leash bound,
        And his crest was a branch of the yew."

"Thou liest, thou liest, thou little foot-page,
        Loud dost thou lie to me!
For that knight is cold, and low laid in the mould,
        All under the Eildon-tree."

"Yet hear but my word, my noble lord!
        For I heard her name his name;
And that lady bright, she called the knight
        Sir Richard of Coldinghame."

The bold Baron's brow then changed, I trow,
        From high blood-red to pale—

"The grave is deep and dark, and the corpse is stiff and stark,
    So I may not trust thy tale.

"Where fair Tweed flows round holy Melrose,
    And Eildon slopes to the plain,
Full three nights ago, by some secret foe,
    That gay gallant was slain.

"The varying light deceived thy sight,
    And the wild winds drown'd the name;
For the Dryburgh bells ring and the white monks do sing
    For Sir Richard, of Coldinghame!"

He pass'd the court-gate, and he oped the tower-grate,
    And he mounted the narrow stair
To the bartizan-seat, where, with maids that on her wait
    He found his lady fair.

That lady sat in mournful mood,
    Look'd over hill and vale,
Over Tweed's fair flood and Mertoun's wood
    And all down Teviotdale.

"Now hail, now hail, thou lady bright!"
    "Now hail, thou Baron true!
What news, what news from Ancram fight?
    What news from the bold Buccleuch?"

"The Ancram Moor is red with gore,
    For many a southron fell;
And Buccleuch has charged us evermore
    To watch our beacons well."

The lady blush'd red, but nothing she said;
    Nor added the Baron a word.
Then she stepp'd down the stair to her chamber fair,
    And so did her moody lord.

In sleep the lady mourn'd, and the Baron toss'd and turn'd,
    And oft to himself he said,
"The worms around him creep, and his bloody grave is deep—
    It cannot give up the dead!"

It was near the ringing of matin-bell,
    The night was wellnigh done,
When a heavy sleep on that Baron fell,
    On the eve of good Saint John.

The lady look'd through the chamber fair,
    By the light of a dying flame;
And she was aware of a knight stood there—
    Sir Richard of Coldinghame!

"Alas! away, away!" she cried,
    "For the holy Virgin's sake!"
"Lady, I know who sleeps by thy side;
    But, lady, he will not awake.

"By Eildon-tree, for long nights three,
    In bloody grave have I lain;
The mass and the death-prayer are said for me,
    But, lady, they are said in vain.

"By the Baron's brand, near Tweed's fair strand,
    Most foully slain I fell;
And my restless sprite on the beacon's height
    For a space is doom'd to dwell.

"At our trysting-place, for a certain space,
    I must wander to and fro;
But I had not had power to come to thy bower
    Had'st thou not conjured me so."

Love master'd fear; her brow she cross'd—
    "How, Richard, hast thou sped?

And art thou saved, or art thou lost?"
　　The vision shook his head!

"Who spilleth life shall forfeit life;
　　So bid thy lord believe;
That lawless love is guilt above,
　　This awful sign receive."

He laid his left palm on an oaken beam,
　　His right upon her hand—
The lady shrunk, and fainting sunk,
　　For it scorch'd like a fiery brand.

The sable score of fingers four
　　Remains on that board impress'd;
And for evermore that lady wore
　　A covering on her wrist.

There is a nun in Dryburgh bower,
　　Ne'er looks upon the sun;
There is a monk in Melrose tower,
　　He speaketh word to none;

That nun who ne'er beholds the day,
　　That monk who speaks to none—
That nun was Smaylho'me's Lady gay,
　　That monk the bold Baron.

Glenfinlas; or, Lord Ronald's Coronach

"For them the viewless forms of air obey,
        Their bidding heed, and at their beck repair;
They know what spirit brews the stormful day,
        And heartless oft, like moody madness stare,
To see the phantom-train their secret work prepare."

COLLINS.

O hone a rie'! O hone a rie'!
        The pride of Albin's line is o'er,
And fall'n Glenartney's stateliest tree;
        We ne'er shall see Lord Ronald more!

O, sprung from great Macgillianore,
        The chief that never fear'd a foe,
How matchless was thy broad claymore,
        How deadly thine unerring bow!

Well can the Saxon widows tell,
        How on the Teith's resounding shore
The boldest Lowland warriors fell,
        As down from Lenny's pass you bore.

But o'er his hills, in festal day,
        How blazed Lord Ronald's beltane-tree,
While youths and maids the light strathspey
        So nimbly danced with Highland glee!

Cheer'd by the strength of Ronald's shell,
        E'en age forgot his tresses hoar;
But now the loud lament we swell,
        O ne'er to see Lord Ronald more!

From distant isles a chieftain came,
    The joys of Ronald's halls to find,
And chase with him the dark-brown game,
    That bounds o'er Albin's hills of wind.

'Twas Moy; whom in Columba's isle
    The seer's prophetic spirit found,
As, with a minstrel's fire the while,
    He waked his harp's harmonious sound.

Full many a spell to him was known,
    Which wandering spirits shrink to hear;
And many a lay of potent tone
    Was never meant for mortal ear.

For there, 'tis said, in mystic mood,
    High converse with the dead they hold,
And oft espy the fated shroud,
    That shall the future corpse enfold.

O so it fell, that on a day,
    To rouse the red deer from their den,
The Chiefs have ta'en their distant way,
    And scour'd the deep Glenfinlas glen.

No vassals wait their sports to aid,
    To watch their safety, deck their board;
Their simple dress the Highland plaid,
    Their trusty guard the Highland sword.

Three summer days, through brake and dell,
    Their whistling shafts successful flew;
And still, when dewy evening fell,
    The quarry to their hut they drew.

In grey Glenfinlas' deepest nook
    The solitary cabin stood,

Fast by Moneira's sullen brook,
    Which murmurs through that lonely wood.

Soft fell the night, the sky was calm,
    When three successive days had flown;
And summer mist in dewy balm
    Steep'd heathy bank and mossy stone.

The moon, half-hid in silvery flakes,
    Afar her dubious radiance shed,
Quivering on Katrine's distant lakes,
    And resting on Benledi's head.

Now in their hut, in social guise,
    Their silvan fare the Chiefs enjoy;
And pleasure laughs in Ronald's eyes,
    As many a pledge he quaffs to Moy.

"What lack we here to crown our bliss,
    While thus the pulse of joy beats high?
What, but fair woman's yielding kiss,
    Her panting breath and melting eye!

"To chase the deer of yonder shades,
    This morning left their father's pile
The fairest of our mountain maids,
    The daughters of the proud Glengyle.

"Long have I sought sweet Mary's heart,
    And dropp'd the tear, and heaved the sigh:
But vain the lover's wily art,
    Beneath a sister's watchful eye.

"But thou mayst teach that guardian fair,
    While far with Mary I have flown,
Of other hearts to cease her care,
    And find it hard to guard her own.

"Touch but thy harp—thou soon shalt see
  The lovely Flora of Glengyle,
Unmindful of her charge and me,
  Hang on thy notes 'twixt tear and smile.

"Or, if she choose a melting tale,
  All underneath the greenwood bough,
Will good Saint Oran's rule prevail,
  Stern huntsman of the rigid brow?"

"Since Enrick's fight, since Morna's death,
  No more on me shall rapture rise,
Responsive to the panting breath,
  Or yielding kiss, or melting eyes.

"E'en then, when o'er the heath of woe,
  Where sunk my hopes of love and fame,
I bade my harp's wild wailings flow,
  On me the Seer's sad spirit came.

"The last dread curse of angry heaven,
  With ghastly sights and sounds of woe,
To dash each glimpse of joy, was given;
  The gift—the future ill to know.

"The bark thou saw'st yon summer morn
  So gaily part from Oban's bay,
My eye beheld her dash'd and torn,
  Far on the rocky Colonsay.

"Thy Fergus too, thy sister's son,—
  Thou saw'st with pride the gallant's power,
As marching 'gainst the Lord of Downe
  He left the skirts of huge Benmore.

"Thou only saw'st their tartans wave,
  As down Benvoirlich's side they wound,

Heard'st but the pibroch answering brave
    To many a target clanking round.

"I heard the groans, I mark'd the tears,
    I saw the wound his bosom bore,
When on the serried Saxon spears
    He pour'd his clan's resistless roar.

"And thou who bidst me think of bliss,
    And bidst my heart awake to glee,
And court like thee the wanton kiss—
    That heart, O Ronald, bleeds for thee!

"I see the death-damps chill thy brow;
    I hear thy Warning Spirit cry;
The corpse-lights dance! they're gone! and now—
    No more is given to gifted eye!

"Alone enjoy thy dreary dreams,
    Sad prophet of the evil hour!
Say, should we scorn joy's transient beams,
    Because to-morrow's storm may lour?

"Or false or sooth thy words of woe,
    Clangillian's Chieftain ne'er shall fear;
His blood shall bound at rapture's glow,
    Though doom'd to stain the Saxon spear.

"E'en now, to meet me in yon dell,
    My Mary's buskins brush the dew."
He spoke, nor bade the Chief farewell,
    But called his dogs, and gay withdrew.

Within an hour return'd each hound;
    In rush'd the rousers of the deer;
They howl'd in melancholy sound,
    Then closely couch'd beside the Seer.

No Ronald yet—though midnight came,
    And sad were Moy's prophetic dreams,
As, bending o'er the dying flame,
    He fed the watch-fire's quivering gleams.

Sudden the hounds erect their ears,
    And sudden cease their moaning howl;
Close press'd to Moy, they mark their fears
    By shivering limbs and stifled growl.

Untouch'd, the harp began to ring,
    As softly, slowly, oped the door;
And shook responsive every string,
    As, light, a footstep press'd the floor.

And by the watch-fire's glimmering light,
    Close by the minstrel's side was seen
An huntress maid in beauty bright,
    All dropping wet her robes of green.

All dropping wet her garments seem;
    Chill'd was her cheek, her bosom bare,
As, bending o'er the dying gleam,
    She wrung the moisture from her hair.

With maiden blush, she softly said,
    "O gentle huntsman, hast thou seen,
In deep Glenfinlas' moonlight glade,
    A lovely maid in vest of green:

"With her a Chief in Highland pride;
    His shoulders bear the hunter's bow,
The mountain dirk adorns his side,
    Far on the wind his tartans flow?"

"And who art thou? and who are they?"
    All ghastly gazing, Moy replied:

"And why, beneath the moon's pale ray,
    Dare ye thus roam Glenfinlas' side?"

"Where wild Loch Katrine pours her tide,
    Blue, dark, and deep, round many an isle,
Our father's towers o'erhang her side,
    The castle of the bold Glengyle.

"To chase the dun Glenfinlas deer
    Our woodland course this morn we bore,
And haply met, while wandering here,
    The son of great Macgillianore.

"O aid me, then, to seek the pair,
    Whom, loitering in the woods, I lost;
Alone, I dare not venture there,
    Where walks, they say, the shrieking ghost."

"Yes, many a shrieking ghost walks there;
    Then, first, my own sad vow to keep,
Here will I pour my midnight prayer,
    Which still must rise when mortals sleep."

"O first, for pity's gentle sake,
    Guide a lone wanderer on her way!
For I must cross the haunted brake,
    And reach my father's towers ere day."

"First, three times tell each Ave-bead,
    And thrice a Pater-noster say,
Then kiss with me the holy rede;
    So shall we safely wend our way."

"O shame to knighthood, strange and foul!
    Go, doff the bonnet from thy brow,
And shroud thee in the monkish cowl,
    Which best befits thy sullen vow.

"Not so, by high Dunlathmon's fire,
　　Thy heart was froze to love and joy,
When gaily rung thy raptured lyre
　　To wanton Morna's melting eye."

Wild stared the minstrel's eyes of flame,
　　And high his sable locks arose,
And quick his colour went and came,
　　As fear and rage alternate rose.

"And thou! when by the blazing oak
　　I lay, to her and love resign'd,
Say, rode ye on the eddying smoke,
　　Or sail'd ye on the midnight wind?

"Not thine a race of mortal blood,
　　Nor old Glengyle's pretended line;
Thy dame, the Lady of the Flood—
　　Thy sire, the Monarch of the Mine."

He mutter'd thrice Saint Oran's rhyme,
　　And thrice Saint Fillan's powerful prayer;
Then turn'd him to the eastern clime,
　　And sternly shook his coal-black hair.

And, bending o'er his harp, he flung
　　His wildest witch-notes on the wind;
And loud and high and strange they rung,
　　As many a magic change they find.

Tall wax'd the Spirit's altering form,
　　Till to the roof her stature grew;
Then, mingling with the rising storm,
　　With one wild yell away she flew.

Rain beats, hail rattles, whirlwinds tear:
　　The slender but in fragments flew;

But not a lock of Moy's loose hair
    Was waved by wind, or wet by dew.

Wild mingling with the howling gale,
    Loud bursts of ghastly laughter rise;
High o'er the minstrel's head they sail,
    And die amid the northern skies.

The voice of thunder shook the wood,
    As ceased the more than mortal yell;
And, spattering foul, a shower of blood
    Upon the hissing firebrands fell.

Next dropp'd from high a mangled arm;
    The fingers strain'd an half-drawn blade:
And last, the life-blood streaming warm,
    Torn from the trunk, a gasping head.

Oft o'er that head, in battling field,
    Stream'd the proud crest of high Benmore;
That arm the broad claymore could wield,
    Which dyed the Teith with Saxon gore.

Woe to Moneira's sullen rills!
    Woe to Glenfinlas' dreary glen!
There never son of Albin's hills
    Shall draw the hunter's shaft agen!

E'en the tired pilgrim's burning feet
    At noon shall shun that sheltering den,
Lest, journeying in their rage, he meet
    The wayward Ladies of the Glen.

And we—behind the Chieftain's shield
    No more shall we in safety dwell;
None leads the people to the field—
    And we the loud lament must swell.

O hone a rie'! O hone a rie'!
 The pride of Albin's line is o'er!
And fall'n Glenartney's stateliest tree;
 We ne'er shall see Lord Ronald more!

ESSAYS AND REVIEWS

[Review of Maturin's *Fatal Revenge*]

Fatal Revenge; or, the Family of Montorio: a Romance. By Dennis Jasper Murphy. 3 vols. 8vo. London. Longman and Co. 1807.

J'apprends d'être vif. Such was the noted answer of a German baron who had alarmed a whole Parisian hotel by leaping over joint-stools in his solitary apartment. This mode of qualifying himself for the lively conversation of the French was probably attended with some fatigue to the worthy *Frei-herr's* person, and perhaps some damage to his shins; with which we the more readily sympathise, as, in compliance with the hint of several well-meaning friends, we are just taking the pen after some desperate efforts *pour apprendre à être vif.* It was whispered to us, in no unfriendly voice, that we were respectable classical scholars, divines at least as serious as was necessary, tolerable politicians considering the old-fashioned nature of our principles, and as good philosophers as could be expected of persons obviously trammeled by belief in the tenets which, in compliance with ancient custom, are still delivered once in seven days to those who chuse to hear them. It seemed farther to be allowed, that we were indifferent good hands at a sarcasm, and displayed some taste for poetry; but still we were not lively—that is, we had none of those light and airy articles which a young lady might read while her hair was papering. To sum up all in one dismal syllable, it was insinuated that we were *dull.* To prove the futility of the charge, we resolved to extend the sphere of our inquiries; and to review not only the grave and weighty, but the flitting and evanescent productions of the times; for the purpose of giving full scope to our ingenuity, and evincing the vivacity of our talents, so wantonly called in question. The want of proper subjects for the exercise of our powers was the first dilemma. We had no friendly correspondent at the court of Paris who, with a sentimental flourish on the peace which ought to subsist in the republic of letters, though war raged between the respective countries of the sages, might forward, through some kind neutral, the last new novel or the latest philosophical discovery of the Institute, and only expect us, in requital, to give the wit and learning and science of the Great Nation its reasonable and just precedence over those of our own country. What then was to be done? After some consideration, we sent to our Publisher for an assortment of the newest and most fashionable novels, hoping to find among the frivolous articles of domestic manufacture something to supply the want of foreign importation. It is from a laborious inspection into the contents of this packet, or rather hamper, that we are now risen with the painful conviction that spirits and patience may be as completely exhausted in perusing trifles as in following algebraical calculations. Before proceeding however to the novel, selected almost at random for the subject of a few remarks, we cannot but express our surprise at the present degradation of this class of compositions.

The elegant and fascinating productions which honoured the name of novel, those which Richardson, Mackenzie, and Burney gave to the public; of which it was the object to exalt virtue and degrade vice; to which no fault could be objected unless that they unfitted here and there a romantic mind for the common intercourse of life, while they refined perhaps a thousand whose faculties could better bear the fair ideal which they presented—these have entirely vanished from the shelves of the circulating library. It may indeed be fairly alleged in defence of those who decline attempting this higher and more refined species of composition, that the soil was in some degree exhausted by overcropping—that the multitude of base and tawdry imitations obscured the merit of the few which are tolerable, as the overwhelming blaze of blue, red, green, and yellow, at the Exhibition, vitiates our taste for the few good paintings which show their modest hues upon its walls. The public was indeed weary of the protracted embarrassments of lords and ladies who spoke such language as was never spoken, and still more so of the see-saw correspondence between the sentimental Lady Lucretia and the witty Miss Caroline, who battledored it in the pathetic and the lively, like Morton and Reynolds on the stage. But let us be just to dead and to living merit. In some of the novels of the late Charlotte Smith we found no ordinary portion of that fascinating power which leads us through every various scene of happiness or distress at the will of the author; which places the passions of the wise and grave for a time under the command of ideal personages; and perhaps has more attraction for the public at large than any other species of literary composition, the drama not excepted. Nor do we owe less to Miss Edgeworth, whose true and vivid pictures of modern life contain the only sketches reminding us of human beings, whom, secluded as we are, we have actually seen and conversed with in various parts of this great metropolis.

When we had removed from the surface of our hamper a few thin volumes of simple and insipid sentiment; taken a moment's breath; and exclaimed "O Athenians, how hard we labour for your applause!" we lighted upon a class of books which excited sterner sensations. There existed formerly a species of novel of a tragi-comic nature, which, far from pretending to the extreme sentiment and delicacy of the works last mentioned, admitted, like the elder English comedy, a considerable dash of coarse and even indelicate humour. Such were the compositions of Fielding; and such of Smollet, the literary Hogarth, whose figures, though they seldom attained grace or elegance, were marked with indelible truth and peculiarity of character. Instead of this kind of comic satire, in which, to borrow a few words of Old Withers, abuses, when whipped, were perhaps stripped a little too bare, we have now the lowest denizens of Grub Street narrating, under the flimsy veil of false names, and through the medium of a fictitious tale, all that malevolence can invent and stupidity propagate concerning private misfortunes and personal characters. We have our Winters in London, Bath, and Brighton, of which it is the dirty object to drag forth the secret history of the day, and to give to Scandal a court of written record. The talent which most of these things indicate is that of the lowest news-paper composition, and the acquaintance with the fashionable world precisely what might be gleaned from the footman or porter; while the portraits of Bow-street officers, swindlers, and bailiffs, are possibly drawn from a more intimate acquaintance. The shortness of our cruize has not yet permitted us to fall in with any of these picaroons; but let them beware, as Lieutenant Bowling says, how they come athwart our hawser; "we shall mind running them down no more than so many porpoises."

"Plunging from depth to depth a vast profound," we at length imagined ourselves arrived at the Limbus Patrum in good earnest. The imitators of Mrs. Radcliffe and Mr. Lewis were before us; personages, who to all the faults and extravagances of their originals, added that of dulness, with which they can seldom be charged. We strolled through a variety of castles, each of which was regularly called Il Castello; met with as many captains of con-dottieri; heard various ejaculations of Santa Maria and Diavolo; read by a decaying lamp, and in a tapestried chamber, dozens of legends as stupid as the main history; examined such suites of deserted apartments as might fit up a reasonable barrack, and saw as many glimmering lights as would make a respectable illumination—Amid these flat imitations of the Castle of Udolpho we lighted unexpectedly upon the work which is the subject of the present article, and, in defiance of the very bad taste in which it is com-posed, we found ourselves insensibly involved in the perusal, and at times impressed with no common degree of respect for the powers of the author. We have at no time more earnestly desired to extend our voice to a bewil-dered traveller, than towards this young man, whose taste is so inferior to his powers of imagination and expression, that we never saw a more re-markable instance of genius degraded by the labour in which it is em-ployed. It is the resentment and regret which we experience at witnessing the abuse of these qualities, as well as the wish to hazard a few remarks up-on the romantic novel in general, which has induced us (though we are obliged to go back a little) to offer our criticism on the "Fatal Revenge, or the Family of Montorio."

It is scarcely possible to abridge the narrative, nor would the attempt be edifying or entertaining. A short abstract of the story is all for which we can afford room. It is introduced in the following striking manner.

"At the siege of Barcelona by the French, in the year 1697, two young officers entered into the service at its most hot and critical period. Their appearance excited some surprise and perplexity. Their melancholy was Spanish, their accent Italian, their names and habits French.

"They distinguished themselves in the service by a kind of careless and desperate courage, that appeared equally insensible of praise or of danger. They forced themselves into all the *coups de main,* the wild and perilous sallies, that abound in a spirited siege, and mark it with a greater variety and vivacity of character than a regular campaign. *Here* they were in their element. But among their brother officers, so cold, so distant, so repulsive, that even *they* who loved their courage, or were interested in their melancholy, stood aloof in awkward and hesitating sympathy. Still, though they would not accept the offices of the benevolence their appear-ance inspired, they were involuntarily always conciliating. Their figures and

motions were so eminently noble and striking, their affection for each other so conspicuous, and their youthful melancholy so deep and hopeless,
that every one inquired, and sought intelligence of them from an impulse
stronger than curiosity. Nothing could be learnt; nothing was known, or
even conjectured of them.

"During the siege, an Italian officer, of middle age, arrived to assume
the command of a post of distinction. His first meeting with these young
men was remarkable. They stood speechless and staring at each other for
some time. In the mixture of emotions that passed over their counte-
nances, no one predominant or decisive could be traced by the many and
anxious witnesses that surrounded them.

"As soon as they separated, the Italian officer was persecuted with inquiries about the strangers. He answered none of them; yet he admitted
that he knew circumstances sufficiently extraordinary relating to the young
men, who, he said, were natives of Italy.

"A few days after, Barcelona was taken by the French forces. The as-
sault was terrible; the young officers were in the very rage of the fight; they
coveted and courted danger; they stood amid showers of grape and ball; they
rushed into the heart of crater and explosions; they literally 'wrought in the
fire.' The effects of their dreadful courage were foreseen by all; and cries of
recall and expostulation sounded around them on every side, in vain.

"On the French taking possession of the town, there was a general demand for the *brothers.* With difficulty the bodies were discovered, and
brought with melancholy pomp into the commander's presence. The Italian
officer was there; every eye was turned on him." Introd. pp. ix–xiii.

The history of these mysterious brethren is told by the officer who
had recognised them, and runs briefly thus: Orazio, Count of Montorio—for we begin our story with the explanation, which in the original
concludes it—possessed of wealth, honours, and ancestry, is married to a
beautiful woman, whom he loves doatingly, but of whose affections he is
not possessed. A villanous brother instils into his mind jealousy of a
cavalier to whom the Countess had formerly been attached. Orazio
causes the supposed paramour to be murdered in the presence of the
lady, who also dies: he then flies from his country with feelings of des-
peration thus forcibly described:—

"My reason was not suspended, it was totally *changed.* I had become a
kind of intellectual savage; a being that, with the malignity and depravation

of inferior natures, still retains the reason of a man, and retains it only for his curse. Oh! that midnight darkness of the soul, in which it seeks for something whose loss has carried away every sense but one of utter and desolate privation; in which it traverses leagues in motion and worlds in thought, without consciousness of relief, yet with a dread of pausing. I had nothing to seek, nothing to recover; the whole world could not restore me an atom, could not shew me again a glimpse of what I had been or lost; yet I rushed on as if the next step would reach shelter and peace." Vol. iii. p. 380.

In this maniac state he reaches an uninhabited islet in the Grecian archipelago, where, from a conversation accidentally overheard between two assassins sent by his brother to murder him, the wretched Orazio learns the innocence of his victims, and the full extent of his misery. He contrives to murder his murderers, and the effect of the subsequent discovery upon his feelings is described in a strain of language which we were alternately tempted to admire as sublime and to reprobate as bombastic.

Orazio determines on revenge, and his plan is diabolically horrid. He resolved to accomplish the murder of his treacherous brother, who, in consequence of his supposed death, had now assumed the honours of the family; and he farther determined that this act of vengeance should be perpetrated by the hands of that very brother's own sons, two amiable youths, who had no cloud upon their character excepting an attachment to mysterious studies, and a strong propensity to superstition.

We do not mean to trace this agent of vengeance through the various devices and stratagems by which he involved in his toils his unsuspecting nephews, assumed in their apprehension the character of an infernal agent, and decoyed them first to meditate upon, and at length actually to perpetrate, the parricide which was the crown and summit of his wishes. The doctrine of fatalism, on which he principally relied for reconciling his victims to his purpose, is in various passages detailed with much gloomy and terrific eloquence. The rest of his machinery is composed of banditti, caverns, dungeons, inquisitors, trap-doors, ruins, secret passages, soothsayers, and all the usual accoutrements from the property-room of Mrs. Radcliffe. The horror of the piece is completed by the murderer discovering that the youths whom he has taken such pains to involve in parricide are not the sons of his brother, but his own offspring by his unfortunate wife. We do not dwell upon any of these particulars, because the observations which we have to hazard upon this neglected novel apply to a numerous class of the same kind, and because the incidents are such as are to be found in most of them.

In the first place, then, we disapprove of the mode introduced by Mrs. Radcliffe, and followed by Mr. Murphy and her other imitators, by winding up their story with a solution by which all the incidents appearing to partake of the mystic and marvellous are resolved by very simple and natural causes. This seems, to us, to savour of the precaution of Snug the Joiner; or, rather, it is as if the machinist, when the pantomime was over, should turn his scenes "the seamy side without," and expose the mechanical aids by which the delusions were accomplished. In one respect, indeed, it is worse management; because the understanding spectator might be in some degree gratified by the view of engines which, however rude, were well adapted to produce the effects which he had witnessed. But the machinery of the castle of Montorio, when exhibited, is wholly inadequate to the gigantic operations ascribed to it. There is a total and absolute disproportion between the cause and effect, which must disgust every reader much more than if he were left under the delusion of ascribing the whole to supernatural agency. The latter resource has indeed many disadvantages; some of which we shall briefly notice. But it is an admitted expedient; appeals to the belief of all ages but our own; and still produces, when well managed, some effect even upon those who are most disposed to contemn its influence. We can therefore allow of supernatural agency to a certain extent and for an appropriate purpose, but we never can consent that the effect of such agency shall be finally attributable to natural causes totally inadequate to its production. We can believe, for example, in Macbeth's witches, and tremble at their spells; but had we been informed, in the conclusion of the piece, that they were only three of his wife's chamber-maids disguised for the purpose of imposing on the Thane's credulity, it would have added little to the credibility of the story, and entirely deprived it of the interest. In like manner we fling back upon the Radcliffe school their flat arid ridiculous explanations, and plainly tell them that they must either confine themselves to ordinary and natural events, or find adequate causes for those horrors and mysteries in which they love to involve us. Yet another word on this subject. We know not if a novel writer of the present day expects or desires his labours to be perused oftener than once; but as there may be here and there a maiden aunt in a family, for whose advantage it must be again read over by the young lady who has already devoured it in secret, we advise them to consider how much they suffer from their adherence to this unfortunate system. We will instance the incident of the black veil in the castle of Udolpho. Attention is excited, and afterwards recalled, by a hundred indirect artifices, to the dreadful and unexplained mystery which the heroine had seen beneath it; and which, after all, proves to be nothing more nor less than a waxen doll. This trick may indeed for once answer the writer's purpose; and has, we suppose, cost many an extra walk to the circulating library, and many a curse upon the malicious concurrent who always has the fourth volume in hand. But it is as impossible to reperuse the book without feeling the contempt awakened by so pitiful a contrivance as it is for a child to regain its original respect for King Solomon after he has seen the monarch disrobed of all his glory, and deposited in the same box with Punch and his wife. And, in fact, we feel inclined to abuse the author in such a case as the watch do Harlequin, when they find out his trick of frightening them by mimicking the report of a pistol.

> Faquin, maraud, pendard, impudent, téméraire,
> Vous osez nous faire peur!

In the second place, we are of opinion that the terrors of this class of novel writers are too accumulated and unremitting. The influence of fear—and here we extend our observations as well to those romances which actually ground it upon supernatural prodigy as to those which attempt a subsequent explanation—is indeed a faithful and legitimate key to unlock every source of fancy and of feeling. Mr. Murphy's introduction is expressed with the spirit and animation which, though often misdirected, pervade his whole work.

> "I question whether there be a source of emotion in the whole mental frame so powerful or universal as *the fear arising from objects of invisible terror.* Perhaps there is no other that has been, at some period or other of life, the predominant and indelible sensation of every mind, of every class, and under every circumstance. Love, supposed to be the most general of passions, has certainly been felt in its purity by very few, and by some not at all, even in its most indefinite and simple state.
>
> "The same might be said, *à fortiori,* of other passions. But who is

there that has never feared? Who is there that has not involuntarily remembered the gossip's tale in solitude or in darkness? Who is there that has not sometimes shivered under an influence he would scarce acknowledge to himself? I might trace this passion to a high and obvious source.

"It is enough for my purpose to assert its existence and prevalency, which will scarcely be disputed by those who remember it. It is absurd to depreciate this passion, and deride its influence. It is *not* the weak and trivial impulse of the nursery, to be forgotten and scorned by manhood. It is the aspiration of a spirit; 'it is the passion of immortals,' that dread and desire of their final habitations." Pref. pp. 4 & 5.

We grant there is much truth in this proposition taken generally. But the finest and deepest feelings are those which are most easily exhausted. The chord which vibrates and sounds at a touch, remains in silent tension under continued pressure. Besides, terror, as Bob Acres says of its counterpart, courage, will come and go; and few people can afford timidity enough for the writer's purpose who is determined on "horrifying" them through three thick volumes. The vivacity of the emotion also depends greatly upon surprize, and surprize cannot be repeatedly excited during the perusal o the same work. It is said respecting the cruel punishment of breaking alive upon the wheel, the sufferer's nerves are so much jarred by the first blow, that he feels comparatively little pain from those which follow. There is something of this in moral feeling; nor do we see a better remedy for it than to recommend the cessation of these experiments upon the public, until their sensibility shall have recovered its original tone. The taste for the marvellous has been indeed compared to the habit of drinking ardent liquors. But it fortunately differs in having its limits: he upon whom one dram does not produce the effect, can attain the desired degree of inebriation by doubling the dose. But when we have ceased to start at one ghost, we are callous to the exhibition of a whole Pandemonium. In short, the sensation is generally as transient as it is powerful, and commonly depends upon some slight circumstances which cannot be repeated.

> The time has been our senses would have cool'd
> To hear a night-shriek, and our fell of hair
> Would at a dismal treatise rouse and stir
> As life were in't. We have supped full with horrors;

And direness, now familiar to our thoughts,
Cannot once start us.

These appear to us the greatest disadvantages under which any author must at present struggle, who chuses supernatural terror for his engine of moving the passions. We dare not call them insurmountable, for how shall we dare to limit the efforts of genius, or shut against its possessor any avenue to the human heart, or its passions? Mr. Murphy himself, for aught we know, may be destined to shew us the prudence of this qualification. He possesses a strong and vigorous fancy, with great command of language. He has indeed regulated his incidents upon those of others, and therefore added to the imperfections which we have pointed out, the want of originality. But his feeling and conception of character are his own, and from these we judge of his powers. In truth we rose from his strange chaotic novel romance as from a confused and feverish dream, unrefreshed, and unamused, yet strongly impressed by many of the ideas which had been so vaguely and wildly presented to our imagination.

It remains to notice the pieces of poetry scattered through these volumes, many of which claim our attention: but we cannot stop to criticise them. There is a wild and desultory elegy, vol. ii. pp. 305–309, which, though not always strictly metrical, has passages of great pathos, as well as fancy. If the author of it be indeed, as he describes himself, young and inexperienced, without literary friend, or counsellor, we earnestly exhort him to seek one on whose taste and judgment he can rely. He is now, like an untutored colt, wasting his best vigour in irregular efforts without either grace or object; but there is much in these volumes which promises a career that may at some future time astonish the public.

Remarks on *Frankenstein*

Frankenstein; or, the Modern Prometheus. 3 vols. 12mo. 16s. 6d. Lackington and Co., London, 1818.

> Did I request thee, Maker, from my clay
> To mould me man? Did I solicit thee
> From darkness to promote me?——
> *Paradise Lost.*

This is a novel, or more properly a romantic fiction, of a nature so peculiar, that we ought to describe the species before attempting any account of the individual production.

The first general division of works of fiction, into such as bound the events they narrate by the actual laws of nature, and such as, passing these limits, are managed by marvellous and supernatural machinery, is sufficiently obvious and decided. But the class of marvellous romances admits of several subdivisions. In the earlier productions of imagination, the poet or tale-teller does not, in his own opinion, transgress the laws of credibility, when he introduces into his narration the witches, goblins, and magicians, in the existence of which he himself, as well as his hearers, is a firm believer. This good faith, however, passes away, and works turning upon the marvellous are written and read merely on account of the exercise which they afford to the imagination of those who, like the poet Collins, love to riot in the luxuriance of oriental fiction, to rove through the meanders of enchantment, to gaze on the magnificence of golden palaces, and to repose by the water-falls of Elysian gardens. In this species of composition, the marvellous is itself the principal and most important object both to the author and reader. To describe its effect upon the mind of the human personages engaged in its wonders, and dragged along by its machinery, is comparatively an inferior object. The hero and heroine, partakers of the supernatural character which belongs to their adventures, walk the maze of

147

enchantment with a firm and undaunted step, and appear as much at their ease, amid the wonders around them, as the young fellow described by the Spectator, who was discovered taking a snuff with great composure in the midst of a stormy ocean, represented on the stage of the opera.

A more philosophical and refined use of the supernatural in works of fiction, is proper to that class in which the laws of nature are represented as altered, not for the purpose of pampering the imagination with wonders, but in order to shew the probable effect which the supposed miracles would produce on those who witnessed them. In this case, the pleasure ordinarily derived from the marvellous incidents is secondary to that which we extract from observing how mortals like ourselves would be affected,

> By scenes like these which, daring to depart
> From sober truth, are still to nature true.

Even in the description of his marvels, however, the author who manages this style of composition with address, gives them an indirect importance with the reader, when he is able to describe with nature, and with truth, the effects which they are calculated to produce upon his dramatis personæ. It will be remembered, that the sapient Partridge was too wise to be terrified at the mere appearance of the ghost of Hamlet, whom he knew to be a man dressed up in pasteboard armour for the nonce—it was when he saw the "little man," as he called Garrick, so frightened, that a sympathetic horror took hold of him. Of this we shall presently produce some examples from the narrative before us. But success in this point is still subordinate to the author's principal object, which is less to produce an effect by means of the marvels of the narrations, than to open new trains and channels of thought, by placing men in supposed situations of an extraordinary and preternatural character, and then describing the mode of feeling and conduct which they are most likely to adopt.

To make more clear the distinction we have endeavoured to draw between the marvellous and the effects of the marvellous, considered as separate objects, we may briefly invite our readers to compare the common tale of Tom Thumb with Gulliver's Voyage to Brobdingnag; one of the most childish fictions, with one which is pregnant with wit and satire, yet both turning upon the same assumed possibility of the existence of a pigmy among a race of giants. In the former case, when the imagination of the story-teller has exhausted itself in every species of hyperbole, in order to describe the diminutive size of his hero, the interest of the tale is at an end; but in the romance of the Dean of St. Patrick's, the exquisite humour with which the natural consequences of so strange and unusual a situation is detailed, has a canvass on which to expand itself, as broad as the luxuriance even of the author's talents could desire. Gulliver stuck into a marrow bone, and Master Thomas Thumb's disastrous fall into the bowl of hasty-pudding, are, in the general outline, kindred incidents; but the jest is exhausted in the latter case, when the accident is told; whereas in the former, it lies not so much in the comparatively pigmy size which subjected Gulliver to such a ludicrous misfortune, as in the tone of grave and dignified feeling with which he resents the disgrace of the incident.

In the class of fictitious narrations to which we allude, the author opens a sort of account-current with the reader; drawing upon him, in the first place, for credit to that degree of the marvellous which he proposes to employ; and becoming virtually bound, in consequence of this indulgence, that his personages shall conduct themselves, in the extraordinary circumstances in which they are placed, according to the rules of probability, and the nature of the human heart. In this view, the *probable* is far from being laid out of sight even amid the wildest freaks of imagination; on the contrary, we grant the extraordinary postulates which the author demands as the foundation of his narrative, only on condition of his deducing the consequences with logical precision.

We have only to add, that this class of fiction has been sometimes applied to the purposes of political satire, and sometimes to the general illustration of the powers and workings of the human mind. Swift, Bergerac, and others, have employed it for the former purpose, and a good illustration of the latter is the well known *Saint Leon* of William Godwin. In this latter work, assuming the possibility of the transmutation of metals, and of the *elixir vitæ,* the author has deduced, in the course of his narrative, the probable consequences of the possession of such secrets upon the fortunes and mind of him who might enjoy them. *Frankenstein* is a novel upon the same plan with *Saint Leon;* it is said to be written by Mr. Percy Bysshe Shelley, who, if we are rightly informed, is son-in-law to Mr. Godwin; and it is inscribed to that ingenious author.

In the preface, the author lays claim to rank his work among the class which we have endeavoured to describe.

> "The event on which this fiction is founded has been supposed by Dr. Darwin, and some of the physiological writers of Germany, as not of impossible occurrence. I shall not be supposed as according the remotest degree of serious faith to such an imagination; yet, in assuming it as the basis of a work of fancy, I have not considered myself as merely weaving a series of supernatural terrors. The event on which the interest of the story depends is exempt from the disadvantages of a mere tale of spectres or enchantment. It was recommended by the novelty of the situations which it developes; and, however impossible as a physical fact, affords a point of view to the imagination for the delineating of human passions more comprehensive and commanding than any which the ordinary relations of existing events can yield.
>
> "I have thus endeavoured to preserve the truth of the elementary principles of human nature, while I have not scrupled to innovate upon their combinations. *The Iliad,* the tragic poetry of Greece,—Shakspeare, in the *Tempest* and *Midsummer's Night's Dream,*—and most especially Milton, in *Paradise Lost,* conform to this rule; and the most humble novelist, who seeks to confer or receive amusement from his labours, may, without presumption, apply to prose fiction a license, or rather a rule, from the adoption of which so many exquisite combinations of human feeling have resulted in the highest specimens of poetry."

We shall, without farther preface, detail the particulars of the singular story which is thus introduced.

A vessel, engaged in a voyage of discovery to the North Pole, having become embayed among the ice at a very high latitude, the crew, and particularly the captain or owner of the ship, are surprised at perceiving a gigantic form pass at some distance from them, on a car drawn by dogs, in a place where they conceived no mortal could exist. While they are speculating on this singular apparition, a thaw commences, and disengages them from their precarious situation. On the next morning they pick up, upon a floating fragment of the broken ice, a sledge like that they had before seen, with a human being in the act of perishing. He is with difficulty recalled to life, and proves to be a young man of the most amiable manners and extended acquirements, but, extenuated by fatigue, wrapped in dejection and gloom of the darkest kind. The captain of the ship, a gentleman whose ardent love of science had engaged him on an expedition so dangerous, becomes attached to the stranger, and at length extorts from him the wonderful tale of his misery, which he thus attains the means of preserving from oblivion.

Frankenstein describes himself as a native of Geneva, born and bred up in the bosom of domestic love and affection. His father—his friend Henry Clerval—Elizabeth, an orphan of extreme beauty and talent, bred up in the same house with him, are possessed of all the qualifications which could render him happy as a son, a friend, and a lover. In the course of his studies he becomes acquainted with the works of Cornelius Agrippa, and other authors treating of occult philosophy, on whose venerable tomes modern neglect has scattered no slight portion of dust. Frankenstein remains ignorant of the contempt in which his favourites are held, until he is separated from his family to pursue his studies at the university of Ingolstadt. Here he is introduced to the wonders of modern chemistry, as well as of natural philosophy in all its branches. Prosecuting these sciences into their innermost and most abstruse recesses, with unusual talent and unexampled success, he at length makes that discovery on which the marvellous part of the work is grounded. His attention had been especially bound to the structure of the human frame and of the principle of life. He engaged in physiological researches of the most recondite and abstruse nature, searching among charnel vaults and in dissection rooms, and the objects most insupportable to the delicacy of human feelings, in order to trace the minute chain of causation which takes place in the change from life to death, and from death to life. In the midst of this darkness a light broke in upon him.

> "Remember," says his narrative, "I am not recording the vision of a madman. The sun does not more certainly shine in the heavens than that which I now affirm is true. Some miracle might have produced it, yet the stages of the discovery were distinct and probable. After days and nights of incredible labour and fatigue, I succeeded in discovering the cause of generation and life; nay, more, I became myself capable of bestowing animation upon lifeless matter."

This wonderful discovery impelled Frankenstein to avail himself of his art by the creation (if we dare to call it so) or formation of a living and sentient being. As the minuteness of the parts formed a great difficulty, he constructed the figure which he proposed to animate of a gigantic size, that is, about eight feet high, and strong and large in proportion. The feverish anxiety with which the young philosopher toils through the horrors of his secret task, now dabbling among the unhallowed reliques of the grave, and now torturing the living animal to animate the lifeless clay, are described generally, but with great vigour of language. Although supported by the hope of producing a new species that should bless him as its creator and source, he nearly sinks under the protracted labour, and loathsome details, of the work he had undertaken; and scarcely is his fatal enthusiasm sufficient to support his nerves, or animate his resolution. The result of this extraordinary discovery it would be unjust to give in any words save those of the author. We shall give it at length, as an excellent specimen of the style and manner of the work.

"It was on a dreary night of November that I beheld the accomplishment of my toils. With an anxiety that almost amounted to agony, I collected the instruments of life around me, that I might infuse a spark of being into the lifeless thing that lay at my feet. It was already one in the morning; the rain pattered dismally against the panes, and my candle was nearly burnt out, when, by the glimmer of the half-extinguished light, I saw the dull yellow eye of the creature open; it breathed hard, and a convulsive motion agitated its limbs.

"How can I describe my emotions at this catastrophe, or how delineate the wretch whom with such infinite pains and care I had endeavoured to form? His limbs were in proportion, and I had selected his features as beautiful. Beautiful!—Great God! His yellow skin scarcely covered the work of muscles and arteries beneath; his hair was of a lustrous black, and flowing; his teeth of a pearly whiteness; but these luxuriances only formed a more horrid contrast with his watery eyes, that seemed almost of the same colour as the dun white sockets in which they were set—his shrivelled complexion, and straight black lips.

"The different accidents of life are not so changeable as the feelings of human nature. I had worked hard for nearly two years, for the sole purpose of infusing life into an inanimate body. For this I had deprived myself of rest and health. I had desired it with an ardour that far exceeded moderation; but now that I had finished, the beauty of the dream vanished, and breathless horror and disgust filled my heart. Unable to endure the aspect of the being I had created, I rushed out of the room, and continued a long time traversing my bed-chamber, unable to compose my mind to sleep. At length lassitude succeeded to the tumult I had before endured; and I threw myself on the bed in my clothes, endeavouring to seek a few moments of forgetfulness. But it was in vain; I slept indeed, but I was disturbed by the wildest dreams. I thought I saw Elizabeth, in the bloom of health, walking in the streets of Ingolstadt. Delighted and surprised, I embraced her; but as I imprinted the first kiss on her lips, they became livid with the hue of death; her features appeared to change, and I thought that I held the corpse of my dead mother in my arms; a shroud enveloped her form, and I saw the grave-worms crawling in the folds of the flannel. I started from my sleep with horror; a cold dew covered my forehead, my teeth chattered, and every limb became convulsed; when, by the dim and yellow light of the moon, as it forced its way through the window-shutters, I beheld the wretch—the miserable monster whom I had created. He held up the curtain of the bed; and his eyes, if eyes they may be called, were fixed on me. His jaws opened, and he muttered some inarticulate sounds, while a grin wrinkled his cheeks. He might have spoken, but I did not hear; one hand was stretched out, seemingly to detain me, but I escaped, and rushed down stairs. I took refuge in the court-yard belonging to the house which I inhabited; where I remained during the rest of the night, walking up and down in the greatest agitation, listening attentively, catching and fearing each sound as if it were to announce the approach of the demoniacal corpse to which I had so miserably given life.

"Oh! no mortal could support the horror of that countenance. A mummy again endued with animation could not be so hideous as that wretch. I had gazed on him while unfinished; he was ugly then; but when those muscles and joints were rendered capable of motion, it became a thing such as even Dante could not have conceived.

"I passed the night wretchedly. Sometimes my pulse beat so quickly and hardly, that I felt the palpitation of every artery; at others, I nearly sank to the ground, through languor and extreme weakness. Mingled with this horror, I felt the bitterness of disappointment: dreams that had been my food and pleasant rest for so long a space, were now become a hell to me; and the change was so rapid, the overthrow so complete!

"Morning, dismal and wet, at length dawned, and discovered, to my sleepless and aching eyes, the church of Ingolstadt, its white steeple and clock, which indicated the sixth hour. The porter opened the gates of the court, which had that night been my asylum, and I issued into the streets, pacing them with quick steps, as if I sought to avoid the wretch whom I feared every turning of the street would present to my view. I did not dare return to the apartment which I inhabited, but felt impelled to hurry on, although wetted by the rain, which poured from a black and comfortless sky.

"I continued walking in this manner for some time, endeavouring, by bodily exercise, to ease the load that weighed upon my mind. I traversed the streets without any clear conception of where I was or what I was doing. My heart palpitated in the sickness of fear; and I hurried on with irregular steps, not daring to look about me.

> 'Like one who on a lonely road
>   Doth walk in fear and dread,
> And, having once turn'd round, walks on,
>   And turns no more his head:
> Because he knows a frightful fiend
>   Doth close behind him tread.'"

He is relieved by the arrival of the diligence from Geneva, out of which jumps his friend Henry Clerval, who had come to spend a season at the college. Compelled to carry Clerval to his lodgings, which, he supposed, must still contain the prodigious and hideous specimen of his Promethean art, his feelings are again admirably described, allowing always for the extraordinary cause supposed to give them birth.

"I trembled excessively; I could not endure to think of, and far less to allude to, the occurrences of the preceding night. I walked with a quick pace, and we soon arrived at my college. I then reflected, and the thought made me shiver, that the creature whom I had left in my apartment might still be there, alive, and walking about. I dreaded to behold this monster; but I feared still more that Henry should see him. Entreating him, therefore, to remain a few minutes at the bottom of the stairs, I darted up towards my own room. My hand was already on the lock of the door before I recollected myself. I then paused; and a cold shivering came over me. I threw the door forcibly open, as children are accustomed to do when they expect a spectre to stand in waiting for them on the other side; but nothing appeared. I stepped fearfully in: the apartment was empty; and my bedroom was also freed from its hideous guest. I could hardly believe that so great a good fortune could have befallen me; but when I became assured that my enemy had indeed fled, I clapped my hands for joy, and ran down to Clerval."

The animated monster is heard of no more for a season. Frankenstein pays the penalty of his rash researches into the *arcana* of human nature, in a long illness, after which the two friends prosecute their studies for two years in uninterrupted quiet. Frankenstein, as may be supposed, abstaining, with a sort of abhorrence, from those in which he had once so greatly delighted. At the lapse of this period, he is made acquainted with a dreadful misfortune which has befallen his family, by the violent death of his youngest brother, an interesting child, who, while straying from his keeper, had been murdered by some villain in the walks of Plainpalais. The marks of strangling were distinct on the neck of the unfortunate infant, and a gold ornament which it wore, and which was amissing, was supposed to have been the murderer's motive for perpetrating the crime.

At this dismal intelligence Frankenstein flies to Geneva, and impelled by fraternal affection, visits the spot where this horrid accident had happened. In the midst of a thunder-storm, with which the evening had closed, and just as he had attained the fatal spot on which Victor had been murdered, a flash of lightning displays to him the hideous demon to which he had given life, gliding towards a neighbouring precipice. Another flash shews him hanging among the cliffs, up which he scrambles with far more than mortal agility, and is seen no more. The inference, that this being was the murderer of his brother, flashed on Frankenstein's mind as irresistibly as the lightning itself, and he was tempted to consider the creature whom he had cast among mankind to work, it would seem, acts of horror and depravity, nearly in the light of his own vampire let loose from the grave, and destined to destroy all that was dear to him.

Frankenstein was right in his apprehensions. Justine, the maid to whom the youthful Victor had been intrusted, is found to be in possession of the golden trinket which had been taken from the child's person; and, by a variety of combining circumstances of combined evidence, she is concluded to be the murderess, and, as such, condemned to death and executed. It does not appear that Frankenstein attempted to avert her fate, by communicating his horrible secret; but, indeed, who would have given him credit, or in what manner could he have supported his tale?

In a solitary expedition to the top of Mount Aveyron, undertaken to dispel the melancholy which clouded his mind, Frankenstein unexpectedly meets with the monster he had animated, who compels him to a conference and a parley. The material demon gives an account, at great length, of his history since his animation, of the mode in which he acquired various points of knowledge, and of the disasters which befell him, when, full of benevolence and philanthropy, he endeavoured to introduce himself into human society. The most material part of his education was acquired in a ruinous pig-stye—a Lyceum which this strange student occupied, he assures us, for a good many months undiscovered, and in constant observance of the motions of an amiable family, from imitating whom he learns the use of language, and other accomplishments, much more successfully than Caliban, though the latter had a conjuror to his tutor. This detail is not only highly improbable, but it is injudicious, as its unnecessary minuteness tends rather too much to familiarize us with the being whom it regards, and who loses, by this *lengthy* oration, some part of the mysterious sublimity annexed to his first appearance. The result is, this monster; who was at first, according to his own account, but a harmless monster, becomes ferocious and malignant, in consequence of finding all his approaches to human society repelled with injurious violence and offensive marks of disgust. Some papers concealed in his dress acquainted him with the circumstances and person to whom he owed his origin; and the hate which he felt towards the whole human race was now concentrated in resentment against Frankenstein. In this humour he murdered the child, and disposed the picture so as to induce a belief of Justine's guilt. The last is an inartificial circumstance; this indirect mode of mischief was not likely to occur to the being the narrative presents to us. The conclusion of this strange narrative is a peremptory demand on the part of the demon, as he is usually termed, that Frankenstein should renew his fearful experiment, and create for him an helpmate hideous as himself, who should have no pretence for shunning his society. On this condition he promises to withdraw to some distant desert, and shun the human race for ever. If his creator shall refuse him this consolation, he vows the prosecution of the most frightful vengeance. Frankenstein, after a long pause of reflection, imagines he sees that the justice due to the miserable being, as well as to mankind, who might be exposed to so much misery, from the power and evil dispositions of a creature who could climb perpendicular cliffs and exist among glaciers, demanded that he should comply with the request; and granted his promise accordingly.

Frankenstein retreats to one of the distant islands of the Orcades, that in secrecy and solitude he might resume his detestable and ill-omened labours, which now were doubly hideous, since he was deprived of the enthusiasm with which he formerly prosecuted them. As he is sitting one night in his laboratory, and recollecting the consequences of his first essay in the Promethean art, he begins to hesitate concerning the right he had to form another being as malignant and blood-thirsty as that he had unfortunately already animated. It is evident, that, he would thereby give the demon the means of propagating a hideous race, superior to mankind in strength and hardihood, who might render the very existence of the present human race a condition precarious and full of terror. Just as these reflections lead him to the conclusion that his promise was criminal, and ought not to be kept, he looks up, and sees, by the light of the moon, the demon at the casement.

> "A ghastly grin wrinkled his lips as he gazed on me, where I sat fulfilling the task which he allotted to me. Yes, he had followed me in my travels; he had loitered in forests, hid himself in caves, or taken refuge in wide and desert heaths; and he now came to mark my progress, and claim the fulfilment of my promise.
>
> "As I looked on him, his countenance expressed the utmost extent of malice and treachery. I thought with a sensation of madness on my promise of creating another like to him, and, trembling with passion, tore to pieces the thing on which I was engaged. The wretch saw me destroy the creature on whose future existence he depended for happiness, and, with a howl of devilish despair and revenge, withdrew."

At a subsequent interview, described with the same wild energy, all treaty is broken off betwixt Frankenstein and the work of his hands, and they part on terms of open and declared hatred and defiance. Our limits do not allow us to trace in detail the progress of the demon's vengeance, Clerval falls its first victim, and under circumstances which had very nearly conducted the new Prometheus to the gallows as his supposed murderer. Elizabeth, his bride, is next strangled on her wedding-night; his father dies of grief; and at length Frankenstein, driven to despair and distraction, sees nothing left for him in life but vengeance on the singular cause of his misery. With this purpose he pursues the monster from clime to clime, receiving only such intimations of his being on the right scent, as served to shew that the demon delighted in thus protracting his fury and his sufferings. At length, after the flight and pursuit had terminated among the frost-fogs, and icy islands of the northern ocean, and just when he had a glimpse of his adversary, the ground sea was heard, the ice gave way, and Frankenstein was placed in the perilous situation in which he is first introduced to the reader.

Exhausted by his sufferings, but still breathing vengeance against the being which was at once his creature and his persecutor, this unhappy victim to physiological discovery expires, just as the clearing away of the ice permits Captain Walton's vessel to hoist sail for their return to Britain. At midnight, the demon, who had been his destroyer, is discovered in the cabin, lamenting over the corpse of the person who gave him being. To Walton he attempts to justify his resentment towards the human race, while, at the same time, he acknowledges himself a wretch who had murdered the lovely and the helpless, and pursued to irremediable ruin his creator, the select specimen of all that was worthy of love and admiration.

"Fear not," he continues, addressing the astonished Walton, "that I shall be the instrument of future mischief. My work is nearly complete. Neither yours nor any man's death is needed to consummate the series of my being, and accomplish that which must be done; but it requires my own. Do not think that I shall be slow to perform this sacrifice. I shall quit your vessel on the ice-raft which brought me hither, and shall seek the most northern extremity of the globe; I shall collect my funeral pile, and consume to ashes this miserable frame, that its remains may afford no light to any curious and unhallowed wretch, who would create such another as I have been—"

"He sprung from the cabin-window, as he said this, upon the ice-raft which lay close to the vessel. He was soon borne away by the waves, and lost in darkness and distance."

Whether this singular being executed his purpose or no must necessarily remain an uncertainty, unless the voyage of discovery to the North Pole should throw any light on the subject.

So concludes this extraordinary tale, in which the author seems to us to disclose uncommon powers of poetic imagination. The feeling with which we perused the unexpected and fearful, yet, allowing the possibility of the event, very natural conclusion of Frankenstein's experiment, shook a little even our firm nerves; although such and so numerous have been the expedients for exciting terror employed by the romantic writers of the age, that the reader may adopt Macbeth's words with a slight alteration:

> "We have supp'd full with horrors;
> Direness, familiar to our 'callous' thoughts,
> Cannot once startle us."

It is no slight merit in our eyes, that the tale, though wild in incident, is written in plain and forcible English, without exhibiting that mixture of hyperbolical Germanisms with which tales of wonder are usually told, as if it were necessary that the language should be as extravagant as the fiction. The ideas of the author are always clearly as well as forcibly expressed; and his descriptions of landscape have in them the choice requisites of truth, freshness, precision, and beauty. The self-education of the monster, considering the slender opportunities of acquiring knowledge that he possessed, we have already noticed as improbable and overstrained. That he should have not only learned to speak, but to read, and, for aught we know, to write—that he should have become acquainted with *Werter,* with Plutarch's Lives, and with *Paradise Lost,* by listening through a hole in a wall, seems as unlikely as that he should have acquired, in the same way, the problems of Euclid, or the art of book-keeping by single and double entry. The author has however two apologies—the first, the necessity that his monster should acquire those endowments, and the other, that his neighbours were engaged in teaching the language of the country to a young foreigner. His progress in self-knowledge, and the acquisition of information, is, after all, more wonderful than that of Hai Eben Yokhdan, or Automathes, or the hero of the little romance called *The Child of Nature,* one of which works might perhaps suggest the train of ideas followed by the author of *Frankenstein.* We should also be disposed, in support of the principles with which we set out, to question whether the monster, how tall, agile, and strong however, could have perpetrated so much mischief undiscovered, or passed through so many countries without being secured, either on account of his crimes, or for the benefit of some such speculator as Mr. Polito, who would have been happy to have added to his museum so curious a specimen of natural history. But as we have consented to admit the leading incident of the work, perhaps some of our readers may be of opinion, that to stickle upon lesser improbabilities, is to incur the censure bestowed by the Scottish proverb on those who start at straws after swallowing *windlings.*

The following lines which occur in the second volume, mark, we think, that the author possesses the same facility in expressing himself in verse as in prose.

> We rest; a dream has power to poison sleep.
>> We rise; one wand'ring thought pollutes the day.
> We feel, conceive, or reason; laugh, or weep,
>> Embrace fond woe, or cast our cares away;
> It is the same: for, be it joy or sorrow,
>> The path of its departure still is free.
> Man's yesterday may ne'er be like his morrow;
>> Nought may endure but mutability!

Upon the whole, the work impresses us with a high idea of the author's original genius and happy power of expression. We shall be delighted to hear that he has aspired to the *paullo majora;* and, in the meantime, congratulate our readers upon a novel which excites new reflections and untried sources of emotion. If Gray's definition of Paradise, to lie on a couch, namely, and read new novels, come any thing near truth, no small praise is due to him, who, like the author of *Frankenstein,* has enlarged the sphere of that fascinating enjoyment.

Horace Walpole

*T*he *Castle of Otranto* is remarkable, not only for the wild interest of the story, but as the first modern attempt to found a tale of amusing fiction upon the basis of the ancient romances of chivalry. The neglect and discredit of these venerable legends had commenced so early as the reign of Queen Elizabeth, when, as we learn from the criticism of the times, Spenser's fairy web was approved rather on account of the mystic and allegorical interpretation, than the plain and obvious meaning of his chivalrous pageant. The drama, which shortly afterwards rose into splendour, and English versions from the innumerable novelists of Italy, supplied to the higher class the amusement which their fathers received from the legends of Don Belianis and the Mirror of Knighthood; and the huge volumes, which were once the pastime of nobles and princes, shorn of their ornaments, and shrunk into abridgements, were banished to the kitchen or nursery, or, at best, to the hall-window of the old-fashioned country manor-house. Under Charles II., the prevailing taste for French literature dictated the introduction of those dullest of dull folios, the romances of Calprenede and Scuderi, works which hover between the ancient tale of chivalry and the modern novel. The alliance was so ill conceived, that these ponderous tomes retained all the insufferable length and breadth of the prose volumes of chivalry, the same detailed account of reiterated and unvaried combats, the same unnatural and extravagant turn of incident, without the rich and sublime strokes of genius, and vigour of imagination, which often distinguish the early romance; while they exhibited all the metaphysical jargon, sentimental languor, and flat love-intrigue of the novel, without being enlivened by its variety of character, just traits of feeling, or acute views of life. Such an ill-imagined species of composition retained its ground longer than might have been expected, only because these romances were called works of entertainment, and there was nothing better to supply their room. Even in the days of the *Spectator,* Clelia, Cleopatra, and the Grand Cyrus, (as that precious folio is christened by its butcherly translator,) were the favourite closet companions of the fair sex. But this unnatural taste began to give way early in the eighteenth century; and, about the middle of it, was entirely superseded by the works of Le Sage, Richardson, Fielding, and Smollett; so that even the very name of romance, now so venerable in the ear of antiquaries and book-collectors, was almost forgotten at the time *The Castle of Otranto* made its first appearance.

The peculiar situation of Horace Walpole, the ingenious author of this work, was such as gave him a decided predilection for what may be called the Gothic style, a term which he contributed not a little to rescue from the bad fame into which it had fallen, being currently used before his time to express whatever was in pointed and diametrical opposition to the rules of true taste.

Horace Walpole, it is needless to remind the reader, was the son of Sir Robert Walpole, that celebrated minister, who held the reins of government under two successive monarchs, with a grasp so firm and uncontrolled, that his power seemed entwined with the rights of the Brunswick family. Horace was born in the year 1716–17; was educated at Eton, and formed, at that celebrated seminary, a school-boy acquaintance with the celebrated Gray, which continued during the earlier part of their residence together at Cambridge, so that they became fellow-travellers by joint consent in 1739. They disagreed and parted on the continent; the youthful vivacity, and, perhaps, the aristocratic assumption of Walpole, not agreeing with the somewhat formal opinions and habits of the professed man of letters. In the reconciliation afterwards effected between them, Walpole frankly took on himself the blame of the rupture, and they continued friends until Gray's death.

When Walpole returned to England, he obtained a seat in Parliament, and entered public life as the son of a prime minister as powerful as England had known for more than a century. When the father occupied such a situation, his sons had necessarily their full share of that court which is usually paid to the near connections of those who have the patronage of the state at their disposal. To the feeling of importance inseparable from the object of such attention, was added the early habit of connecting and associating the interest of Sir Robert Walpole, and even the domestic affairs of his family, with the parties in the Royal Family of England, and with the changes in the public affairs of Europe. It is not therefore wonderful, that the turn of Horace Walpole's mind, which was naturally tinged with the love of pedigree, and a value for family honours, should have been strengthened in that bias by circumstances, which seemed, as it were, to implicate the fate of his own house with that of princes, and to give the shields of the Walpoles, Shorters, and Robsarts, from whom he descended, an added dignity, unknown to their original owners. If Mr. Walpole ever founded hopes of raising himself to political eminence, and turning his family importance to advantage in his career, the termination of his father's power, and the personal change with which he felt it attended, disgusted him with active life, and early consigned him to literary retirement. He had, indeed, a seat in Parliament for many years; but, unless upon one occasion, when he vindicated the memory of his father with great dignity and elo-quence, he took no share in the debates of the House, and not much inter-est in the parties which maintained them. Indeed, in the account which he has himself rendered us of his own views and dispositions with respect to state affairs, he seems rather to have been bent on influencing party spirit, and bustling in public affairs, for the sake of embroilment and intrigue, than in order to carry any particular measure, whether important to him-self, or of consequence to the state. In the year 1758, and at the active age of forty-one, secured from the caprices of fortune, he retired altogether from public life, to enjoy his own pursuits and studies in retirement. His father's care had invested him with three good sinecure offices, so that his income, managed with economy, which no one understood better how to practise, was sufficient for his expense in matters of *virtù,* as well as for maintaining his high rank in society.

The subjects of Horace Walpole's studies were, in a great measure, dictated by his habits of thinking and feeling, operating upon an animated imagination, and a mind, acute, active, penetrating, and fraught with a great variety of miscellaneous knowledge. Travelling had formed his taste for the fine arts; but his early predilection in favour of birth and rank connected even those branches of study with that of Gothic history and antiquities. His *Anecdotes of Painting and Engraving* evince many marks of his favourite pursuits; but his *Catalogue of Royal and Noble Authors,* and his *Historical Doubts,* we owe entirely to his pursuits as an antiquary and genealogist.

The former work evinces, in a particular degree, Mr. Walpole's respect for birth and rank; yet is, perhaps, ill calculated to gain much sympathy for either. It would be difficult, by any process or principle of subdivision, to select a list of as many plebeian authors, containing so very few whose genius was worthy of commemoration; but it was always Walpole's foible to disclaim a professed pursuit of public favour, for which, however, he earnestly thirsted, and to hold himself forth as a privileged author, "one of the right-hand file," who did not mean to descend into the common arena, where professional authors contend before the public eye, but wrote merely to gratify his own taste, by throwing away a few idle hours on literary composition. There was much affectation in this, which accordingly met the reward which affectation usually incurs; as Walpole seems to have suffered a good deal from the criticism which he affected to despise, and occasionally from the neglect which he appeared to court.

The *Historical Doubts* are an acute and curious example how minute antiquarian research may shake our faith in the facts most pointedly averred by general history. It is remarkable also to observe, how, in defending a system which was probably at first adopted as a mere literary exercise, Mr. Walpole's doubts acquired, in his own eyes, the respectability of certainties, in which he could not brook controversy.

Mr. Walpole's domestic occupations, as well as his studies, bore evidence of a taste for English antiquities, which was then uncommon. He loved, as a satirist has expressed it, "to gaze on Gothic toys through Gothic glass;" and the villa at Strawberry Hill, which he chose for his abode, gradually swelled into a feudal castle, by the addition of turrets, towers, galleries, and corridors, whose fretted roofs, carved panels, and illuminated windows, were garnished with the appropriate furniture of scutcheons, armorial bearings, shields, tilting lances, and all the panoply of chivalry. The Gothic order of architecture is now so generally, and, indeed, indiscriminately used, that we are rather surprised if the country-house of a tradesman retired from business does not exhibit lanceolated windows, divided by stone shafts, and garnished by painted glass, a cupboard in the form of a cathedral-stall, and a pig-house with a front borrowed from the façade of an ancient chapel. But, in the middle of the eighteenth century, when Mr. Walpole began to exhibit specimens of the Gothic style, and to show how patterns, collected from cathedrals and monuments, might be applied to chimney-pieces, ceilings, windows, and balustrades, he did not comply with the dictates of a prevailing fashion, but pleased his own taste, and realized his own visions, in the romantic cast of the mansion which he erected.

Mr. Walpole's lighter studies were conducted upon the same principle which influenced his historical researches, and his taste in architecture. His extensive acquaintance with foreign literature, on which he justly prided himself, was subordinate to his pursuits as an English antiquary and genealogist, in which he gleaned subjects for poetry and for romantic fiction, as well as for historical controversy. These are studies, indeed, proverbially dull; but it is only when they are pursued by those whose fancies nothing can enliven. A Horace Walpole, or a Thomas Warton, is not a mere collector of dry and minute facts, which the general historian passes over with disdain. He brings with him the torch of genius, to illuminate the ruins through which he loves to wander; nor does the classic scholar derive more inspiration from the pages of Virgil, than such an antiquary from the glowing, rich, and powerful feudal painting of Froissart. His mind being thus stored with information, accumulated by researches into the antiquities of the middle ages, and inspired, as he himself informs us, by the romantic cast of his own habitation, Mr. Walpole resolved to give the public a specimen of the Gothic style adapted to modern literature, as he had already exhibited its application to modern architecture.

As, in his model of a Gothic modern mansion, our author had studiously endeavoured to fit to the purposes of modern convenience, or luxury, the rich, varied, and complicated tracery and carving of the ancient cathedral, so, in *The Castle of Otranto,* it was his object to unite the marvellous turn of incident, and imposing tone of chivalry, exhibited in the ancient romance, with that accurate display of human character, and contrast of feelings and passions, which is, or ought to be, delineated in the modern novel. But Mr. Walpole, being uncertain of the reception which a work upon so new a plan might experience from the world, and not caring, perhaps, to encounter the ridicule which would have attended its failure, *The Castle of Otranto* was, in 1764, ushered into the world, as a translation, by William Marshall, from the Italian of Onuphrio Muralto, a sort of anagram, or translation, of the author's own name, It did not, however, long impose upon the critics of the day. It was soon suspected to proceed from a more elegant pen than that of any William Marshall, and, in the second edition, Walpole disclosed the secret. In a private letter, he gave the following account of the origin of the composition, in which he contradicts the ordinary assertion, that it was completed in eight days.

"9th March, 1763.

"Shall I confess to you what was the origin of this romance? I waked one morning in the beginning of last June from a dream, of which all I could recover was, that I had thought myself in an ancient castle, (a very natural dream for a head filled like mine with Gothic story,) and that on the uppermost bannister of a great staircase, I saw a gigantic hand in armour. In the evening I sat down and began to write, without knowing in the least what I intended to say or relate. The work grew on my hands, and I grew fond of it. Add, that I was very glad to think of any thing rather than politics. In short, I was so engrossed with my tale, which I completed in less than two months, that one evening I wrote from the time I had drank my tea, about six o'clock, till half an hour after one in the morning, when my hands and fingers were so weary, that I could not hold the pen to finish the sentence, but left Matilda and Isabella talking in the middle of a paragraph."

It does not seem that the authenticity of the narrative was at first suspected. Mr. Gray writes to Mr. Walpole, on 30th December, 1764:

"I have received *The Castle of Otranto,* and return you my thanks for it. It engages our attention here, (*i. e.* at Cambridge,) makes some of us cry a little; and all, in general, afraid to go to bed o'nights. We take it for a translation; and should believe it to be a true story, if it were not for St. Nicholas."

The friends of the author, as appears from the letter already quoted, were probably soon permitted to peep beneath the veil he had thought proper to assume; and, in the second edition, it was altogether withdrawn by a preface, in which the tendency and nature of the work are shortly commented upon and explained. From the following passage, translated from a letter by the author to Madame Deffand, it would seem that he repented of having laid aside his incognito; and sensitive to criticism, like most dilettante authors, was rather more hurt by the raillery of those who liked not his tale of chivalry, than gratified by the applause of his admirers.

"So they have translated my *Castle of Otranto,* probably in ridicule of the author. So be it;—however, I beg you will let their raillery pass in silence. Let the critics have their own way; they give me no uneasiness. I have not written the book for the present age, which will endure nothing but *cold common sense.* I confess to you, my dear friend, (and you will think me madder than ever,) that this is the only one of my works with which I am myself pleased; I have given reins to my imagination till I became on fire with the visions and feelings which it excited. I have composed it in defiance of rules, of critics, and of philosophers; and it seems to me just so much the better for that very reason. I am even persuaded, that some time hereafter, when taste shall resume the place which philosophy now occupies, my poor *Castle* will find admirers; we have actually a few among us already, for I am just publishing the third edition. I do not say this in order to mendicate your approbation.[9] I told you from the beginning you would not like the book,—your visions are all in a different style. I am not sorry that the translator has given the Second Preface; the first, however, accords best with the style of the fiction. I wished it to be believed ancient, and almost every body was imposed upon."

If the public applause, however, was sufficiently qualified by the voice of censure to alarm the feelings of the author, the continued demand for various editions of *The Castle of Otranto* showed how high the work really stood in popular estimation, and probably eventually reconciled Mr. Walpole to the taste of his own age. This romance has been justly considered not only as the original and model of a peculiar species of composition, attempted and successfully executed by a man of great genius, but as one of the standard works of our lighter literature.

Horace Walpole continued the mode of life which he had adopted so early as 1753, until his death, unless it may be considered as an alteration, that his sentiments of Whiggism, which, he himself assures us, almost amounted to Republicanism, received a shock from the French Revolution, which he appears from its commencement to have thoroughly detested. The tenor of his life could be hardly said to suffer interruption by his father's earldom of Orford devolving upon him when he had reached his

---

9. Madame Deffand had mentioned having read *The Castle of Otranto,* twice over; but she did not add a word of approbation. She blamed the translator for giving the Second Preface, chiefly because she thought it might commit Walpole with Voltaire.

seventy-fourth year, by the death of his nephew. He scarce assumed the title, and died a few years after it had descended to him, 2nd March, 1797, at his house in Berkeley square.

While these sheets are passing through the press, we have found in Miss Hawkins's very entertaining reminiscences of her early abode at Twickenham, the following description of the person of Horace Walpole, before 1772, giving us the most lively idea of the person and manners of a Man of Fashion about the middle of the last century:—

> "His figure was not merely tall, but more properly long and slender to excess; his complexion, and particularly his hands, of a most unhealthy paleness. His eyes were remarkably bright and penetrating, very dark and lively: his voice was not strong, but his tones were extremely pleasant, and, if I may so say, highly gentlemanly. I do not remember his common gait; he always entered a room in that style of affected delicacy, which fashion had then made almost natural; *chapeau bras* between his hands, as if he wished to compress it, or under his arm; knees bent, and feet on tiptoe, as if afraid of a wet floor.—His dress in visiting was most usually, in summer, when I most saw him, a lavender suit, the waistcoat embroidered with a little silver, or of white silk worked in the tambour, partridge silk stockings, and gold buckles, ruffles and frill generally lace. I remember, when a child, thinking him very much under-dressed, if at any time, except in mourning, he wore hemmed cambric. In summer no powder, but his wig combed straight, and showing his very smooth pale forehead, and queued behind; in winter, powder."

We cannot help thinking that this most respectable lady, by whose communications respecting eminent individuals the public has been so much obliged, has been a little too severe on the Gothic whims of the architecture at Strawberry Hill. The admirers of the fine arts should have forbearance for each other, when their fervent admiration of a favourite pursuit leads them into those extremes which are caviar to the multitude. And as the ear of the architect should not be hasty to condemn the over-learned conceits of the musician, so the eye of the musician should have some toleration for the turrets and pinnacles of the fascinated builder.

It is foreign to our plan to say much of Horace Walpole's individual character. His works bear evidence to his talents; and, even striking out the horribly impressive but disgusting drama of *The Mysterious Mother,* and the excellent romance which we are about to analyze more critically, they must leave him the reputation of a man of excellent taste, and certainly of being the best letter-writer in the English language.

In private life, his temper appears to have been precarious; and though expensive in indulging his own taste, he always seems to have done so on the most economical terms possible. He is often, in his epistolary correspondence, harsh and unkind to Madame Deffand, whose talents, her blindness, and her enthusiastic affection for him, claimed every indulgence from a warm-hearted man. He is also severe and rigid towards Bentley, whose taste and talents he had put into continual requisition for the ornaments of his house. These are unamiable traits of character, and they have been quoted often, and exaggerated much. But his memory has suffered most on account of his conduct towards Chatterton, in which we have always thought he was perfectly defensible. That unhappy son of genius endeavoured to impose upon Walpole a few stanzas of very inferior merit as ancient; and sent him an equally gross and palpable imposture under the shape of a pretended List of Painters. Walpole's sole crime lies in not patronising at once a young man, who only appeared before him in the character of a very inartificial impostor, though he afterwards proved himself a gigantic one. The fate of Chatterton lies, not at the door of Walpole, but of the public at large, who, two years (we believe) afterwards, were possessed of the splendid proofs of his natural powers, and any one of whom was as much called upon as Walpole to prevent the most unhappy catastrophe.

Finally, it must be recorded, to Walpole's praise, that, though not habitually liberal, he was strictly just, and readily parted with that portion of his income which the necessities of the state required. He may, perhaps, have mistaken his character when he assumes as its principal characteristic, "disinterestedness and contempt of money," which, he intimates, was with him less "a virtue than a passion." But by the generous and apparently most sincere offer to divide his whole income with Marshal Conway, he showed, that if there existed in his bosom more love of money than perhaps he was himself aware of, it was subjugated to the influence of the nobler virtues and feelings.

We are now to offer a few remarks on *The Castle of Otranto,* and on the class of compositions to which it belongs, and of which it was the precursor.

It is doing injustice to Mr. Walpole's memory to allege, that all which he aimed at in *The Castle of Otranto,* was "the art of exciting surprise and horror;" or, in other words, the appeal to that secret and reserved feeling of love for the marvellous and supernatural, which occupies a hidden corner in almost every one's bosom. Were this all which he had attempted, the means by which he sought to attain his purpose might, with justice, be termed both clumsy and puerile. But Mr. Walpole's purpose was both more difficult of attainment, and more important when attained. It was his object to draw such a picture of domestic life and manners, during the feudal times, as might actually have existed, and to paint it checkered and agitated by the action of supernatural machinery, such as the superstition of the period received as matter of devout credulity. The natural parts of the narrative are so contrived, that they associate themselves with the marvellous occurrences; and, by the force of that association, render those *speciosa miracula* striking and impressive, though our cooler reason admits their impossibility. Indeed, to produce, in a well-cultivated mind, any portion of that surprise and fear which are founded on supernatural events, the frame and tenor of the whole story must be adjusted in perfect harmony with this main-spring of the interest. He who, in early youth, has happened to pass a solitary night in one of the few ancient mansions which the fashion of more modern times has left undespoiled of their original furniture, has probably experienced, that the gigantic and preposterous figures dimly visible in the defaced tapestry,—the remote clang of the distant doors which divide him from living society,—the deep darkness which involves the high and fretted roof of the apartment,—the dimly seen pictures of ancient knights, renowned for their valour, and perhaps for their crimes,—the varied and indistinct sounds which disturb the silent desolation of a half-deserted mansion,—and, to crown all, the feeling that carries us back to ages of feudal power and papal superstition, join together to excite a corresponding sensation of supernatural awe, if not of terror. It is in such situations, when superstition becomes contagious, that we listen with respect, and even with dread, to the legends which are our sport in the garish light of sunshine, and amid the dissipating sights and sounds of everyday life. Now, it seems to have been Walpole's object to attain, by the minute accuracy of a fable, sketched with singular attention to the costume of the period in which the scene was laid, that same association, which might prepare his reader's mind for the reception of prodigies congenial to the creed and feelings of the actors. His feudal tyrant, his distressed damsel, his resigned yet digni-fied churchman,—the Castle itself, with its feudal arrangements of dun-geons, trap-doors, oratories, and galleries,—the incidents of the trial, the chivalrous procession, and the combat;—in short, the scene, the perform-ers, and action, so far as it is natural, form the accompaniments of his spec-tres and his miracles, and have the same effect on the mind of the reader, that the appearance and drapery of such a chamber as we have described may produce upon that of a temporary inmate. This was a task which re-quired no little learning, no ordinary degree of fancy, no common portion of genius, to execute. The association of which we have spoken is of a na-ture peculiarly delicate, and subject to be broken and disarranged. It is, for instance, almost impossible to build such a modern Gothic structure as shall impress us with the feelings we have endeavoured to describe. It may be grand, or it may be gloomy; it may excite magnificent or melancholy ideas; but it must fail in bringing forth the sensation of supernatural awe, connected with halls that have echoed to the sounds of remote generations, and have been pressed by the footsteps of those who have long since passed away. Yet Horace Walpole has attained in composition, what, as an architect, he must have felt beyond the power of his art. The remote and superstitious period in which his scene is laid,—the art with which he has furnished forth its Gothic decorations,—the sustained, and, in general, the dignified tone of feudal manners,—prepare us gradually for the favourable reception of prodigies, which, though they could not really have happened at any period, were consistent with the belief of all mankind at that in which the action is placed. It was, therefore, the author's object, not merely to ex-cite surprise and terror, by the introduction of supernatural agency, but to wind up the feelings of his reader till they became for a moment identified with those of a ruder age, which

"Held each strange tale devoutly true."

The difficulty of attaining this nice accuracy of delineation may be best estimated by comparing *The Castle of Otranto* with the less successful ef-forts of later writers; where, amid all their attempts to assume the tone of antique chivalry, something occurs in every chapter so decidedly incongru-ous, as at once reminds us of an ill-sustained masquerade, in which ghosts, knights-errant, magicians, and damsels gent, are all equipped in hired dresses from the same warehouse in Tavistock Street.

There is a remarkable particular in which Mr. Walpole's steps have been departed from by the most distinguished of his followers.

Romantic narrative is of two kinds,—that which, being in itself possible, may be matter of belief at any period; and that which, though held impossible by more enlightened ages, was yet consonant with the faith of earlier times. The subject of *The Castle of Otranto* is of the latter class. Mrs. Radcliffe, a name not to be mentioned without the high respect due to genius, has endeavoured to effect a compromise between those different styles of narrative, by referring her prodigies to an explanation founded on natural causes, in the latter chapters of her romances. To this improvement upon the Gothic romance there are so many objections, that we own ourselves inclined to prefer, as more simple and impressive, the narrative of Walpole, which details supernatural incidents as they would have been readily believed and received in the eleventh or twelfth century. In the first place, the reader feels indignant at discovering that he has been cheated into sympathy with terrors, which are finally explained as having proceeded from some very simple cause; and the interest of a second reading is entirely destroyed by his having been admitted behind the scenes at the conclusion of the first. Secondly, the precaution of relieving our spirits from the influence of supposed supernatural terror, seems as unnecessary in a work of professed fiction, as that of the prudent Bottom, who proposed that the human face of the representative of his lion should appear from under his masque, and acquaint the audience plainly that he was a man as other men, and nothing more than Snug the joiner. Lastly, these substitutes for supernatural agency are frequently to the full as improbable as the machinery which they are introduced to explain away and to supplant. The reader, who is required to admit the belief of supernatural interference, understands precisely what is demanded of him; and, if he be truly a gentle reader, throws his mind into the attitude best adapted to humour the deceit which is presented for his entertainment, and grants, for the time of perusal, the premises on which the fable depends.[10] But if the author voluntarily binds

---

10. There are instances, to the contrary, however. For example, that stern votary of severe truth, who cast aside *Gulliver's Travels* as containing a parcel of improbable fictions.

himself to account for all the wondrous occurrences which he introduces, we are entitled to exact that the explanation shall be natural, easy, ingenious, and complete. Every reader of such works must remember instances, in which the explanation of mysterious circumstances in the narrative has proved equally, nay, even more incredible, than if they had been accounted for by the agency of supernatural beings; for the most incredulous must allow, that the interference of such agency is more possible than that an effect resembling it should be produced by an utterly inadequate cause. But it is unnecessary to enlarge farther on a part of the subject, which we have only mentioned to exculpate our author from the charge of using machinery more clumsy than his tale from its nature required. The bold assertion of the actual existence of phantoms and apparitions seems to us to harmonize much more naturally with the manners of feudal times, and to produce a more powerful effect upon the reader's mind, than any attempt to reconcile the superstitious credulity of feudal ages with the philosophic scepticism of our own, by referring those prodigies to the operation of fulminating powder, combined mirrors, magic lanterns, trap-doors, speaking-trumpets, and such-like apparatus of German phantasmagoria.

It cannot, however, be denied, that the character of the supernatural machinery in *The Castle of Otranto* is liable to objections. Its action and interference is rather too frequent, and presses too hard and constantly upon the same feelings in the reader's mind, to the hazard of diminishing the elasticity of the spring upon which it should operate. The fund of fearful sympathy which can be afforded by a modern reader to a tale of wonder, is much diminished by the present habits of life, and modes of education. Our ancestors could wonder and thrill through all the mazes of an interminable metrical romance of fairy land, and of an enchantment, the work perhaps of some

> "Prevailing poet whose undoubting mind
> Believed the magic wonders which he sung."

But our own habits and feelings and belief are different, and a transient, though vivid impression, is all that can be excited by a tale of wonder, even in the most fanciful mind of the present day. By the too frequent recurrence of his prodigies, Mr. Walpole ran, perhaps, his greatest risk of awakening *la raison froide,* that "cold common sense" which he justly deemed the greatest enemy of the effect which he hoped to produce. It may be added also, that the supernatural occurrences of *The Castle of Otranto* are brought forward into too strong daylight, and marked by an over degree of distinctness and accuracy of outline. A mysterious obscurity seems congenial at least, if not essential, to our ideas of disembodied spirits; and the gigantic limbs of the ghost of Alphonso, as described by the terrified domestics, are somewhat too distinct and corporeal to produce the feelings which their appearance is intended to excite. This fault, however, if it be one, is more than compensated by the high merit of many of the marvellous incidents in the romance. The descent of the picture of Manfred's ancestor, although it borders on extravagance, is finely introduced, and interrupts an interesting dialogue with striking effect. We have heard it observed, that the animated figure should rather have been a statue than a picture. We greatly doubt the justice of the criticism. The advantages of the colouring induce us decidedly to prefer Mr. Walpole's fiction to the proposed substitute. There are few who have not felt, at some period of their childhood, a sort of terror from the manner in which the eye of an ancient portrait appears to fix that of the spectator from every point of view. It is, perhaps, hypercritical to remark, (what, however, Walpole of all authors might have been expected to attend to,) that the time assigned to the action, being about the eleventh century, is rather too early for the introduction of a full-length portrait. The apparition of the skeleton hermit to the Prince of Vicenza was long accounted a master-piece of the horrible; but of late the valley of Jehoshaphat could hardly supply the dry bones necessary for the exhibition of similar spectres, so that injudicious and repeated imitation has, in some degree, injured the effect of its original model. What is more striking in *The Castle of Otranto,* is the manner in which the various prodigious appearances, bearing each upon the other, and all upon the accomplishment of the ancient prophecy, denouncing the ruin of the house of Manfred, gradually prepare us for the grand catastrophe. The moonlight vision of Alphonso dilated to immense magnitude, the astonished group of spectators in the front, and the shattered ruins of the castle in the background, are briefly and sublimely described. We know no passage of similar merit, unless it be the apparition of

Fadzean, or Fadoun, in an ancient Scottish poem.[11]

That part of the romance which depends upon human feelings and agency, is conducted with the dramatic talent which afterwards was so conspicuous in *The Mysterious Mother.* The persons are indeed rather generic than individual; but this was in a degree necessary to a plan, calculated rather to exhibit a general view of society and manners during the times which the author's imagination loved to contemplate, than the more minute shades and discriminating points of particular characters. But the actors in the romance are strikingly drawn, with bold outlines becoming the age and nature of the story. Feudal tyranny was, perhaps, never better exemplified, than in the character of Manfred. He has the courage, the art, the duplicity, the ambition of a barbarous chieftain of the dark ages, yet with touches of remorse and natural feeling, which preserve some sympathy for him when his pride is quelled, and his race extinguished. The pious Monk, and the patient Hippolita, are well contrasted with this selfish and tyrannical Prince. Theodore is the juvenile hero of a romantic tale, and Matilda has more interesting sweetness than usually belongs to its heroine. As the character of Isabella is studiously kept down, in order to relieve that of the daughter of Manfred, few readers are pleased with the concluding insinuation, that she became at length the bride of Theodore. This is in some degree a departure from the rules of chivalry; and, however natural an occurrence in common life, rather injures the magic illusions of romance. In other respects, making an allowance for the extraordinary incidents of a dark and tempestuous age, the story, so far as within the course of natural events, is happily detailed, its progress is uniform, its events interesting and well combined, and the conclusion grand, tragical, and affecting.

The style of *The Castle of Otranto* is pure and correct English of the earlier and more classical standard. Mr. Walpole rejected, upon taste and principle, those heavy though powerful auxiliaries which Dr. Johnson imported from the Latin language, and which have since proved to many a luckless wight, who has essayed to use them, as unmanageable as the gauntlets of Eryx,

---

11. This spectre, the ghost of a follower whom he had slain upon suspicion of treachery, appeared to no less a person than Wallace, the champion of Scotland, in the ancient castle of Gask-hall.—See Ellis's *Specimens,* vol. i.

—et pondus et ipsa
Huc illuc vinclorum immensa volumina versat.

Neither does the purity of Mr. Walpole's language, and the simplicity of his narrative, admit that luxuriant, florid, and high-varnished landscape painting, with which Mrs. Radcliffe often adorned, and not unfrequently encumbered, her kindred romances. Description, for its own sake, is scarcely once attempted in *The Castle of Otranto;* and if authors would consider how very much this restriction tends to realize narrative, they might be tempted to abridge at least the showy and wordy exuberance of a style fitter for poetry than prose. It is for the dialogue that Walpole reserves his strength; and it is remarkable how, while conducting his mortal agents with all the art of a modern dramatist, he adheres to the sustained tone of chivalry which marks the period of the action. This is not attained by patching his narrative or dialogue with glossarial terms, or antique phraseology, but by taking care to exclude all that can awaken modern associations. In the one case his romance would have resembled a modern dress, preposterously decorated with antique ornaments; in its present shape, he has retained the form of the ancient armour, but not its rust and cobwebs. In illustration of what is above stated, we refer the reader to the first interview of Manfred with the Prince of Vicenza, where the manners and language of chivalry are finely painted, as well as the perturbation of conscious guilt, confusing itself in attempted exculpation, even before a mute accuser. The characters of the inferior domestics have been considered as not bearing a proportion sufficiently dignified to the rest of the story. But this is a point on which the author has pleaded his own cause fully in the original Prefaces.

We have only to add, in conclusion to these desultory remarks, that if Horace Walpole, who led the way in this new species of literary composition, has been surpassed by some of his followers in diffuse brilliancy of description, and perhaps in the art of detaining the mind of the reader in a state of feverish and anxious suspense, through a protracted and complicated narrative, more will yet remain with him than the single merit of originality and invention. The applause due to chastity and precision of style,—to a happy combination of supernatural agency with human interest,—to a tone of feudal manners and language, sustained by characters strongly drawn and well discriminated,—and to unity of action, producing scenes alternately of interest and of grandeur;—the applause, in fine, which cannot be denied to him who can excite the passions of fear and of pity, must be awarded to the author of *The Castle of Otranto.*

Clara Reeve

Clara Reeve, the ingenious authoress of *The Old English Baron,* was the daughter of the Reverend William Reeve, M.A., Rector of Freston, and of Kerton, in Suffolk, and perpetual Curate of Saint Nicholas. Her grandfather was the Reverend Thomas Reeve, Rector of Storeham Aspal, and afterwards of St. Mary Stoke, in Ipswich, where the family had been long resident, and enjoyed the rights of free burghers. Miss Reeve's mother's maiden name was Smithies, daughter of —— Smithies, goldsmith and jeweller to King George I.

In a letter to a friend, Mrs. Reeve thus speaks of her father:—"My father was an old Whig; from him I have learned all that I know; he was my oracle; he used to make me read the Parliamentary debates while he smoked his pipe after supper. I gaped and yawned over them at the time, but, unawares to myself, they fixed my principles once and for ever. He made me read Rapin's *History of England;* the information it gave made amends for its dryness. I read *Cato's Letters,* by Trenchard and Gordon; I read the Greek and Roman Histories, and *Plutarch's Lives;*—all these at an age when few people of either sex can read their names."

The Reverend Mr. Reeve, himself one of a family of eight children, had the same numerous succession; and it is therefore likely, that it was rather Clara's strong natural turn for study, than any degree of exclusive care which his partiality bestowed, that enabled her to acquire such a stock of early information. After his death, his widow resided in Colchester with three of their daughters; and it was here that Miss Clara Reeve first became an authoress, by translating from Latin Barclay's fine old romance, entitled *Argenis,* published in 1772, under the title of *The Phoenix.* It was in 1777, five years afterwards, that she produced her first and most distinguished work. It was published by Mr. Dilly of the Poultry (who gave ten pounds for the copyright) under the title of *The Champion of Virtue, a Gothic Story.* The work came to a second edition in the succeeding year, and was then first called *The Old English Baron*. The cause of the change we do not pretend to guess; for if Fitzowen be considered as the Old English Baron, we do not see wherefore a character, passive in himself from beginning to end, and only acted upon by others, should be selected to give a name to the story. We ought not to omit to mention, that this work is inscribed to Mrs. Brigden, the daughter of Richardson, who is stated to have lent her assistance to the revisal and correction of the work.

The success of *The Old English Baron* encouraged Miss Reeve to devote more of her leisure hours to literary composition, and she published in succession the following works:—*The Two Mentors, a Modern Story; The Progress of Romance, through Times, Countries, and Manners; The Exile, or Memoirs of the Count de Cronstadt,* the principal incidents of which are borrowed from a novel by M. D'Arnaud; *The School for Widows, a Novel; Plans of Education, with Remarks on the System of other Writers,* in a duodecimo volume; and *The Memoirs of Sir Roger de Clarendon, a natural Son of Edward the Black Prince; with Anecdotes of many other eminent Persons of the fourteenth Century.*

To these works we have to add another tale, of which the interest turned upon supernatural appearances. Miss Reeve informs the public, in a preface to a late edition of *The Old English Baron,* that, in compliance with the suggestion of a friend, she had composed *Castle Connor, an Irish Story,* in which apparitions were introduced. The manuscript, being intrusted to some careless or unfaithful person, fell aside, and was never recovered.

The various novels of Clara Reeve are all marked by excellent good sense, pure morality, and a competent command of those qualities which constitute a good romance. They were, generally speaking, favourably received at the time, but none of them took the same strong possession of the public mind as *The Old English Baron,* upon which the fame of the author may be considered as now exclusively rested.

Miss Reeve, respected and beloved, led a retired life, admitting no materials for biography, until 3rd December, 1803, when she died at Ipswich, her native city, at the advanced age of seventy-eight years. She was buried in the churchyard of St. Stephens, according to her particular direction, near to the grave of her friend, the Reverend Mr. Derby. Her brother, the Reverend Thomas Reeve, still lives, as also her sister, Mrs. Sarah Reeve, both advanced in life. Another brother, bred to the navy, attained the rank of vice-admiral in that service.

Such are the only particulars which we have been able to collect concerning this accomplished and estimable woman, and, in their simplicity, the reader may remark that of her life and of her character. As critics, it is our duty to make some farther observations, which shall be entirely confined to her most celebrated work, upon which her fame arose, and on which, without meaning disparagement to her other compositions, we conceive it entitled to rest.

The authoress has herself informed us that *The Old English Baron* is the "literary offspring of *The Castle of Otranto*," and she has obliged us by pointing out the different and more limited view which she had adopted, of the supernatural machinery employed by Horace Walpole. She condemns the latter for the extravagance of several of his conceptions; for the gigantic size of his sword and helmet; and for the violent fictions of a walking picture, and a skeleton in a hermit's cowl. A ghost, she contends, to be admitted as an ingredient in romance, must behave himself like ghosts of sober demeanour, and subject himself to the common rules still preserved in grange and hall, as circumscribing beings of his description.

We must, however, notwithstanding her authority, enter our protest against fettering the realm of shadows by the opinions entertained of it in the world of realities. If we are to try ghosts by the ordinary rules of humanity, we bar them of their privileges entirely. For instance, why admit the existence of an aerial phantom, and deny it the terrible attribute of magnifying its stature? why admit an enchanted helmet, and not a gigantic one? why allow as an impressive incident the fall of a suit of armour, thrown down, we must suppose, by no mortal hand, and at the same time deny the same supernatural influence the power of producing the illusion (for it is only represented as such) upon Manfred, which gives seeming motion and life to the portrait of his ancestor? It may be said, and it seems to be Miss Reeve's argument, that there is a verge of probability, which even the most violent figment must not transgress; but we reply by the cross question, that if we are once to subject our preternatural agents to the limits of human reason, where are we to stop? We might, under such a rule, demand of ghosts an account of the very circuitous manner in which they are pleased to open their communications with the living world. We might, for example, move a *quo warranto* against the spectre of the murdered Lord Lovel, for lurking about the eastern apartment, when it might have been reasonably expected, that if he did not at once impeach his murderers to the next magistrate, he might at least have put Fitzowen into the secret, and thus obtained the succession of his son more easily than by the dubious and circuitous route of a single combat. If there should be an appeal against this imputation, founded on the universal practice of ghosts, in such circumstances, who always act with singular obliquity in disclosing the guilt of which they complain, the matter becomes a question of precedent; in which view of the case, we may vindicate Horace Walpole for the gigantic exaggeration of his phantom, by the similar expansion of the terrific vision of Fadoun, in Blind Harry's *Life of Wallace;* and we could, were we so disposed, have paralleled his moving picture, by the example of one with which we ourselves had some acquaintance, which was said both to move and to utter groans, to the great alarm of a family of the highest respectability.

Where, then, may the reader ask, is the line to be drawn? or what are the limits to be placed to the reader's credulity, when those of common sense and ordinary nature are once exceeded? The question admits only one answer, namely, that the author himself, being in fact the magician, shall evoke no spirits whom he is not capable of endowing with manners and language corresponding to their supernatural character. Thus Shakspeare, drawing such characters as Caliban and Ariel, gave them reality, not by appealing to actual opinions, which his audience might entertain respecting the possibility or impossibility of their existence, but by investing them with such attributes as all readers and spectators recognised as those which must have corresponded to such extraordinary beings, had their existence been possible. If he had pleased to put into language the "squeaking and gibbering" of those disembodied phantoms which haunted the streets of Rome, no doubt his wonderful imagination could have filled up the sketch, which, marked by these two emphatic and singularly felicitous expressions, he has left as characteristic of the language of the dead.

In this point of view, our authoress has, with equal judgment and accuracy, confined her flight within those limits on which her pinions could support her; and though we are disposed to contest her general principle, we are willing to admit it as a wise and prudent one, so far as applied to regulate her own composition. In no part of *The Old English Baron,* or of any other of her works, does Miss Reeve show the possession of a rich or powerful imagination. Her dialogue is sensible, easy, and agreeable, but neither marked by high flights of fancy, nor strong bursts of passion. Her apparition is an ordinary fiction, of which popular superstition used to furnish a thousand instances, when nights were long, and a family, assembled round a Christmas log, had little better to do than to listen to such tales. Miss Reeve has been very felicitously cautious in showing us no more of Lord Lovel's ghost than she needs must—he is a silent apparition, palpable to the sight only, and never brought forward into such broad daylight as might have dissolved our reverence. And so far, we repeat, the authoress has used her own power to the utmost advantage, and gained her point by not attempting a step beyond it. But we cannot allow that the rule which, in her own case, has been well and wisely adopted, ought to circumscribe a bolder and a more imaginative writer.

In what may be called the costume, or keeping, of the chivalrous period in which the scene of both is laid, the language and style of Horace Walpole, together with his intimate acquaintance with the manners of the middle ages, form an incalculable difference betwixt *The Castle of Otranto* and *The Old English Baron.* Clara Reeve, probably, was better acquainted with Plutarch and Rapin, than with Froissart or Olivier de la Marche. This is no imputation on the taste of that ingenious lady. In her days, Macbeth was performed in a general's full uniform, and Lord Hastings was dressed like a modern high chamberlain going to court. Or, if she looked to romances for her authority, those of the French school were found introducing, under the reign of Cyrus or of Faramond, or in the early republic at Rome, the sentiments and manners of the court of Louis XIV. In the present day, more attention to costume is demanded, and authors, as well as players, are obliged to make attempts, however fantastic or grotesque, to imitate the manners, on the one hand, and the dress on the other, of the times in which the scene is laid. Formerly, nothing of this kind was either required or expected; and it is not improbable that the manner in which Walpole circumscribes his dialogue (in most instances) within the stiff and stern precincts prescribed by a strict attention to the manners and language of the times, is the first instance of such restrictions. In *The Old English Baron,* on the contrary, all parties speak and act much in the fashion of the seventeenth century; employ the same phrases of courtesy; and adopt the same tone of conversation. Baron Fitzowen, and the principal characters, talk after the fashion of country squires of that period, and the lower personages like gaffers and gammers of the same era. And "were but the combat in lists left out," or converted into a modern duel, the whole train of incidents might, for any peculiarity to be traced in the dialect or narration, have taken place in the time of Charles II., or in either of the two succeeding reigns. As it is, the story reads as if it had been transcribed into the language, and remodelled according to the ideas, of this latter period. Yet we are uncertain whether, upon the whole, this does not rather add to, than diminish the interest of the work;—at least it gives an interest of a different kind, which, if it cannot compete with that which arises out of a highly exalted and poetical imagination, and a strict attention to the character and manners of the middle ages, has yet this advantage, that it reaches its point more surely than had a higher, more difficult, and more ambitious line of composition been attempted.

To explain our meaning:—He that would please the modern world, yet present the exact impression of a tale of the middle ages, will repeatedly find that he will be obliged, in despite of his utmost exertions, to sacrifice the last to the first object, and eternally expose himself to the just censure of the rigid antiquary, because he must, to interest the readers of the present time, invest his characters with language and sentiments unknown to the period assigned to his story; and thus his utmost efforts only attain a sort of composition between the true and the fictitious,—just as the dress of Lear, as performed on the stage, is neither that of a modern sovereign, nor the cerulean painting and bear-hide with which the Britons, at the time when that monarch is supposed to have lived, tattooed their persons, and sheltered themselves from cold. All this inconsistency is avoided by adopting the style of our grandfathers and great-grandfathers, sufficiently antiquated to accord with the antiquated character of the narrative, yet copious enough to express all that is necessary to its interest, and to supply that deficiency of colouring which the more ancient times do not afford.

It is no doubt true that *The Old English Baron,* written in the latter and less ambitious taste, is sometimes tame and tedious, not to say mean and tiresome. The total absence of peculiar character (for every person introduced is rather described as one of a genus than as an original, discriminated, and individual person) may have its effect in producing the tædium which loads the story in some places. This is a general defect in the novels of the period, and it was scarce to be expected that the amiable and accomplished authoress, in her secluded situation, and with acquaintance of events and characters derived from books alone, should have rivalled those authors who gathered their knowledge of the human heart from having, like Fielding and Smollett, become acquainted, by sad experience, with each turn of "many-coloured life." Nor was it to be thought that she should have emulated in this particular her prototype Walpole, who, as a statesman, a poet, and a man of the world, "who knew the world like a man," has given much individual character to his sketch of Manfred. What we here speak of is not the deficiency in the style and costume, but a certain creeping and low line of narrative and sentiment; which may be best illustrated by the grave and minute accounting into which Sir Philip Harclay and the Baron Fitzowen enter,—after an event so unpleasant as the judgment of Heaven upon a murderer, brought about by a judicial combat, and that combat occasioned by the awful and supernatural occurrences in the eastern chamber,—where we find the arrears of the estate gravely set off against the education of the heir, and his early maintenance in the Baron's family. Yet even these prolix, minute, and unnecessary details are precisely such as would occur in a similar story told by a grandsire or grandame to a circle assembled round a winter's fire; and while they take from the dignity of the composition, and would therefore have been rejected by a writer of more exalted imagination, do certainly add in some degree to its reality, and bear in that respect a resemblance to the art with which De Foe impresses on his readers the truth of his fictions, by the insertion of many minute, and immaterial, or unnatural circumstances, which we are led to suppose could only be recorded because they are true. Perhaps, to be circumstantial and abundant in minute detail, and in one word, though an unauthorized one, to be somewhat *prosy,* is a secret mode of securing a certain necessary degree of credulity from the hearers of a ghost-story. It gives a sort of quaint antiquity to the whole, as belonging to the times of "superstitious elde," and those whom we have observed to excel in oral narratives of such a nature, usually study to secure the attention of their audience by employing this art. At least, whether owing to this mode of telling her tale, or to the interest of the story itself, and its appeal to the secret reserve of superstitious feeling which maintains its influence in most bosoms, *The Old English Baron* has

always produced as strong an effect as any story of the kind, although liable to the objections which we have freely stated, without meaning to impeach the talents of the amiable authoress.

Dismissing this interesting subject for the present, we trust we may find some future opportunity to offer a few more general remarks on the introduction of supernatural machinery into modern works of fiction.

Ann Radcliffe

The life of Mrs. Ann Radcliffe, spent in the quiet shade of domestic privacy, and in the interchange of familiar affections and sympathies, appears to have been as retired and sequestered, as the fame of her writings was brilliant and universal. The most authentic account of her birth, family, and personal appearance, seems to be that contained in the following communication to a work of contemporary biography.

"She was," (says this writer,) "born in London, in the year 1764, [9th July;] the daughter of William and Ann Ward, who, though in trade, were nearly the only persons of their two families not living in handsome, or at least easy independence. Her paternal grandmother was a Cheselden, the sister of the celebrated surgeon, of whose kind regard her father had a grateful recollection, and some of whose presents, in books, I have seen. The late Lieutenant-Colonel Cheselden, of Somerby in Leicestershire, was, I think, another nephew of the surgeon. Her father's aunt, the late Mrs. Barwell, first of Leicester, and then of Duffield in Derbyshire, was one of the sponsors at her baptism. Her maternal grandmother was Anne Oates, the sister of Dr. Samuel Jebb, of Stratford, who was the father of Sir Richard: on that side she was also related to Dr. Halifax, Bishop of Gloucester, and to Dr. Halifax, Physician to the King. Perhaps it may gratify curiosity to state farther, that she was descended from a near relative of the De Witts of Holland. In some family papers which I have seen, it is stated, that a De Witt, of the family of John and Cornelius, came to England, under the patronage of government, upon some design of draining the fens in Lincolnshire, bringing with him a daughter, Amelia, then an infant. The prosecution of the plan is supposed to have been interrupted by the rebellion, in the time of Charles the First; but De Witt appears to have passed the remainder of his life in a mansion near Hull, and to have left many children, of whom Amelia was the mother of one of Mrs. Radcliffe's ancestors.

"This admirable writer, whom I remember from about the time of her twentieth year, was, in her youth, of a figure exquisitely proportioned; while she resembled her father, and his brother and sister, in being low of stature. Her complexion was beautiful, as was her whole countenance, especially her eyes, eyebrows, and mouth. Of the faculties of her mind, let her works speak. Her tastes were such as might be expected from those works. To contemplate the glories of creation, but more particularly the grander features of their display, was one of her chief delights: to listen to fine music was another. She had also a gratification in listening to any good verbal sounds; and would desire to hear passages repeated from the Latin and Greek classics; requiring, at intervals, the most literal translations that could be given, with all that was possible of their idiom, how much soever the version might be embarrassed by that aim at exactness. Though her fancy was prompt, and she was, as will readily be supposed, qualified in many respects for conversation, she had not the confidence and presence of mind, without which, a person conscious of being observed, can scarcely be at ease, except in long-tried society. Yet she had not been without some good examples of what must have been ready conversation in more extensive circles. Besides that a great part of her youth had been passed in the residence of her superior relatives, she had the advantage of being much loved, when a child, by the late Mr. Bentley; to whom, on the establishment of the fabric known by the name of Wedgwood and Bentley's, was appropriated the superintendence of all that related to form and design. Mr. Wedgwood was the intelligent man of commerce, and the able chemist; Mr. Bentley the man of more general literature, and of taste in the arts. One of her mother's sisters was married to Mr. Bentley; and, during the life of her aunt, who was accomplished 'according to the moderation,'—may I say, the *wise* moderation?—of that day, the little niece was a favourite guest at Chelsea, and afterwards at Turnham Green, where Mr. and Mrs. Bentley resided. At their house she saw several persons of distinction for literature; and others who, without having been so distinguished, were beneficial objects of attention for their minds and their manners. Of the former class the late Mrs. Montague, and once, I think, Mrs. Piozzi; of the latter, Mrs. Ord. The gentleman, called Athenian Stuart, was also a visitor there."

Thus respectably born and connected, Miss Ward, at the age of twenty-three, acquired the name which she has made so famous, by marrying William Radcliffe, Esq., graduated at Oxford, and a student of law. He renounced, however, the prosecution of his legal studies, and became afterwards proprietor and editor of the *English Chronicle.*

Thus connected in a manner which must have induced her to cherish her literary powers, Mrs. Radcliffe first came before the public as a novelist in 1789, only two years after her marriage, and when she was twenty-five years old. The romance, entitled *The Castles of Athlin and Dunbayne,* which she then produced, gave, however, but moderate intimation of the author's eminent powers. The scene is laid in Scotland, during the dark ages, but without any attempt to trace either the peculiar manners or scenery of the country; and although, in reading the work with that express purpose, we can now trace some germs of that taste and talent for the wild, romantic, and mysterious, which the authoress afterwards employed with such effect, we cannot consider it, on the whole, as by any means worthy of her pen. It is nevertheless curious to compare this sketch with Mrs. Radcliffe's more esteemed productions, since it is of consequence to the history of human genius to preserve its earlier efforts, that we may trace, if possible, how the oak at length germinates from the unmarked acorn.

Mrs. Radcliffe's genius was more advantageously displayed in the *Sicilian Romance,* which appeared in 1790, and which, as we ourselves (then novel-readers of no ordinary appetite) well recollect, attracted in a considerable degree the attention of the public. This work displays the exuberance and fertility of imagination, which was the author's principal characteristic. Adventures heaped on adventures, in quick and brilliant succession, with all the hair-breadth charms of escape or capture, hurry the reader along with them, and the imagery and scenery by which the action is relieved, are like those of a splendid Oriental tale. Still this work had marked traces of the defects natural to an unpractised author. The scenes were inartificially connected, and the characters hastily sketched, without any attempt at individual distinctions; being cast in the usual mould of ardent lovers, tyrannical parents, with domestic ruffians, guards, and others, who had wept or stormed through the chapters of romance, without much alteration in their family habits or features, for a quarter of a century before Mrs. Radcliffe's time. Nevertheless, the *Sicilian Romance* attracted much notice among the novel-readers of the day, as far excelling the ordinary meagreness of stale and uninteresting incident with which they were at that time regaled from the Leadenhall press. Indeed, the praise may be claimed for Mrs. Radcliffe, of having been the first to introduce into her prose fictions a beautiful and fanciful tone of natural description and impressive narrative, which had hitherto been exclusively applied to poetry. Fielding, Richardson, Smollett, even Walpole, though writing upon an imaginative subject, are decidedly prose authors. Mrs. Radcliffe has a title to be considered as the first poetess of romantic fiction, that is, if actual rhythm shall not be deemed essential to poetry.

The Romance of the Forest, which appeared in 1791, placed the author at once in that rank and preeminence in her own particular style of composition, which her works have ever since maintained. Her fancy, in this new effort, was more regulated, and subjected to the fetters of a regular story. The persons, too, although perhaps there is nothing very original in the conception, were depicted with skill far superior to that which the author had hitherto displayed, and the work attracted the public attention in proportion. That of La Motte, indeed, is sketched with particular talent, and most part of the interest of the piece depends upon the vacillations of a character, who, though upon the whole we may rather term him weak and vicious, than villanous, is, nevertheless, at every moment on the point of becoming an agent in atrocities which his heart disapproves of. He is the exact picture "of the needy man who has known better days;" one who, spited at the world, from which he has been expelled with contempt, and condemned by circumstances to seek an asylum in a desolate mansion full of mysteries and horrors, avenges himself, by playing the gloomy despot within his own family, and tyrannizing over those who were subjected to him only by their strong sense of duty. A more powerful agent appears on the scene—obtains the mastery over this dark but irresolute spirit, and, by alternate exertion of seduction and terror, compels him to be his agent in schemes against the virtue, and even the life of an orphan whom he was bound in gratitude, as well as in honour and hospitality, to cherish and protect.

The heroine, too, wearing the usual costume of innocence, purity, and simplicity, as proper to heroines as white gowns are to the sex in general, has some pleasant touches of originality. Her grateful affection for the La Motte family—her reliance on their truth and honour, when the wife had become unkind, and the father treacherous towards her, is an interesting and individual trait in her character.

But although undoubtedly the talents of Mrs. Radcliffe, in the important point of drawing and finishing the characters of her narrative, were greatly improved since her earlier attempts, and manifested sufficient power to raise her far above the common crowd of novelists, this was not the department of art on which her popularity rested. The public were chiefly aroused, or rather fascinated, by the wonderful conduct of a story, in which the author so successfully called out the feelings of mystery and of awe, while chapter after chapter, and incident after incident, maintained the thrilling attraction of awakened curiosity and suspended interest. Of these, every reader felt the force, from the sage in his study, to the family group in middle life, which assembles round the evening taper, to seek a solace from the toils of ordinary existence by an excursion into the regions of imagination. The tale was the more striking, because varied and relieved by descriptions of the ruined mansion, and the forest with which it is surrounded, under so many different points of view, now pleasing and serene, now gloomy, now terrible—scenes which could only have been drawn by one to whom nature had given the eye of a painter, with the spirit of a poet.

In 1793, Mrs. Radcliffe had the advantage of visiting the scenery of the Rhine, and, although we are not positive of the fact, we are strongly inclined to suppose, that *The Mysteries of Udolpho* were written, or at least corrected, after the date of this journey; for the mouldering castles of the robber-chivalry of Germany, situated on the wild and romantic banks of that celebrated stream, seem to have given a bolder flight to her imagination, and a more glowing character to her colouring, than are exhibited in *The Romance of the Forest.* The scenery on the Lakes of Westmoreland, which Mrs. Radcliffe visited about the same time, was also highly calculated to awaken her fancy, as nature has in these wild but beautiful regions realized the descriptions in which this authoress loved to indulge. Her remarks upon these countries were given to the public in 1794, in a very well-written work, entitled, *A Journey through Holland, &c.*

Much was of course expected from Mrs. Radcliffe's next effort, and the booksellers felt themselves authorized in offering what was then considered as an unprecedented sum, £500, for *The Mysteries of Udolpho.* It often happens, that a writer's previous reputation proves the greatest enemy which, in a second attempt upon public favour, he has to encounter. Exaggerated expectations are excited and circulated, and criticism, which had been seduced into former approbation by the pleasure of surprise, now stands awakened and alert to pounce upon every failing. Mrs. Radcliffe's popularity, however, stood the test, and was heightened rather than diminished by *The Mysteries of Udolpho.* The very name was fascinating; and the public, who rushed upon it with all the eagerness of curiosity, rose from it with unsated appetite. When a family was numerous, the volumes always flew, and were sometimes torn, from hand to hand; and the complaints of those whose studies were thus interrupted were a general tribute to the genius of the author. Another might be found of a different and higher description, in the dwelling of the lonely invalid, or unregarded votary of celibacy, who was bewitched away from a sense of solitude, of indisposition, of the neglect of the world, or of secret sorrow, by the potent charm of this mighty enchantress. Perhaps the perusal of such works may, without injustice, be compared with the use of opiates, baneful, when habitually and constantly resorted to, but of most blessed power in those moments of pain and of languor, when the whole head is sore, and the whole heart sick. If those who rail indiscriminately at this species of composition, were to consider the quantity of actual pleasure which it produces, and the much greater proportion of real sorrow and distress which it alleviates, their philanthropy ought to moderate their critical pride, or religious intolerance.

To return to *The Mysteries of Udolpho.* The author, pursuing her own favourite bent of composition, and again waving her wand over the world of wonder and imagination, had judiciously used a spell of broader and more potent command. The situation and distresses of the heroines, have here, and in *The Romance of the Forest,* a general aspect of similarity. Both are divided from the object of their attachment by the gloomy influence of unfaithful and oppressive guardians, and both become inhabitants of time-stricken towers, and witnesses of scenes now bordering on the supernatural, and now upon the horrible. But this general resemblance is only such as we love to recognise in pictures which have been painted by the same hand, and as companions for each other. Every thing in *The Mysteries of Udolpho* is on a larger and more sublime scale, than in *The Romance of the Forest;* the interest is of a more agitating and tremendous nature; the scenery of a wilder and more terrific description; the characters distinguished by fiercer and more gigantic features. Montoni, a lofty-souled desperado, and Captain of Condottieri, stands beside La Motte and his Marquis, like one of Milton's fiends beside a witch's familiar. Adeline is confined within a ruined manor-house, but her sister heroine, Emily, is imprisoned in a huge castle, like those of feudal times; the one is attacked and defended by bands of armed banditti, the other only threatened by a visit from constables and thief-takers. The scale of the landscape is equally different; the quiet and limited woodland scenery of the one work forming a contrast with the splendid and high-wrought descriptions of Italian mountain grandeur which occur in the other.

In general, *The Mysteries of Udolpho* was, at its first appearance, considered as a step beyond Mrs. Radcliffe's former work, high as that had justly advanced her. We entertain the same opinion in again reading them both, even after some years' interval. Yet there were persons of no mean judgment, to whom the simplicity of *The Romance of the Forest* seemed preferable to the more highly coloured and broader style of *The Mysteries of Udolpho;* and it must remain matter of opinion, whether their preference be better founded than in the partialities of a first love, which in literature, as in life, are often unduly predominant. With the majority of readers, the superior magnificence of landscape, and dignity of conception of character, secured the palm for the more recent work.

The fifth production by which Mrs. Radcliffe arrested the attention of the public, was fated to be her last. *The Italian,* which appeared in 1797, was purchased by the booksellers for £800, and obtained a share of public favour equal to any of its predecessors. Here, too, the author had, with much judgment, taken such a point of distance and distinction, that while employing her own peculiar talent, and painting in the style of which she may be considered the inventor, she cannot be charged with repeating or copying herself. She selected the new and powerful machinery afforded her by the Popish religion, when established in its paramount superiority, and thereby had at her disposal, monks, spies, dungeons, the mute obedience of the bigot, the dark and dominating spirit of the crafty priest,—all the thunders of the Vatican, and all the terrors of the Inquisition. This fortunate adoption placed in the hands of the authoress a powerful set of agents, who were at once supplied with means and motives for bringing forward scenes of horror; and thus a tinge of probability was thrown over even those parts of the story, which are most inconsistent with the ordinary train of human events.

Most writers of romance have been desirous to introduce their narrative to the reader, in some manner which might at once excite interest, and prepare his mind for the species of excitation which it was the author's object to produce. In *The Italian,* this has been achieved by Mrs. Radcliffe with an uncommon degree of felicity; nor is there any part of the romance itself which is more striking, than its impressive commencement.

A party of English travellers visit a Neapolitan church:—

"Within the shade of the portico, a person with folded arms, and eyes directed towards the ground, was pacing behind the pillars the whole extent of the pavement, and was apparently so engaged by his own thoughts, as not to observe that strangers were approaching. He turned, however, suddenly. as if startled by the sound of steps, and then, without farther pausing, glided to a door that opened into the church, and disappeared.

"There was something too extraordinary in the figure of this man, and too singular in his conduct, to pass unnoticed by the visitors. He was of a tall thin figure, bending forward from the shoulders; of a sallow complexion, and harsh features, and had an eye which, as it looked up from the cloak that muffled the lower part of his countenance, was expressive of uncommon ferocity.

"The travellers, on entering the church, looked round for the stranger, who had passed thither before them, but he was nowhere to be seen; and, through all the shade of the long aisles, only one other person appeared. This was a friar of the adjoining convent, who sometimes pointed out to strangers the objects in the church which were most worthy of attention, and who now, with this design, approached the party that had just entered.

"When the party had viewed the different shrines and whatever had been judged worthy of observation, and were returning through an obscure aisle towards the portico, they perceived the person who had appeared upon the steps, passing towards a confessional on the left, and, as he entered it, one of the party pointed him out to the friar, and enquired who he was; the friar turning to look after him, did not immediately reply, but, on the question being repeated, he inclined his head, as in a kind of obeisance, and calmly replied, 'He is an assassin.'

"'An assassin!' exclaimed one of the Englishmen; 'an assassin, and at liberty!'

"An Italian gentleman, who was of the party, smiled at the astonishment of his friend.

"'He has sought sanctuary here,' replied the friar; 'within these walls he may not be hurt.'

"'Do your altars, then, protect a murderer!' said the Englishman.

"'He could find shelter nowhere else,' answered the friar, meekly.

*   *   *

"'But observe yonder confessional,' added the Italian, 'that beyond the pillars on the left of the aisle, below a painted window. Have you discovered it? The colours of the glass throw, instead of a light, a shade over that part of the church, which, perhaps, prevents your distinguishing what I mean.'

"The Englishman looked whither his friend pointed, and observed a confessional of oak, or some very dark wood, adjoining the wall, and remarked also, that it was the same which the assassin had just entered. It consisted of three compartments, covered with a black canopy. In the central division was the chair of the confessor, elevated by several steps above the pavement of the church; and on either hand was a small closet, or box, with steps leading up to a grated partition, at which the penitent might kneel, and, concealed from observation, pour into the ear of the confessor, the consciousness of crimes that lay heavy at his heart.

"'You observe it?' said the Italian.

"'I do,' replied the Englishman: 'it is the same which the assassin had passed into; and I think it one of the most gloomy spots I ever beheld; the view of it is enough to strike a criminal with despair!'

"'We, in Italy, are not so apt to despair,' replied the Italian, smilingly.

"'Well, but what of this confessional?' enquired the Englishman. 'The assassin entered it.'

"'He has no relation with what I am about to mention,' said the Italian; 'but I wish you to mark the place, because some very extraordinary circumstances belong to it.'

"'What are they?' said the Englishman.

"'It is now several years since the confession, which is connected with them, was made at that very confessional,' added the Italian; 'the view of it, and the sight of the assassin, with your surprise at the liberty which is allowed him, led me to a recollection of the story. When you return to the hotel, I will communicate it to you, if you have no pleasanter mode of engaging your time.'

"'After I have taken another view of this solemn edifice,' replied the Englishman, 'and particularly of the confessional you have pointed to my notice.'

"While the Englishman glanced his eye over the high roofs, and along the solemn perspectives of the Santa del Pianto, he perceived the figure of the assassin stealing from the confessional across the choir, and, shocked on again beholding him, he turned his eyes, and hastily quitted the church.

"The friends then separated, and the Englishman, soon after returning to his hotel, received the volume. He read as follows."

This introductory passage, which, for the references which it bears to the story, and the anxious curiosity it excites in the reader's mind, may be compared to the dark and vaulted gateway of an ancient castle, is followed by a tale of corresponding mystery and terror; in detailing which, the art of Mrs. Radcliffe, who was so great a mistress of throwing her narrative into mystery, affording half intimations of veiled and secret horrors, is used perhaps to the very uttermost. And yet, though our reason ultimately presents us with this criticism, we believe she generally suspends her remonstrance till the perusal is ended; and it is not until the last page is read, and the last volume closed, that we feel ourselves disposed to censure that which has so keenly interested us. We become then at length aware, that there is no uncommon merit in the general contrivance of the story; that many of the incidents are improbable, and some of the mysteries left unexplained; yet the impression of general delight which we have received from the perusal, remains unabated, for it is founded on recollection of the powerful emotions of wonder, curiosity, even fear, to which we have been subjected during the currency of the narrative.

A youth of high birth and noble estates becomes enamoured of a damsel of low fortunes, unknown race, and all that portion of beauty and talents which belongs to a heroine of romance. Their union is opposed by his family, and chiefly by the pride of his mother, who calls to her aid the real hero of the tale, her confessor, Father Schedoni, a strongly drawn character as ever stalked through the regions of romance, equally detestable for the crimes he has formerly perpetrated, and those which he is willing to commit; formidable from his talents and energy; at once a hypocrite and a profligate, unfeeling, unrelenting, and implacable. With the aid of this agent, Vivaldi, the lover, is thrown into the dungeons of the Inquisition, while Ellena, his bride, is carried by the pitiless monk to an obscure den, where, finding the services of an associate likely to foil his expectation, he resolves to murder her with his own hand. Hitherto the story, or, at least, the situation, is not altogether dissimilar from the *Mysteries of Udolpho;* but the fine scene, where the monk, in the act of raising his arm to murder his sleeping victim, discovers her to be his own child, is of a new, grand, and powerful character;

and the horrors of the wretch, who, on the brink of murder, has but just escaped from committing a crime of yet more exaggerated horror, constitute the strongest painting which has been produced by Mrs. Radcliffe's pencil, and form a crisis well fitted to be actually embodied on canvas by some great master. In the prisons of the Inquisition, the terrific Schedoni is met, counterplotted, and at length convicted, by the agency of a being as wicked as himself, who had once enjoyed his confidence. Several pauses of breathless suspense are thrown in, during the detail of these intrigues, by which Mrs. Radcliffe knew so well how to give interest to the work.

On reconsidering the narrative, we indeed discover that many of the incidents are imperfectly explained, and that we can distinguish points upon which the authoress had doubtless intended to lay the foundation of something which she afterwards forgot or omitted. Of the first class, is the astonishment testified by the Grand Inquisitor with such striking effect, when a strange voice was heard, even in the awful presence of that stern tribunal, to assume the task of interrogation proper to its judges. The incident in itself is most impressive. As Vivaldi is blindfolded, and bound upon the rack, the voice of a mysterious agent, who had repeatedly crossed his path, and always eluded his search, is heard to mingle in his examination, and strikes the whole assembly with consternation.

> "'Who is come amongst us?' he [the Grand Inquisitor] repeated, in a louder tone. Still no answer was returned; but again a confused murmur sounded from the tribunal, and a general consternation seemed to prevail. No person spoke with sufficient preeminence to be understood by Vivaldi; something extraordinary appeared to be passing, and he awaited the issue with all the patience he could command. Soon after he heard the doors opened, and the noise of persons quitting the chamber. A deep silence followed; but he was certain that the familiars were still beside him, waiting to begin their work of torture."

This is all unquestionably very impressive; but no other explanation of the intruder's character is given, than that he is an officer of the Inquisition; a circumstance which may explain his being present at Vivaldi's examination, but by no means his interference with it, against the pleasure of the Grand Inquisitor. The latter certainly would neither have been surprised at the presence of one of his own officials, nor overawed by his deportment; since the one was a point of ordinary duty, and the other must have been accounted as an impertinence. It may be added also, that there is no full or satisfactory reason assigned for the fell and unpitying hostility of Zampari to Schedoni, and that the reasons which can be gathered are inadequate and trivial.

We may notice an instance of even greater negligence, in the passages respecting the ruined palace of the Baron di Cambrusca, where the imperfect tale of horror hinted at by a peasant, the guide of Schedoni, appears to jar upon the galled conscience of the monk, and induces the reader to expect a train of important consequences. Unquestionably, the ingenious authoress had meant this half-told tale to correspond with some particulars in the proposed development of the story, which having been finished more hastily, or in a different manner from what she intended, she had, like a careless knitter, neglected to take up her "loose stitches." It is, however, a baulking of the reader's imagination, which authors in this department would do well to guard against. At the same time, critics are bound in mercy to remember, how much more easy it is to devise a complicated chain of interest, than to disentangle it with perfect felicity. Dryden, it is said, used to curse the inventors of fifth acts in the drama, and romance-writers owe no blessings to the memory of him who devised explanatory chapters.

We have been told that, in this beautiful romance, the customs and rules of the Inquisition have been violated; a charge more easily made than proved, and which, if true, is of minor importance, because its code is happily but little known to us. It is matter of more obvious criticism, and therefore a greater error, that the scraps of Italian language introduced to give locality to the scene, are not happily chosen, and savour of affectation. But if Mrs. Radcliffe did not intimately understand the language and manners of Italy, the following extract may prove how well she knew how to paint Italian scenery, which she could only have seen in the pictures of Claude or Poussin.

> "These excursions sometimes led to Puzzuoli, Baia, or the woody cliffs of Pausilippo; and as, on their return, they glided along the moonlight bay, the melodies of Italian strains seemed to give enchantment to the scenery of its shore. At this cool hour the voices of the vine-dressers were frequently heard in trio, as they reposed, after the labour of the day, on some pleasant promontory, under the shade of poplars; or the brisk music of the dance from fishermen, on the margin of the waves below. The

boatmen rested on their oars, while their company listened to voices modulated by sensibility to finer eloquence, than it is in the power of art alone to display; and at others, while they observed the airy natural grace, which distinguishes the dance of the fishermen and peasant girls of Naples. Frequently, as they glided round a promontory, whose shaggy masses impended far over the sea, such magic scenes of beauty unfolded, adorned by these dancing groups on the bay beyond, as no pencil could do justice to. The deep clear waters reflected every image of the landscape; the cliffs, branching into wild forms, crowned with groves, whose rough foliage often spread down their steeps in picturesque luxuriance; the ruined villa, on some bold point, peeping through the trees; peasants' cabins hanging on the precipices, and the dancing figures on the strand—all touched with the silvery tint and soft shadows of moonlight. On the other hand, the sea, trembling with a long line of radiance, and showing in the clear distance the sails of vessels stealing in every direction along its surface, presented a prospect as grand as the landscape was beautiful."

There are other descriptive passages, which, like those in *The Mysteries of Udolpho,* approach more nearly to the style of Salvator Rosa.

The Italian was received with as much ardour as Mrs. Radcliffe's two previous novels, and it was from no coldness on the part of the public, that, like an actress in full possession of applauded powers, she chose to retreat from the stage in the blaze of her fame. After publication of *The Italian,* in 1797, the public were not favoured with any more of Mrs. Radcliffe's works.

We are left in vain to conjecture the reasons, which, for more than twenty years, condemned an imagination so fertile, so far as the public were concerned, to sterility. The voice of unfriendly criticism, always as sure an attendant upon merit as envy herself, may perhaps have intimidated the gentleness of her character; or Mrs. Radcliffe, as frequently happens, may have been disgusted at seeing the mode of composition, which she had brought into fashion, profaned by the host of servile imitators, who could only copy and render more prominent her defects, without aspiring to her merits. But so steadily did she keep her resolution, that for more than twenty years the name of Mrs. Radcliffe was never mentioned, unless with reference to her former productions, and in general (so retired was the current of her life) there was a belief that Fate had removed her from the scene.

Notwithstanding her refraining from publication, it is impossible to believe that an imagination so strong, supported by such ready powers of expression, should have remained inactive during so long a period; but the manuscripts on which she was occasionally employed, have as yet been withheld from the public. We have reason to believe, that arrangements were at one time almost concluded between Mrs. Radcliffe and a highly respectable publishing-house, respecting a poetical romance, but were broken off in consequence of the author changing or delaying her intention of publication. It is to be hoped, that the world will not be ultimately deprived of what undoubtedly must be the source of much pleasure whenever it shall see the light.

The tenor of Mrs. Radcliffe's private life seems to have been peculiarly calm and sequestered. She probably declined the sort of personal notoriety which, in London society, usually attaches to persons of literary merit; and, perhaps, no author whose works were so universally read and admired, was so little personally known even to the most active of that class of people of distinction, who rest their peculiar pretensions to fashion upon the selection of literary society. Her estate was certainly not the less gracious; and it did not disturb Mrs. Radcliffe's domestic comforts, although many of her admirers believed, and some are not yet undeceived, that, in consequence of brooding over the terrors which she depicted, her reason had at length been overturned, and that the author of *The Mysteries of Udolpho* only existed as the melancholy inmate of a private mad-house. This report was so generally spread, and so confidently repeated in print, as well as in conversation, that the Editor believed it for several years, until, greatly to his satisfaction, he learned, from good authority, that there neither was, nor ever had been, the most distant foundation for this unpleasing rumour.

A false report of another kind gave Mrs. Radcliffe much concern. In Miss Seward's Correspondence, among the literary gossip of the day, it is roundly stated, that the *Plays upon the Passions* were Mrs. Radcliffe's, and that she owned them. Mrs. Radcliffe was much hurt at being reported capable of borrowing from the fame of a gifted sister; and the late Miss Seward would, no doubt, have suffered equally, had she been aware of the pain she inflicted by giving currency to a rumour so totally unfounded. The truth is, that, residing at a distance from the metropolis, and living upon literary intelligence as her daily food, Miss Seward was sometimes imposed upon by those friendly caterers who were more anxious to supply her with the newest intelligence, than solicitous about its accuracy.

During the last twelve years of her life, Mrs. Radcliffe suffered from a spasmodic asthma, which considerably affected her general health and spirits. This chronic disorder took a more fatal turn upon the 9th of January, 1823; and upon the 7th of February following, terminated the life of this ingenious and amiable lady, at her own house in London.

Mrs. Radcliffe, as an author, has the most decided claim to take her place among the favoured few, who have been distinguished as the founders of a class, or school. She led the way in a peculiar style of composition, affecting powerfully the mind of the reader, which has since been attempted by many, but in which no one has attained or approached the excellences of the original inventor, unless perhaps the author of *The Family of Montorio.*

The species of romance which Mrs. Radcliffe introduced, bears nearly the same relation to the novel that the modern anomaly entitled a melodrame does to the proper drama. It does not appeal to the judgment by deep delineations of human feeling, or stir the passions by scenes of deep pathos, or awaken the fancy by tracing out, with spirit and vivacity, the lighter marks of life and manners, or excite mirth by strong representations of the ludicrous or humorous. In other words, it attains its interest neither by the path of comedy nor of tragedy; and yet it has, notwithstanding, a deep, decided, and powerful effect, gained by means independent of both—by an appeal, in one word, to the passion of fear, whether excited by natural dangers, or by the suggestions of superstition. The force, therefore, of the production, lies in the delineation of external incident, while the characters of the agents, like the figures in many landscapes, are entirely subordinate to the scenes in which they are placed; and are only distinguished by such outlines as make them seem appropriate to the rocks and trees, which have been the artist's principal objects. The persons introduced—and here also the correspondence holds betwixt the melo-drame and the romantic novel—bear the features, not of individuals, but of the class to which they belong. A dark and tyrannical count; an aged crone of a housekeeper, the depositary of many a family legend; a garrulous waiting-maid; a gay and lighthearted valet; a villain or two of all work; and a heroine, fulfilled with all perfections, and subjected to all manner of hazards, form the stock-in-trade of a romancer or a melodramatist; and if these personages be dressed in the proper costume, and converse in language sufficiently appropriate to their stations and qualities, it is not expected that the audience shall shake their sides at the humour of the dialogue, or weep over its pathos.

On the other hand, it is necessary that these characters, though not delineated with individual features, should be truly and forcibly sketched in the outline; that their dress and general appearance should correspond with and support the trick of the scene; and that their language and demeanour should either enhance the terrors amongst which they move, or form, as the action may demand, a strong and vivid contrast to them. Mrs. Radcliffe's powers of fancy were particularly happy in depicting such personages, in throwing upon them and their actions just enough of that dubious light which mystery requires, and in supplying them with language and manners which correspond with their situation and business upon the scene. We may take, as an example, the admirable description of the monk Schedoni:

> "His figure was striking, but not so from grace; it was tall, and, though extremely thin, his limbs were large and uncouth, and as he stalked along, wrapt in the black garments of his order, there was something terrible in his air; something almost superhuman. His cowl, too, as it threw a shade over the livid paleness of his face, increased its severe character, and gave an effect to his large melancholy eye, which approached to horror. His was not the melancholy of a sensible and wounded heart, but apparently that of a gloomy and ferocious disposition. There was something in his physiognomy extremely singular, and that cannot easily be defined. It bore the traces of many passions, which seemed to have fixed the features they no longer animated. An habitual gloom and severity prevailed over the deep lines of his countenance; and his eyes were so piercing, that they seemed to penetrate, at a single glance, into the hearts of men, and to read their most secret thoughts; few persons could support their scrutiny, or even endure to meet them twice. Yet, notwithstanding all this gloom and austerity, some rare occasions of interest had called forth a character upon his countenance entirely different; and he could adapt himself to the tempers and passions of persons whom he wished to conciliate with astonishing facility, and generally with complete triumph. This monk, this Schedoni, was the confessor and secret adviser of the Marchesa di Vivaldi."

To draw such portraits as Schedoni's, and others which occur in Mrs. Radcliffe's novels, requires no mean powers; and although they belong rather to romance than to real life, the impression which they make upon the imagination is scarce lessened by the sense, that they are in some sort as fabulous as fairies or ogres. But when the public have been surprised into a universal burst of applause, it is their custom to indemnify themselves by a corresponding degree of censure; just as children, when tired of admiring a new plaything, find a fresh and distinct pleasure in breaking it to pieces. Mrs. Radcliffe, who had afforded such general delight to the public, was not doomed to escape the common fate; and the criticism with which she was assailed, was the more invidious, that it was inflicted, in more than one case, by persons of genius, who followed the same pursuit with herself. It was the cry at the period, and has sometimes been repeated since, that the romances of Mrs. Radcliffe, and the applause with which they were received, were evil signs of the times, and argued a great and increasing degradation of the public taste, which, instead of banqueting as heretofore upon scenes of passion, like those of Richardson, or of life and manners, as in the pages of Smollett and Fielding, was now coming back to the fare of the nursery, and gorged upon the wild and improbable fictions of an overheated imagination. There might be some truth in this, if it were only applied to the crowd of copyists who came forward in imitation of Mrs. Radcliffe, and assumed her magic wand, without having the power of wielding it with effect. No author can be arraigned for the deficiencies of those who servilely copy his style, and, following their original as the shadow follows the substance, present an obscure, distorted, and indistinct outline of what is in itself clear, precise, and distinct. But the inferiority of this servile race is much more like to put the particular style they imitate out of fashion, than to engraft its peculiarities upon the public taste.

When applied to Mrs. Radcliffe herself, the tone of criticism which we allude to will, when justly examined, be found to rest chiefly on that depreciating spirit, which would undermine the fair fame of an accomplished writer, by showing that she does not possess the excellences proper to a style of composition totally different from that which she has attempted. The question is neither, whether the romances of Mrs. Radcliffe possess merits which her plan did not require, nay, almost excluded; nor whether hers is to be considered as a department of fictitious composition, equal in dignity and importance to those where the great ancient masters have long pre-occupied the ground. The real and only point is, whether, considered as a separate and distinct species of writing, that introduced by Mrs. Radcliffe possesses merit, and affords pleasure; for, these premises being admitted, it is as unreasonable to complain of the absence of advantages foreign to her style and plan, and proper to those of another mode of composition, as to regret that the peach-tree does not produce grapes, or the vine peaches. A glance upon the face of nature is, perhaps, the best cure for this unjust and unworthy system of criticism. We there behold, that not only each star differs from another in glory, but that there is spread over the face of Nature a boundless variety; and that as a thousand different kinds of shrubs and flowers, not only have beauties independent of each other, but are more delightful from that very circumstance than if they were uniform, so the fields of literature admit the same variety; and it may be said of the Muse of Fiction, as well as of her sisters,

"Mille habet ornatus, mile decenter habet."

It may be stated, to the additional confusion of such hypercritics as we allude to, that not only does the infinite variety of human tastes require different styles of composition for their gratification; but if there were to be selected one particular structure of fiction, which possesses charms for the learned and unlearned, the grave and gay, the gentleman and the clown, it would be perhaps that of those very romances which the severity of their criticism seeks to depreciate. There are many men too mercurial to be delighted by Richardson's beautiful, but protracted display of the passions; and there are some too dull to comprehend the wit of Le Sage, or too saturnine to relish the nature and spirit of Fielding: And yet these very individuals will with difficulty be divorced from *The Romance of the Forest,* or *The Mysteries of Udolpho;* for curiosity and a lurking love of mystery, together with a germ of superstition, are more general ingredients in the human mind, and more widely diffused through the mass of humanity, than either genuine taste for the comic, or true feeling of the pathetic. The unknown author of *The Pursuits of Literature,* who, in respect to common tales of terror,

"boasts an English heart,
 Unused at ghosts or rattling bones to start,"

acknowledges, nevertheless, the legitimate character of Mrs. Radcliffe's art, and pays no mean tribute to her skill. Of some sister novelists he talks with slight regard.

> "Though all of them are ingenious ladies, yet they are too frequently whining and frisking in novels, till our girls' heads turn wild with impossible adventures; and now and then are tainted with democracy. Not so the mighty magician of *The Mysteries of Udolpho,* bred and nourished by the Florentine muses in their secret solitary caverns, amid the paler shrines of Gothic superstition, and in all the dreariness of enchantment; a poetess whom Ariosto would with rapture have acknowledged as,

> ——'La nudrita
> Damigella Trivulzia AL SACRO SPECO."—O. F. c. xlvi."

Mrs. Radcliffe was not made acquainted with this high compliment till long after the satire was published; and its value was enhanced by the author's general severity of judgment, and by his perfect acquaintance with the manners and language of Italy, in which she had laid her scene.

It is farther to be observed, that the same class of critics who ridiculed these romances as unnatural and improbable, were disposed to detract from the genius of the author, on account of the supposed facility of her task. Art or talent, they said, was not required to produce that sort of interest and emotion, which is perhaps, after all, more strongly excited by a vulgar legend of a village ghost, than by the high painting and laboured descriptions of Mrs. Radcliffe. But this criticism is not much better founded than the former. The feelings of suspense and awful attention which she excites, are awakened by means of springs which lie open indeed to the first touch, but which are peculiarly liable to be worn out by repeated pressure. The public soon, like Macbeth, become satiated with horrors, and indifferent to the strongest *stimuli* of that kind. It shows, therefore, the excellence and power of Mrs. Radcliffe's genius, that she was able three times to bring back her readers with fresh appetite to a banquet of the same description; while of her numerous imitators, who rang the changes upon old castles and forests, and "antres dire," scarcely one attracted attention, until Mr. Lewis published his *Monk,* several years after she had resigned her pen.

The materials of these celebrated romances, and the means employed in conducting the narrative, are all selected with a view to the author's primary object, of moving the reader by ideas of impending danger, hidden guilt, supernatural visitings,—by all that is terrible, in short, combined with much that is wonderful. For this purpose, her scenery is generally as gloomy as her tale, and her personages are those at whose frown that groom grows darker. She has uniformly (except in her first effort) selected for her place of action the south of Europe, where the human passions, like the weeds of the climate, are supposed to attain portentous growth under the fostering sun; which abounds with ruined monuments of antiquity, as well as the more massive remnants of the middle ages; and where feudal tyranny and Catholic superstition still continue to exercise their sway over the slave and bigot, and to indulge to the haughty lord, or more haughty priest, that sort of despotic power, the exercise of which seldom fails to deprave the heart, and disorder the judgment. These circumstances are skilfully selected, to give probability to events which could not, without great violation of truth, be represented as having taken place in England. Yet, even with the allowances which we make for foreign minds and manners, the unterminating succession of misfortunes which press upon the heroine, strikes us as unnatural. She is continually struggling with the tide of adversity, and hurried downwards by its torrent; and if any more gay description is occasionally introduced, it is only as a contrast, and not a relief, to the melancholy and gloomy tenor of the narrative.

In working upon the sensations of natural and superstitious fear, Mrs. Radcliffe has made much use of obscurity and suspense, the most fertile source, perhaps, of sublime emotion; for there are few dangers that do not become familiar to the firm mind, if they are presented to consideration as certainties, and in all their open and declared character; whilst, on the other hand, the bravest have shrunk from the dark and the doubtful. To break off the narrative, when it seemed at the point of becoming most interesting—to extinguish a lamp, just when a parchment containing some hideous secret ought to have been read—to exhibit shadowy forms and half-heard sounds of woe, are resources which Mrs. Radcliffe has employed with more effect than any other writer of romance. It must be confessed, that in order to bring about these situations, some art or contrivance, on the part of the author, is rather too visible. Her heroines voluntarily expose themselves to situations which in nature a lonely female would certainly have avoided.

They are too apt to choose the midnight hour for investigating the mysteries of a deserted chamber or secret passage, and generally are only supplied with an expiring lamp, when about to read the most interesting documents. The simplicity of the tale is thus somewhat injured—it is as if we witnessed a dressing up of the very phantom by which we are to be startled; and the imperfection, though redeemed by many beauties, did not escape the censure of criticism.

A principal characteristic of Mrs. Radcliffe's romances is the rule which the author imposed upon herself, that all the circumstances of her narrative, however mysterious, and apparently superhuman, were to be accounted for on natural principles, at the winding up of the story. It must be allowed, that this has not been done with uniform success, and that the author has been occasionally more successful in exciting interest and apprehension, than in giving either interest or dignity of explanation to the means she has made use of. Indeed, we have already noticed, as the torment of romance-writers, those necessary evils, the concluding chapters, when they must unravel the skein of adventures which they have been so industrious to perplex, and account for all the incidents which they have been at so much pains to render unaccountable. Were these great magicians, who deal in the wonderful and fearful, permitted to dismiss their spectres as they raise them, amidst the shadowy and indistinct light so favourable to the exhibition of phantasmagoria, without compelling them into broad daylight, the task were comparatively easy, and the fine fragment of *Sir Bertrand* might have rivals in that department. But the modern author is not permitted to escape in that way. We are told of a formal old judge before whom evidence was tendered, of the ghost of a murdered person having declared to a witness, that the prisoner at the bar was guilty: the judge admitted the evidence of the spirit to be excellent, but denied his right to be heard through the mouth of another, and ordered the spectre to be summoned into open court. The public of the current day deal as rigidly, in moving for a *quo warranto* to compel an explanation from the story-teller; and the author must either at once represent the knot as worthy of being severed by supernatural aid, and bring on the stage his actual fiend or ghost, or, like Mrs. Radcliffe, explain by natural agency the whole marvels of his story.

We have already, in some brief remarks on *The Castle of Otranto,* avowed some preference for the more simple mode, of boldly avowing the use of supernatural machinery. Ghosts and witches, and the whole tenets of superstition, having once, and at no late period, been matter of universal belief, warranted by legal authority, it would seem no great stretch upon the reader's credulity to require him, while reading of what his ancestors did, to credit for the time what those ancestors devoutly believed in. And yet, notwithstanding the success of Walpole and Maturin, (to whom we may add the author of *Forman,*) the management of such machinery must be acknowledged a task of a most delicate nature. "There is but one step," said Bonaparte, "betwixt the sublime and the ridiculous;" and in an age of universal incredulity, we must own it would require, at the present day, the support of the highest powers, to save the supernatural from slipping into the ludicrous. The *Incredulus odi* is a formidable objection.

There are some modern authors, indeed, who have endeavoured, ingeniously enough, to compound betwixt ancient faith and modern incredulity. They have exhibited phantoms, and narrated prophecies strangely accomplished, without giving a defined or absolute opinion, whether these are to be referred to supernatural agency, or whether the apparitions were produced (no uncommon case) by an overheated imagination, and the presages apparently verified by a casual, though singular, coincidence of circumstances. This is, however, an evasion of the difficulty, not a solution; and besides, it would be leading us too far from the present subject, to consider to what point the author of a fictitious narrative is bound by his charter to gratify the curiosity of the public, and whether, as a painter of actual life, he is not entitled to leave something in shade, when the natural course of events conceals so many incidents in total darkness. Perhaps, upon the whole, this is the most artful mode of terminating such a tale of wonder, as it forms the means of compounding with the taste of two different classes of readers; those who, like children, demand that each particular circumstance and incident of the narrative shall be fully accounted for; and the more imaginative class, who, resembling men that walk for pleasure through a moonlight landscape, are more teazed than edified by the intrusive minuteness with which some well-meaning companion disturbs their reveries, divesting stock and stone of the shadowy semblances in which fancy had dressed them, and pertinaciously restoring to them the ordinary forms and commonplace meanness of reality.

It may indeed be claimed as meritorious in Mrs. Radcliffe's mode of expounding her mysteries, that it is founded in possibilities. Many situations have occurred, highly tinctured with romantic incident and feeling, the mysterious obscurity of which has afterwards been explained by deception and confederacy. Such have been the impostures of superstition in all ages, and such delusions were also practised by the members of the Secret Tribunal, in the middle ages, and in more modern times by the Rosicrucians and Illuminati, upon whose machinations Schiller has founded the fine romance of *The Ghost-Seer*. But Mrs. Radcliffe has not had recourse to so artificial a solution. Her heroines often sustain the agony of fear, and her readers that of suspense, from incidents which, when explained, appear of an ordinary and trivial nature; and in this we do not greatly applaud her art. A stealthy step behind the arras, may doubtless, in some situations, and when the nerves are tuned to a certain pitch, have no small influence upon the imagination; but if the conscious listener discovers it to be only the noise made by the cat, the solemnity of the feeling is gone, and the visionary is at once angry with his senses for having been cheated, and with his reason for having acquiesced in the deception.[12] We fear that some such feeling of disappointment and displeasure attends most readers, when they read for the first time the unsatisfactory solution of the mysteries of the black pall and the wax figure, which has been adjourned from chapter to chapter, like something suppressed, because too horrible for the ear.

There is a separate inconvenience attending a narrative where the imagination has been long kept in suspense, and is at length imperfectly gratified by an explanation falling short of what the reader has expected; for, in such a case, the interest terminates on the first reading of the volumes, and cannot, so far as it rests upon a high degree of excitation, be recalled upon a second perusal. A plan of narrative, happily complicated and ingeniously resolved, continues to please after many readings; for, although the interest of eager curiosity is no more, it is supplied by the rational pleasure, which admires the author's art, and traces a thousand minute passages, which render the catastrophe probable, yet escape notice in the eagerness of a first perusal. But it is otherwise, when some inadequate cause is assigned for a strong emotion; the reader feels tricked, and as in the case of a child who

12. By a singular coincidence, the late lamented author of *Don Juan* has introduced this very idea into the last canto of that poem.

has once seen the scenes of a theatre too nearly, the idea of pasteboard, cords, and pullies, destroys for ever the illusion with which they were first seen from the proper point of view. Such are the difficulties and dilemmas which attend the path of the professed story-teller, who, while it is expected of him that his narrative should be interesting and extraordinary, is neither permitted to explain its wonders, by referring them to ordinary causes, on account of their triteness, nor to supernatural agency, because of its incredibility. It is no wonder that, hemmed in by rules so strict, Mrs. Radcliffe, a mistress of the art of exciting curiosity, has not been uniformly fortunate in the mode of gratifying it.

The best and most admired specimen of her art is the mysterious disappearance of Ludovico, after having undertaken to watch for a night in a haunted apartment; and the mind of the reader is finely wound up for some strange catastrophe, by the admirable ghost-story which he is represented as perusing to amuse his solitude, as the scene closes upon him. Neither can it be denied, that the explanation afforded of this mysterious incident is as probable as romance requires, and in itself completely satisfactory. As this is perhaps the most favourable example of Mrs. Radcliffe's peculiar skill in composition, the incidents of the black veil and the waxen figure, may be considered as instances where the explanation falls short of expectation, and disappoints the reader entirely. On the other hand, her art is at once, according to the classical precept, exerted and concealed in the beautiful and impressive passage, where the Marchesa is in the choir of the convent of San Nicolo, contriving with the atrocious Schedoni the murder of Ellena.

> "'Avoid violence, if that be possible,' she added, immediately comprehending him, 'but let her die quickly! The punishment is due to the crime.'
>
> "The Marchesa happened, as she said this, to cast her eyes upon the inscription over a confessional, where appeared, in black letters, these awful words, 'GOD *hears thee!'* It appeared an awful warning; her countenance changed; it had struck upon her heart. Schedoni was too much engaged by his own thoughts to observe, or understand her silence. She soon recovered herself; and, considering that this was a common inscription for confessionals, disregarded what she had at first considered as a peculiar admonition; yet some moments elapsed before she could renew the subject.

"'You were speaking of a place, father,' resumed the Marchesa—'you mentioned a—'

"'Ay,' muttered the confessor, still musing—'in a chamber of that house there is—'

"'What noise is that?' said the Marchesa, interrupting him. They listened. A few low and querulous notes of the organ sounded at a distance, and stopped again.

"'What mournful music is that?' said the Marchesa, in a faltering voice; 'it was touched by a fearful hand! Vespers were over long ago?'

"'Daughter,' said Schedoni, somewhat sternly, 'you said you had a man's courage. Alas! you have a woman's heart.'

"'Excuse me, father; I know not why I feel this agitation, but I will command it.—That chamber?'

"'In that chamber,' resumed the confessor, 'is a secret door, constructed long ago.'

"'And for what purpose constructed?' said the fearful Marchesa.

"'Pardon me, daughter; 'tis sufficient that it is there; we will make a good use of it. Through that door—in the night—when she sleeps—'

"'I comprehend you,' said the Marchesa, 'I comprehend you. But why,—you have your reasons, no doubt,—but why the necessity of a secret door in a house which you say is so lonely—inhabited by only one person?'

"'A passage leads to the sea,' continued Schedoni, without replying to the question. 'There, on the shore, when darkness covers it; there, plunged amidst the waves, no stain shall hint of—'

"'Hark!' interrupted the Marchesa, starting, 'that note again!'

"The organ sounded faintly from the choir, and paused, as before. In the next moment, a slow chanting of voices was heard, mingling with the rising peal, in a strain particularly melancholy and solemn.

"'Who is dead?' said the Marchesa, changing countenance: 'it is a requiem!'

"'Peace be with the departed!' exclaimed Schedoni, and crossed himself; 'peace rest with his soul!'

"'Hark! to that chant,' said the Marchesa, in a trembling voice; 'it is a first requiem; the soul has but just quitted the body!'

"They listened in silence. The Marchesa was much affected; her complexion varied at every instant; her breathings were short and interrupted, and she even shed a few tears, but they were those of despair, rather than of sorrow."

Mrs. Radcliffe's powers, both of language and description, have been justly estimated very highly. They bear, at the same time, considerable marks of that warm, and somewhat exuberant imagination, which dictated her works. Some artists are distinguished by precision and correctness of outline, others by the force and vividness of their colouring; and it is to the latter class that this author belongs. The landscapes of Mrs. Radcliffe are far from equal in accuracy and truth to those of her contemporary, Mrs. Charlotte Smith, whose sketches are so very graphical, that an artist would find little difficulty in actually painting from them. Those of Mrs. Radcliffe, on the contrary, while they would supply the most noble and vigorous ideas, for producing a general effect, would leave the task of tracing a distinct and accurate outline to the imagination of the painter. As her story is usually enveloped in mystery, so there is, as it were, a haze over her landscapes, softening indeed the whole, and adding interest and dignity to particular parts, and thereby producing every effect which the author desired, but without communicating any absolutely precise or individual image to the reader. The beautiful description of the Castle of Udolpho, upon Emily's first approach to it, is of this character. It affords a noble subject for the pencil: but were six artists to attempt to embody it upon canvass, they would probably produce six drawings entirely dissimilar to each other, yet all of them equally authorized by the printed description, which, although a long one, is so beautiful a specimen of Mrs. Radcliffe's peculiar talents, that we do not hesitate to insert it.

"Towards the close of the day, the road wound into a deep valley. Mountains, whose shaggy steeps appeared to be inaccessible, almost surrounded it. To the east, a vista opened, and exhibited the Apennines in their darkest horrors; and the long perspective of retiring summits rising over each other, their ridges clothed with pines, exhibited a stronger image of grandeur, than any that Emily had yet seen. The sun had just sunk below the top of the mountains she was descending, whose long shadow stretched athwart the valley, but his sloping rays, shooting through an opening of the cliffs, touched with a yellow gleam the summits of the forest that hung upon the opposite steeps, and streamed in full splendour upon the towers and battlements of a castle that spread its extensive ramparts along the brow of a precipice above. The splendour of these illumined objects was heightened by the contrasted shade which involved the valley below.

"'There,' said Montoni, speaking for the first time in several hours, 'is Udolpho.'

"Emily gazed with melancholy awe upon the castle, which she understood to be Montoni's; for, though it was now lighted up by the setting sun, the Gothic greatness of its features, and its mouldering walls of dark grey stone, rendered it a gloomy and sublime object. As she gazed, the light died away on its walls, leaving a melancholy purple tint, which spread deeper and deeper, as the thin vapour crept up the mountain, while the battlements above were still tipped with splendour. From these, too, the rays soon faded, and the whole edifice was invested with the solemn duskiness of evening. Silent, lonely, and sublime, it seemed to stand the sovereign of the scene, and to frown defiance on all who dared to invade its solitary reign. As the twilight deepened, its features became more awful in obscurity, and Emily continued to gaze, till its clustering towers were alone seen rising over the tops of the woods, beneath whose thick shade the carriages soon after began to ascend.

"The extent and darkness of these tall woods awakened terrific images in her mind, and she almost expected to see banditti start up from under the trees. At length the carriages emerged upon a heathy rock, and soon after reached the castle gates, where the deep tone of the portal bell, which was struck upon to give notice of their arrival, increased the fearful emotions that had assailed Emily. While they waited till the servant within should come to open the gates, she anxiously surveyed the edifice; but the gloom that overspread it, allowed her to distinguish little more than a part of its outline, with the massy walls of the ramparts, and to know that it was vast, ancient, and dreary. From the parts she saw, she judged of the heavy strength and extent of the whole. The gateway before her, leading into the courts, was of gigantic size, and was defended by two round towers, crowned by overhanging turrets, embattled, where, instead of banners, now waved long grass and wild plants, that had taken root among the mouldering stones, and which seemed to sigh, as the breeze rolled past, over the desolation around them. The towers were united by a curtain, pierced and embattled also, below which appeared the pointed arch of a huge portcullis, surmounting the gates: from these, the walls of the ramparts extended to other towers, overlooking the precipice, whose shattered outline, appearing on a gleam that lingered in the west, told of the ravages of war.—Beyond these all was lost in the obscurity of evening."

We think it interesting to compare this splendid and beautiful fancy-picture with the precision displayed by the same author's pencil, when she was actually engaged in copying nature, and probably the reader will be of opinion, that *Udolpho* is an exquisite effect-piece, *Hardwick* a striking and faithful portrait.

"Northward, beyond London, we may make one stop, after a country, not otherwise necessary to be noticed, to mention Hardwick, in Derbyshire, a seat of the Duke of Devonshire, once the residence of the Earl of Shrewsbury, to whom Elizabeth deputed the custody of the unfortunate Mary. It stands on an easy height, a few miles to the left of the road from Mansfield to Chesterfield, and is approached through shady lanes, which conceal the view of it, till you are on the confines of the park. Three towers of hoary grey then rise with great majesty among old woods, and their summits appear to be covered with the lightly shivered fragments of battlements, which, however, are soon discovered to be perfectly carved open work, in which the letters E. S. frequently occur under a coronet, the initials, and the memorials of the vanity, of Elizabeth, Countess of Shrewsbury, who built the present edifice. Its tall features, of a most picturesque tint, were finely disclosed between the luxuriant woods and over the lawns of the park, which every now and then let in a glimpse of the Derbyshire hills. The scenery reminded us of the exquisite descriptions of Harewood.

"The deep embowering shades that veil Elfrida and those of Hardwick, once veiled a form as lovely as the ideal graces of the poet, and conspired to a fate more tragical than that which Harewood witnessed.

"In front of the great gates of the castle court, the ground, adorned by old oaks, suddenly sinks to a darkly shadowed glade, and the view opens over the vale of Scarsdale, bounded by the wild mountains of the Peak. Immediately to the left of the present residence, some ruined features of the ancient one, enwreathed with the rich drapery of ivy, give an interest to the scene, which the later, but more historical structure, heightens and prolongs. We followed, not without emotion, the walk which Mary had so often trodden, to the folding-doors of the great hall, whose lofty grandeur, aided by silence, and seen under the influence of a lowering sky, suited the temper of the whole scene. The tall windows, which half subdue the light they admit, just allowed us to distinguish the large figures in the tapestry, above the oak wainscoting, and showed a colonnade of oak supporting a gallery along the bottom of the hall, with a pair of gigantic elk's horns flourishing between the windows opposite to the entrance. The scene of Mary's arrival, and her feelings upon entering this solemn shade, came involuntarily to the mind; the noise of horses' feet, and many voices from the court; her proud, yet gentle and melancholy look, as, led by my Lord Keeper, she passed slowly up the hall; his somewhat obsequious, yet jealous and vigilant air, while, awed by her dignity and beauty, he remembers the terrors of his own queen; the silence and anxiety of her maids, and the bustle of the surrounding attendants.

"From the hall, a staircase ascends to the gallery of a small chapel, in which the chairs and the cushions used by Mary still remain, and proceeds to the first story, where only one apartment bears memorials of her imprisonment,—the bed, tapestry, and chairs having been worked by herself. This tapestry is richly embossed with emblematic figures, each with its title worked above it, and, having been scrupulously preserved, is still entire and fresh.

"Over the chimney of an adjoining dining-room, to which, as well as to other apartments on this floor, some modern furniture has been added, is this motto carved in oak:—

"'There is only this: To fear God, and keep his Commandments.' So much less valuable was timber than workmanship, when this mansion was constructed, that, where the staircases are not of stone, they are formed of solid oaken steps, instead of planks; such is that from the second, or state story, to the roof, whence, on clear days, York and Lincoln Cathedrals are said to be included in the extensive prospect. This second floor is that which gives its chief interest to the edifice. Nearly all the apartments of it were allotted to Mary; some of them for state purposes; and the furniture is known by other proof than its appearance, to remain as she left it. The chief room, or that of audience, is of uncommon loftiness, and strikes by its grandeur, before the veneration and tenderness arise, which its antiquities, and the plainly told tale of the sufferings they witnessed, excite."[13]

The contrast of these two descriptions will satisfy the reader, that Mrs. Radcliffe knew as well how to copy nature, as when to indulge imagination. The towers of Udolpho are undefined, boundless, and wreathed in mist and obscurity; the ruins of Hardwick are as fully and boldly painted, but with more exactness of outline, and perhaps less warmth and magnificence of colouring.

It is singular, that though Mrs. Radcliffe's beautiful descriptions of foreign scenery, composed solely from the materials afforded by travellers,

---

13. *Journey through Holland and the Western Frontier of Germany, with a Return down the Rhine. To which are added, Observations during a Tour to the Lakes of Lancashire, Westmoreland, and Cumberland.* By Ann Radcliffe. 4to, 1795. Page 371.

collected and embodied by her own genius, were marked in a particular degree (to our thinking at least) with the characteristics of fancy-portraits; yet many of her contemporaries conceived them to be exact descriptions of scenes which she had visited in person. One report, transmitted to the public by the *Edinburgh Review,* stated, that Mr. and Mrs. Radcliffe had visited Italy; that Mr. Radcliffe had been attached to one of the British Embassies in that country; and that it was there his gifted consort imbibed the taste for picturesque scenery, for mouldering ruins, and for the obscure and gloomy anecdotes which tradition relates of their former inhabitants. This is so far a mistake, as Mrs. Radcliffe never was in Italy; but we have already mentioned the probability of her having availed herself of the acquaintance she formed in 1793 with the magnificent scenery on the banks of the Rhine, and the frowning remains of feudal castles with which it abounds. The inaccuracy of the reviewer is of no great consequence; but a more absurd report found its way into print, namely, that Mrs. Radcliffe, having visited the fine old Gothic mansion of Haddon House, had insisted upon remaining a night there, in the course of which she had been inspired with all that enthusiasm for Gothic residences, hidden passages, and mouldering walls, which marks her writings. Mrs. Radcliffe, we are assured, never saw Haddon House; and although it was a place excellently worth her attention, and could hardly have been seen by her without suggesting some of those ideas in which her imagination naturally revelled, yet we should suppose the mechanical aid to invention—the recipe for fine writing—the sleeping in a dismantled and unfurnished old house, was likely to be rewarded with nothing but a cold, and was an affectation of enthusiasm to which Mrs. Radcliffe would have disdained to have recourse.

The warmth of imagination which Mrs. Radcliffe manifests, was naturally connected with an inclination towards poetry, and accordingly songs, sonnets, and pieces of fugitive verse, amuse and relieve the reader in the course of her volumes. These are not, in this place, the legitimate subject of criticism; but it may be remarked, that they display more liveliness and richness of fancy, than correctness of taste, or felicity of expression. The language does not become pliant in Mrs. Radcliffe's hands; and, unconscious of this defect, she has attempted, nevertheless, to bend it into new structures of verse, for which the English is not adapted. The song of the glow-worm is an experiment of this nature. It must also be allowed, that the imagination

of the author sometimes carries her on too fast, and that if she herself
formed a competent and perfect idea of what she meant to express, she has
sometimes failed to convey it to the reader. At other and happier times, her
poetry partakes of the rich and beautiful colouring which distinguishes her
prose composition, and has, perhaps, the same fault, of not being in every
case quite precise in expressing the meaning of the author. The following address to Melancholy may be fairly selected as a specimen of her powers.

"Spirit of love and sorrow—hail!
    Thy solemn voice from far I hear,
Mingling with evening's dying gale:
    Hail, with this sadly-pleasing tear!

"O! at this still, this lonely hour,
    Thine own sweet hour of closing day,
Awake thy lute, whose charmful power
    Shall call up fancy to obey;

"To paint the wild romantic dream,
    That meets the poet's musing eye,
As on the bank of shadowy stream
    He breathes to her the fervid sigh.

"O lonely spirit! let thy song
    Lead me through all thy sacred haunt;
The minster's moonlight aisles along,
    Where spectres raise the midnight chaunt.

"I hear their dirges faintly swell!
    Then, sink at once in silence drear,
While, from the pillar'd cloister's cell,
    Dimly their gliding forms appear!

"Lead where the pine-woods wave on high,
    Whose pathless sod is darkly seen,
As the cold moon, with trembling eye,
    Darts her long beams the leaves between.

"Lead to the mountain's dusky head,
        Where, far below, in shades profound,
Wide forests, plains, and hamlets spread,
        And sad the chimes of vesper sound.

"Or guide me where the dashing oar
        Just breaks the stillness of the vale,
As slow it tracks the winding shore,
        To meet the ocean's distant sail:

"To pebbly banks that Neptune laves,
        With measured surges, loud and deep,
Where the dark cliff bends o'er the waves,
        And wild the winds of autumn sweep.

"There pause at midnight's spectred hour,
        And list the long-resounding gale;
And catch the fleeting moonlight's power,
        O'er foaming seas and distant sail."

It cannot, we think, be denied, that we have here beautiful ideas expressed in appropriate versification; yet here, as in her prose compositions, the poetess is too much busied with external objects, too anxious to describe the outward accompaniments of melancholy, to write upon the feeling itself; and although the comparison be made at the expense of a favourite author, we cannot help contrasting the poetry we have just inserted, with a song, by Fletcher, on a similar subject.

    PAS. (*Sings.*)
        "Hence, all you vain delights,
            As short as are the nights
                Wherein you spend your folly!
            There's nought in this life sweet,
            If man were wise to see't,
                But only melancholy!

        Welcome, folded arms, and fixed eyes,
            A sigh that piercing mortifies,

A look that's fasten'd to the ground,
A tongue chain'd up without a sound!
Fountain heads, and pathless groves,
Places which pale passion loves!
Moonlight walks, when all the fowls
Are warmly housed, save bats and owls!
A midnight bell, a parting groan!
These are the sounds we feed upon;
Then stretch our bones in a still gloomy valley,
Nothing's so dainty sweet as lovely melancholy."
The Nice Valour.

In these last verses the reader may observe, that the human feeling of the votary of melancholy, or rather the pale passion itself, is predominant; that our thoughts are of, and with, the pensive wanderer; and that the "fountain heads and pathless groves," like the landscape in a portrait, are only secondary parts of the picture. In Mrs. Radcliffe's verses, it is different. The accessaries and accompaniments of melancholy are well described, but they call for so much of our attention, that the feeling itself scarce solicits due regard. We are placed among melancholy objects, but our sadness is reflected from the scene, it is not the growth of our own minds. Something like this may be observed in Mrs. Radcliffe's romances, where our curiosity is too much interested about the evolution of the story, to permit our feelings to be acted upon by the distresses of the hero or heroine. We do not acknowledge them as personal objects of our interest, and, convinced that the authoress will extricate them from their embarrassments, we are more concerned about the course of the story, than the feelings or fate of those of whom it is told.

But we must not take farewell of a favourite author with a depreciating sentiment. It may be true, that Mrs. Radcliffe rather walks in fairy-land than in the region of realities, and that she has neither displayed the command of the human passions, nor the insight into the human heart, nor the observation of life and manners, which recommend other authors in the same line. But she has taken the lead in a line of composition, appealing to those powerful and general sources of interest, a latent sense of supernatural awe, and curiosity concerning whatever is hidden and mysterious; and if she has been ever nearly approached in this walk, which we should hesitate to affirm, it is at least certain that she has never been excelled or even equalled.

We have been given to understand, we trust from good authority, that a posthumous work of Mrs. Radcliffe's is likely soon to make its appearance. Come when it will, and contain almost what it may, it must be an acquisition to the public of no common interest.

On the Supernatural in Fictitious Composition

1. Hoffmann's *Leben und Nachlass.* 2 vols. Berlin, 1823.
2. Hoffmann's *Scrapions-brüder.* 6 vols. 1819–26.
3. Hoffmann's *Nachtstücke.* 2 vols. 1816.

No source of romantic fiction, and no mode of exciting the feelings of interest which the authors in that description of literature desire to produce, seems more directly accessible than the love of the supernatural. It is common to all classes of mankind, and perhaps is to none so familiar as to those who assume a certain degree of scepticism on the subject; since the reader may have often observed in conversation, that the person who professes himself most incredulous on the subject of marvellous stories, often ends his remarks by indulging the company with some well-attested anecdote, which it is difficult or impossible to account for on the narrator's own principles of absolute scepticism. The belief itself, though easily capable of being pushed into superstition and absurdity, has its origin not only in the facts upon which our holy religion is founded, but upon the principles of our nature, which teach us that while we are probationers in this sublunary state, we are neighbours to, and encompassed by the shadowy world, of which our mental faculties are too obscure to comprehend the laws, our corporeal organs too coarse and gross to perceive the inhabitants.

All professors of the Christian Religion believe that there was a time when the Divine Power showed itself more visibly on earth than in these our latter days; controlling and suspending, for its own purposes, the ordinary laws of the universe; and the Roman Catholic Church, at least, holds it as an article of faith, that miracles descend to the present time. Without entering into that controversy, it is enough that a firm belief in the great truths of our religion has induced wise and good men, even in Protestant countries, to subscribe to Dr. Johnson's doubts respecting supernatural appearances.

"That the dead are seen no more, said Imlac, I will not undertake to maintain against the concurrent and unvaried testimony of all ages, and of all nations. There is no people, rude or learned, among whom apparitions of the dead are not related and believed. This opinion, which perhaps prevails as far as human nature is diffused, could become universal only by its truth; those that never heard of one another could not have agreed in a tale which nothing but experience can make credible. That it is doubted by single cavillers, can very little weaken the general evidence; and some who deny it with their tongues, confess it by their fears."

Upon such principles as these there lingers in the breasts even of philosophers, a reluctance to decide dogmatically upon a point where they do not and cannot possess any, save negative, evidence. Yet this inclination to believe in the marvellous gradually becomes weaker. Men cannot but remark that (since the scriptural miracles have ceased,) the belief in prodigies and supernatural events has gradually declined in proportion to the advancement of human knowledge; and that since the age has become enlightened, the occurrence of tolerably well attested anecdotes of the supernatural character are so few, as to render it more probable that the witnesses have laboured under some strange and temporary delusion, rather than that the laws of nature have been altered or suspended. At this period of human knowledge, the marvellous is so much identified with fabulous, as to be considered generally as belonging to the same class.

It is not so in early history, which is full of supernatural incidents; and although we now use the word *romance* as synonymous with fictitious composition, yet as it originally only meant a poem, or prose work contained in the Romaunce language, there is little doubt that the doughty chivalry who listened to the songs of the minstrel, "held each strange tale devoutly true," and that the feats of knighthood which he recounted, mingled with tales of magic and supernatural interference, were esteemed as veracious as the legends of the monks, to which they bore a strong resemblance. This period of society, however, must have long past before the Romancer began to select, and arrange with care, the nature of the materials out of which he constructed his story. It was not when society, however differing in degree and station, was levelled and confounded by one dark cloud of ignorance, involving the noble as well as the mean, that it need be scrupulously considered to what class of persons the author addressed himself, or with what species of decoration he ornamented his story. "Homo was then a common name for all men," and all were equally pleased with the same style of composition. This, however, was gradually altered. As the knowledge to which we have before alluded made more general progress, it became impossible to detain the attention of the better instructed class by the simple and gross fables to which the present generation would only listen in childhood, though they had been held in honour by their fathers during youth, manhood, and old age.

It was also discovered that the supernatural in fictitious composition requires to be managed with considerable delicacy, as criticism begins to be more on the alert. The interest which it excites is indeed a powerful spring; but it is one which is peculiarly subject to be exhausted by coarse handling and repeated pressure. It is also of a character which it is extremely difficult to sustain, and of which a very small proportion may be said to be better than the whole. The marvellous, more than any other attribute of fictitious narrative, loses its effect by being brought much into view. The imagination of the reader is to be excited if possible, without being gratified. If once, like Macbeth, we "sup full with horrors," our taste for the banquet is ended, and the thrill of terror with which we hear or read of a night-shriek, becomes lost in that sated indifference with which the tyrant came at length to listen to the most deep catastrophes that could affect his house. The incidents of a supernatural character are usually those of a dark and undefinable nature, such as arise in the mind of the Lady in the Mask of Comus,— incidents to which our fears attach more consequence, as we cannot exactly tell what it is we behold, or what is to be apprehended from it:—

> "A thousand fantasies
> Begin to throng into my memory,
> Of calling shapes and beck'ning shadows dire,
> And aery tongues that syllable men's names
> On sands, and shores, and desart wildernesses."

Burke observes upon obscurity, that it is necessary to make anything terrible, and notices "how much the notions of ghosts and goblins, of which none can form clear ideas, affect minds which give credit to the popular tales concerning such sorts of beings." He represents also, that no person "seems better to have understood the secret of heightening, or of setting terrible things in their strongest light, by the force of a judicious obscurity, than Milton. His description of Death, in the second book, is admirably studied; it is astonishing with what a gloomy pomp, with what a significant and expressive uncertainty of strokes and colouring, he has finished the portrait of the king of terrors.

> 'The other shape,—
> If shape it might be called, which shape had none
> Distinguishable in member, joint, or limb:
> Or substance might be called that shadow seemed,—
> For each seemed either; black he stood as night;
> Fierce as ten furies; terrible as hell;
> And shook a deadly dart. What seemed his head
> The likeness of a kingly crown had on.'

In this description all is dark, uncertain, confused, terrible and sublime to the last degree."

The only quotation worthy to be mentioned along with the passage we have just taken down, is the well-known apparition introduced with circumstances of terrific obscurity in the book of Job:—

"Now a thing was secretly brought to me, and mine ears received a little thereof. In thoughts from the visions of the night, when deep sleep falleth on men, fear came upon me, and trembling which made all my bones to shake. Then a spirit passed before my face: the hair of my flesh stood up. It stood still, but I could not discern the form thereof: an image was before mine eyes; there was silence, and I heard a voice."

From these sublime and decisive authorities, it is evident that the exhibition of supernatural appearances in fictitious narrative ought to be rare, brief, indistinct, and such as may become a being to us so incomprehensible, and so different from ourselves, of whom we cannot justly conjecture whence he comes, or for what purpose, and of whose attributes we can have no regular or distinct perception. Hence it usually happens, that the first touch of the supernatural is always the most effective, and is rather weakened and defaced, than strengthened, by the subsequent recurrence of similar incidents. Even in Hamlet, the second entrance of the ghost is not nearly so impressive as the first; and in many romances to which we could refer, the supernatural being forfeits all claim both to our terror and veneration, by condescending to appear too often; to mingle too much in the events of the story, and above all, to become loquacious, or, as it is familiarly called, *chatty.* We have, indeed, great doubts whether an author acts wisely in permitting his goblin to speak at all, if at the same time he renders him subject to human sight. Shakspeare, indeed, has contrived to put such language in the mouth of the buried majesty of Denmark, as befits a supernatural being, and is by the style distinctly different from that of the living persons in the drama. In another passage he has had the boldness to intimate, by two expressions of similar force, in what manner and with what tone supernatural beings would find utterance:

> "And the sheeted dead
>   Did *squeak* and *gibber* in the Roman streets."

But the attempt in which the genius of Shakspeare has succeeded would probably have been ridiculous in any meaner hand; and hence it is, that, in many of our modern tales of terror, our feelings of fear have, long before the conclusion, given way under the influence of that familiarity which begets contempt.

A sense that the effect of the supernatural in its more obvious application is easily exhausted, has occasioned the efforts of modern authors to cut new walks and avenues through the enchanted wood, and to revive, if possible, by some means or other, the fading impression of its horrors.

The most obvious and inartificial mode of attaining this end is, by adding to, and exaggerating the supernatural incidents of the tale. But far from increasing its effect, the principles which we have laid down, incline us to consider the impression as usually weakened by exaggerated and laborious description. Elegance is in such cases thrown away, and the accumulation of superlatives, with which the narrative is encumbered, renders it tedious, or perhaps ludicrous, instead of becoming impressive or grand.

There is indeed one style of composition, of which the supernatural forms an appropriate part, which applies itself rather to the fancy than to the imagination, and aims more at amusing than at affecting or interesting the reader. To this species of composition belong the eastern tales, which contribute so much to the amusement of our youth, and which are recollected, if not reperused, with so much pleasure in our more advanced life. There are but few readers of any imagination who have not at one time or other in their life sympathized with the poet Collins, "who," says Dr. Johnson, "was eminently delighted with those flights of imagination, which pass the bounds of nature, and to which the mind is reconciled only by a passive acquiescence in popular traditions. He loved fairies, genii, giants, and monsters; he delighted to rove through the meadows of enchantment, to gaze on the magnificence of golden palaces, to repose by the waterfalls of Elysian gardens." It is chiefly the young and the indolent who love to be soothed by works of this character, which require little attention in the perusal. In our riper age we remember them as we do the joys of our infancy, rather because we loved them once, than that they still continue to afford us amusement. The extravagance of fiction loses its charms for our riper judgment; and notwithstanding that these wild fictions contain much that is beautiful and full of fancy, yet still, unconnected as they are with each other, and conveying no result to the understanding, we pass them by as the championess Britomart rode along the rich strand.

> Which as she overwent,
> She saw bestrewed all with rich array
> Of pearls and precious stones of great assay,
> And all the gravel mixt with golden ore:
> Whereat she wondered much, but would not stay
> For gold, or pearls, or precious stones, one hour;
> But them despised all, for all was in her power.

With this class of supernatural composition may be ranked, though inferior in interest, what the French call *Contes des Fées;* meaning, by that title, to distinguish them from the ordinary popular tales of fairy folks which are current in most countries. The *Conte des Fées* is itself a very different composition, and the fairies engaged are of a separate class from those whose amusement is to dance round the mushroom in the moonlight, and mislead the belated peasant. The French *Fée* more nearly resembles the Peri of Eastern, or the Fata of Italian poetry. She is a superior being, having the nature of an elementary spirit, and possessing magical powers enabling her, to a considerable extent, to work either good or evil. But whatever merit this species of writing may have attained in some dexterous hands, it has, under the management of others, become one of the most absurd, flat, and insipid possible. Out of the whole *Cabinet des Fées,* when we get beyond our old acquaintances of the nursery, we can hardly select five volumes, from nearly fifty, with any probability of receiving pleasure from them.

It often happens that when any particular style becomes somewhat antiquated and obsolete, some caricature, or satirical imitation of it, gives rise to a new species of composition. Thus the English Opera arose from the parody upon the Italian stage, designed by Gay, in the Beggar's Opera. In like manner, when the public had been inundated, *ad nauseam,* with Arabian tales, Persian tales, Turkish tales, Mogul tales, and legends of every nation east of the Bosphorus, and were equally annoyed by the increasing publication of all sorts of fairy tales,—Count Anthony Hamilton, like a second Cervantes, came forth with his satirical tales, destined to overturn the empire of Dives, of Genii, of Peris, *et hoc genus omne.*

Something too licentious for a more refined age, the Tales of Count Hamilton subsist as a beautiful illustration, showing that literary subjects, as well as the fields of the husbandman, may, when they seem most worn out and effete, be renewed and again brought into successful cultivation by a new course of management. The wit of Count Hamilton, like manure applied to an exhausted field, rendered the eastern tale more piquant, if not more edifying, than it was before. Much was written in imitation of Count Hamilton's style; and it was followed by Voltaire in particular, who in this way rendered the supernatural romance one of the most apt vehicles for circulating his satire. This, therefore, may be termed the comic side of the supernatural, in which the author plainly declares his purpose to turn into jest the miracles which he relates, and aspires to awaken ludicrous sensations without affecting the fancy—far less exciting the passions of the reader. By this species of delineation the reader will perceive that the supernatural style of writing is entirely travestied and held up to laughter, instead of being made the subject of respectful attention, or heard with at least that sort of imperfect excitement with which we listened to a marvellous tale of fairyland. This species of satire—for it is often converted to satirical purposes—has never been more happily executed than by the French authors, although Wieland, and several other German writers, treading in the steps of Hamilton, have added the grace of poetry to the wit and to the wonders with which they have adorned this species of composition. Oberon, in particular, has been identified with our literature by the excellent translation of Mr. Sotheby, and is nearly as well known in England as in Germany. It would, however, carry us far too wide from our present purpose, were we to consider the comi-heroic poetry which belongs to this class, and which includes the well-known works of Pulci, Berni—perhaps, in a certain degree, of Ariosto himself, who, in some passages at least, lifts his knightly visor so far as to give a momentary glimpse of the smile which mantles upon his countenance.

One general glance at the geography of this most pleasing "Londe of Faery," leads us into another province, rough as it may seem and uncultivated, but which, perhaps, on that very account, has some scenes abounding in interest. There are a species of antiquarians who, while others laboured to re-unite and ornament highly the ancient traditions of their country, have made it their business, *antiquos accedere fontes,* to visit the ancient springs and sources of those popular legends which, cherished by the grey and superstitious Elde, had been long forgotten in the higher circles, but are again brought forward and claim, like the old ballads of a country, a degree of interest even from their rugged simplicity. The Deutsche Sagen of the brothers Grimm, is an admirable work of this kind; assembling, without any affectation either of ornamental diction or improved incident, the various traditions existing in different parts of Germany respecting popular superstitions and the events ascribed to supernatural agency. There are other works of the same kind, in the same language, collected with great care and apparent fidelity. Sometimes trite, sometimes tiresome, sometimes childish, the legends which these authors have collected with such indefatigable zeal form nevertheless a step in the history of the human race; and, when compared with similar collections in other countries, seem to infer traces of a common descent which has placed one general stock of superstition within reach of the various tribes of mankind. What are we to think when we find the Jutt and the Fin telling their children the same traditions which are to be found in the nurseries of the Spaniard and Italian; or when we recognize in our own instance the traditions of Ireland or Scotland as corresponding with those of Russia? Are we to suppose that their similarity arises from the limited nature of human invention, and that the same species of fiction occurs to the imaginations of different authors in remote countries as the same species of plants are found in different regions without the possibility of their having been propagated by transportation from the one to others? Or ought we, rather, to refer them to a common source, when mankind formed but the same great family, and suppose that as philologists trace through various dialects the broken fragments of one general language, so antiquaries may recognize in distant countries parts of what was once a common stock of tradition? We will not pause on this inquiry, nor observe more than generally that, in collecting these traditions, the industrious editors have been throwing light, not only on the history of their own country in particular, but on that of mankind in general. There is generally some truth mingled with the abundant falsehood, and still more abundant exaggeration of the oral legend; and it may be frequently and unexpectedly found to confirm or confute the meagre statement of some ancient chronicle. Often, too, the legend of the common people, by assigning peculiar features, localities, and specialities to the incidents which it holds in memory, gives life and spirit to the frigid and dry narrative which tells the fact alone, without the particulars which render it memorable or interesting.

It is, however, in another point of view, that we wish to consider those popular traditions in their collected state: namely, as a peculiar mode of exhibiting the marvellous and supernatural in composition. And here we must acknowledge, that he who peruses a large collection of stories of fiends, ghosts, and prodigies, in hopes of exciting in his mind that degree of shuddering interest approaching to fear, which is the most valuable triumph of the supernatural, is likely to be disappointed. A whole collection of ghost stories inclines us as little to fear as a jest book moves us to laughter. Many narratives, turning upon the same interest, are apt to exhaust it: as in a large collection of pictures an ordinary eye is so dazzled with the variety of brilliant or glowing colours as to become less able to distinguish the merit of those pieces which are possessed of any.

But notwithstanding this great disadvantage, which is inseparable from the species of publication we are considering, a reader of imagination, who has the power to emancipate himself from the chains of reality, and to produce in his own mind the accompaniments with which the simple or rude popular legend ought to be attended, will often find that it possesses points of interest, of nature, and of effect, which, though irreconcilable to sober truth, carry with them something that the mind is not averse to believe, something in short of plausibility, which, let poet or romancer do their very best, they find it impossible to attain to. An example may, in a case of this sort, be more amusing to the reader than mere disquisition, and we select one from a letter received many years since from an amiable and accomplished nobleman some time deceased, not more distinguished for his love of science, than his attachment to literature in all its branches:—

"It was in the night of, I think, the 14th of February, 1799, that there came on a dreadful storm of wind and drifting snow from the south-east, which was felt very severely in most parts of Scotland. On the preceding day a Captain M——, attended by three other men, had gone out a deer-shooting in that extensive tract of mountains which lies to the west of Dal-nacardoch. As they did not return in the evening, nothing was heard of them. The next day, people were sent out in quest of them, as soon as the storm abated. After a long search, the bodies were found, in a lifeless state, lying among the ruins of a *bothy,* (a temporary hut,) in which it would seem Captain M—— and his party had taken refuge. The bothy had been destroyed by the tempest, and in a very astonishing manner. It had been built partly of stone, and partly of strong wooden uprights driven into the ground; it was not merely blown down, but quite torn to pieces. Large stones, which had formed part of the walls, were found lying at the distance of one or two hundred yards from the site of the building, and the wooden uprights appeared to have been rent asunder by a force that had twisted them off as in breaking a tough stick. From the circumstances in which the bodies were found, it appeared that the men were retiring to rest at the time the calamity came upon them. One of the bodies, indeed, was found at a distance of many yards from the bothy; another of the men was found upon the place where the bothy had stood, with one stocking off, as if he had been undressing; Captain M—— was lying without his clothes, upon the wretched bed which the bothy had afforded, his face to the ground, and his knees drawn up. To all appearance the destruction had been quite sudden: yet the situation of the building was such as promised security against the utmost violence of the wind. It stood in a narrow recess, at the foot of a mountain, whose precipitous and lofty declivities sheltered it on every side, except in the front, and here, too, a hill rose before it, though with a more gradual slope. This extraordinary wreck of a building so situated, led the common people to ascribe it to a supernatural power. It was recollected by some who had been out shooting with Captain M— about a month before, that while they were resting at this bothy, a shepherd lad had come to the door and inquired for Captain M—, and that the captain went out with the shepherd, and they walked away together, leaving the rest of the party in the bothy. After a time, Captain M— returned alone; he said nothing of what had passed between him and the lad, but looked very grave and thoughtful, and from that time there was observed to be a mysterious anxiety hanging about him. It was remembered, that one evening after dusk, when Captain M— was in the bothy, some of his party that were standing before the door saw a fire blazing on the top of the hill which rises in front of it. They were much surprised to see a fire in such a solitary place, and at such a time, and set out to inquire into the cause of it, but when they reached the top of the hill, there was no fire to be seen! It was remembered, too, that on the day before the fatal night, Captain M— had shown a singular obstinacy in going forth upon his expedition. No representations of the inclemency of the weather, and of the dangers he would be exposed to, could restrain him. He said he *must* go, and was resolved to go. Captain M.'s character was likewise remembered; that he was popularly reported to be a man of no principles, rapacious, and cruel; that he had got money by procuring recruits from the highlands,—an unpopular mode of acquiring wealth; and that, amongst other base measures for his purpose, he had gone so far as to leave a purse upon the road, and to threaten the man who had picked it up with an indictment for robbery if he did not enlist.[14] Our informer added nothing more; he neither told us his own opinion nor that of the country; but left it to our own notions of the manner in which good and evil is rewarded in this life, to suggest the Author of the miserable event. He seemed impressed with superstitious awe on the subject, and said, 'There was na' the like seen in a' Scotland.' The man is far advanced in years, and is a schoolmaster in the neighbourhood of Rannoch. He was employed by us as a guide upon Schehallion; and he told us the story one day as we walked before our horses, while we slowly wound up the road on the northern declivity of Rannoch. From this elevated ground he commanded an extensive prospect over the dreary mountains to the north, and amongst them our guide pointed out that at the foot of which was the scene of his dreadful tale. The account is, to the

---

14. It is needless to say that this was a mere popular report, which might greatly misrepresent the character of the unfortunate sufferer.

best of my recollection, just what I received from my guide. In some tri-fling particulars, from defect of memory, I may have misrepresented or added a little, in order to connect the leading circumstances; and I fear, al-so, that something may have been forgotten. Will you ask Mr. P——whether Captain M——, on leaving the bothy after his conversation with the shepherd lad, did not say that he must return there in a month after? I have a faint idea that it was so; and, if true, it would be a pity to lose it. Mr. P—— may, perhaps, be able to correct or enlarge my account for you in other instances."

The reader will, we believe, be of our opinion, that the feeling of su-perstitious awe annexed to the catastrophe contained in this interesting nar-rative, could not have been improved by any circumstances of additional horror which a poet could have invented; that the incidents and the gloomy simplicity of the narrative are much more striking than they could have been rendered by the most glowing description; and that the old highland school-master, the outline of whose tale is so judiciously preserved by the narrator, was a better medium for communicating such a tale than would have been the form of Ossian, could he have arisen from the dead on purpose.

It may however be truly said of the muse of romantic fiction,

"Mille habet ornatus."

The Professor Musaeus, and others of what we may call his school, con-ceiving, perhaps, that the simplicity of the unadorned popular legend was like to obstruct its popularity, and feeling, as we formerly observed, that though individual stories are sometimes exquisitely impressive, yet collec-tions of this kind were apt to be rather bald and heavy, employed their tal-ents in ornamenting them with incident in ascribing to the principal agents a peculiar character, and rendering the marvellous more interesting by the individuality of those in whose history it occurs. Two volumes were tran-scribed from the Volksmarchen of Musaeus by the late Dr. Beddoes, and published under the title of "Popular Tales of the Germans," which may afford the English reader a good idea of the stile of that interesting work. It may, indeed, be likened to the Tales of Count Anthony Hamilton, already mentioned, but there is great room for distinction. "Le Belier," and, "Fleur d'Epine," are mere parodies arising out of the fancy, indebted for their interest to his wit. Musaeus, on the other hand, takes the narration of the common legend, dresses it up after his own fashion, and describes, according to his own pleasure, the personages of his drama. Hamilton is a cook who compounds his whole banquet out of materials used for the first time; Musaeus brings forward ancient traditions, like yesterday's cold meat from the larder, and, by dint oil skill and seasoning, gives it a new relish for the meal of to-day. Of course the merit of the rifaciamento will fall to be divided in this case betwixt the effect attained by the ground-work of the story, and that which is added by the art of the narrator. In the tale, for example, of the "Child of Wonder," what may be termed the raw material is short, simple, and scarce rising beyond the wonders of a nursery tale, but it is so much enlivened by the vivid sketch of the selfish old father who barters his four daughters against golden eggs and sacks of pearls, as to give an interest and zest to the whole story. "The Spectre Barber" is another of these popular tales, which, in itself singular and fantastic, becomes lively and interesting from the character of a good-humoured, well-meaning, thick-skulled burgher of Bremen, whose wit becomes sharpened by adversity, till he learns gradually to improve circumstances as they occur, and at length recovers his lost prosperity by dint of courage, joined with some degree of acquired sagacity.

A still different management of the wonderful and supernatural has, in our days, revived the romance of the earlier age with its history and its antiquities. The Baron de la Motte Fouqué has distinguished himself in Germany by a species of writing which requires at once the industry of the scholar, and the talents of the man of genius. The efforts of this accomplished author aim at a higher mood of composition than the more popular romancer. He endeavours to recall the history, the mythology, the manners of former ages, and to offer to the present time a graphic description of those which have passed away. The travels of Thioldolf, for example, initiate the reader into that immense storehouse of Gothic superstition which is to be found in the Edda and the Sagas of northern nations; and to render the bold, honest, courageous character of his gallant young Scandinavian the more striking, the author has contrasted it forcibly with the chivalry of the south, over which he asserts its superiority. In some of his works the baron has, perhaps, been somewhat profuse of his historical and antiquarian lore; he wanders where the reader has not skill to follow him; and we lose interest in the piece because we do not comprehend the scenes through which we are conducted. This is the case with some of the volumes where the interest turns on the ancient German history, to understand which, a much deeper acquaintance with the antiquities of that dark period is required than is like to be found in most readers. It would, we think, be a good rule in this style of composition, were the author to confine his historical materials to such as are either generally understood as soon as mentioned, or at least can be explained with brief trouble in such a degree as to make a reader comprehend the story. Of such happy and well-chosen subjects, the Baron de la Motte Fouqué has also shown great command on other occasions. His story of "Sintram and his Followers" is in this respect admirable; and the tale of his Naiad, Nixie, or Water-Nymph, is exquisitely beautiful. The distress of the tale—and, though relating to a fantastic being, it is *real distress*—arises thus. An elementary spirit renounces her right of freedom from human passion to become the spouse of a gallant young knight, who requites her with infidelity and ingratitude. The story is the contrast at once and the *pendant* to the "Diable Amoureux" of Cazotte, but is entirely free from a tone of *polissonnerie* which shocks good taste in its very lively prototype.

The range of the romance, as it has been written by this profusely inventive author, extends through the half-illumined ages of ancient history into the Cimmerian frontiers of vague tradition; and, when traced with a pencil of so much truth and spirit as that of Fouqué, affords scenes of high interest, and forms, it cannot be doubted, the most legitimate species of romantic fiction, approaching in some measure to the epic in poetry, and capable in a high degree of exhibiting similar beauties.

We have thus slightly traced the various modes in which the wonderful and supernatural may be introduced into fictitious narrative; yet the attachment of the Germans to the mysterious has invented another species of composition, which, perhaps, could hardly have made its way in any other country or language. This may be called the FANTASTIC mode of writing,— in which the most wild and unbounded license is given to an irregular fancy, and all species of combination, however ludicrous, or however shocking, are attempted and executed without scruple. In the other modes of treating the supernatural, even that mystic region is subjected to some laws, however slight; and fancy, in wandering through it, is regulated by some probabilities in the wildest flight. Not so in the fantastic style of composition, which has no restraint save that which it may ultimately find in the exhausted imagination of the author. This style bears the same proportion to the more regular romance, whether ludicrous or serious, which Farce, or rather Pantomime, maintains to Tragedy and Comedy. Sudden transformations are introduced of the most extraordinary kind, and wrought by the most inadequate means; no attempt is made to soften their absurdity, or to reconcile their inconsistencies; the reader must be contented to look upon the gambols of the author as he would behold the flying leaps and incongruous transmutations of Harlequin, without seeking to discover either meaning or end further than the surprise of the moment.

Our English severity of taste will not easily adopt this wild and fantastic tone into our own literature; nay, perhaps will scarce tolerate it in translations. The only composition which approaches to it is the powerful romance of Frankenstein, and there, although the formation of a thinking and sentient being by scientific skill is an incident of the fantastic character, still the interest of the work does not turn upon the marvellous creation of Frankenstein's monster, but upon the feelings and sentiments which that creature is supposed to express as most natural—if we may use the phrase—to his unnatural condition and origin. In other words, the miracle is not wrought for the mere wonder, but is designed to give rise to a train of acting and reasoning in itself just and probable, although the *postulatum* on which it is grounded is in the highest degree extravagant. So far Frankenstein, therefore, resembles the "Travels of Gulliver," which suppose the existence of the most extravagant fictions, in order to extract from them philosophical reasoning and moral truth. In such cases the admission of the marvellous expressly resembles a sort of entry-money paid at the door of a lecture-room,—it is a concession which must be made to the author, and for which the reader is to receive value in moral instruction. But the *fantastic* of which we are now treating encumbers itself with no such conditions, and claims no further object than to surprise the public by the wonder itself. The reader is led astray by a freakish goblin, who has neither end nor purpose in the gambols which he exhibits, and the oddity of which must constitute their own reward. The only instance we know of this species of writing in the English language, is the ludicrous sketch in Mr. Geoffrey Crayon's tale of "The Bold Dragoon," in which the furniture dances to the music of a ghostly fiddler. The other ghost-stories of this well-known and admired author come within the legitimate bounds which Glanville, and other grave established authors, ascribe to the shadowy realms of spirits; but we suppose Mr. Crayon to have exchanged his pencil in the following scene, in order to prove that the pandours, as well as the regular forces of the ghostly world, were alike under his command:—

"By the light of the fire he saw a pale, weazon-faced fellow, in a long flannel gown, and a tall white night-cap with a tassel to it, who sat by the fire with a bellows under his arm by the way of bagpipe, from which he forced the asthmatical music that had bothered my grandfather. As he played, too, he kept twitching about with a thousand queer contortions, nodding his head, and bobbing about his tasselled night-cap.

"From the opposite side of the room, a long-backed, bandy-legged chair, covered with leather, and studded all over in a coxcombical fashion with little brass nails, got suddenly into motion, thrust out first a claw-foot, then a crooked arm, and at length making a leg, slided gracefully up to an easy chair of tarnished brocade, with a hole in its bottom, and led it gallantly out in a ghostly minuet about the floor.

"The musician now played fiercer and fiercer, and bobbed his head and his night-cap about like mad. By degrees, the dancing mania seemed to seize upon all the other pieces of furniture. The antique long-bodied chairs paired off in couples and led down a country-dance; a three-legged stool danced a hornpipe, though horribly puzzled by its supernumerary leg; while the amorous tongs seized the shovel round the waist, and whirled it about the room in a German waltz. In short, all the moveables got in motion, pirouetting, hands across, right and left, like so many devils: all except a great clothes-press, which kept curtseying and curtseying in a corner like a dowager, in exquisite time to the music; being rather too corpulent to dance, or, perhaps, at a loss for a partner."

This slight sketch, from the hand of a master, is all that we possess in England corresponding to the Fantastic style of composition which we are now treating of. "Peter Schlemil," "The Devil's Elixir," and other German works of the same character, have made it known to us through the medium of translation. The author who led the way in this department of literature was Ernest Theodore William Hoffmann; the peculiarity of whose genius, temper, and habits, fitted him to distinguish himself where imagination was to be strained to the pitch of oddity and bizarrerie. He appears to have been a man of rare talent,—a poet, an artist, and a musician, but unhappily of a hypochondriac and whimsical disposition, which carried him to extremes in all his undertakings; so his music became capricious,—his drawings caricatures,—and his tales, as he himself termed them, fantastic extravagances. Bred originally to the law, he at different times enjoyed, under the Prussian and other governments, the small appointments of a subordinate magistrate; at other times he was left entirely to his own exertions, and supported himself as a musical composer for the stage, as an author, or as a draughtsman. The shifts, the uncertainty, the precarious nature of this kind of existence, had its effect, doubtless, upon a mind which nature had rendered peculiarly susceptible of elation and depression; and a temper, in itself variable, was rendered more so by frequent change of place and of occupation, as well as by the uncertainty of his affairs. He cherished his fantastic genius also with wine in considerable quantity, and indulged liberally in the use of tobacco. Even his outward appearance bespoke the state of his nervous system: a very little man with a quantity of dark-brown hair, and eyes looking through his elf-locks, that

"E'en like grey goss-hawk's stared wild,"

indicated that touch of mental derangement, of which he seems to have been himself conscious, when entering the following fearful memorandum in his diary:—

"Why, in sleeping and in waking, do I, in my thoughts, dwell upon the subject of insanity? The out-pouring of the wild ideas that arise in my mind may perhaps operate like the breathing of a vein."

Circumstances arose also in the course of Hoffmann's unsettled and wandering life, which seemed to his own apprehension to mark him as one who "was not in the roll of common men." These circumstances had not so much of the extraordinary as his fancy attributed to them. For example; he was present at deep play in a watering-place, in company with a friend, who was desirous to venture for some of the gold which lay upon the table. Betwixt hope of gain and fear of loss, distrusting at the same time his own luck, he at length thrust into Hoffmann's hand six gold pieces, and requested him to stake for him. Fortune was propitious to the young visionary, though he was totally inexperienced in the game, and he gained for his friend about thirty Fredericks d'or. The next evening Hoffmann resolved to try fortune on his own account. This purpose, he remarks, was not a previous determination, but one which was suddenly suggested by a request of his friend to undertake the charge of staking a second time on his behalf. He advanced to the table on his own account, and deposited on one of the cards the only two Fredericks d'or of which he was possessed. If Hoffmann's luck had been remarkable on the former occasion, it now seemed as if some supernatural power stood in alliance with him. Every attempt which he made succeeded—every card turned up propitiously.—

"My senses," he says, "became unmanageable, and as more and more gold streamed in upon me, it seemed as I were in a dream, out of which I only awaked to pocket the money. The play was given up, as is usual, at two in the morning. In the moment when I was about to leave the room, an old officer laid his hand upon my shoulder, and regarding me with a fixed and severe look, said: 'Young man, if you understand this business so well, the bank, which maintains free table, is ruined; but if you do so understand the game, reckon upon it securely that the devil will be as sure of you as of all the rest of them.' Without waiting an answer, he turned away. The morning was dawning when I came home, and emptied from every pocket heaps of gold on the table. Imagine the feelings of a lad in a state of absolute dependance, and restricted to a small sum of pocket-money, who finds himself, as if by a thunder-clap, placed in possession of a sum enough to be esteemed absolute wealth, at least for the moment! But while I gazed on the treasure, my state of mind was entirely changed by a sudden and singular agony so severe, as to force the cold sweat-drops from my brow. The words of the old officer now, for the first time, rushed upon my mind in their fullest and most terrible acceptation. It seemed to me as if the gold, which glittered upon the table, was the earnest of a bargain by which the Prince of Darkness had obtained possession of my soul, which never more could escape eternal destruction. It seemed as if some poisonous reptile was sucking my heart's blood, and I felt myself fall into an abyss of despair."

Then the ruddy dawn began to gleam through the window, wood and plain were illuminated by its beams, and the visionary begun to experience the blessed feeling of returning strength, to combat with temptations, and to protect himself against the infernal propensity, which must have been attended with total destruction. Under the influence of such feelings Hoffmann formed a vow never again to touch a card, which he kept till the end of his life. "The lesson of the officer," says Hoffmann, "was good, and its effect excellent." But the peculiar disposition of Hoffmann made it work upon his mind more like an empiric's remedy than that of a regular physician. He renounced play less from the conviction of the wretched moral consequences of such a habit, than because he was actually afraid of the Evil Spirit in person.

In another part of his life Hoffmann had occasion to show, that his singularly wild and inflated fancy was not accessible to that degree of timidity connected with insanity, and to which poets, as being of "imagination all compact," are sometimes supposed to be peculiarly accessible. The author was in Dresden during the eventful period when the city was nearly taken by the allies, but preserved by the sudden return of Buonaparte and his guards from the frontiers of Silesia. He then saw the work of war closely carried on, venturing within fifty paces of the French sharp-shooters while skirmishing with those of the allies in front of Dresden. He had experience of a bombardment: one of the shells exploding before the house in which Hoffmann and Keller, the comedian, with bumpers in their hands to keep up their spirits, watched the progress of the attack from an upper window. The explosion killed three persons; Keller let his glass fall,—Hoffmann had more philosophy; he tossed off his bumper and moralized: "What is life!" said he, "and how frail the human frame that cannot withstand a splinter of heated iron!" He saw the field of battle when they were cramming with naked corpses the immense fosses which form the soldier's grave; the field covered with the dead and the wounded,—with horses and men; powder-waggons which had exploded, broken weapons, schakos, sabres, cartridge-boxes, and all the relics of a desperate fight. He saw, too, Napoleon in the midst of his triumph, and heard him ejaculate to an adjutant, with the look and the deep voice of the lion, the single word "Voyons." It is much to be regretted that Hoffmann preserved but few memoranda of the eventful weeks which he spent at Dresden during this period, and of which his turn for remark and powerful description would have enabled him to give so accurate a picture. In general, it may be remarked of descriptions concerning warlike affairs, that they resemble plans rather than paintings; and that, however calculated to instruct the tactician, they are little qualified to interest the general reader. A soldier, particularly, if interrogated upon the actions which he has seen, is much more disposed to tell them in the dry and abstracted style of a gazette, than to adorn them with the remarkable and picturesque circumstances which attract the general ear. This arises from the natural feeling, that, in speaking of what they have witnessed in any other than a dry and affected professional tone, they may be suspected of a desire to exaggerate their own dangers,—a suspicion which, of all others, a brave man is most afraid of incurring, and which, besides, the present spirit of the military profession holds as amounting to bad taste. It is, therefore, peculiarly unfortunate, that when a person unconnected with the trade of war, yet well qualified to describe its terrible peculiarities, chances to witness events so remarkable as those to which Dresden was exposed in the memorable 1813, he should not have made a register of what could not have failed to be deeply interesting. The battle of Leipsic, which ensued shortly after, as given to the public by an eye-witness—M. Shoberl, if we recollect the name aright—is an example of what we might have expected from a person of Hoffmann's talents, giving an account of his personal experience respecting the dreadful events which he witnessed. We could willingly have spared some of his grotesque works of *diablerie,* if we had been furnished, in their place, with the genuine description of the attack upon, and the retreat from Dresden, by the allied army, in the month of August, 1813. It was the last decisive advantage which was obtained by Napoleon, and being rapidly succeeded by the defeat of Vandamme, and the loss of his whole *corps d'armée,* was the point from which his visible declension might be correctly dated. Hoffmann was also a high-spirited patriot,—a true, honest, thorough-bred German, who had set his heart upon the liberation of his country, and would have narrated with genuine feeling the advantages which she obtained over her oppressor. It was not, however, his fortune to attempt any work, however slight, of an historical character, and the retreat of the French army soon left him to his usual habits of literary industry and convivial enjoyment.

It may, however, be supposed, that an imagination which was always upon the stretch received a new impulse from the scenes of difficulty and danger through which our author had so lately passed. Another calamity of a domestic nature must also have tended to the increase of Hoffmann's morbid sensibility. During a journey in a public carriage, it chanced to be overturned, and the author's wife sustained a formidable injury on the head, by which she was a sufferer for a length of time.

All these circumstances, joined to the natural nervousness of his own temper, tended to throw Hoffmann into a state of mind very favourable, perhaps, to the attainment of success in his own peculiar mode of composition, but far from being such as could consist with that right and well-balanced state of human existence, in which philosophers have been disposed to rest the attainment of the highest possible degree of human happiness. Nerves which are accessible to that morbid degree of acuteness, by which the mind is incited, not only without the consent of our reason, but even contrary to its dictates, fall under the condition deprecated in the beautiful Ode to Indifference:

> "Nor peace, nor joy, the heart can know,
>   Which, like the needle, true,
>   Turns at the touch of joy or woe,
>   But, turning, trembles too."

The pain which in one case is inflicted by an undue degree of bodily sensitiveness, is in the other the consequence of our own excited imagination; nor is it easy to determine in which the penalty of too much acuteness or vividness of perception is most severely exacted. The nerves of Hoffmann in particular were strung to the most painful pitch which can be supposed. A severe nervous fever, about the year 1807, had greatly increased the fatal sensibility under which he laboured, which acting primarily on the body speedily affected the mind. He had himself noted a sort of graduated scale concerning the state of his imagination, which, like that of a thermometer, indicated the exaltation of his feelings up to a state not far distant, probably, from that of actual mental derangement. It is not, perhaps, easy to find expressions corresponding in English to the peculiar words under which Hoffmann classified his perceptions: but we may observe that he records, as the humour of one day, a deep disposition towards the romantic and religious; of a second, the perception of the exalted or excited humorous; of a third, that of the satirical humorous; of a fourth, that of the excited or extravagant musical sense; of a fifth, a romantic mood turned towards the unpleasing and the horrible; of a sixth, bitter satirical propensities excited to the most romantic, capricious, and exotic degree; of a seventh, a state of quietism of mind open to receive the most beautiful, chaste, pleasing, and imaginative impressions of a poetical character; of an eighth, a mood equally excited, but accessible only to ideas the most unpleasing, the most horrible, the most unrestrained at once and most tormenting. At other times, the feelings which are registered by this unfortunate man of genius, are of a tendency exactly the opposite to those which he marks as characteristic of his state of nervous excitement. They indicate a depression of spirits, a mental callousness to those sensations to which the mind is at other times most alive, accompanied with that melancholy and helpless feeling which always attends the condition of one who recollects former enjoyments in which he is no longer capable of taking pleasure. This species of moral palsy is, we believe, a disease which more or less affects every one, from the poor mechanic who finds that his *hand,* as he expresses it, *is out,* that he cannot discharge his usual task with his usual alacrity, to the poet whose muse deserts him when perhaps he most desires her assistance. In such cases wise men have recourse to exercise or change of study; the ignorant and infatuated seek grosser means of diverting the paroxysm. But that which is to the person whose mind is in a healthy state, but a transitory though disagreeable feeling, becomes an actual disease in such minds as that of Hoffmann, which are doomed to experience in too vivid perceptions in alternate excess, but far most often and longest in that which is painful,—the influence of an over-excited fancy. It is minds so conformed to which Burton applies his abstract of Melancholy, giving alternately the joys and the pains which arise from the influence of the imagination. The verses are so much to the present purpose, that we cannot better describe this changeful and hypochondriac system of mind than by inserting them:

> "When to myself I act and smile,
>   With pleasing thoughts the time beguile,
>   By a brook-side or wood so green,
>   Unheard, unsought for, and unseen,
>   A thousand pleasures do me bless,
>   And crown my soul with happiness;
>   All my joys besides are folly,
>   None so sweet as Melancholy.

"When I lye, sit, or walk alone,
  I sigh, I grieve, making great moan,
  In a dark grove, or irksome den,
  With discontents and furies; then
  A thousand miseries at once
  Mine heavy heart and soul ensconce;
      All my griefs to this are jolly,
      None so sour as Melancholy.

"Methinks I hear, methinks I see,
  Sweet musick, wonderous melody,
  Towns, palaces, and cities fine;
  Here now, then, then, the world is mine,
  Rare beauties, gallant ladies shine,
  Whate'er is lovely or divine;
      All other joys to this are folly,
      None so sweet as Melancholy.

"Methinks I hear, methinks I see
  Ghosts, goblins, fiends; my phantasie
  Presents a thousand ugly shapes,
  Headless bears, black men and apes,
  Doleful outcries and fearful sights
  My sad and dismal soul affrights;
      All my griefs to this are jolly,
      None so damn'd as Melancholy."

In the transcendental state of excitation described in these verses, the painful and gloomy mood of the mind is, generally speaking, of much more common occurrence than that which is genial, pleasing, or delightful. Every one who chooses attentively to consider the workings of his own bosom, may easily ascertain the truth of this assertion, which indeed appears a necessary accompaniment of the imperfect state of humanity, which usually presents to us, in regard to anticipation of the future, so much more that is unpleasing than is desirable; in other words, where fear has a far less limited reign than the opposite feeling of hope. It was Hoffmann's misfortune to be peculiarly sensible of the former passion, and almost instantly to combine with any pleasing sensation, as it arose, the idea of mischievous or dangerous consequences. His biographer has given a singular example of this unhappy disposition, not only to apprehend the worst when there was real ground for expecting evil, but also to mingle such apprehension, capriciously and unseasonably, with incidents which were in themselves harmless and agreeable. "The devil," he was wont to say, "will put his hoof into every thing, how good soever in the outset." A trifling but whimsical instance will best ascertain the nature of this unhappy propensity to expect the worst. Hoffmann, a close observer of nature, chanced one day to see a little girl apply to a market-woman's stall to purchase some fruit which had caught her eye and excited her desire. The wary trader wished first to know what she was able to expend on the purchase; and when the poor girl, a beautiful creature, produced with exultation and pride a very small piece of money, the market-woman gave her to understand that there was nothing upon her stall which fell within the compass of her customer's purse. The poor little maiden, mortified and affronted, as well as disappointed, was retiring with tears in her eyes, when Hoffmann called her back, and arranging matters with the dealer filled the child's lap with the most beautiful fruit. Yet he had hardly time to enjoy the idea that he had altered the whole expression of the juvenile countenance from mortification to extreme delight and happiness, than he became tortured with the idea that he might be the cause of the child's death, since the fruit he had bestowed upon it might occasion a surfeit or some other fatal disease. This presentiment haunted him until he reached the house of a friend, and it was akin to many which persecuted him during life, never leaving him to enjoy the satisfaction of a kind or benevolent action, and poisoning with the vague prospect of imaginary evil whatever was in its immediate tendency productive of present pleasure or promising future happiness.

We cannot here avoid contrasting the character of Hoffmann with that of the highly imaginative poet Wordsworth, many of whose smaller poems turn upon a sensibility affected by such small incidents as that above-mentioned, with this remarkable difference—that the virtuous, and manly, and well regulated disposition of the author leads him to derive pleasing, tender, and consoling reflections from those circumstances which induced Hoffmann to anticipate consequences of a different character. Such petty incidents are passed noteless over by men of ordinary minds. Observers of poetical imagination, like Wordsworth and Hoffmann, are the chemists who can distil them into cordials or poisons.

We do not mean to say that the imagination of Hoffmann was either wicked or corrupt, but only that it was ill-regulated and had an undue tendency to the horrible and the distressing. Thus he was followed, especially in his hours of solitude and study, by the apprehension of mysterious danger to which he conceived himself exposed; and the whole tribe of demigorgons, apparitions, and fanciful spectres and goblins of all kinds with which he has filled his pages, although in fact the children of his own imagination, were no less discomposing to him than if they had had a real existence and actual influence upon him. The visions which his fancy excited are stated often to be so lively, that he was unable to endure them; and in the night, which was often his time of study, he was accustomed frequently to call his wife up from bed, that she might sit by him while he was writing, and protect him by her presence from the phantoms conjured up by his own excited imagination.

Thus was the inventor, or at least first distinguished artist who exhibited the fantastic or supernatural grotesque in his compositions, so nearly on the verge of actual insanity, as to be afraid of the beings his own fancy created. It is no wonder that to a mind so vividly accessible to the influence of the imagination, so little under the dominion of sober reason, such a numerous train of ideas should occur in which fancy had a large share and reason none at all. In fact, the grotesque in his compositions partly resembles the arabesque in painting, in which is introduced the most strange and complicated monsters, resembling centaurs, griffins, sphinxes, chimeras, rocs, and all other creatures of romantic imagination, dazzling the beholder as it were by the unbounded fertility of the author's imagination, and sating it by the rich contrast of all the varieties of shape and colouring, while there is in reality nothing to satisfy the understanding or inform the judgment. Hoffmann spent his life, which could not be a happy one, in weaving webs of this wild and imaginative character, for which after all he obtained much less credit with the public, than his talents must have gained if exercised under the restraint of a better taste or a more solid judgment. There is much reason to think that his life was shortened not only by his mental malady, of which it is the appropriate quality to impede digestion and destroy the healthful exercise of the powers of the stomach, but also by the indulgences to which he had recourse in order to secure himself against the melancholy, which operated so deeply upon the constitution of his mind.

This was the more to be regretted, as, notwithstanding the dreams of an overheated imagination, by which his taste appears to have been so strangely misled, Hoffmann seems to have been a man of excellent disposition, a close observer of nature, and one who, if this sickly and disturbed train of thought had not led him to confound the supernatural with the absurd, would have distinguished himself as a painter of human nature, of which in its realities he was an observer and an admirer.

Hoffmann was particularly skilful in depicting characters arising in his own country of Germany. Nor is there any of her numerous authors who have better and more faithfully designed the upright honesty and firm integrity which is to be met with in all classes which come from the ancient Teutonic stock. There is one character in particular in the tale called "Der Majorat"—the Entail,—which is perhaps peculiar to Germany, and which makes a magnificent contrast to the same class of persons as described in romances, and as existing perhaps in real life in other countries. The justiciary B—— bears about the same office in the family of the baron Roderick von R——, a nobleman possessed of vast estates in Courland, which the generally-known Baillie Macwheeble occupied on the land of the baron of Bradwardine. The justiciary, for example, was the representative of the Seigneur in his feudal courts of justice; he superintended his revenues, regulated and controlled his household, and from his long acquaintance with the affairs of the family, was entitled to interfere both with advice and assistance in any case of peculiar necessity. In such a character, the Scottish author has permitted himself to introduce a strain of the roguery supposed to be incidental to the inferior classes of the law,—may be no unnatural ingredient. The Baillie is mean, sordid, a trickster, and a coward, redeemed only from our dislike and contempt by the ludicrous qualities of his character, by a considerable degree of shrewdness, and by the species of almost instinctive attachment to his master and his family which seem to overbalance in quality the natural selfishness of his disposition. The justiciary of R—— is the very reverse of this character. He is indeed an original: having the peculiarities of age and some of its satirical peevishness; but in his moral qualities he is well described by La Motte Fouqué, as a hero of ancient days in the night-gown and slippers of an old lawyer of the present age. The innate worth, independence, and resolute courage of the justiciary seem to be rather enhanced than diminished by his education and profession, which naturally infers an accurate knowledge of mankind, and which, if practised without honour and honesty, is the basest and most dangerous fraud which an individual can put upon the public. Perhaps a few lines of Crabbe may describe the general tendency of the justiciary's mind, although marked, as we shall show, by loftier traits of character than those which the English poet has assigned to the worthy attorney of his borough:

> "He, roughly honest, has been long a guide
> In borough business on the conquering side;
> And seen so much of both sides and so long,
> He thinks the bias of man's mind goes wrong:
> Thus, though he's friendly, he is still severe,
> Surly, though kind, suspiciously sincere:
> So much he's seen of baseness in the mind,
> That while a friend to man, he scorns mankind;
> He knows the human heart, and sees with dread
> By slight temptation how the strong are led;
> He knows how interest can asunder rend
> The bond of parent, master, guardian, friend,
> To form a new and a degrading tie
> 'Twixt needy vice and tempting villainy."

The justiciary of Hoffmann, however, is of a higher character than the person distinguished by Crabbe. Having known two generations of the baronial house to which he is attached, he has become possessed of their family secrets, some of which are of a mysterious and terrible nature. This confidential situation, but much more the nobleness and energy of his own character, gives the old man a species of authority even over his patron himself, although the baron is a person of stately manners, and occasionally manifests a fierce and haughty temper. It would detain us too long to communicate a sketch of the story, though it is, in our opinion, the most interesting contained in the reveries of the author. Something, however, we must say to render intelligible the brief extracts which it is our purpose to make, chiefly to illustrate the character of the justiciary.

The principal part of the estate of the baron consisted in the Castle of R—sitten, a majorat, or entailed property, which gives name to the story, and which, as being such, the baron was under the necessity of making his place of residence for a certain number of weeks in every year, although it had nothing inviting in its aspect or inhabitants. It was a huge old pile over-hanging the Baltic Sea, silent, dismal, almost uninhabited, and surrounded, instead of gardens and pleasure-grounds, by forests of black pines and firs which came up to its very walls. The principal amusement of the baron and his guests was to hunt the wolves and bears which tenanted these woods during the day, and to conclude the evening with a boisterous sort of festivi-ty, in which the efforts made at passionate mirth and hilarity showed that, on the baron's side at least, they did not actually exist. Part of the castle was in ruins; a tower built for the purpose of astrology by one of its old posses-sors, the founder of the majorat in question, had fallen down, and by its fall made a deep chasm, which extended from the highest turret down to the dungeon of the castle. The fall of the tower had proved fatal to the unfor-tunate astrologer; the abyss which it occasioned was no less so to his eldest son. There was a mystery about the fate of the last, and all the facts known or conjectured respecting the cause of his fatal end were the following.

The baron had been persuaded by some expressions of an old steward, that treasures belonging to the deceased astrologer lay buried in the gulf which the tower had created by its fall. The entrance to this horrible abyss lay from the knightly hall of the castle, and the door, which still remained there, had once given access to the stair of the tower, but since its fall only opened on a yawning gulf full of stones. At the bottom of this gulf the sec-ond baron, of whom we speak, was found crushed to death, holding a wax-light fast in his hand. It was imagined that he had risen to seek a book from a library which also opened from the hall, and, mistaking the one door for the other, had met his fate by falling into the yawning gulf. Of this, however, there could be no certainty.

This double accident, and the natural melancholy attached to the place, occasioned the present Baron Roderick residing so little there; but the title under which he held the estate laid him under the necessity of making it his residence for a few weeks every year. About the same time when he took up his abode there, the justiciary was accustomed to go thith-er for the purpose of holding baronial courts, and transacting his other offi-cial business. When the tale opens he sets out upon his journey to R—sitten, accompanied by a nephew, the narrator of the tale, a young man, en-tirely new to the world, trained somewhat in the school of Werter,—romantic, enthusiastic, with some disposition to vanity,—a musician, a poet, and a coxcomb; upon the whole, however, a very well-disposed lad, with great respect for his grand-uncle, the justiciary, by whom he is regarded with kindness, but also as a subject of raillery. The old man carries him along with him partly to assist in his professional task, partly that he might get somewhat case-hardened by feeling the cold wind of the north whistle about his ears, and undergoing the fatigue and dangers of a wolf-hunt.

They reach the old castle in the midst of a snow-storm, which added to the dismal character of the place, and which lay piled thick up by the very gate by which they should enter. All knocking of the postilion was in vain; and here we shall let Hoffmann tell his own story.

"The old man then raised his powerful voice: 'Francis! Francis! where are you then? be moving; we freeze here at the door: the snow is peeling our faces raw; be stirring;—the devil!' A watch-dog at length began to bark, and a wandering light was seen in the lower story of the building,—keys rattled, and at length the heavy folding-doors opened with difficulty. 'A fair welcome t'ye in this foul weather!' said old Francis, holding the lantern so high as to throw the whole light upon his shrivelled countenance, the features of which were twisted into a smile of welcome; the carriage drove into the court, we left it, and I was then for the first time aware that the ancient domestic was dressed in an old-fashioned Iägger-livery, adorned with various loops and braids of lace. Only one pair of grey locks now remained upon his broad white forehead; the lower part of his face retained the colouring proper to the hardy huntsman; and, in spite of the crumpled muscles which writhed the countenance into something resembling a fantastic mask, there was an air of stupid yet honest kindness and good-humour, which glanced from his eyes, played around his mouth, and reconciled you to his physiognomy.

"'Well, old Frank!' said my great-uncle, as entering the anti-chamber he shook the snow from his pelisse, 'well, old man, is all ready in my apartments? Have the carpets been brushed,—the beds properly arranged,—and good fires kept in my room yesterday and to-day?' 'No!' answered Frank with great composure, 'no, worthy sir! not a bit of all that has been done.' 'Good God!' said my uncle, 'did not I write in good time,—and do not I come at the exact day? Was ever such a piece of stupidity? And now I must sleep in rooms as cold as ice!' 'Indeed, worthy Mr. Justiciary,' said Francis with great solemnity, while he removed carefully with the snuffers a glowing waster from the candle, flung it on the floor, and trod cautiously upon it, 'you must know that the airing would have been to no purpose, for the wind and snow have driven in, in such quantities through the broken window-frames: so—' 'What!' said my uncle, interrupting him, throwing open his pelisse, and placing both arms on his sides, 'what! the windows are broken, and you, who have charge of the castle, have not had them repaired?' 'That would have been done, worthy sir,' answered Francis, with the same indifference, 'but people could not get rightly at them on account of the heaps of rubbish and stone that are lying in the apartment.' 'And how, in a thousand devils' names,' said my great-uncle, 'came rubbish and stones into my chamber?' 'God bless you, my young master,' said the old man, episodically to me, who happened at the moment to sneeze, then proceeded gravely to answer the justiciary, that the stones and rubbish were those of a partition-wall which had fallen in the last great tempest. 'What, the devil! have you had a earthquake?' said my uncle, angrily. 'No, worthy sir,' replied the old man, 'but three days ago the heavy paved roof of the justice-hall fell in with a tremendous crash.' 'May the devil—,' said my uncle, breaking out in a passion, and about to let fly a heavy oath; but suddenly checking himself, he lifted submissively his right hand towards Heaven, while he moved with his left his fur cap from his forehead, was silent for an instant, then turned to me and spoke cheerfully: 'In good truth, kinsman, we had better hold our tongues and ask no further questions, else we shall only learn greater mishaps, or perhaps the whole castle may come down upon our heads. But Frank,' said he, 'how could you be so stupid as not to get another apartment arranged and aired for me and this youth? Why did you not put some large room in the upper-story of the castle in order for the court-day?' 'That is already done,' said the old man, pointing kindly to the stairs, and beginning to ascend with the light. 'Now, only think of the old houlet, that could not say this at once,' said my uncle, while we followed the domestic. We passed through many long, high, vaulted corridors,—the flickering light carried by Francis throwing irregular gleams on the thick darkness; pillars, capitals, and arches of various shapes appeared to totter as we passed them; our own shadows followed us with giant steps, and the singular pictures on the wall, across which these shadows passed, seemed to waver and to tremble, and their voices to whisper amongst the heavy echoes of our footsteps, saying— 'Wake us not, wake us not, the enchanted inhabitants of this ancient fabric!' At length, after we had passed along the range of cold and dark apartments, Francis opened a saloon in which a large blazing fire received us with a merry crackling, resembling a hospitable welcome. I felt myself cheered on the instant I entered the apartment; but my great-uncle remained standing in the middle of the hall, looked round him, and spoke with a very serious and almost solemn tone: 'This, then, must be our hall of justice!' Francis raising the light so that it fell upon an oblong whitish patch of the large dark wall, which patch had exactly the size and form of a walled-up or condemned door, said in a low and sorrowful tone, 'Justice has been executed here before now.' 'How came you to say that, old man?' said my uncle, hastily throwing the pelisse from his shoulders. 'The word escaped me,' said Francis, as he lighted the candles on the table, and opened the door of a neighbouring apartment where two beds were comfortably prepared for the reception of the guests. In a short time a good supper smoked before us in the hall, to which succeeded a bowl of punch, mixed according to the right northern fashion, and it may therefore be presumed none of the weakest. Tired with his journey, my uncle betook himself to bed; but the novelty and strangeness of the situation and even the excitement of the liquor I had drank, prevented me from thinking of sleep. The old domestic removed the supper-table, made up the fire in the chimney, and took leave of me after his manner with many a courteous bow.

"And now I was left alone in the wide high hall of chivalry; the hailstorm had ceased to patter, and the wind to howl; the sky was become clear without-doors, and the full moon streamed through the broad transome windows, illumining, as if by magic, all those dark corners of the singular apartment into which the imperfect light of the wax candles and the chimney-fire could not penetrate. As frequently happens in old castles, the walls and roof of the apartment were ornamented,—the former with heavy panelling, the latter with fantastic carving and painted of different colours. The subjects chiefly presented the desperate hunting matches with bears and wolves, and the heads of the animals, being in many cases carved, projected strangely from the painted bodies, and even, betwixt the fluttering and uncertain light of the moon and of the fire, gave a grisly degree of reality. Amidst these pieces were hung portraits, as large as life, of knights striding forth in hunting-dresses, probably the chase-loving ancestors of the present baron. Every thing, whether of painting or of carving, showed the dark and decayed colours of times long passed, and rendered more conspicuous the blank and light-coloured part of the wall before noticed. It was in the middle space betwixt two doors which led off through the hall into side-apartments, and I could now see that it must itself have been a door, built up at a later period, but not made to correspond with the rest of the apartment, either by being painted over or covered with carved work. Who knows not that an unwonted and somewhat extraordinary situation possesses a mysterious power over the human spirit? Even the dullest fancy will awake in a secluded valley surrounded with rocks, or within the walls of a gloomy church, and will be taught to expect in such a situation things different from those encountered in the ordinary course of human life. Conceive too that I was only a lad of twenty years of age, and that I had drunk several glasses of strong liquor, and it may easily be believed that the knight's hall in which I sat made a singular impression on my spirit. The stillness of the night is also to be remembered,—broken, as it was, only by the heavy waving of the billows of the sea, and the solemn piping of the wind, resembling the tones of a mighty organ touched by some passing spirit; the clouds wandering across the moon, drifted along the arched windows, and seemed giant shapes gazing through the rattling casements; in short, in the slight shuddering which crept over me I felt as if an unknown world was about to expand itself visibly before me. This feeling, however silly, only resembled the slight and not unpleasing shudder with which we read or hear a well-told ghost story. It occurred to me in consequence that I could find no more favourable opportunity for reading the work to which, like most young men of a romantic bias, I was peculiarly partial, and which I happened to have in my pocket. It was 'the Ghost Seer' of Schiller: I read—and read, and in doing so excited my fancy more and more, until I came to that part of the tale which seizes on the imagination with so much fervour, viz. the wedding feast in the house of the Count von B——. Just at the very moment when I arrived at the passage where the bloody spectre of Gironimo entered the wedding apartment, the door of the knights' hall, which led into an anti-chamber, burst open with a violent shock;—I started up with astonishment and the book dropped from my hand; but, as in the same moment all was again still, I became ashamed of my childish terror;—it might be by the impulse of the rushing night-wind, or by some other natural cause, that the door was flung open. 'It is nothing,' I said aloud, 'my overheated fancy turns the most natural accidents into the supernatural.' Having thus re-assured myself, I picked up the book and again sat down in the elbow-chair; but then I heard something move in the apartment with measured steps, sighing at the same time, and sobbing in a manner which seemed to express at once the extremity of inconsolable sorrow, and the most agonizing pain which the human bosom could feel. I tried to believe that this could only be the moans of some animal enclosed somewhere near our part of the house, I reflected upon the mysterious power of the night, which makes distant sounds appear as if they were close beside us, and I expostulated with myself for suffering the sounds to affect me with terror. But as I thus debated the point, a sound like that of scratching mixed with louder and deeper sighs, such as could only be extracted by the most acute mental agony, or during the parting pang of life, was indisputably heard upon the very spot where the door appeared to have been built up: 'Yet it *can* only be some poor animal in confinement,—I shall call out aloud, or I shall stamp with my foot upon the ground, and then either every thing will be silent or the animal will make itself be known;' so I purposed, but the blood stopped in my veins,—a cold sweat stood upon my forehead,—I remained fixed in my chair, not daring to rise, far less to call out. The hateful sounds at last ceased,—the steps were again distinguished,—it seemed as if life and the power of motion returned to me,—I started up and walked two paces forward, but in that moment an ice-cold night-breeze whistled through the hall, and at the same time the moon threw a bright light upon the picture of a very grave, well-nigh terrible looking man, and it seemed to me as if I plainly heard a warning voice amid the deep roar of the sea and the shriller whistle of the night-wind speaking the warning—'No farther! No farther! Lest thou encounter the terrors of the spiritual world!' The door now shut with the same violent clash with which it had burst open; I heard the sound of steps retiring along the anti-room and descending the staircase: the principal door of the castle was opened and shut with violence; then it seemed as if a horse was led out of the stable, and, after a short time, as if it was again conducted back to its stall. After this, all was still, at the same time I became aware that my uncle in the neighbouring apartment was struggling in his sleep and groaned like a man afflicted with a heavy dream. I hastened to awake him, and when I had succeeded, I received his thanks for the service. 'Thou hast done well, kinsman, to awake me,' he said; 'I have had a detestable dream, the cause of which is this apartment and the hall, which set me a thinking upon past times and upon many extraordinary events which have here happened. But now we shall sleep sound till morning.'"

With morning the business of the justiciary's office began. But abridging the young lawyer's prolonged account of what took place, the mystic terror of the preceding evening retained so much effect on his imagination, that he was disposed to find out traces of the supernatural in every thing which met his eyes; even two respectable old ladies, aunts of Baron Roderick von R——, and the sole old-fashioned inhabitants of the old-fashioned castle, had in their French caps and furbelows a ghostly and phantom-like appearance in his prejudiced eyes. The justiciary becomes disturbed by the strange behaviour of his assistant; he enters into expostulation upon the subject so soon as they were in private:

"'What is the matter with you?' he said; 'thou speakest not; thou eatest not; thou drinkest not;—art thou sick; or dost thou lack any thing? in short, what a fiend ails thee?' I embraced the opportunity to communicate all the horrible scenes of the preceding night; not even concealing from my grand-uncle that I had drunk a good deal of punch, and had been reading 'the Ghost Seer' of Schiller. This, I must allow,' I added, 'because it is possible, that my toiling and overheated fancy might have created circumstances which had no other existence.' I now expected that my kinsman would read me a sharp lecture on my folly, or treat me with some bitter jibes: but he did neither; he became very grave, looked long on the ground, then suddenly fixed a bold and glowing look upon me. 'Kinsman,' said he, 'I am unacquainted with your book; but you have neither it nor the liquor to thank for the ghostly exhibition you have described. Know, that I had a dream to the self-same purpose. I thought I sat in the hall as thou didst; but whereas *thou* only heardest sounds, *I* beheld, with the eyes of my spirit, the appearances which these voices announced. Yes! I beheld the inhuman monster as he entered,—saw him glide to the condemned door,—saw him scratch on the wall in comfortless despair until the blood burst from under his wounded nails; then I beheld him lead a horse from the stable and again conduct it back;—didst thou not hear the cock crow in the distant village? it was then that thou didst awake me, and I soon got the better of the terrors by which this departed sinner is permitted to disturb the peace of human life.' The old man stopped, and I dared not ask further questions, well knowing he would explain the whole to me when it was proper to do so. After a space, during which he appeared wrapt in thought, my uncle proceeded: 'Kinsman, now that thou knowest the nature of this disturbance, hast thou the courage once more to encounter it, having me in thy company?' It was natural that I should answer in the affirmative, the rather as I found myself mentally strengthened to the task: 'Then will we,' proceeded the old man, 'watch together this ensuing night. There is an inward voice which tells me this wicked spirit must give way, not so much to the force of my understanding, as to my courage, which is built upon a firm confidence in God. I feel, too, that it is no rash or criminal undertaking, but a bold and pious duty that I am about to discharge. When I risk body and life to banish the evil spirit who would drive the sons from the ancient inheritance of their fathers, it is in no spirit of presumption or vain curiosity: since, in the firm integrity of mind, and the pious confidence which lives within me, the most ordinary man is and remains a victorious hero. But should it be God's will that the wicked spirit shall have power over me, then shalt thou, kinsman, make it known that I died in honourable

Christian combat with the hellish spectre which haunts this place. For thee, thou must keep thyself at a distance, and no ill will befall thee.'

"The evening was spent in various kinds of employment; the supper was set as before in the knight's hall; the full moon shone clear through the glimmering clouds; the billows of the sea roared; and the night-wind shook the rattling casements. However inwardly excited, we compelled ourselves to maintain an indifferent conversation. The old man had laid his repeating watch on the table; it struck twelve,—then the door flew open with a heavy crash, and, as on the former night, slow and light footsteps traversed the hall, and the sighs and groans were heard as before. My uncle was pale as death; but his eyes streamed with unwonted fire, and as he stood upright, his left arm dropped by his side and his right uplifted toward heaven, he had the air of a hero in the act of devotion. The sighs and groans became louder and more distinguishable, and the hateful sounds of scratching upon the wall were again heard more odiously than on the former night. The old man then strode forward right towards the condemned door, with a step so bold and firm that the hall echoed back his tread. He stopped close before the spot where the ghostly sounds were heard yet more and more wildly, and spoke with a strong and solemn tone such as I never heard him before use: 'Daniel! Daniel!' he said, 'what makest thou here at this hour?' A dismal screech was the reply, and a sullen heavy sound was heard, as when a weighty burden is cast down upon the floor. 'Seek grace and mercy before the throne of the Highest!' continued my uncle, with a voice even more authoritative than before, 'there is thy only place of appeal! Hence with thee out of the living world in which thou hast no longer a portion!' It seemed as if a low wailing was heard to glide through the sky and to die away in the roaring of the storm which began now to awaken. Then the old man stepped to the door of the hall and closed it with such vehemence that the whole place echoed. In his speech, in his gestures, there seemed something almost superhuman which filled me with a species of holy fear. As he placed himself in the arm chair, the fixed sternness of his rigid brow began to relax; his look appeared more clear; he folded his hands and prayed internally. Some minutes passed away ere he said, with that mild tone which penetrates so deeply into the heart, the simple words, 'now, kinsman?' Overcome by horror, anxiety, holy reverence and love, I threw myself on my knees, and moistened with warm tears the hand which he stretched out to me; the old man folded me in his arms, and, after he had pressed me to his bosom with heartfelt affection, said, with a feeble and exhausted voice, 'Now, kinsman, shall we sleep soft and undisturbed!'"

The spirit returned no more. It was the ghost—as may have been anticipated—of a false domestic, by whose hand the former baron had been precipitated into the gulf which yawned behind the new wall so often mentioned in the narrative.

The other adventures in the castle of R—sitten are of a different cast, but strongly mark the power of delineating human character which Hoffmann possessed. Baron Roderick and his lady arrive at the castle with a train of guests. The lady is young, beautiful, nervous, and full of sensibility,—fond of soft music, pathetic poetry, and walks by moonlight; the rude company of huntsmen by which the baron is surrounded, their boisterous sports in the morning, and their no less boisterous mirth in the evening, is wholly foreign to the disposition of the Baroness Seraphina, who is led to seek relief in the society of the nephew of the justiciary, who can make sonnets, repair harpsichords, sustain a part in an Italian duet, or in a sentimental conversation. In short, the two young persons, without positively designing any thing wrong, are in a fair way of rendering themselves guilty and miserable, were they not saved from the snare which their passion was preparing by the calm observation, strong sense, and satirical hints of our friend the justiciary.

It may therefore be said of this personage, that he possesses that true and honourable character which we may conceive entitling a mortal as well to overcome the malevolent attacks of evil beings from the other world as to stop and control the course of moral evil in that we inhabit, and the sentiment is of the highest order by which Hoffmann ascribes to unsullied masculine honour and integrity that same indemnity from the power of evil which the poet claims for female purity:

> "Some say no evil thing that walks by night
> In fog, or fire, by lake or moorish fen,
> Blue meagre hag, or stubborn unlaid ghost
> That breaks his magic chain at curfew time,
> No goblin, nor swart faery of the mine,
> Hath hurtful power o'er true virginity."

What we admire, therefore, in the extracts which we have given is not the mere wonderful or terrible part of the story, though the circumstances are well narrated; it is the advantageous light in which it places the human character as capable of being armed with a strong sense of duty, and of opposing itself, without presumption but with confidence, to a power of which it cannot estimate the force, of which it hath every reason to doubt the purpose, and at the idea of confronting which our nature recoils.

Before we leave the story of "the Entail," we must notice the conclusion, which is beautifully told, and will recall to most readers who are passed the prime of life, feelings which they themselves must occasionally have experienced. Many, many years after the baronial race of R—— had become extinguished, accident brought the young nephew, now a man in advanced age, to the shores of the Baltic. It was night, and his eye was attracted by a strong light which spread itself along the horizon.

> "'What fire is that before us, postilion?' said I. 'It is no fire,' answered he, 'it is the beacon light of R—sitten.' 'Of R—sitten!' He had scarce uttered the words, when the picture of the remarkable days which I had passed in that place arose in clear light in my memory. I saw the baron,—I saw Seraphina,—I saw the strange-looking old aunts,—I saw myself, with a fair boyish countenance, out of which the mother's milk seemed not yet to have been pressed, my frock of delicate azure blue, my hair curled and powdered with the utmost accuracy, the very image of the lover sighing like a furnace, who tunes his sonnets to his mistress's eye-brows. Amidst a feeling of deep melancholy, fluttered like sparkles of light the recollection of the justiciary's rough jests, which appeared to me now much more pleasant than when I was the subject of them. Next morning I visited the village, and made some inquiries after the baronial steward: 'With your favour, Sir,' said the postilion, taking the pipe out of his mouth, and touching his night-cap, 'there is here no baronial steward; the place belongs to his majesty, and the royal superintendent is still in bed.' On farther questions, I learned that the Baron Roderick von R—— having died without descendants, the entailed estate, according to the terms of the grant, had been vested in the crown. I walked up to the castle, which lay now in a heap of ruins. An old peasant, who came out of the pine wood, informed me that a great part of the stones had been used to build the beacon-tower; he told me too of the spectre which in former times had haunted the spot, and asserted that when the moon was at the full, the voice of lamentation was still heard among the ruins."

If the reader has, in a declining period of his life, revisited the scenes of youthful interest, and received from the mouth of strangers an account of the changes which have taken place, he will not be indifferent to the simplicity of this conclusion.

The passage which we have quoted, while it shows the wildness of Hoffmann's fancy, evinces also that he possessed power which ought to have mitigated and allayed it. Unfortunately, his taste and temperament directed him too strongly to the grotesque and fantastic,—carried him too far "extra mœnia flammantia mundi," too much beyond the circle not only of probability but even of possibility, to admit of his composing much in the better style which he might easily have attained. The popular romance, no doubt, has many walks, nor are we at all inclined to halloo the dogs of criticism against those whose object is merely to amuse a passing hour, It may be repeated with truth, that in this path of light literature, "tout genre est permis hors les genres ennuyeux," and of course, an error in taste ought not to be followed up and hunted down as if it were a false maxim in morality, a delusive hypothesis in science, or a heresy in religion itself. Genius too is, we arc aware, capricious, and must be allowed to take its own flights, however eccentric, were it but for the sake of experiment. Sometimes, also, it may be eminently pleasing to look at the wildness of an Arabesque painting executed by a man of rich fancy. But we do not desire to see genius expand or rather exhaust itself upon themes which cannot be reconciled to taste; and the utmost length in which we can indulge a turn to the fantastic is, where it tends to excite agreeable and pleasing ideas.

We are not called upon to be equally tolerant of such capriccios as are not only startling by their extravagance, but disgusting by their horrible import. Moments there are, and must have been, in the author's life, of pleasing as well as painful excitation; and the Champagne which sparkled in his glass must have lost its benevolent influence if it did not sometimes wake his fancy to emotions which were pleasant as well as whimsical. But as repeatedly the tendency of all overstrained feelings is directed towards the painful, and the fits of lunacy, and the crises of very undue excitement which approach to it, are much more frequently of a disagreeable than of a pleasant character, it is too certain that we possess in a much greater degree the power of exciting in our minds what is fearful, melancholy, or horrible, than of commanding thoughts of a lively and pleasing character. The grotesque, also, has a natural alliance with the horrible; for that which is out of nature can be with difficulty reconciled to the beautiful. Nothing, for instance, could be more displeasing to the eye than the palace of that crack-brained Italian prince, which was decorated with every species of monstrous sculptures which a depraved imagination could suggest to the artist. The works of Callot, though evincing a wonderful fertility of mind, are in like manner regarded with surprise rather than pleasure. If we compare his fertility with that of Hogarth, they resemble each other in extent; but in that of the satisfaction afforded by a close examination the English artist has wonderfully the advantage. Every new touch which the observer detects amid the rich superfluities of Hogarth is an article in the history of human manners, if not of the human heart; while, on the contrary, in examining microscopically the diablerie of Callot's pieces, we only discover fresh instances of ingenuity thrown away, and of fancy pushed into the regions of absurdity. The works of the one painter resemble a garden carefully cultivated, each nook of which contains something agreeable or useful; while those of the other are like the garden of the sluggard, where a soil equally fertile produces nothing but wild and fantastic weeds.

Hoffmann has in some measure identified himself with the ingenious artist upon whom we have just passed a censure by his title of "Night Pieces *after the manner of Callot,*" and in order to write such a tale, for example, as that called "the Sandman," he must have been deep in the mysteries of that fanciful artist, with whom he might certainly boast a kindred spirit. We have given an instance of a tale in which the wonderful is, in our opinion, happily introduced, because it is connected with and applied to human interest and human feeling, and illustrates with no ordinary force the elevation to which circumstances may raise the power and dignity of the human mind. The following narrative is of a different class:

> "half horror and half whim,
>   Like fiends in glee, ridiculously grim."

Nathaniel, the hero of the story, acquaints us with the circumstances of his life in a letter addressed to Lothair, the brother of Clara; the one being his friend, the other his betrothed bride. The writer is a young man of a fanciful and hypochondriac temperament, poetical and metaphysical in an excessive degree, with precisely that state of nerves which is most accessible to the influence of imagination. He communicates to his friend and his mis-

tress an adventure of his childhood. It was, it seems, the custom of his father, an honest watchmaker, to send his family to bed upon certain days
earlier in the evening than usual, and the mother in enforcing this observance used to say, "To-bed, children, *the Sandman* is coming!" In fact,
on such occasions, Nathaniel observed that after their hour of retiring, a
knock was heard at the door, a heavy step echoed on the staircase, some
person entered his father's apartments, and occasionally a disagreeable and
suffocating vapour was perceptible through the house. This then was the
Sandman; but what was his occupation, and what was his purpose? The
nursery-maid being applied to, gave a nursery-maid's explanation, that the
Sandman was a bad man, who flung sand in the eyes of little children who
did not go to bed. This increased the terror of the boy, but at the same time
raised his curiosity. He determined to conceal himself in his father's
apartment and wait the arrival of the nocturnal visitor; he did so, and the
Sandman proved to be no other than the lawyer Copelius, whom he had
often seen in his father's company. He was a huge left-handed, splay-footed
sort of personage, with a large nose, great ears, exaggerated features, and a
sort of ogre-like aspect, which had often struck terror into the children before this ungainly limb of the law was identified with the terrible Sandman.
Hoffmann has given a pencil sketch of this uncouth figure, in which he has
certainly contrived to represent something as revolting to adults as it might
be terrible to children. He was received by the father with a sort of humble
observance; a secret stove was opened and lighted, and they instantly commenced chemical operations of a strange and mysterious description, but
which immediately accounted for that species of vapour which had been
perceptible on other occasions. The gestures of the chemists grew fantastic,
their faces, even that of the father, seemed to become wild and terrific as
they prosecuted their labours; the boy became terrified, screamed and left
his hiding-place;—was detected by the alchemist, for such Copelius was,
who threatened to pull out his eyes, and was with some difficulty prevented
by the father's interference from putting hot ashes in the child's face. Nathaniel's imagination was deeply impressed by the terror he had undergone, and a nervous fever was the consequence, during which the horrible
figure of the disciple of Paracelsus was the spectre which tormented his imagination.

After a long interval, and when Nathaniel was recovered, the nightly visits of Copelius to his pupil were renewed, but the latter promised his wife that it should be for the last time. It proved so, but not in the manner which the old watchmaker meant. An explosion took place in the chemical laboratory which cost Nathaniel's father his life; his instructor in the fatal art, to which he had fallen a victim, was no where to be seen. It followed from these incidents, calculated to make so strong an impression upon a lively imagination, that Nathaniel was haunted through life by the recollections of this horrible personage, and Copelius became in his mind identified with the evil principle.

When introduced to the reader, the young man is studying at the university, where he is suddenly surprised by the appearance of his old enemy, who now personates an Italian or Tyrolese pedlar, dealing in optical glasses and such trinkets, and, although dressed according to his new profession, continuing under the Italianized name of Guiseppe Coppola to be identified with the ancient adversary. Nathaniel is greatly distressed at finding himself unable to persuade either his friend or his mistress of the justice of the horrible apprehensions which he conceives ought to be entertained from the supposed identity of this terrible jurisconsult with his double-ganger the dealer in barometers. He is also displeased with Clara, because her clear and sound good sense rejects not only his metaphysical terrors, but also his inflated and affected strain of poetry. His mind gradually becomes alienated from the frank, sensible, and affectionate companion of his childhood, and he grows in the same proportion attached to the daughter of a professor called Spalanzani, whose house is opposite to the windows of his lodging. He has thus an opportunity of frequently remarking Olympia as she sits in her apartment; and although she remains there for hours without reading, working, or even stirring, he yet becomes enamoured of her extreme beauty in despite of the insipidity of so inactive a person. But much more rapidly does this fatal passion proceed when he is induced to purchase a perspective glass from the pedlar, whose resemblance was so perfect to his old object of detestation. Deceived by the secret influence of the medium of vision, he becomes indifferent to what was visible to all others who approach Olympia,—to a certain stiffness of manner which made her walk as if by the impulse of machinery,—to a paucity of ideas which induced her to express herself only in a few short but reiterated phrases,—in short, to all that indicated Olympia to be what she ultimately proved, a mere literal puppet, or automaton, created by the mechanical skill of Spalanzani, and inspired with an appearance of life by the devilish arts we may suppose of the alchemist, advocate, and weather-glass seller Copelius, alias Coppola. At this extraordinary and melancholy truth the enamoured Nathaniel arrives by witnessing a dreadful quarrel between the two imitators of Prometheus, while disputing their respective interests in the subject of their creative power. They uttered the wildest imprecations, and tearing the beautiful automaton limb from limb, belaboured each other with the fragments of their clockwork figure. Nathaniel, not much distant from lunacy before, became frantic on witnessing this horrible spectacle.

But we should be mad ourselves were we to trace these ravings any farther. The tale concludes with the moon-struck scholar attempting to murder Clara by precipitating her from a tower. The poor girl being rescued by her brother, the lunatic remains alone on the battlements, gesticulating violently and reciting the gibberish which he had acquired from Copelius and Spalanzani. At this moment, and while the crowd below are devising means to secure the maniac, Copelius suddenly appears among them, assures them that Nathaniel will presently come down of his own accord, and realizes his prophecy by fixing on the latter a look of fascination, the effect of which is instantly to compel the unfortunate young man to cast himself headlong from the battlements.

This wild and absurd story is in some measure redeemed by some traits in the character of Clara, whose firmness, plain good sense, and Frank affection are placed in agreeable contrast with the wild imagination, fanciful apprehensions, and extravagant affection of her crazy-pated admirer.

It is impossible to subject tales of this nature to criticism. They are not the visions of a poetical mind, they have scarcely even the seeming authenticity which the hallucinations of lunacy convey to the patient; they are the feverish dreams of a light-headed patient, to which, though they may sometimes excite by their peculiarity, or surprise by their oddity, we never feel disposed to yield more than momentary attention. In fact, the inspirations of Hoffmann so often resemble the ideas produced by the immoderate use of opium, that we cannot help considering his case as one requiring the assistance of medicine rather than of criticism; and while we acknowledge that with a steadier command of his imagination he might have been an author of the first distinction, yet situated as he was, and indulging the diseased state of his own system, he appears to have been subject to that undue vividness of thought and perception of which the celebrated Nicolai became at once the victim and the conqueror. Phlebotomy and cathartics, joined to sound philosophy and deliberate observation, might, as in the case of that celebrated philosopher, have brought to a healthy state a mind which we cannot help regarding as diseased, and his imagination soaring with an equal and steady flight might have reached the highest pitch of the poetical profession.

The death of this extraordinary person took place in 1822. He became affected with the disabling complaint called *tabes dorsalis,* which gradually deprived him of the power of his limbs. Even in this melancholy condition he dictated several compositions, which indicate the force of his fancy, particularly one fragment entitled "The Recovery," in which are many affecting allusions to the state of his own mental feelings at this period; and a novel called "The Adversary," on which he had employed himself even shortly before his last moments. Neither was the strength of his courage in any respect abated; he could endure bodily agony with firmness, though he could not bear the visionary terrors of his own mind. The medical persons made the severe experiment whether by applying the actual cautery to his back by means of glowing iron, the activity of the nervous system might not be restored. He was so far from being cast down by the torture of this medical martyrdom, that he asked a friend who entered the apartment after he had undergone it, whether he did not smell the roasted meat. The same heroic spirit marked his expressions, that "he would be perfectly contented to lose the use of his limbs, if he could but retain the power of working constantly by the help of an amanuensis." Hoffman died at Berlin, upon the 25th June, 1822, leaving the reputation of a remarkable man, whose temperament and health alone prevented his arriving at a great height of reputation, and whose works as they now exist ought to be considered less as models for imitation than as affording a warning how the most fertile fancy may be exhausted by the lavish prodigality of its possessor.

Appendix

Narrative of a Fatal Event

[The following melancholy relation has been sent us without a signature or reference. It is contrary to our general rule to insert any communication under such circumstances, but we are unwilling to give any additional pain, and besides, there is something in the querulous tone of it, that seems to plead for indulgence, &c. and we would be glad to have it in our power to "administer to a mind diseased."]

If it could alleviate in the smallest degree the intense sufferings that have preyed upon my mind, and blasted my hope, during a period now of almost seven-and-thirty years, I would account the pain I may feel, during the time I am attempting to narrate the following occurrence, of no more consequence than the shower of sleet that drives in my face while I am walking home from the parish church to my parlour fire.

I already remarked, it is within a few months of being thirty-seven years since I left the university of Glasgow, in company with a young person of my own age, and from the same part of the country. I shall speak of him by the name of Campbell; it can interest few but myself now, to say that it is not his real name. We had been intimately acquainted for years before we came together to the college, and a predilection for the same studies, a strong bias for general literature, and more especially for those courses of inquiry which are the amusement rather than the task of minds given to the pursuit of knowledge, had, in the course of four swift years, bound us together in one of those friendships which young men are apt to persuade themselves can never possibly be dissolved, while no sooner are they separated for a time, than every event they meet with in the course of common life tends ins sensibly to obliterate this youthful union; as the summer

263

showers so imperceptibly melt the wreath of snow upon the mountain, that the evening on which the last speck disappears passes unnoticed.

But our friendship was not destined to be subjected to this slow and wasting process: it was suddenly and fearfully broken off. It is now seven-and-thirty years, next June, since the event I allude to; and I still flatter myself, that had I had the courage to have saved Campbell's life when probably it was in my power, our mutual regard would have suffered no diminution, wherever our future lots might have been cast.

The teachers of youth, in the university of the western capital of the kingdom, had fallen, about that time, into the great and presumptuous error of letting their pupils loose in a desert and boundless field, as if the truth could be found every where by searching the wilderness; and error was only to be stumbled upon by chance, and immediately detected and avoided. Wiser surely it had been to consider truth and error as at least equally obvious to the youthful mind, and therefore to rein in the minds of their pupils, and oblige them to conform to the safe and long established modes of reasoning and thinking.

One lamentable consequence of this presumptuous system was, the effect it had upon the young men of my own age, in arousing in our minds a disregard for the standards of our faith in religion; for instead of studying nature by the help of revelation, we reversed the order of induction, and, pretending to follow the works of the Deity as our principal guide, endeavoured to illustrate the revealed will of God by the analogy of nature. This may appear somewhat foreign to the subject, but a similar train of thought always mingles with my recollections, and it is not the least cause of my unceasing regret, that I should, in the pride and rashness of youthful enthusiasm, have encouraged Campbell, and even often led the way in these dangerous speculations. It was our last year at Principal ——'s[15] class! and, alas! I have to endure the remembrance that my friend was snatched to a premature death, while he was yet an unbeliever in some of the most sublime mysteries of our holy faith.

As I said already, Campbell and I, after a winter of hard study, proposed to ourselves, and set out on, a journey of six weeks, in order to in-

---

15. Last year of attendance on the course of Theology. EDITOR.

dulge our predilection for natural history, among the mountains and isles of the Highlands.

We had one morning ascended a high mountain in Knapdale. Many objects were either new to us or unobserved before, or we saw them under new views. Poor Campbell's spirits seemed to rise, and his mind to take wilder flights, in proportion as he looked to the barometer that he carried, and observed the sinking of the mercury. "This *Cannach,*" said he, "that blooms here on the mountains of Scotland, unseen, save by the deer and the ptarmagan, is not it more delicately beautiful than the *gloriosa* of Siam, or the rose of Cashmere? and if, as philosophers assert, there is an analogy through all the works of nature, and the meaner animals proceed from the parent as slumbering embryos, and the more perfect are produced nearly as they afterwards exist—why do we meet here in this cold and stormy region with the *Festuca vivipira,* which has flowers and seeds in the warmer valleys below? Does this puny grass adapt its economy to its circumstances, and finding that the cold and the winds render its flowers abortive, does it resolve to continue its species by these buds and little plants, which it is observed to shake off when they can provide for themselves?" These and similar speculations enlivened our botanical labours.

The day was calm, the sky resplendent, and a view of the sea and the islands, from the point of Cantyre, on the south to Tiree and Coll on the N. West (the most picturesque and singular portion of our native country), was pourtrayed on the expanse before us. The scene had its full effect upon the mind of my friend, fitted alike to concentrate itself upon the most minute, and expand itself to grasp the most magnificent, objects in nature; he had not been more charmed with the most diminutive plants than now, when he took a rapid review of the vast ocean, with all its mighty movements of tides and currents; of the joint and contending influence of the sun and moon; of the agency of a mass of matter, inert in itself, revolving at a distance, and with a velocity alike inconceivable, and even moving, as by a mysterious cord, the vast pivot around which it rolled; and of the progressive power of man, originally fixed below his tree, and comparatively ignorant, listless, and blind, who had formed unto himself new senses, and new powers and instruments of thought, until he at last weighed the sun as in a balance, and seemed to have gained a view of the infinitude of space, and was lost in the fearful extent of his own discoveries.

We descended towards the shore of what is called the Sound of Jura, through many a dell and bosky wood, sometimes loitering as we stopped to examine the objects of our study—sometimes gayly walking over the barren moor.

The sea-shore presented us with a new field of inquiry, and a new class of objects; many curious and beautiful species of *fuci* grow on these shores, and of several of the smaller and finer kinds we were enabled to acquire specimens, with the view of enriching our common herbarium. "On the summit of Knockmordhu," said Campbell, "we were talking of the wonderful adaptation of plants, but is there not something in the economy of these algæ, that shews a wise and intelligent provision, as clearly as does the conformation of any part of the human body? How comes it that the invisible seed of the lichens should be of the same specific weight, or lighter than the air, so that the most precipitous rock that the wind blows upon is furnished with them in abundance? And their sister tribe, these *fuci,* that thrive only within reach of the wave, the seeds of these are almost equally minute, that they too may be fitted to lodge in the asperities of the rock, and they are of the same weight of the sea water, and float about in it continually; so that every dash of the spray is full of them, and they fix upon every fragment that is detached from the cliff."

As the ebbing tide began to discover to us the black side of the rocky islets, we procured a boat at a small hamlet that overhung a little bay, and went on a mimic voyage of discovery. While we returned again to the main land, the warmth of the day, and the beautiful transparency of the water, which, as the whole extent of the west coast is rocky shore, is highly remarkable, tempted Campbell to propose that we should amuse ourselves with swimming. Owing to a horror I had acquired when a boy, from an exaggerated description of the danger of the convulsive grasp of a person drowning, or *dead grip* as it is called, I always felt an involuntary repugnance to practise this exercise in company with others. However, we now indulged in it so long, that I began to feel tired, and was swimming towards the rocky shore, which was at no great distance. Campbell, who had now forgot his philosophical reveries, in the pleasure of a varied and refreshing amusement, was sporting in all the gayety of exuberant spirits, when I heard a sudden cry of fear. I turned, and saw him struggling violently, as if in the act of sinking. I immediately swam towards him. He had been seized with cramp, which suspends all power of regular exertion, while at the same time it commonly deprives its victim of presence of mind; and as poor Campbell alternately sunk and rose, his wild looks as I approached him, and convulsed cries for assistance, struck me with a sudden and involuntary panic, and I hesitated to grasp the extended hand of my drowning friend. After a moment's struggle he sunk, exclaiming, My God! with a look at me of such an expression, that it has ten thousand times driven me to wish my memory was a blank. A dreadful alarm now struck my heart, like the stab of a dagger, and with almost a similar sensation of pain; I rushed to the place where he disappeared, the boiling of the water, caused by his descending body, prevented a distinct view, but on looking down, I thought I saw three or four corpses, struggling with each other, while, at the same moment, I heard a loud and melancholy cry from the bushes on the steep bank that overhung the shore. As the boiling of the water settled, I was partly relieved from extreme horror; but I had the misery to see Campbell again; for the water was as clear as the air. He stood upright at the bottom among the large sea-weeds—he even reached up his arms and exerted himself, as if endeavouring fruitlessly to climb to the surface. I looked in despair towards the shore, and all around. The feeling of hopeless loneliness was dreadful. I again distinctly heard the same melancholy cry. A superstitious dread came over me as before, for a few seconds; but I observed an old gray goat, which had advanced to the jutting point of a rock; he had perhaps been alarmed from the unusual appearance in the sea below, and was bleating for his companions. I now recollected the boat, and swam exhausted to the shore, while every moment I imagined I saw before me the extended hand of my friend which I should never more grasp. I rowed back more than half distracted. The water, when Campbell had sunk, was between twelve and fourteen feet deep, and, as I said before, remarkably transparent. Some people are capable of sustaining life under water far longer than others, and poor Campbell was of an extremely vigorous constitution. I saw him again more distinctly, and his appearance was in the utmost degree affecting. He seemed to be yet alive, for he sat upright, and grasped with one hand the stem of a large tangle; the broad frond of which waved sometimes over him as it was moved by the tide, while he moved convulsively his other arm and one of his legs.[16]

---

16. This appearance might arise from the refraction of the agitated water, as well as from the excited imagination of the narrator. EDITOR.

I remember well, I cried out in agony, O if I had a rope! With great exertion, and by leaning over the boat with my arm and face under water, I tried to arouse his attention, by touching his hands with the oar. I was convinced that, had there been length of rope in the boat, I could have saved him. He evidently was not quite insensible, for upon repeatedly touching his hand, he let go his hold of the angle, and after feebly and ineffectually grasping at the oar, I saw him once more stretch up his hand, as if conscious that some person was endeavouring to assist him. He then fell slowly on his back, and lay calm, and still, among the sea weed.

Unconnected ravings, and frantic cries, could alone express the unsufferable anguish I endured.—His stretched out hand!—I often, often see it still! yet it is nearly thirty-seven years ago. But the heart that would not save his friend, that saw him about to perish, yet kept aloof in his last extremity, perhaps deserves that suffering which time seems rather to increase than alleviate.

It is in vain that I reason with myself,—that I say, "all this is too true,—I hesitated to save him,—I kept aloof from him,—I answered not his last cry for help,—I refused his outstretched hand, and saw him engulphed in the cruel waters,—but yet surely this did not spring from selfish or considerate care for my own safety. Before and since I have hazarded my life, with alertness and enthusiasm, to rescue others,—no cold calculating prudence kept me back; it was an instinctive and involuntary impulse, originating from a strong early impression, and on finding myself suddenly placed in circumstances which had been long dreaded in imagination!"

But all this reasoning avails nothing. I still recollect the inestimable endowments and amiable disposition of my early and only friend,—memory still dwells upon our taking leave of the city,—our passage of the Clyde,—our researches and walks in the woodlands and sequestered glens of Cowal,—our moonlight sail on Lochfine,—our ascent of the mountain,—the splendid view of the sea and islands,—and our conversation on the summit,—the first cry of alarm,—the out-stretched hand and upbraiding look,—the appearance of the sinking body,—the bleating of the goat,—my friend's dying efforts among the sea-weed!

It is nearly seven and thirty years now; yet, day or night, I may almost say, a waking hour has not passed in which I have not felt part of the suffering that I witnessed convulsing the body of my poor friend, under the agonies of a strangely protracted death. Why then, will the reader say, does the writer of this melancholy story now communicate his miseries to the public? This natural question I will endeavour to answer. The body of Campbell was found, but the distracting particulars of his fate were unknown. They were treasured in my own bosom with the same secrecy with which a catholic bigot conceals the *discipline,* or whip of wire, which, in execution of his private penance, is so often dyed in his blood. I avoided every allusion to the subject, when the ordinary general inquiries had been answered, and it was too painful a subject for any one to press upon me for particulars. It was soon forgotten by all but me; and a long period has passed away, if not of secret guilt, at least of secret remorse. Accident led me, about a month since, to disclose the painful state of my mind to a friend in my neighbourhood, who pretends to some philosophy and knowledge of the human heart. I hardly knew how I was surprised into the communication of feelings which I had kept so long secret. The discourse happened to turn upon such moods of the mind as that under which I have suffered. I was forced into my narrative almost involuntarily, and might apply to myself the well-known lines:

> Forthwith this frame of mine was wrenched
> > With a strange agony,
> Which forc'd me to begin my tale,
> > And then it left me free.

My friend listened to the detail of my feelings with much sympathy. "I do not," he said, when my horrid narrative was closed, "attempt by reasoning to eradicate from your mind feelings so painfully disproportioned to the degree of blame which justly attaches to your conduct. I do not remind you, that your involuntary panic palsied you as much as the unfortunate sufferer's cramp, and that you were in the moment as little able to give him effectual assistance, as he was to keep afloat without it. I might add in your apology, that the instinct of self-preservation is uncommonly active in cases where we ourselves are exposed to the same sort of danger with that in which we see others perishing. I once witnessed a number of swimmers amusing themselves in the entrance of Leith harbour, when one was seized with the cramp and went down. In one instant the pier was crowded with naked figures, who had fled to the shore to escape the supposed danger;

and in the next as many persons, who were walking on the pier, had thrown off part of their clothes and plunged in to assist the perishing man. The different effect upon the bystanders, and on those who shared the danger, is to be derived from their relative circumstances, and from no superior benevolence of the former, or selfishness of the latter. Your own understanding must have often suggested these rational grounds of consolation, though the strong impression made on your imagination by circumstances so deplorable, has prevented your receiving benefit from them. The question is, how this disease of the mind (for such it is) can be effectually removed?"

I looked anxiously in his face, as if in expectation of the relief he spoke of. "I was once," said he, "when a boy, in the company of an old military officer, who had been, in his youth, employed in the service of apprehending some outlaws, guilty of the most deliberate cruelties. The narrative, told by one so nearly concerned with it, and having all those minute and circumstantial particulars which seize forcibly on the imagination, placed the shocking scene as it were before my very eyes. My fancy was uncommonly lively at that period of my life, and it was strongly affected. The tale cost me a sleepless night, with fervor and tremor on the nerves. My father, a man of uncommonly solid sense, discovered, with some difficulty, the cause of my indisposition. Instead of banishing the subject which had so much agitated me, he entered upon the discussion, shewed me the volume of the state trials which contained the case of the outlaws, and, by enlarging repeatedly upon the narrative, rendered it familiar to my imagination, and of consequence more indifferent to it. I would advise you, my friend, to follow a similar course. It is the secrecy of your sufferings which goes far to prolong them. Have you never observed, that the mere circumstance of a fact, however indifferent in itself, being known to one, and one only, gives it an importance in the eyes of him who possesses the secret, and renders it of much more frequent occurrence as the progress of his thoughts, than it could have been from any direct interest which it possesses. Shake these fetters therefore from your mind, and mention this event to one or two of our common friends; hear them, as you now hear me, treat your remorse, relatively to its extent and duration, as a mere disease of the mind, the consequence of the impressive circumstances of that melancholy event over which you have suffered your fancy to brood in solemn silence and secrecy. Hearing it thus spoken of by others, their view of the case will end by be-

coming familiar and habitual to you, and you will then get rid of the agonies which have hitherto operated like a night-mare to hag-ride your imagination."

Such was my friend's counsel, which I heard in silence, inclined to believe his deductions, yet feeling abhorrent to make the communications he advised. I had been once surprised into such a confession, but to tell my tale again deliberately, and face to face,—to avow myself guilty of something approaching at once to cowardice and to murder,—I felt myself incapable of the resolution necessary to the disclosure. As a middle course I send you this narrative; my name will be unknown, for the event passed in a distant country from that in which I now live. I shall hear, perhaps, the unfortunate survivor censured, or excused; the wholesome effect may be produced in my mind which my friend expects from the narrative becoming the theme of public discussion; and to him who can best pity and apologise for my criminal weakness, I may perhaps find courage to whisper, "the unhappy object of your compassion is now before you."

TWEEDSIDE.

Bibliography

"Ann Radcliffe." In *Ballantyne's Novelist's Library*. London: Hurst, Robinson & Co., 1821-24. 10.i-xxxix.

"Clara Reeve." In *Ballantyne's Novelist's Library*. London: Hurst, Robinson & Co., 1821-24. 4.lxxix-lxxxvii.

"The Erl-King." *Kelso Mail* (1 March 1798). In *Tales of Terror*, [ed. M. G. Lewis]. Kelso, Scotland: James Ballantyne, 1799. In [Sir Walter Scott and others]. *An Apology for Tales of Terror*. Kelso, Scotland: James Ballantyne, 1799.

"The Eve of St. John." Kelso: James Ballantyne, 1800. In *Tales of Wonder*, ed. M. G. Lewis. London: W. Bulmer & Co., 1801. 1.153-64. In Scott's *Minstrelsy of the Scottish Border*. Kelso, Scotland: James Ballantyne, 1802. 2.309-21.

"The Fire-King." In *Tales of Wonder* (q.v.). 1.62-69.

"Glenfinlas." In Scott's *Minstrelsy of the Scottish Border* (q.v.). 2.374-89.

"Horace Walpole." In Walpole's *The Castle of Otranto*. Kelso, Scotland: James Ballantyne, 1811. In *Ballantyne's Novelist's Library*. London: Hurst, Robinson & Co., 1821-24. 4.lx-lxxviii.

"My Aunt Margaret's Mirror." In *The Keepsake for 1829,* ed. Frederic Mansell Reynolds. London: Published for the Proprietor by Hurst, Chance & Co., [1828]. 1-44.

"Narrative of a Fatal Event." *Blackwood's Edinburgh Magazine* 2 (March 1818): 630-35.

"On the Supernatural in Fictitious Composition." *Foreign Quarterly Review* 1 (July 1827): 60–98.

"Phantasmagoria." *Blackwood's Edinburgh Magazine* 3 (May 1818): 211–15.

"Remarks on *Frankenstein.*" *Blackwood's Edinburgh Magazine* 2 (March 1818): 613–20.

Review of Maturin's *The Fatal Revenge. Quarterly Review* 3 (May 1810): 339–47.

"Story of an Apparition." *Blackwood's Edinburgh Magazine* 3 (September 1818): 705–7.

"The Tapestried Chamber." In *The Keepsake for 1829,* ed. Frederic Mansell Reynolds. London: Published for the Proprietor by Hurst, Chance & Co., [1828]. 123–42.

"Wandering Willie's Tale." In *Redgauntlet.* Edinburgh: Archibald Constable & Co., 1824. 1.225–61.

"The Wild Huntsman." In *The Chase, and William and Helen.* Edinburgh: Printed by Mundell & Son for Manners & Miller, 1796 (as "The Chase"). In *Tales of Terror* (q.v.). In *An Apology for Tales of Terror* (q.v.).

"William and Helen." In *The Chase, and William and Helen* (q.v.) In *Tales of Terror* (q.v.). In *An Apology for Tales of Terror* (q.v.).

About S. T. Joshi

S. T. Joshi is the author of *The Weird Tale* (1990), *H. P. Lovecraft: The Decline of the West* (1990), and *Unutterable Horror: A History of Supernatural Fiction* (2012). He has prepared corrected editions of H. P. Lovecraft's work for Arkham House and annotated editions of Lovecraft's stories for Penguin Classics. He has also prepared editions of Lovecraft's collected essays and poetry. His exhaustive biography, *H. P. Lovecraft: A Life* (1996), was expanded as *I Am Providence: The Life and Times of H. P. Lovecraft* (2010). He is the editor of the anthologies *American Supernatural Tales* (Penguin, 2007), *Black Wings* I–VI (PS Publishing, 2010, 2012, 2013), *A Mountain Walked: Great Tales of the Cthulhu Mythos* (Centipede Press, 2014), *The Madness of Cthulhu* (Titan Books, 2014–15), and *Searchers After Horror: New Tales of the Weird and Fantastic* (Fedogan & Bremer, 2014). He is the editor of the *Lovecraft Annual, Spectral Realms,* and *Penumbra* (all published by Hippocampus Press). Among his works of fiction are *The Recurring Doom: Tales of Mystery and Horror* (Sarnath Press, 2019) and *Something from Below* (PS Publishing, 2019).

www.ingramcontent.com/pod-product-compliance
Lightning Source LLC
Chambersburg PA
CBHW070447030726
47503CB00004B/941